CRIMSON SHORE

DOUGLAS PRESTON and LINCOLN CHILD are the number one bestselling co-authors of the celebrated Pendergast novels, as well as the Gideon Crew books. Preston and Child's *Relic* and *The Cabinet of Curiosities* were chosen by readers in a National Public Radio poll as being among the one hundred greatest thrillers ever written, and *Relic* was made into a number one box office hit movie. Readers can sign up for their monthly newsletter, The Pendergast File, at www.PrestonChild.com and follow them on Facebook.

Also by Douglas Preston and Lincoln Child

Agent Pendergast Novels

Relic
Reliquary
The Cabinet of Curiosities
Still Life with Crows
Brimstone
Dance of Death
The Book of the Dead
The Wheel of Darkness
Cemetery Dance
Fever Dream
Cold Vengeance
Two Graves
White Fire
Blue Labyrinth

Gideon Crew Novels

Gideon's Sword
Gideon's Corpse
The Lost Island

Other Novels

Mount Dragon
Riptide
Thunderhead
The Ice Limit

PRESTON & CHILD

CRIMSON SHORE

HEAD
ZEUS

First published in the USA in 2015 by Grand Central Publishing,
a division of Hachette Book Group, Inc.

First published in the UK in 2015 by Head of Zeus, Ltd.

9 7 5 3 1 2 4 6 8

A catalogue record for this book is available from
the British Library.

ISBN (HB): 9781784974206
ISBN (XTPB): 9781784974213
ISBN (E): 9781784974596

Typeset by Adrian McLaughlin

Printed and bound in Germany
by GGP Media GmbH, Pössneck

Head of Zeus Ltd
Clerkenwell House
45–47 Clerkenwell Green
London EC1R 0HT

WWW.HEADOFZEUS.COM

Lincoln Child dedicates this book to
his daughter, Veronica

Douglas Preston dedicates this book to
Ed and Daria White

1

When the doorbell chimed, Constance Greene stopped playing the Flemish virginal and the library fell silent and tense. She glanced in the direction of Special Agent A. X. L. Pendergast, sitting by a dying fire, wearing thin white gloves, having gone quite still while leafing through an illuminated manuscript, a glass of Amontillado half-finished on the side table. Constance recalled the last time someone had rung the doorbell at 891 Riverside Drive—the rarest of occurrences at the Pendergast mansion. The memory of that awful moment now hung in the room like a miasma.

Proctor, Pendergast's chauffeur, bodyguard, and general factotum, appeared. "Shall I answer the door, Mr. Pendergast?"

"Please. But do not let the person in; get their name and business and report back."

Three minutes later, Proctor returned. "It is a man named Percival Lake, and he wishes to hire you for a private investigation."

Pendergast raised a palm, about to dismiss this out of hand. Then he paused. "Did he mention the nature of the crime?"

"He declined to go into any details."

Pendergast seemed to fall into a reverie, his spidery fingers lightly tapping on the gilded spine of the manuscript. "Percival Lake... The name is familiar. Constance, would you be so good as to look that up on... What is that website? It was named after a large mathematical number."

"Google?"

"Ah, yes. *Google* him for me, if you please."

Constance raised her fingers from the age-yellowed ivory keys, moved away from the instrument, opened a small cupboard, and slid out a laptop on a retracting table. She typed for a moment.

"There's a sculptor of that name who does monumental work in granite."

"I thought it rang a bell." Pendergast plucked off the gloves and laid them aside. "Show him in."

As Proctor left, Constance turned to Pendergast with a frown. "Are our finances so sadly reduced that you must resort to moonlighting?"

"Of course not. But the man's work—though rather old-fashioned—is stimulating. As I recall, his figures emerge from the stone much like Michelangelo's *Slave Awakening*. The least I can do is give him an audience."

Moments later Proctor returned. A striking man stood in the doorway behind him: perhaps sixty-five, with a great shock of white hair. The hair was the only thing that looked at all old about him; he was close to six and a half feet tall, with a craggy, handsome face bronzed by the sun, a trim, athletic bearing, wearing a blue blazer over a crisp white cotton shirt and tan slacks. He radiated good health and vigorous living. His hands were massive.

"Inspector Pendergast?" He came striding over with his arm extended and enveloped Pendergast's pale hand in his own gigantic paw, giving it such a shake that it almost knocked over Pendergast's sherry.

Inspector? Constance winced. It looked as if her guardian was going to get his stimulation.

"Pray sit down, Mr. Lake," said Pendergast.

"Thank you!" Lake took a seat, threw one leg over the other, and leaned back.

"Can I offer you anything to drink? Sherry?"

"Don't mind if I do."

Proctor silently poured him a small glass, placing it by his elbow. The sculptor took a sip. "Excellent stuff, thanks. And thank you for agreeing to see me."

Pendergast inclined his head. "Before you tell me your story, I'm afraid I can't claim the title Inspector. That would be British. I am merely a special agent of the FBI."

"I guess I read too many murder mysteries." The man shifted in his chair. "Let me get right to the point. I live in a little seaside town in northern Massachusetts called Exmouth. It's a quiet place, off the tourist trail, and not well known even among the summer crowd. About thirty years ago, my wife and I bought the old lighthouse and keeper's quarters on Walden Point, and I've been there ever since. It's proven an excellent spot for my work. I've always been someone who appreciates fine wine—red, don't bother with white—and the basement of the old house was a perfect place for my rather large collection, being dug into the ground with stone walls and floor, fifty-six degrees summer and winter. Anyway, a few weeks ago, I went away for a long weekend to Boston. When I returned, I found a rear window broken. Nothing had been taken in the house, but when we went to the basement, it was cleaned out. My wine cellar was gone!"

"How terrible for you."

Constance thought she could just detect the faintest note of contemptuous amusement in Pendergast's voice.

"Tell me, Mr. Lake, are you still married?"

"My wife died several years back. I now have a, well, lady friend who lives with me."

"And she was with you the weekend the cellar was stolen?"

"Yes."

"Tell me about your wine."

"Where to start? I had a vertical collection of Chateau Léoville Poyferré going back to 1955, along with excellent collections of all the notable years of Chateau Latour, Pichon-Longueville, Petrus, Dufort-Viviens, Lascombes, Malescot-Saint-Exupéry, Chateau Palmer, Talbot—"

Pendergast stemmed this flood with an upraised hand.

"Sorry," Lake said with a sheepish smile. "I tend to go overboard when it comes to wine."

"Only French Bordeaux?"

"No. More recently I had been collecting some wonderful Italian wines as well, Brunellos, Amarones, and Barolos mostly. All gone."

"Did you go to the police?"

"The Exmouth police chief is worthless. An ass, in fact. He came out of Boston, and he's going through the motions, but it's clear to me he isn't taking it seriously. I suppose if it was a collection of Bud Light he might be more concerned. I need someone who's going to find that wine before it gets dispersed or, God forbid, drunk up."

Pendergast nodded slowly. "So why come to me?"

"I read those books about your work. The ones by Smithback. William Smithback, I believe."

A moment passed before Pendergast replied. "I fear those books grossly distorted the facts. In any case, to the degree

4

that they are true, you must realize I focus my attention on human deviancy—not purloined wine. I'm sorry I cannot be of more assistance."

"Well, I hoped you might, since I understood from those books that you're a bit of a connoisseur yourself." Lake leaned forward in his chair. "Agent Pendergast, I'm a desperate man. My wife and I spent untold hours assembling that collection. Every bottle has a memory, a history, especially of my wonderful years with her. In some ways I feel like she's died all over again. I'd pay you a very good fee."

"I'm indeed sorry I can't help you in the matter. Mr. Proctor will show you out."

The sculptor rose. "Well, I knew it was a long shot. Thanks for listening." His troubled look eased slightly. "All I can say is, thank God the thieves missed the Haut-Braquilanges!"

The room fell silent.

"Chateau Haut-Braquilanges?" Pendergast said faintly.

"Yes, indeed. A full case of '04. My prized possession. It was set aside, in one corner of the cellar, in the original wooden case. The damned idiots just overlooked it."

Proctor opened the door to the library, waiting.

"How did you happen on a case of the '04? I thought it was long gone."

"And so did everyone else. I'm always on the lookout for wine collections for sale, especially when the owner dies and his heirs want to turn it into cash. My wife and I found this case in an old wine collection in New Orleans."

Pendergast raised his eyebrows. "New Orleans?"

"An ancient French family of means that fell onto hard times."

As Constance watched, a look of irritation crossed Pendergast's face—or was it vexation?

Lake turned toward the open door just as Pendergast rose from his chair. "On second thought, I *will* take on your little problem."

"Really?" Lake turned back, his face breaking into a smile. "Wonderful! As I said, whatever your fee is I will be glad—"

"My fee is simple: a bottle of the Haut-Braquilanges."

Lake hesitated. "I was thinking more along the lines of a financial arrangement."

"The bottle is my fee."

"But to break up the case ..." His voice trailed off and a long silence ensued. At last, Lake smiled. "Ah, well, why not? You obviously aren't in need of ready funds. I should be glad to have your help. In fact, you can have your pick of the case!" Flushed with his own gesture of generosity, Lake extended his hand once again.

Pendergast shook it. "Mr. Lake, please leave your address and contact information with Proctor. I will join you in Exmouth tomorrow."

"I'll look forward to seeing you. I haven't touched any-thing in the basement; I left it just as is. The police came through, of course, but they did precious little besides take a few photographs with a cell phone—if you can believe it."

"It would be helpful if you found an excuse to keep them out, should they return."

"Return? Little chance of that."

In a moment he had left, trailed by Proctor. Constance turned toward Pendergast. He returned her look with amused, silvery eyes.

"May I ask what you're doing?" she said.

"Taking a private case."

"Stolen wine?"

"My dear Constance, New York City has been depressingly free of serial murders these last few months. My plate, as they say, is empty. This is a perfect vacation opportunity: a week or two in a charming seaside town, in the off-season, with an amuse-bouche of a case to occupy one's time. Not to mention a congenial client."

"Blustery and self-aggrandizing would be a more suitable characterization."

"You're a worse misanthrope than I am. I for one could use the bracing, autumnal air of the seaside after the events of late."

She glanced at him privately. It was true—after the ordeal he'd endured over the summer, any diversion might be welcome. "But a bottle of wine as payment? Next you'll be offering your services in exchange for a Shake Shack hamburger."

"Unlikely. That wine is the reason, the *only* reason, I took the case. In the nineteenth century, Chateau Haut-Braquilanges produced the finest wines in France. Their signature claret was the product of a single vineyard, of about two acres, planted in Cabernet Sauvignon, Cabernet Franc, and Merlot. It was situated on a hill near Fronsac. Unfortunately, that hill was violently contested in World War I, drenched with mustard gas and poisoned forever, and the chateau leveled. There are at most two dozen bottles left of the vintages from that chateau known to exist. But none from the greatest vintage of all—1904. It was believed extinct. Extraordinary that this fellow has a case of it. You saw how reluctant he was to part with even the one bottle."

Constance shrugged. "I hope you enjoy the vacation."

"I have no doubt it will be a most amiable holiday for us."

"Us? You want me to go with you?" She felt a creeping sensation of heat in her face.

2

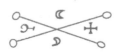

C onstance Greene could smell the sea air as soon as Pendergast turned their vintage Porsche roadster onto the Metacomet Bridge, a decaying pile of rusted trestles and struts that spanned a broad salt marsh. The mid-October sun momentarily glittered off the water as they sped along. On the far side of the marsh, the road plunged momentarily through a dark pine wood, then broke free again. There, lying along a curve where the marshlands met the ocean, lay the town of Exmouth, Massachusetts. To Constance, it looked as she imagined a typical New England town should: a cluster of shingled houses along a main street; several church steeples; a brick town hall. As they slowed and passed down the main street, she examined her surroundings with interest.

The town had a faint air of benign neglect that only added to its charm: a seaside village with white clapboard buildings, seagulls wheeling overhead, uneven brick sidewalks and local shops. They passed a gas station, several old storefronts with plate-glass windows, a diner, a funeral parlor, a movie theater turned into a bookstore, and an eighteenth-century sea captain's mansion, complete with widow's walk. A sign out front identified it as the Exmouth Historical Society and Museum.

The few townspeople strolling on the sidewalks stopped and stared at them as they passed by. Constance found herself surprised at her own curiosity. Although she'd never admit it, she knew that, despite her voluminous reading, she had seen so very little of the world that she felt like a Marco Polo in her own land.

"Do you see any likely wine criminals?" Pendergast asked.

"That elderly gentleman in the madras jacket with the purple bow tie looks suspicious."

Pendergast slowed and carelessly eased the roadster to the curb.

"We're stopping?"

"We have a little time. Let us try what I understand to be a local delicacy: the lobster roll." As they got out, the gentleman in the madras jacket passed with a nod and smile, and continued on.

"Definitely suspicious," murmured Constance.

"He should be locked up on the strength of that bow tie alone."

They walked along the sidewalk and turned down a lane leading to the waterfront. A cluster of fishing shacks mingled with shops and a few restaurants, and a row of piers led into a bay at the mouth of the tidal marshes. Beyond, over the waving sea grasses, Constance could see a bright line of ocean. Could she live in a town like this? Absolutely not. But it was an interesting place to visit.

Alongside the commercial pier stood a seafood shack, with a hand-painted sign of a lobster and a clam dancing to a row of mussels playing instruments.

"Two lobster rolls, please," said Pendergast as they stepped up to the shack.

The food quickly arrived: massive chunks of lobster in a creamy sauce, overstuffed into a buttered, split-top hot dog roll and spilling out into their cardboard trays.

"How does one eat it?" Constance said, eyeing hers.

"I am at a loss."

A two-toned police squad car eased into the nearby parking lot and made a circuit. The car slowed and the driver, a large man with captain's bars on his shoulder, eyed them for a moment, gave a knowing smile, then continued on.

"The chief himself," Pendergast said, tossing his uneaten lobster roll into a trash can.

"Something seemed to have amused him."

"Yes, and I believe we shall soon discover why."

As they strolled back up the main street, Constance saw a ticket fluttering on the Porsche's windscreen. Pendergast pulled it out and examined it. "It seems I parked straddling two spaces. How remiss of me."

Constance saw that Pendergast had indeed parked the car squarely across two painted parking-space lines. "But the entire street is practically free of parked cars."

"One must obey the law."

Pendergast tucked the ticket into his suit pocket and they got into the car. He started it up and eased back out into the main street. In a moment they had passed through town and were out the other side, the shop buildings already giving way to modest shingled houses. The road rose up through grassy meadows bordered by massive oaks before coming out on higher land overlooking the Atlantic. Ahead, toward the bluffs, Constance could see the Exmouth lighthouse—their destination. It was painted bone white with a black top and stood out against the blue sky. Next to it rose the keeper's residence, austere as an Andrew Wyeth painting.

As they approached, Constance also made out a scattering of sculptures in a meadow along the edges of the bluff—rough-cut granite forms with polished and somewhat sinister shapes emerging from the stone: faces, body forms, mythical sea creatures. It was a striking location for a sculpture garden.

Pendergast brought the roadster to a halt in the graveled drive alongside the house. As they got out, Percival Lake appeared in the door, then strode onto the porch.

"Welcome! Good Lord, you certainly travel in style. That's a '55 Spyder 550, if I'm not mistaken," he said as he came down the steps.

"A '54, actually," Pendergast replied. "It's my late wife's car. I prefer something more comfortable, but my associate, Miss Greene, insisted on it."

"I did not," she interjected.

"Your associate." Constance did not like the way the man's eyebrows rose in ironical amusement as he looked at her. "Pleased to see you again."

She shook his hand rather coldly.

"Let us visit the scene of the crime," said Pendergast.

"You don't waste any time."

"In a criminal investigation, there is an inverse relationship between the quality of evidence and the length of time it has been awaiting examination."

"Right." Lake led them into the house. They passed through a front hall and parlor with sweeping views of the ocean. The old house had been immaculately kept up, airy and fresh, with the sea breeze swelling the lace curtains. In the kitchen, an attractive bleached blonde in her thirties, slender and fit, was dicing carrots.

"This is *my* associate, Carole Hinterwasser," Lake told them. "Please meet Agent Pendergast and Constance Greene. They are here to find my wine collection."

The woman turned with a smile, displaying white teeth, dried her hands on a cloth, and shook their hands in turn. "Excuse me, I'm just making a mirepoix. I'm so glad you could come! Perce is really devastated. Those wines meant a lot to him—way more than the value."

"Indeed," said Pendergast. Constance could see his silvery eyes darting about.

"This way," said Lake.

At the back of the kitchen stood a narrow door. Lake opened it, flicked on a light switch. It illuminated a set of steep, rickety stairs going down into darkness. A rich, cool smell of damp earth and stone rose up.

"Take care," he cautioned. "These stairs are steep."

They descended into a mazelike space, with stone walls covered in niter, and a stone floor. In one alcove was a furnace and water heater, in another a finished room with a collection of air tools, sandbags, protection suits, and equipment for polishing stone.

They turned a corner and came into the largest room in the basement. One wall was covered, floor to ceiling, with empty wooden wine racks. Curling yellow labels were tacked to the wood or strewn about the floor, along with broken bottles and a heavy perfume of wine.

Pendergast picked up a piece of a broken bottle, reading the label. "Chateau Latour, '61. These burglars were singularly careless."

"They made a mess of the place, the cretins."

Pendergast knelt before the closest rack, examining it with a bright LED penlight. "Tell me about the weekend of the theft."

"Carole and I had gone away to Boston. We do that frequently, to dine, go to the symphony or a museum—recharge our batteries. We left Friday afternoon and returned Sunday evening."

The light probed here and there. "Who knew you were gone?"

"Pretty much the whole village, I imagine. We have to drive through town on our way out, and as you can see Exmouth is a small place. Everyone knows we make frequent trips to Boston."

"You said they broke a window. I assume the house was locked?"

"Yes."

"Is there an alarm system?"

"No. I suppose in retrospect that seems stupid. But crime is almost nonexistent here. I can't remember the last time there was a burglary in Exmouth."

Now a test tube and tweezers appeared from somewhere in Pendergast's suit. Using the tweezers, he plucked something from the wine rack and put it in the tube.

"What is the history of the house?" he asked.

"It's one of the oldest north of Salem. As I mentioned, it was the lighthouse keeper's place, built in 1704, and added on to at various later dates. My wife and I bought it and took our time with the renovations. As a sculptor I can work anywhere, but we found this to be an idyllic location—quiet, off the beaten track yet close to Boston. Charming and undiscovered. And the local granite is splendid. There's a quarry just on the far side of the salt marshes. Some of the pink granite used to build the Museum of Natural History in New York came out of that quarry. Lovely stuff."

"I should like a tour of your sculpture garden sometime."

"Absolutely! You're staying at the Inn, I assume? I'll be sure to arrange a viewing."

While Lake was praising the local granite, Constance watched as Pendergast moved about on his knees, getting his suit filthy, scrutinizing the cellar floor. "And the bottles of Braquilanges? I assume they are in that case in the far corner?"

"Yes, and thank God they missed them!"

Pendergast rose again. His pale face seemed troubled. He went over to the wine, which sat by itself in a wooden crate with the crest of the chateau stamped on it. The top was loose, and he lifted it up and peered inside. Ever so gently he reached in and removed a bottle, cradling it almost like a baby.

"Who would have believed it?" he murmured.

He put it back.

Crossing the floor, feet crunching on glass, Pendergast returned to the empty wine racks. This time he examined the upper sections. He took a few more samples, shone his light along the ceiling, and then along the floor, where the racks were anchored. Suddenly, he grasped two wooden braces holding up the center part of the racks and gave a mighty pull. With a cracking and groaning of wood the rack came away, exposing the wall behind, laid with dressed stone.

"What in the world—?" Lake began.

But Pendergast ignored him, pulling more pieces of the wine rack away, until the entire central area of the mortared wall behind the rack was exposed. Now, taking out a small penknife, he inserted it between two of the stones and began to scrape and cut, wiggling free one stone and pulling it out. He laid it with care on the ground and shone his penlight through the hole he'd made. With surprise, Constance realized there was a space behind.

"I'll be damned," said Lake, coming forward to look.

"Step back," said Pendergast sharply.

He now removed a pair of latex gloves from a suit pocket and snapped them on. Then he took off his jacket and spread it on the grimy floor, placing the stone upon it. Working more rapidly, but still with great care, he removed another block of stone, and then another, arranging them faceup on his jacket. Constance winced; already the English bespoke suit looked beyond redemption.

A shallow niche gradually became exposed. It was empty, save for chains set into the stone at the top and bottom of the back wall, from which dangled wrist and leg irons. Constance contemplated these with cool detachment; she had long ago discovered similar articles in the subbasement spaces of Pendergast's own Riverside Drive mansion. The FBI agent himself, however, had grown even paler than usual.

"I'm floored," said Lake. "I had no idea—"

"Silence, if you please," Constance interrupted. "My guardian—that is, Mr. Pendergast—is occupied."

Pendergast continued removing stones until the entire niche was exposed. It was about six feet tall, three feet wide, and three feet deep. It was as ancient as the house, and had clearly been built to contain a person. The leg and wrist irons had rusted shut in the closed position, but contained no skeleton. The niche, she noticed, was inexplicably clean, not a speck of dust visible.

Now Pendergast knelt within the niche and probed every little crack and fissure with a magnifying loupe and the small set of tweezers, test tube at the ready. Constance watched him work for ten minutes, before—finding very little—he transferred his attention to the floor immediately in front of the niche. Another lengthy period of probing and poking followed. Lake looked on, clearly having a difficult time remaining silent.

"Ah!" Pendergast suddenly said. He rose, holding what appeared to be a tiny bone in the tweezers. He affixed the loupe to his eye and examined the bone at some length. Then he knelt again, and—almost genuflecting over the stones he'd removed—examined their rear faces with the light and the loupe.

And then he glanced up, silvery eyes fixing on Constance.

"What is it?" she asked.

"The vacation is over."

"What do you mean?"

"This is no mere theft of wine. This is far bigger—and far more dangerous. You can't stay here. You must return to Riverside Drive."

3

C onstance stared at Pendergast's dust-coated face. After a moment, she replied: "Too dangerous? For me? Aloysius, you forget whom you're speaking to."

"I do not."

"Then perhaps you might explain."

"I shall." He dropped the tiny bone into the glass test tube, stoppered it, and handed it to her. "Take this."

She took it, along with the loupe.

"That is the distal phalanx of the left index finger of a human being. You will note the very tip of the bone is chipped, scraped, and fractured. That was done perimortem—at the time of death."

She handed it back. "I can see that."

"Now let us look at the building stones." He pivoted with the penlight. "I've arranged them on my jacket as they were in situ, with the inside face towards us. Note the deep gouges, scratches, and those splatters of a dark substance." She watched as he used the LED as a pointer. "What do they tell you?"

Constance had seen this coming. "That someone, many

years ago, was chained and walled up in that niche alive, and tried to claw his way out."

A mirthless smile gathered on Pendergast's face. "Excellent."

"That's awful," Lake broke in, undisguised shock on his face. "Just *awful*. I had no idea! But...how did you know that niche was there?"

"The thieves did not take the Braquilanges. That was my first clue. Anyone who goes to the trouble of stealing an entire wine cellar is going to know about such a legendary vintage. And they would not have been so clumsy as to break that magnum of '61 Chateau Latour"—here, Pendergast indicated a mess on the floor—"which is worth at least fifteen thousand dollars. So I knew from the start that, though we were undoubtedly dealing with thieves, we were most certainly not dealing with *wine* thieves. No—they were here to get something far more valuable, at least to them. Naturally, this led me to look behind the wine racks, where I saw evidence of recent activity—which in turn led to the niche."

Lake peered a little gingerly into the space. "And you really think a person was walled up in there?"

"Yes."

"And that this whole robbery was staged to...to remove the skeleton?"

"Undoubtedly." Pendergast tapped the test tube in Constance's hand that contained the finger bone.

"Good Lord."

"The walling-up was clearly an ancient crime. Yet the people who took the skeleton must have known about that crime, and either wished to cover it up or wanted to retrieve something in the niche, or both. They went to great lengths to hide their activity. Pity for them they missed this bone. It should prove most eloquent."

"And the danger?" asked Constance.

"My dear Constance! This crime is the work of local people—or, at the very least, someone with a deep history in this town. I'm certain they also knew of something else walled up with the skeleton—presumably something of great value. Since they had to move the wine rack, and would be unable to disguise the disturbance, they staged a theft to cover it up."

"They?" asked Lake. "There was more than one?"

"A presumption on my part. This took a significant amount of effort."

"You still have not addressed the element of danger," said Constance.

"The danger comes from the fact that I will now investigate. Whoever did this will not be happy. They will take steps to protect themselves."

"And you think *I'm* vulnerable?"

The silence stretched on until Constance realized Pendergast was not going to answer the question.

"The only real danger here," she said in a low voice, "is what might happen to the criminals if they make the mistake of crossing swords with you. In that case, they will answer to *me*."

Pendergast shook his head. "That, frankly, is what I fear most." He paused, considering. "If I allow you to remain here, you must keep yourself...under control."

Constance ignored the implication. "I'm confident you'll find me a great help, particularly with the historical aspects—since obviously there's a history here."

"A valid point: no doubt I could benefit from your assistance. But please—no freelancing. I had enough of that with Corrie."

"I am, thankfully, not Corrie Swanson."

A silence fell in the room. "Well," Lake said at last. "Let's get out of this dank basement, have a drink, watch the sun set, and talk about what comes next. I have to say I'm totally floored by this discovery. Rather macabre, but a fascinating diversion nonetheless."

"Fascinating, yes," Pendergast told him. "Dangerous, even more so. Do not forget that, Mr. Lake."

They settled on the porch looking out over the sea while the sun set behind them, shooting purple, orange, and scarlet light into the clouds piled on the eastern horizon. Lake opened a bottle of Veuve Clicquot.

Pendergast accepted a glass. "Mr. Lake, I have to ask you a few more questions, if you don't mind."

"I don't mind the questions, but I do mind the 'Mr. Lake' bit. Call me Perce."

"I am from the South. I would be obliged if I could be indulged and we address each other formally."

Lake rolled his eyes. "Fine, if that's what you want."

"Thank you. You mentioned the unhelpfulness of the police several times. What have they done so far in the case?"

"Not a damned thing! We've only got two cops in town, the chief of police and a young sergeant. They came over, poked around for about fifteen minutes, took some photos, and that was it. No fingerprinting, no nothing."

"Tell me about them."

"The chief, Mourdock, is a bully and dumber than a granite curbstone. He's essentially been on vacation ever since coming up from the Boston PD. Lazy bastard, especially now that he's six months from retirement."

"What about his deputy? The sergeant?"

"Gavin? Not nearly as dumb as his boss. Seems a good fellow—just too much under the chief's thumb." Lake hesitated.

Constance noticed the hesitation. "And the chief knows we're here, does he not?"

"The other day, I'm afraid I put my foot in it. I got a bit hot under the collar with Mourdock. I told him I was going to hire a private detective."

"And his reaction?" Pendergast asked.

"Hot air. Threats."

"What kind of threats?"

"Said if any private dick set foot in his town, he'd arrest him on the spot. I doubt he'd actually do it, of course. But he's bound to cause trouble. I'm sorry—I should have kept my mouth shut."

"And from now on you will—particularly regarding the discovery made today."

"I promise."

Pendergast took a sip of champagne. "Moving on, how much do you know about the specific history of this house and its inhabitants?"

"Not all that much. It was the lightkeeper's house until the 1930s, when the light was automated. The house grew badly neglected. When I bought it, it was practically falling apart."

"And the lighthouse? Does it still operate?"

"Oh, yes. It comes on at dusk. It's no longer needed, of course, but all the lighthouses along the New England coast still run—for nostalgic reasons. I don't actually own the lighthouse itself—it's owned by the U.S. Coast Guard and licensed to the American Lighthouse Foundation, which keeps it up. It's got a fourth-order Fresnel lens, flashing white, nine seconds character. The historical society should have a list of all the lighthouse keepers."

Pendergast glanced at Constance. "There's your first assignment: find out who was keeper of the light when this atrocity occurred in the basement. I will have the finger bone analyzed and get you a date."

She nodded.

He turned back to Lake. "And the town's history? Anything that might shed light on the crypt downstairs?"

Lake shook his head, ran a big, veined hand through his white hair. Constance noticed he had massive arms— probably a result of being a stone sculptor. "Exmouth is a very old fishing and whaling town, established in the early 1700s. I'm not sure what genius decided to situate it on these salt marshes, but it wasn't a great idea. The whole area is plagued by greenheads. Although the fishing was lucrative for decades, it never took off as a summer resort, like Rockport or Marblehead."

"Greenheads?" Pendergast asked. "Is that some type of biting fly?"

"The worst. *Tabanus nigrovittatus*. It's the female of the species who bite and drink blood—naturally."

"Naturally," said Constance dryly. "Only females do the real work."

Lake laughed. "Touché."

"Any dark history to the town? Tales, rumors, murders, intrigue?"

Lake waved his hand. "Rumors."

"Such as?"

"About what you'd expect, given that Salem is just south of here. Stories that a band of witches settled nearby, in the 1690s, trying to escape the trials. Rubbish, of course. Basically, we're what's left of an old New England fishing village. Although the west part of town—they call it Dill Town, but it was incorporated into Exmouth back in the '40s—has its petty crimes now and then. The other side of the tracks, you might say." He took a greedy sip of his champagne. "I must tell you, finding a torture chamber in my basement is quite a shock. I can hardly believe it. It's like that gruesome story by Poe, 'The Cask of Amontillado.'" He paused, looked at Pendergast. "You say there was something of value inside, too? Like a pirate treasure, maybe? The skeleton guarding the chest of gold?"

"It's too early to speculate."

Lake turned to Constance, a twinkle in his eye. "What do you think? Any speculations?"

Constance gazed back at him. "No. But a certain phrase does come to mind."

"Which is?"

"*For the love of God, Montresor!*"

Pendergast looked at her sharply, then at Lake, whose startled face had momentarily gone pale. "You'll have to excuse my associate," Pendergast said. "She has a rather mordant sense of humor."

Constance smoothed down her dress with a prim gesture.

4

Pendergast pulled the Porsche roadster—its top down to greet the late-morning sunlight—into a parking space along Main Street.

"Automobiles are still something of a novelty to me," Constance said as she got out. "But even I can tell you've parked improperly. You've straddled the line again."

Pendergast merely smiled. "Let us go shopping."

"You can't be serious."

"Constance, one of the first things you must learn when on a case with me is not to question every little thing. Now...I see some lovely Hawaiian shirts in that shop window—and they're even on sale!"

She followed him into the shop and pretended to look through a rack of tennis whites while Pendergast went through the Hawaiian shirts, selecting several of them, apparently at random. She heard him chatting up the clerk, asking her if they ever had problems with shoplifting and whether the security camera clearly visible in the front window was really necessary. She frowned as she heard the clerk ringing up his purchases. She assumed he was taking the measure of the town, but it seemed so random, so unfocused, given the fact there were many other pressing matters to investigate. For example, the list of lighthouse keepers, awaiting her in the Historical Society's archives—and the carbon 14 dating of the finger bone.

Soon they were back out on the street, Pendergast holding a shopping bag. He loitered in the doorway of the shop, checking his watch.

"How many yards of execrable taste, exactly, did you buy?" Constance asked, eyeing the bag.

"I didn't notice. Let us linger here for a moment."

Constance peered at him. Perhaps it was her imagination, but he seemed to have a look of anticipation on his face.

And then she saw, rolling down Main Street, the two-toned police car.

Pendergast checked his watch again. "New Englanders are so wonderfully punctual."

The car slowed and pulled to the curb. A policeman got out; the chief they had seen the day before. Constance was not a great judge of twentieth-century masculinity, but this fellow looked like a 1950s college football star gone to seed: crew cut, thick neck, and square jaw, perched atop an enormous, lumpy frame. Hiking up his jangling belt, the man pulled out a thick ticket book and began writing a ticket for the roadster.

Pendergast approached. "May I inquire as to the problem?"

The policeman turned to him, rubbery lips distending into a smile. "Slow learner?"

"What do you mean?"

"Straddling the spaces again. I guess one citation wasn't enough."

Pendergast pulled out the previous ticket. "You mean this?"

"That's right."

Pendergast neatly tore it in half and tucked the pieces back into his pocket.

The chief frowned. "Cute."

Constance winced at the man's heavy South Boston accent. Was there an accent in English more grating? Pendergast was being his provocative self, and she began to understand his look of anticipation. This might prove enjoyable. At the right moment, he would pull his FBI shield and put this verminous cop in his place.

The man finished writing the ticket, slid it up under the windshield wipers. "There you go." He grinned. "Another one for you to tear up."

"Don't mind if I do." Pendergast plucked it out, tore it in half, and pushed the pieces into his pocket, giving it a little pat with his hand.

"You can tear them up all day, but that won't make them go away." The chief leaned forward. "Let me give you a little free advice. We don't appreciate some wannabe private dick coming into our town and interfering with our investigation. So watch your step."

"I am acting as a private investigator, yes," Pendergast said. "I do, however, take exception to the use of the term 'dick.'"

"My sincere apologies for using the term '*dick*.'"

"Several hundred thousand dollars' worth of wine were stolen," Pendergast said, his voice taking on a pompous tone. "This is grand larceny at the highest level. Since the police seem unable, or unwilling, to make any progress on solving this case, *I* have been called in."

The chief frowned. Despite the autumnal warmth, beads of sweat began to appear on his greasy brow. "All right. You know what? I'm going to be watching everything you do.

One step, one *toe*, over the line and I'll run you out of this town so fast your head will spin. Is that clear?"

"Certainly. And while I investigate grand larceny, you may continue to protect the town from the scourge of straddled parking."

"You're quite the comedian."

"That was an observation, not a pleasantry."

"Well, observe this: next time you straddle a parking space, I'll tow your vehicle." He ran a pair of thick fingers along the side of the car. "Now, please move it into a legal parking place."

"You mean, right now?"

The cop's breath was coming harder. "Right now," he said.

Pendergast got in, started the car, and moved it back, but he stopped prematurely, leaving the rear bumper just on the line.

He got out. "There."

The cop stared at him. "You're still over the line."

Pendergast looked at the Porsche in an exaggerated fashion, scrutinizing the bumper and the painted line and frowning. "It's *on* the line—not over. Besides, look at all the parking spaces on the street. Who's going to care?"

The cop's breathing had become a wheeze. "You little prick, you think you're funny?"

"First you called me a 'dick.' Now you've called me a 'prick.' I commend you on your poesy. But you seem to forget that a lady is present. Perhaps your mother should have employed the soap treatment more frequently to your rather orotund mouth."

Constance had seen Pendergast deliberately provoke people before, but not quite so belligerently. She wondered why the first thing he'd done in this investigation was to go out of his way to make an enemy of the chief of police.

The chief took a step closer. "Okay. I'm done. I want you

out of this town. *Now.* Get back in your faggoty little vehicle and you and your girlfriend get your asses out."

"Or?"

"Or I'll take you in for loitering and disturbing the peace."

Most uncharacteristically, Pendergast laughed aloud. "No, thank you. I'm going to stay as long as I please. In fact, I'm looking forward to watching the baseball game at the Inn tonight—during which, no doubt, the New York Yankees will firmly insert the Red Sox back into the cesspit they've been trying to crawl out of during the American League championship."

A long, steaming silence. Then the cop, calmly and with deliberation, reached down to his belt and unhooked a pair of handcuffs. "Put your hands behind your back, sir, and turn around."

Pendergast instantly complied. The chief slapped on the cuffs.

"Right this way, *sir.*" He gave Pendergast a gentle nudge toward the patrol car. Constance waited for Pendergast to say something, pull his shield. But he did nothing.

"Just a minute," she said to the cop's retreating back, her voice low.

He stopped and turned.

Constance looked into the man's face. "You do this, and you'll be the sorriest man in the state of Massachusetts."

The chief's eyes widened in mock fear. "Are you threatening me?"

"Constance?" Pendergast asked, his voice managing to be pleasant while at the same time full of warning.

Constance kept her attention on the chief. "I'm not threatening you," she said. "I'm merely predicting a sad and humiliating future for you."

"And who's going to do this, exactly—*you*?"

"Constance?" Pendergast said, a little louder.

She made a great effort to stifle her reply, to stem the furious flow of blood that suddenly thrummed in her ears.

"Bitch." The cop turned and continued to ease Pendergast toward the squad car, the FBI agent going willingly. The chief opened the back door and put his hand on Pendergast's head to push him into the seat.

"Bring the checkbook to the station," Pendergast told Constance, reaching into his pocket with some difficulty and tossing her the car keys, "so you can make bail."

Constance stared as the squad car pulled away from the curb and went speeding down Main Street with a screech of rubber, slowing her breathing, waiting for the red mist to recede from her vision. It wasn't until the car was out of sight that she remembered there was no one to drive their roadster.

5

The Exmouth police station was located in a quaint brick building at the opposite end of town.

"Please take care to park within the lines," said Constance to the young man she had recruited to drive the car the length of town. He'd been gawking at the car while she stood there, wondering what to do, and she had offered to let him drive it. He had leapt at the chance. Only once he was in the car had she noticed he smelled like fish.

He pulled the car into the space and yanked the parking break.

"Wow," he said. "I can't believe it. What a ride." He looked at her. "Where'd you get this car?"

"It isn't mine. Thank you very much for being a gentleman. You may go now."

He hesitated and she had the sense he was noticing her for the first time, his eyes roving over her figure. He was a brawny, honest yeoman type, with a wedding ring on his left hand. "Say, if you're free later—"

"I'm not, and neither are you," she said, plucking the keys from his hand. She exited the car and began walking toward the police station, leaving the man in the parking lot staring after her.

She entered a surprisingly spotless waiting room, presided over by portraits of the governor and the lieutenant governor, with a large gold-fringed American flag in the corner and a wood-paneled wall covered with plaques and commendations. A tiny woman sat behind a desk, answering phones and trying to look busy. Beyond her, through the open door, Constance could hear a television, tuned to a game show of some kind.

"May I help you?" the woman asked.

"I'm here to—what is the term?—make bail for Mr. Pendergast."

The lady looked at her curiously. "He's being processed. Please have a seat. May I have your name?"

"Constance Greene." She seated herself, smoothing her long dress.

A young policeman emerged from the back rooms, then paused, staring at her. Constance returned the look. Was there something strange about this town, or was it she who was strange? He was dark and Italian-looking, with a brooding expression. He seemed to flush at her stare, turned away, gave the receptionist a piece of paper, spoke to her briefly, then turned back to Constance. "Are you here for Pendergast?"

"Yes."

A hesitation. "It may be several hours."

Why on earth hasn't he pulled rank by now? "I'll wait."

He left. She found the lady behind the desk looking at her curiously as well. She seemed eager to talk, and Constance, who normally would have shut her out as one shuts a door, recalled that she was supposed to be investigating, and that this was an opportunity. She gave the lady what she hoped was a welcoming smile.

"Where are you from?" the woman asked.

"New York."

"I didn't know there were Amish in New York."

Constance stared at her. "We're not Amish."

"Oh, I'm so sorry! I just assumed, with the man in the black suit, and you with that dress…" Her voice trailed off. "I hope I didn't offend."

"Not in the least." Constance looked at the woman more closely. She was about fifty. The avid look on her face spoke of dull routine and a thirst for gossip. Here was someone who would know everything going on in the town. "We're just old-fashioned," she said, with another forced smile.

"Are you here on vacation?"

"No. We've investigating the burglary of Percival Lake's wine cellar."

A silence. "The man in the black suit is a private investigator?"

"In a manner of speaking. I'm his assistant."

The woman became nervous. "Well, well," she said, cracking some papers on the desk and shuffling them about, suddenly busy.

Perhaps she should not have been so quick to disclose their purpose in town. She would try a new tack. "How long have you worked here?" Constance asked.

"Twenty-six years."

"Do you like it?"

"It's a nice town. Friendly."

"Do you have much crime here?"

"Oh, no. Hardly any. The last murder we had here was in 1978."

"Other crimes?"

"The usual. Mostly kids. Vandalism, shoplifting, under-age drinking—that's about it."

"So this is unusual? Arresting someone for loitering and disturbing the peace?"

A nervous hand adjusted her hairdo. "I can't say. Excuse me, I have work to take care of." She went back to her paper-work.

Constance felt chagrined. How on earth did Pendergast do it? She would have to pay more attention to his methods.

It was late afternoon when the young policeman came back out and gave some papers to the lady behind the desk.

"Miss Greene?" the lady asked.

She rose.

"Bail has been set. Five hundred dollars."

As Constance wrote out the check, the woman explained the terms and slid the paperwork toward her. She signed it.

"It won't be too much longer," the woman promised.

And it wasn't: five minutes later, Pendergast appeared in the doorway in surprisingly good spirits. The bag with the Hawaiian shirts had vanished.

"Excellent, most excellent," he said. "Let us go."

Constance said nothing as they walked to the car.

"How did you get the car here?" Pendergast asked, seeing it at the curb.

She explained.

Pendergast frowned. "I would have you keep in mind that there are dangerous characters buried in this little town."

"Trust me, he wasn't one of them."

As they got into the car, Constance felt her irritation

rising. He held his hand out for the keys, but she made no move to give them to him.

"Aloysius."

"Yes?"

"What in God's name do you think you're doing?"

"What do you mean?"

"You deliberately provoked the chief and got yourself arrested. Several hours ago. And I assume you didn't tell him you're an FBI agent."

"No."

"How, exactly, is this supposed to help our investigation?"

Pendergast laid a hand on her shoulder. "I want to commend you for your restraint with the chief, by the way. He is a most unpleasant man. Now to answer your question: this will *directly* help our investigation."

"Would you care to explain?"

"I would not. All shall become clear, I promise you."

"Your inscrutability is going to drive me mad."

"Patience! Now, shall we return to the Inn? I have an engagement with Percival Lake. Would you care to join us for some dinner, perhaps? You must be famished."

"I'll have dinner in my room, thank you."

"Very well. Let us hope it proves less disappointing than this morning's breakfast."

They were driving along a narrow lane between old New England stone walls. Now the trees parted, revealing the Captain Hull Inn: a large, rambling Victorian sea captain's house, shingled in gray with white trim, standing by itself in a broad meadow, packed tightly around with Carolina rose bushes heavy with hips. It had a large wraparound porch with white pillars and a dozen rocking chairs looking out to sea, with a view of the Exmouth lighthouse about a half mile down the coast. The crushed-oyster-shell parking lot contained several cars. Constance had found her room, which she'd checked into the night before, pleasantly old-fashioned.

"When is your trial?" Constance asked. "I understand that small towns such as this often believe in dispensing swift justice."

"There will be no trial." Pendergast looked at her, evidently absorbing the expression on her face. "Constance, I'm not trying to be deliberately perverse. It is simply better for your education into my methods if you witness how events unfold naturally. Now, shall we?" And with that he put his hand on the frame of the roadster, got out, and opened the door for her.

6

Percival Lake paused in the doorway of the Chart Room restaurant, spotting Pendergast immediately among the knots of diners. The man stuck out like a sore thumb, all black and white among this crowd of New England folk in madras and seersucker. In Lake's experience, even eccentric and unconventional people carefully curated their persona. Very few truly didn't give a goddamn what others thought. Pendergast was one.

Lake rather liked that.

Pendergast was gazing at the chalkboard—the Chart Room of the Captain Hull Inn had no printed menus—with a frown. As Lake threaded his way through the tables, Pendergast glanced up, then rose. They shook hands.

"I love this room," said Lake as they sat down. "The old sawn pine planks on the floor, the nautical instruments, the stone fireplace. It's very cozy, especially now, in the fall. When it gets chillier they'll light the fire."

"I find it rather like a coffin," said Pendergast.

Lake laughed and glanced at the chalkboard. "The wine in here is rotgut, but the Inn has a nice selection of craft beers. There's a local one I highly recommend—"

"I am not a drinker of beer."

The waitress—a young woman with close-cropped hair almost as blond as Pendergast's—came over to take their orders. "What can I get you gentlemen?" she asked perkily.

A silence as Pendergast glanced over the bottles arrayed behind the bar. Then his pale eyebrows shot up. "I see you have absinthe."

"I think it's sort of an experiment."

"I'll have that, if you please. Make sure the water you bring with it is fresh springwater, not tap, and absolutely ice cold but without ice, along with a few sugar cubes. If you could manage a slotted spoon and a reservoir glass, that would be most appreciated."

"A reservoir glass." The waitress scribbled everything down. "I'll do my best."

"Shall we order dinner?" Lake asked. "The fried clams are a specialty."

Pendergast shot another glance at the chalkboard. "Perhaps later."

"A pint of the Riptide IPA for me, please."

The waitress went away and Lake turned to Pendergast. "Striking-looking girl. She's new."

He could see Pendergast had so little interest he didn't appear to have heard.

Lake cleared his throat. "I hear you got yourself arrested today. It's all over town, of course. You've made quite a splash."

"Indeed."

"I guess you had your reasons."

"Naturally."

The young waitress returned with their drinks, setting everything in front of Pendergast: glass; spoon—not slotted;

a dish of sugar cubes; a small glass pitcher of water; and the absinthe in a tall glass. "I hope this is okay," she said.

"A credible effort," said Pendergast. "Thank you."

"Looks like you're about to conduct a chemistry experiment," said Lake as Pendergast carefully arranged everything.

"There is in fact some chemistry involved," Pendergast said, placing a sugar cube in the spoon, balancing it over the absinthe glass, and carefully dribbling the water over it.

Lake watched the green liquid turn cloudy. The scent of anise drifted across the small table and he shuddered.

"There are certain oil-based herbal extracts in absinthe that dissolve in alcohol but have poor solubility with water," Pendergast explained. "They come out of solution when you add the water, creating the opalescence, or *louche*."

"I'd try it if I didn't hate licorice. Isn't wormwood supposed to cause brain damage?"

"The act of living causes brain damage."

Lake laughed and raised his glass. "In that case: to Exmouth and the mystery of the walled-up skeleton."

They clinked glasses. Pendergast sipped from his and set it down. "I've noticed a somewhat cavalier attitude in you," he said.

"How so?"

"You've just lost a very valuable wine collection. Usually, burglaries leave people feeling unsettled, violated. Yet you appear to be in good spirits."

"And with you on the case, why not?" Lake sipped his beer. "I take life pretty easily, I guess. I learned to do that, growing up."

"And where did you grow up?"

"Outpost, Minnesota. Quite a name, isn't it? Just twenty miles south of International Falls. Population, one hundred and twenty. The winters were right out of Kafka. To cope, you either drank, went crazy, or learned to take life as it comes." Lake chuckled. "Most of us chose the last option." He took another sip of beer. "Had a quarry just outside of town. That's how I got into working with stone. Plenty of time on my hands between November and April."

"And then?"

"Well, there I was—a Midwestern farm boy, gone to New York to make it in the art world. It was in the early '80s and my work somehow struck a chord. What's old is new again, that was the idea. What a crazy place. As I became more successful, it went to my head—the money, the fame, the parties, the whole god-awful, pretentious, downtown-art-gallery world." He shook his head. "Like everyone else, I got into cocaine. I finally woke up. I realized if I didn't do something, get out of that environment, I'd lose my muse entirely."

"How did you pick this place?"

"I'd met this great gal, and she was as sick of New York as I was. She'd spent summers in Newburyport as a child. We bought the lighthouse, restored it, and the rest is history. We had a good run, Elise and me. God, I loved her. Miss her every day."

"How did she die?"

Lake was a bit startled by the directness of the question and the use of the word *die*, when everyone else employed such euphemisms as "passed." "Pancreatic cancer. She was diagnosed, and three months later she was gone."

"You never get bored here?"

"If you're serious about being an artist, you need to work in a quiet place. You've got to retreat from the world, away from the bullshit, the curators, the critics, the trends. And on a practical level, I also needed space. I do big pieces. And

I mentioned the wonderful source of pink granite just up the coast. I can go to the quarry and pick out my stone, and they custom-cut it and deliver. Luscious stuff."

"I'm somewhat familiar with your work," said Pendergast. "You're not afraid to avoid the trendy or the ephemeral. And you have an excellent feeling for the stone."

Lake found himself blushing. He sensed this man rarely, if ever, gave out praise.

"And your new friend, Ms. Hinterwasser? How did you meet her?"

This was becoming a little too direct. "After Elise died, I took a cruise. I met her there. She'd recently divorced."

"She decided to move in with you?"

"I invited her. I don't like being alone. And celibacy does not suit me—not at all."

"Does she share your enthusiasm for wine?"

"She's more a daiquiri and margarita drinker."

"We all have our flaws," said Pendergast. "And the town itself? How would you characterize it?"

"Quiet. Nobody here cares much that I'm a relatively famous sculptor. I can go about my business without being bothered."

"But...?"

"But...I suppose all small towns have a dark side. The affairs and feuds, the crooked real estate deals, the incompetent selectmen—you know, New England's version of town fathers—and of course, a chief of police who spends most of his time ticketing out-of-state cars to collect money for his salary."

"You've told me some of the chief's history already."

"The rumor was he got into trouble down in Boston. It wasn't enough to get him fired, just queered his career prospects. Bit of a yahoo, obviously, although he's acquired a veneer of polish over the years."

"What kind of trouble?"

"They say he put too much muscle on a suspect, coerced or threatened him into confessing to something he didn't do. The guy was later exonerated by DNA and had to be released, won a big lawsuit against the city."

"And his deputy?"

"Gavin?" Lake paused. "He's a good fellow. Quiet. Native of Exmouth. His father used to be chief of police. College educated—U Mass Boston, I believe. Did well enough, majored in Criminal Justice. Everybody expected him to go on to great things. Instead, he came back to work on the same force his father had led—much to the town's delight, I might add. Naturally, he has his eye on Mourdock's job." He paused. "Ready for a bite?"

Another glance at the chalkboard. "May I ask if there is a better restaurant in town?"

Lake laughed. "You're sitting in numero uno. They just can't get past the mind-set of New England pub fare: broiled scrod, burgers, fried clams. But there's a new guy in the kitchen, they say he's retired Navy. Maybe he's going to improve things."

"We shall see."

Lake looked at him. "I'm sort of curious about you, Mr. Pendergast. I've been trying to place your accent. I know it's from the South, but I can't seem to put my finger on it."

"It's a New Orleans accent found in the French Quarter."

"I see. And what brought you to New York? If you don't mind me asking."

Lake could see, from the expression on the man's face, that he did mind.

"I came to New York on an investigation some years ago. The New York Field Office asked me to stay."

Trying to get back on safer ground, Lake asked: "Are you married? Any kids?"

Now he could see this was one question too far. The gracious expression on Pendergast's face vanished and there was a long silence before he said, "No," in a voice that would freeze water.

Lake covered up his embarrassment with another swig of beer. "Let's talk about the case, then. I'm curious if you have any theories about whodunit."

"No theories that rise above the level of rank speculation." Pendergast glanced around, the blank look fading from his face. "Perhaps it would be more efficacious if you'd tell me about the people in this room."

Lake was a little taken aback by this request. "You mean, their names?"

"Names, background précis, peculiarities."

Lake ordered a second beer—this time, a Thunderhead IPA. He had a big appetite and had to eat something soon. He leaned forward. "There's one thing they can't screw up in this restaurant: oysters on the half shell."

At this, Pendergast perked up. "Excellent suggestion. Let us order two dozen."

Lake waved over the waitress and placed the order. He leaned forward. "Let's see. The new waitress—"

"We need not discuss the waitress. Next?"

"Hmmm..." Lake looked around the room. There were only two tables occupied in addition to the bartender and a man at the bar. "The man behind the bar is Joe Dunwoody. The Dunwoodys are an old Exmouth family, go way back to colonial times. His brother Dana is one of the selectmen, and a pretty shrewd lawyer to boot. You don't cross him."

"And if you do?"

"You might not get a permit for that garage you want to build. Or the septic inspector might show up and red-tag your system. Petty stuff—but annoying."

"Next."

Lake looked around. "See that busty woman in the corner nursing a Seven and Seven? Dolores Claybrook. Town busybody. Horrible woman, the very definition of *schadenfreude*. Her family was one of the wealthiest in town, made their money in Gloucester—shipbuilding. A branch moved here and got into the codfishing business. They went into a decline along with the cod. She's the last one left, buried three husbands. If you winked at her and pinched her ass you could really get her talking."

"Perhaps some other time. Next?"

"That couple at the table near the window—Mark and Sarah Lillie. He runs the local insurance agency, dabbles in small-town investments. They own a financial-planning business on the side. His family goes way back, too—guess almost everyone in Exmouth does. Originally from Oldham."

"Oldham?"

"Small town that was situated on Crow Island, south of here. It was destroyed in the hurricane of '38. Most of the residents settled in Dill Town, which had previously been abandoned. The Lillie family has since integrated itself with the blue blood of Exmouth—or what passes for it, anyway."

Pendergast indicated a tweedy man eating dinner at the bar. "And that rather curious fellow, the one with the leather patches on his jacket?"

"He's not from around here—obviously. English. He was here a few weeks ago, doing historical research on a

44

maritime mystery rather famous in these parts. Now it seems he's back, I don't know why."

"A maritime mystery?"

"The 1884 disappearance of the SS *Pembroke Castle*, out of London, bound for Boston. It vanished at night in a nor'easter somewhere along the stretch of coast between Cape Elizabeth and Cape Ann. Not a trace was found, not even a broken spar. You get people coming through from time to time, trying to figure out what happened. It's like the *Flying Dutchman* or the *Marie Celeste*."

"Curious. And the gentleman's name?"

"Morris McCool."

"Have you met him?"

"No. But I must say, there's something suspicious about him. If he wasn't from 'away,' he'd be my first suspect for the theft of my wine cellar. Morris McCool...there's a made-up name if ever I heard one."

"On the contrary, no one would invent a pseudonym like that."

Lake paused while the waitress brought them a large platter of raw oysters on a bed of crushed ice, with a side of cocktail sauce, grated horseradish, and lemon slices.

"How do you like them?" Lake asked.

"Lemon and no more."

"There's my man." Lake squeezed lemon over the glossy, fat oyster-bodies, watching the edges curl as the acid hit them.

"After you."

Pendergast picked up one and, with a quick gesture, brought the shell to his lips, soundlessly sucked in the oyster, laid the empty shell down with feline delicacy, and dabbed at his lips.

Lake took another and they fell into silence as they proceeded to suction in one plump oyster after another in rapid succession until the platter was nothing but glistening, empty shells.

Pendergast gave a final dab to his lips, then folded up the napkin and glanced at his watch. "Now I must be on my way. That was most enjoyable—thank you for the suggestion."

"My pleasure." There was something about this fellow that Lake found curiously attractive: the keen marble face, the black suit, the austere look...and, not least, his avidity for oysters.

7

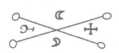

M orris McCool departed the Captain Hull Inn, feeling quite expansive despite the shepherd's pie that lay heavily in his gut. While the meal had been a travesty of the real dish, he was quite surprised at the fine range of local beers and ales now available in America; on his last visit, twenty years before, he'd been hard-pressed to find something other than Coors.

McCool was an enthusiastic walker. Back in his village in Penrith, Cumbria, he always took a walk after dinner to aid digestion. He was a great believer in fresh air and exercise, and it was on these after-dinner walks that he'd had many of his historical insights and ideas.

But this would be a walk with a purpose. Taking a hand-sketched map from his pocket, he perused it, oriented himself, and started toward a silvered wooden staircase leading down the bluffs to the beach below.

The rollers came in on a regular cadence, thundering and hissing up the strand, withdrawing in a sheen and repeating. Keeping to where the sand was still firm from the dampness of the retreating tide, he continued down the beach toward the broad marshes where the river Exmouth flowed into the bay. The infamous "greenheads," which dominated the heat of the day, had retired for the cool October evening.

He inhaled the salt air with satisfaction. He was so close now ... so very close. While there were still some puzzling—indeed, quite inexplicable—aspects, he was sure he had solved the main mystery.

The beach was deserted, save for a small figure behind him enjoying a similar evening stroll. The figure seemed to have appeared rather suddenly, out of the marshes. McCool was not pleased that someone might note where he was going, and he quickened his pace to leave the fellow traveler behind. Even as he walked, the lighthouse on the distant bluff began winking on and off, no doubt automated to come on as the sun set. And the orange globe of the sun was sinking down into the skeleton pines along the verge of the marsh.

The beach turned inward where a ribbon of the Exmouth entered the ocean, the current flowing out of the broad estuary with the ebbing tide, exposing dark gray mudflats. There was a rich but not entirely unpleasant smell coming off the flats. As he made the turn, he glanced back and was considerably startled to see the figure behind him was much closer. The man must have been walking briskly, perhaps even jogging, to have gained on him that much. Was he trying to catch up? Even from a distance McCool didn't like the look of the man.

A faint trail led through the marsh grass along the edge of the trees, and he quickened his pace even more. The man was perhaps a hundred yards behind now, dressed in rough-hewn and rather obscure-looking clothing. Or at least that was McCool's impression from a quick glance.

He walked along the trail, checking the rude map. The

nineteenth-century working waterfront, long abandoned, was around the next bend of the estuary. As he turned the corner, it came into view: a series of old wooden pilings extending in parallel rows of stubs into the bay, the decking long gone. Massive granite pilings, formed of rough-cut blocks, still stood along the shore—and would stand to the end of time—the granite foundations of loading docks and wharves, along with a ruined fish-processing plant. McCool had carefully mapped this area, using historical documents and photographs to re-create the waterfront of the 1880s. This was where the draggers and seiners and coasters had plied their trade, having endured a long economic decline from the whaling heyday of the eighteenth and early nineteenth centuries. The moribund waterfront had finally succumbed to the infamous "Yankee Clipper" hurricane of 1938. The modern waterfront had been rebuilt farther up the estuary, in a more protected location. But the town had never really recovered.

As the rotting piers came into view, McCool heard a sound behind him and turned to find the man approaching him at a determined rate. And now he noticed what a peculiar and frightening figure this was: with a strangely warped face, a Brillo-brush of wiry red hair, disturbing wet lips thicker on one side than the other, a splotch of diseased-like freckles, a three-pointed beard, and a projecting brow with a single bushy eyebrow straight across. McCool thought he knew everyone in town, but he had never seen this fellow before. He was the stuff of nightmares.

He carried a bayonet in one hand, which—as he approached with fast stride and gleaming eyes—he unsheathed with a zing of steel.

With an involuntary cry of confusion and fear, McCool

turned and ran toward the old piers. His pursuer also broke into a run, keeping pace, not closing in or dropping behind, almost as if driving him forward.

McCool cried out for help once, then again, but he was far from the town and his voice was swallowed by the vast marshlands beyond the rotting piers.

In an effort to escape his pursuer, he plunged off the trail, scrambled up an embankment above the first pier, vaulted over a stone foundation, and clawed his way through a thicket of raspberry bushes. He could hear his pursuer crashing along behind.

"What do you want?" McCool cried, but received no answer.

The brambles tore at his pants and shirt, scratching his face and hands. He burst out the other side of the thicket and continued along the contours of the embankment, stumbling past a rotting, caved-in fish house and a tangle of rusted cables and chains.

This was insane. He was being pursued by a lunatic.

He sobbed in panic, gasping, sucking in air. In his terror he tripped over another broken foundation and rolled partway down the embankment, regained his feet, then sprinted into a broad area of marsh grass. Maybe he could lose the man in the grass. He pushed forward, pinwheeling his arms, pressing through the thick grasses. He glanced back; the red-haired lunatic was still following, eyes like coals, sweeping effortlessly along, bayonet in hand.

"Help!" he screamed. "Someone help me!"

A flock of blackbirds burst upward from a swath of cattails in a mass of beating wings. There was no way to outrun this dogged pursuer. He was just being pushed deeper and deeper into the marsh.

The water. If he could just reach the water. He was a strong swimmer. The lunatic might not swim as well.

He veered left, toward the heart of the marsh. Now the grass was so high he couldn't see ahead, and he stumbled forward, bashing aside the sharp grass with his arms, barely noticing the cuts and slashes it inflicted. On and on he plunged, hearing the crash and swish of his pursuer, now only a dozen feet behind. The bay or a marsh channel would be ahead somewhere. Something, for God's sake, *something...*

And suddenly the grasses ended and he burst onto a mud-flat, stretching ahead fifty yards to a swift-flowing channel of water.

No help for it; he leapt into the mud, sinking to his knees. With a cry of fear, he struggled, flopping and sucking and flailing through the muck. He turned and saw the red-haired freak standing at the edge of the grass, bayonet in hand, his entire face distorted into a grotesque grinning visage.

"*Who are you?!*" he screamed.

The man melted back into the grass and disappeared.

For a moment McCool stood in the muck, gasping for breath, coughing, his hands on his knees, feeling as if his lungs might fall out. What to do now? He looked around. The channel lay fifty feet farther on, a muddy stream going out with the tide. On the far side was more endless marsh.

Never would he go back into that nightmare of grass: not with that maniac lurking in there. Never. And yet the only way out of this hell was back through the grass, or else to take to the water and drift out with the tide.

He stood there, heart pounding. The light was fading; the water ran on and the blackbirds wheeled about, crying.

He slopped his way toward the water channel. The mud grew firmer as he approached the edge, where he paused.

The mud was cold—and the water, he knew, would be colder still. But he had no choice.

He waded in. It was very cold. He pushed off, letting the current take him, and he began to swim downstream, burdened by the tweed jacket and mud-soaked trousers and heavy leather shoes. But he was an experienced swimmer and kept himself above water, taking long strokes, making fast time, the marsh grass slipping by. The channel narrowed, the current growing swifter, the grass closing in on both sides. He was heading toward the sea. That was all he could focus on. Thank God, he would soon see the beach, where he could climb out and get back to the safety of the Inn.

As he rounded another bend in the channel, swimming frantically, he saw the wall of grass part to reveal a figure: red hair, distorted grinning face, blazing yellow eyes, gleaming bayonet.

"God, no. *No!*" he screamed, making frantically for the far shore of the channel even as the current swept him toward the embankment where the figure stood—even as the figure leapt like a raptor into the water, crashing down on him—even as the thrust of cold steel felt like a sudden icicle piercing his guts.

8

I ndira Ganesh had received the small bone late the previous
evening and had worked on it all night and throughout the
day. It was now ten pm and she'd been working nearly thirty
hours straight, but she hardly felt tired. She liked working
at night, when her lab, at the Peabody Museum on Divinity
Avenue, Cambridge, was as quiet as a temple. In such an
atmosphere, the work was like meditation or even prayer.
When people were around she was never so productive.

And this little bone was just the sort of puzzle she liked.
Absolutely no information had come in with it—not even
identification that it was human. She had no idea who needed
the analysis or why. Only that Howard Kress, chairman of
Harvard's Department of Human Evolutionary Biology and
her boss, had personally brought her the bone and said, in
mysterious terms, that if he could have a complete and total
analysis by the morning after next, he would consider it the
greatest personal favor.

She had all the equipment and machines she needed at
her disposal and she'd gone right to work. Identifying the
bone as the right distal phalanx of a human index finger had

been easy. From there the questions grew deeper and harder to answer. She always felt as if the bones she studied were whispering to her, eager to tell their stories. Now she had the story of this little bone—or at least, all that she could coax from it in thirty hours.

As Ganesh hunched over her computer, preparing to type up the preliminary report, she had a strange feeling of something behind her, the almost psychic pressure of a person's gaze on her back. She turned and gasped: a tall, pale man with a striking face stood in the doorway.

"Dr. Ganesh? I'm so sorry to disturb you. The name is Pendergast. I am the one interested in the finger bone."

She put her hand on her chest. "You gave me such a start."

"May I take a seat?"

When she hesitated, he reached into his jacket pocket, removed the shield of a special agent with the Federal Bureau of Investigation.

"Please," she said, indicating a chair. "But how did you get in here? The museum's closed."

"Someone must have left a door unlocked. Now, if you don't mind, could we chat about the bone?"

"I was just writing up the results."

The man waved his hand. "I'd much rather hear it from you directly. I'm in something of a hurry."

"All right." She paused, recovering from her surprise, collecting her thoughts, determining where to start. "First of all, the size and robustness of the bone suggests a male. Someone with big, strong hands. The muscle attachments were so pronounced that I can say with confidence this person performed daily work, hard manual work, involving grasping and holding."

"Interesting."

"The distal end of the bone was severely abraded at the time of death. It seems the man literally scratched or clawed his finger to the bone. I've never seen anything like it, and I'm at a loss to explain."

The pale man sat in silence for a moment. Then he spoke. "The gentleman in question was walled up alive."

Ganesh leaned forward. "Really?"

A nod.

"So this is a murder investigation?"

"Of an antique sort."

"I see." She cleared her throat. "The bone was well preserved and had plenty of collagen. I did a radiocarbon date on the sample. It's fairly recent, relatively speaking. Because of that the age was a little hard to measure, but it appears to date back one hundred forty years, plus or minus twenty."

"And there's no way to narrow the margin of error, I understand."

"That's correct. Radiocarbon dating works best on artifacts between five hundred and fifty thousand years old. The error bars get longer at both ends."

"Did you use beta counting or mass spectrometry?"

Ganesh was amused by this. Here was a man trying to show off his knowledge, but he knew just enough to ask a dumb question. "With such a recent date, only accelerator mass spectrometry would give a usable result."

"I see."

And now she wondered if, rather than being dumb, maybe he had been testing her. What a strange and compelling man this was. "With the abundance of collagen and the lack of contamination, I did manage to get some really good DNA results. The individual is definitely male, with seventy-five percent African ancestry, the other twenty-five percent western European."

"Curious."

"This is a typical mix for African Americans, almost all of whom have a proportion of European ancestry. He would have had a dark but probably not black skin color."

"And his age?"

"A histological examination indicated an age of around forty. It also showed he was in excellent health, aside from several short but severe bouts of an illness when he was young. Thin sections I studied indicate the illness might well have been scurvy—a severe vitamin C deficiency."

"The fellow was a sailor, then?"

"The evidence points that way. The same isotope analysis showed a diet high in fish, shellfish, wheat, and barley."

"How can you tell that?"

"The food you eat and the water you drink get broken down and the carbon, oxygen, and nitrogen become incorporated into your bones. Those three elements have various stable isotope ratios, which differ from food to food—and from water sources. Based on the ratios of those isotopes, we can tell what a person was eating and drinking during, say, the last twenty years of his or her life."

"Drinking?"

"Yes. As you go higher in latitude, the ratio of oxygen isotopes in freshwater changes."

"Interesting. And at what latitude did this fellow's drinking water come from?"

"From around 40 to 55 degrees. In North America, that corresponds to an area roughly from New Jersey to Newfoundland and points west. The test is not very accurate."

"And his diet?"

"The wheat came from eating bread, and the barley most likely came from beer. Add the fish and shellfish and you get a classic nineteenth-century coastal diet. I tested the bone for antibodies. They came back positive for malaria."

"Malaria again implies a sailor, no?"

"Absolutely. And he was also positive for TB."

"You mean he had tuberculosis?"

"No. He was far too healthy. Virtually everyone living in seaport cities in the nineteenth century would have tested positive for TB, however. Everyone was exposed."

"I see. Anything else?"

"Putting it all together, I'd say what you have here is a large, strong, healthy, forty-year-old African American male, a sailor by trade who worked with his hands, perhaps a helmsman or foretopman, who probably came from a fairly comfortable socioeconomic class, given there were no signs of malnutrition other than the scurvy. He was born around 1840 and died around 1880. When not at sea he lived in a seaport town or city. He sailed at least part of the time in the tropics."

The FBI agent nodded slowly. "Remarkable, Dr. Ganesh. Truly remarkable."

"The bones speak to me, Mr. Pendergast. They tell me their stories."

The pale man rose. "Thank you. You have been most helpful. And now, if you don't mind, I'd like to retrieve the sample."

Ganesh smiled. "I wish I could oblige. But you see, every question I ask consumes a tiny bit of bone. As the bone tells its story, it dies just a little. I'm afraid the bone gave up its existence along with its story." She spread her hands.

As she did so, the man took one of her hands in his, which felt cool and smooth. "I bow before your ability to speak to the dead, Dr. Ganesh." And he kissed her hand.

Ganesh found herself flushed and warm long after the man had departed.

9

Constance stepped through the door, then stopped and frowned in instinctual disapproval. The place looked more like a rag-and-bone shop than a historical society. A lot of stuff was randomly hung on the wall—faded maps, old nets, buoys, harpoons, gaff hooks, narwhal horns, sail needles, a gigantic lobster shell on a plaque, another wooden plaque covered with sailing knots, and pictures of Exmouth in the old days. The center of the "museum" sported an old dory, about twenty feet long, with several sets of oars between wooden dowels.

She had jingled a door-opening upon entering and was soon confronted by an eager, gray-haired man with fat-lobed ears stuck onto a narrow, bony face. A badge identified him as a volunteer named Ken Worley.

"Greetings," said the volunteer, looming into her field of view and proffering a pamphlet. "Welcome to the Exmouth Historical Society and Museum!"

Trying to be polite, Constance took the pamphlet with a murmured "Thank you." She began an assiduous examination of the dory, hoping he would vanish.

"Nice dory, don't you think? *Disregarded age in corners thrown.* That's the motto of our little museum."

Parsing this inaccurate spouting of Shakespeare, and without thinking, Constance corrected him: "*Unregarded* age."

A sudden silence. "Are you sure? I'll have to double-check that."

"No need to double-check anything," Constance said. "You're wrong."

Temporarily set back, the man retreated to his pile of pamphlets and busied himself with a large register book, opening it and flipping through the pages. Constance, who was studying some old framed maps of Exmouth and its environs, could tell that he was down but not vanquished.

"Would you care to put down your name for special mailings and events?" he asked, pointing at the register book.

"No, thank you. I was wondering—where do you keep your archives?"

The man blinked. "We don't have any archives."

"No town papers? Property maps? Old marriage registers?"

"I'm afraid the town records were lost in the Great Hurricane of '38. They called it the Yankee Clipper. It swept away the old Exmouth docks and wrecked half the town. You can still see the ruins on Exmouth Bay. Picturesque, in its own way."

"So this is it? This is all you have?"

"It may not look like much, but every item here has a story. For example, that Newburyport dory you were admiring was used to hunt great blue whales. When whales were sighted going around Crow Island, the men would rush down to the beach and launch those dories into the surf, chase a whale, harpoon it, and drag it back to the beach, carve it up right there on the shore. Imagine the courage, the pluck, it took—*Disdaining fortune, with his burnished steel, which smoked with bloody execution!*"

"*Brandish'd* steel."

A silence. "I'm quite sure it's *burnished*," said Worley in a stiff voice. "I was a thespian in my youth—and theater director for twenty years at the old Exmouth Playhouse."

Feeling a rising impatience with this tiresome man, Constance ignored him and continued poking around the museum, glancing over the framed pictures of ships, articles about storms and wrecks and legends of buried pirate treasure. Out of the corner of her eye she saw Worley retire to his chair behind the register book and busy himself with addressing envelopes laboriously by hand. She hoped that would keep him quiet at least until she had finished going through the museum.

She was struck with a sudden thought: *How would Pendergast respond to this situation?* Would he be able to glean anything from these shabby artifacts and old newspaper stories? Was there something she, perhaps, was overlooking? As she looked around, it dawned on her how Pendergast would, in fact, profit from this situation. The realization caused her to flush with chagrin. She glanced at Worley, still addressing envelopes.

"Mr. Worley?"

He raised his eyes. "Yes?"

And yet Pendergast's method was difficult. It did not come naturally to her. "On second thought, I think you are right," she managed. "It is *burnished*."

At this his face brightened. "I've played Macbeth many times."

"At the Exmouth Playhouse?"

"Yes, and also once in Boston, at the Market Square Theater. Full house."

"Boston?" A pause. "I've always wanted to go onstage, but I never had the opportunity. One wonders how you remember all those lines."

Surely the motivation behind such a toadyish observation would be obvious. And yet the man was nodding. "There are ways," he said. "Various tricks of the trade. It's really not all that difficult."

Being a lickspittle was mortifying in the extreme, but Constance found the mortification somewhat mitigated by her observation that his stiff, offended manner was quickly dropping away.

"You must know everyone in town," she observed.

"I certainly do! Nothing like theater to bring a town together."

"How fortunate. As it happens, I have a particular interest in lighthouses and was wondering if you knew anything about the one here."

"The Exmouth Light is one of the most historic in New England," Worley opined. "It was built in 1704 by order of Queen Anne herself. This was a dangerous stretch of coast. Many ships were lost."

"I was hoping to find a list of the keepers of the light and their tenures."

"I don't think anyone's compiled an official list."

She thought back to the information Pendergast had given her at breakfast. "Who was keeper around 1880?"

A silence. "Why 1880?"

She'd been pushing too hard. Really, this was most difficult. "No particular reason," she said, forcing a little laugh.

"Let's see. The Slocum family were keepers from around the Civil War—all the way through to 1886, I think. That was when Meade Slocum fell down the lighthouse steps and broke his neck. Afterwards, it was taken over by the McHardies. Jonathan McHardie. They had it up to the time the light was automated in 1934."

"So there are none of Meade Slocum's descendants in town?"

"As far as I'm aware there are none anywhere. Widower, no children. He was a drinker. One of the hazards of the job, up at all hours, lonely, isolated—especially in winter. They say he went crazy in his last few years, claimed the lighthouse was haunted."

"Haunted? How so?"

"The crying of babies at night, or something like that."

"I see." She paused. "Where might I find out more about him?"

Worley peered at her under bushy brows. "Are you by chance working with that historian?"

In addition to the age and racial identity of the finger bone, Pendergast had mentioned Morris McCool to her at breakfast. She simply must learn how to ask questions more nonchalantly. "No. Simple curiosity."

"Because that fellow was asking the same kinds of questions." He took a step closer, his face clouded with suspicion. "Who *are* you with?"

Constance felt confusion mingled with rising annoyance. She was botching this. But she didn't dare lie—not in a small town like this. "I'm here with Mr. Pendergast, the private investigator. He's looking into the theft of the wine cellar."

"Ah! That fellow in the red car who got himself arrested yesterday?"

"Yes."

"Good for him. Chief Mourdock is a horse's ass." Apparently, Worley felt getting arrested by the police chief was something very much in Pendergast's favor. "If you could be more specific about what you're looking for, maybe I could help."

"I wish I could be more specific. I'm trying to learn the history of the town."

"It was a shame someone stole Lake's wine. He's a nice gent. But I'm not sure the town's history has anything to do with it."

"We're trying to be thorough. One of the things I'm interested in is the history of the town's African American population."

"And a very interesting history."

"Please go on."

"Down near the old waterfront was what they called Dill Town. It was the black section of town."

"Why Dill Town?"

"Named after the freed slave who originally settled there. John Dill. Most of the residents were sailors in the early days. That area was actually more prosperous for a time than the white half of town."

"Why was that?"

"They went out to sea longer, worked on whalers and grain ships. When you're out to sea, nobody gives a damn about skin color. It's what you could do. And the crews on those ships were polyglot."

"But back on land—in Exmouth—was there racial tension?"

"Not at first, when there was plenty of work for everyone. But later on there was—resentment about the prosperity of Dill Town. You see, the Exmouth whites were mostly coastal fishermen. They didn't go to sea for years at a time a-whaling, like the blacks did. And then, thanks to Krakatoa, things got bad for everyone."

"Krakatoa?"

"Yes, indeed. Late 1883 it was, the year Krakatoa erupted. There was no summer for Exmouth the following year; folks say there were frosts in every month of 1884. The crops died and the fishing industry failed. By that time the whaling industry was already suffering, and the easy money it once brought in was no more. Things went from bad to worse until there was an incident where a black youth was blamed for raping a white woman. The man was lynched."

"A lynching? In Massachusetts?"

"Yes, ma'am. They strung him up, threw his body in the bay. In 1902, that was. For the blacks, that was the beginning of the end for Dill Town. It was almost empty by the time the Yankee Clipper blew through in '38, flattening Oldham."

"Oldham?"

"A very backward old community that used to exist south of here, on Crow Island. It's part of that wildlife preserve now, you know."

"Let's get back to the lynching. Any idea who was responsible?"

"The usual drunken vigilante types. It's a matter of shame now, and you won't get anyone to talk about it."

"But you're talking about it."

"My family's 'from away,' as they say around here. My parents moved here from Duxbury. And I've seen more of the world than many of these townsfolk. Don't forget, I played Macbeth in Boston."

Constance held out her hand. "I didn't introduce myself. Constance Greene. Thank you for all the information."

He shook it. "Nice to meet you, Constance. Ken Worley, at your service."

"If I have more questions, may I come back?"

"It would be my pleasure. And I hope you and Mr. Pendergast will be able to enjoy our little town while you're here." He threw out a hand and ended with a declamation:

This castle hath a pleasant seat; the breeze
Nimbly and sweetly recommends itself
Unto our gentle senses

Constance knew it was possible the man might be of further use to them. However, her patience was now at an extremity. "Air," she said.

Worley blinked. "Excuse me?"

"'Air.' Not 'breeze.' Thank you again for your help, Mr. Worley." And with the faintest of curtsies she exited the building.

10

Bradley Gavin came out from the back offices, sack lunch in hand. He stopped when he saw a figure lounging in the doorway of the police station's waiting room. It was that strange private investigator, Pendergast. Gavin was already curious about the man who had managed to get the chief so riled up. Not that it was hard to do—all the chief needed to get worked up was to be given some actual work. For the past two years, Gavin had done virtually all the policing in town...while the chief concerned himself with writing up parking tickets. He had six more months of that, and then Mourdock would retire his lazy ass and Gavin would take over as chief. Or so he hoped; it depended, of course, on the town's three selectmen. But he'd been a dedicated officer, his family was old Exmouth stock, he was part of the town's inner circle, and his father had been chief before him, so he felt his chances were good.

Putting his lunch to one side, Gavin glanced back at Pendergast, wondering whether the man wasn't pushing his luck a little, showing up here so soon after his arrest.

"Can I help you?" he asked politely.

The man in the door unbent himself, took a step forward, and extended his hand. "We haven't formally met. I'm Pendergast."

Gavin took it. "I'm Sergeant Gavin."

Now another figure stepped into the waiting room from outside: it was Pendergast's secretary, or assistant, or whatever she was, the petite young woman named Constance. She looked at him silently with her strange violet eyes. Her bobbed hair was a deep, rich mahogany and, though the cut of her clothing was severe, it could not entirely conceal the curvaceous form beneath. With some effort, Gavin returned his gaze to Pendergast.

"Am I correct in my understanding that you and the chief are the entirety of the Exmouth constabulary?"

Constabulary. He could see how this guy could get under the chief's skin. "We're a small department," Gavin said.

"I need access to some files for my investigation. Are you the person who can help me?"

"Um, no, that would have to be the chief."

"Excellent! Could you get him for me?"

Gavin gave the guy a long, steady look. "You really want to go there?"

"Go where? I'm not going anywhere."

Gavin couldn't tell if the guy was a wiseass or a dumbass. He turned. "Sally, would you buzz the chief that Mr., ah, Pendergast is here to see him?"

The receptionist looked nervous. "Are you sure—?"

"Yes, please."

She reluctantly pressed the buzzer and murmured into her headset.

Gavin knew the chief would come out. Locking up Pendergast the day before hadn't gotten the chip off his shoulder, and he'd been grumbling and bitching about the man and his continued presence in town ever since.

This should prove entertaining.

A moment later, Chief Mourdock appeared out of the back offices. He was moving slowly and with gravitas, spoiling for a fight. He stopped at the entrance to the waiting area, looking from Pendergast to Constance Greene and back again. "What is it?"

"Thank you, Chief, for meeting with me." Pendergast stepped forward, whisking a piece of paper out of his pocket. "I have here a list of files I need for my investigation into the wine theft. They consist of your reports on home burglaries and home invasions over the past twelve months. Also, I'd like to know whether there are any ex-convicts living in the town. And I would appreciate borrowing Sergeant Gavin here to help me review these files and answer questions as they arise."

He stopped. There was a long, sizzling silence as Chief Mourdock stared at the man. And then he began to laugh—a loud, mirthless, guttural laugh. "I can't believe it. You, coming in here, making demands of *me*?"

"I have not completed my investigation."

"Get out. Now. I don't want to see your skinny, undertaking ass again until court."

"Or?"

"Or I'll cuff you like I did before and you can spend a night here as my special guest."

"Are you threatening me with another arrest?"

The chief's face had flushed a dark red and his meaty hands were clenched and flexing. Gavin had never seen the man so angry. Mourdock took a step forward. "Last fucking chance, dickhead."

Pendergast did not move. "I am merely asking for cooperation in seeing some files. A simple 'no' would have sufficed."

"That's it. Gavin, put the steel on him."

Gavin, alarmed, had not expected to be dragged into this. "Um, what's the charge, Chief?"

The chief turned on him in a fury. "Don't you question me! He's trespassing. Cuff him."

"Trespassing?" Constance Greene said, her voice low and full of unexpected menace. "In a public place?"

Suddenly, this wasn't as diverting as Gavin had assumed it would be. He stared at the chief, who glared back at him. Reluctantly, he turned to Pendergast. "Turn around, please."

As Gavin removed the cuffs from his belt, Constance Greene moved forward.

Quickly, Pendergast made a kind of suppressing gesture to her. Then he put his hands behind his back and turned around. As Gavin was about to put on the cuffs, Pendergast said, "Could you please remove my badge wallet from my back pocket?"

Badge wallet? The man's tone was suddenly cold, and Gavin felt a prickling premonition that something terrible was about to happen. He removed the leather wallet.

"Transfer it to my jacket pocket, if you will."

As Gavin fumbled with the wallet, the chief snatched it from him and it fell open, exposing a flash of blue and gold.

There was a moment of silence.

"What the hell's this?" the chief asked, staring at it as if he'd never seen anything like it before.

Pendergast remained silent.

Mourdock read the writing on the badge. "You're...an *FBI agent?*"

"So you *are* literate, after all," Constance Greene said.

The chief's face was suddenly almost as white as Pendergast's. "Why didn't you say something?"

"It's irrelevant. I'm not on duty."

"But... Jesus Christ! You should have presented your credentials. You just let me *assume...*"

"Assume what?"

"Assume... that you were just some..." His voice choked up.

"Just some private citizen you could mistreat and bully?" Constance Greene said in her silky, old-fashioned voice. "I warned you of this."

As Gavin watched, Pendergast advanced on the police chief. "Chief Mourdock, in all my years as a special agent, I have rarely seen an abuse of police power such as I have experienced in your town. Yesterday, over a minor parking infraction, you insulted me in vulgar terms, threatened me with physical violence, and arrested and jailed me without cause. Also, you used a pejorative term highly offensive to the LGBT community."

"LBG... What?... I did not!"

"And finally, you failed to Mirandize me."

"Lies. All lies! I *did* Mirandize you. You can't prove any of this."

"Fortunately, the entire interaction was captured on videotape by the security camera of a clothing store directly across the street. I now have a copy of that tape, thanks to Special Agent in Charge Randolph Bulto of the Boston Field Office, who did me the favor of getting the necessary warrant just this morning."

"I...I..." The chief could barely speak.

Turning to Gavin, Pendergast nodded at the cuffs. "Will you put those things away, please?"

Gavin hastily returned them to his service belt.

"Thank you." Pendergast took a step back. "Chief Mourdock, in the words of a certain poet, there are two roads we could take right now. Would you like to know what they are?"

"Roads?" The chief was unable to keep up, almost silly with shock.

"Yes, roads. The first road is the more traveled one, the one where I file a complaint against you for abuse of police authority, with the videotape as proof to back up my own lengthy list of charges. This would end your career on the very cusp of retirement, destroy your reputation, endanger your pension, and quite possibly lead to the shame of community service or even a minor jail sentence. And then there is the other road." He waited, crossing his arms.

"What other road?" the chief finally croaked.

"And you a New Englander... The road less traveled, of course! That is where you throw yourself wholeheartedly into helping me with my investigation. In. *Every*. Way. On this road, my colleague SAC Bulto misplaces the videotape and we never speak of this matter again. Oh, and of course all charges against me are dropped." He paused. "Which road shall we take?"

"That road," the chief said hastily. "I'll take the, uh, road less traveled."

"That road shall make all the difference. Oh, yes, I almost forgot. Here." And Pendergast waved his document under the chief's nose.

Mourdock almost dropped the note in his eagerness to grab it. "I'll have these files for you by tomorrow morning."

The FBI agent exchanged a brief glance with his young assistant. She glanced in the direction of the chief, her expression one of disdainful satisfaction, then turned and left the station without another word.

"Much obliged." Pendergast extended his hand. "I can see that you and I are going to be *fast friends*."

As Gavin watched the two exit, he thought: *He's formidable for sure, but that Constance Greene, she's scary...in a strangely intriguing way.*

11

Walt Adderly, proprietor of the Captain Hull Inn, stepped out of his office and into the narrow passageway that led to the Chart Room restaurant. He peered into the dim confines. It was one thirty pm, and while most of the lunchtime diners had left—people ate their meals early in Exmouth—Adderly knew from checking the receipts that they'd had a decent crowd.

His eye stopped when it reached the figure sitting alone at table 8. It was that fellow who was looking into the wine theft for Lake. Percival had told Adderly the man was an FBI agent, which of course Adderly didn't believe: Lake liked his little jokes. The sculptor had also told him that the man—Pendergast, Adderly recalled from the hotel ledger—was rather eccentric. This, at least, was believable: the guy was dressed in a suit of unrelieved black, like someone in mourning, and even in the dimness of the restaurant his pale face stood out like a harvest moon.

As Adderly watched from the shelter of the passageway, Margie, the senior waitress, bustled up with the man's order. "Here you go," she said. "Fried catfish. Enjoy!"

"Indeed," Adderly heard Pendergast murmur in reply. He eyed the plate for a moment. He picked up a fork, poked here and there at the fish, took a tentative bite. Then he put his fork down again. He glanced around the restaurant—it was now empty except for old Willard Stevens, finishing up his third and last cup of coffee—and motioned the waitress over.

"Yes?" asked Margie as she came back.

"May I inquire as to who prepared this?"

"Who?" Margie blinked at this unexpected question. "Our cook, Reggie."

"Is he your regular cook?"

"These days, yes."

"I see." And with this, the man picked up his plate, stood, and walked past the other tables, around the bar, and through the double doors that led into the kitchen.

This was so unusual that Adderly stood where he was for a moment, perplexed. He'd had people so pleased with their meals that they'd asked the cook to come out and be complimented. He'd also had a few send their meals back for various reasons. But he'd never seen a patron just get up and walk into the kitchen before, carrying his lunch with him.

It occurred to him that he'd better go see what was up.

He stepped out of the passage into the restaurant proper, then into the kitchen. Usually a bustle of activity, the place was now almost still. The dishwasher, the two waitresses, the line cook, and Reggie all stood in a huddle, watching the man named Pendergast as he wandered around the food preparation area, opening drawers, picking up various utensils and examining them before replacing them. Then he turned his attention to Reggie.

"You are the cook, I presume?" Pendergast asked.

Reggie nodded.

"And what, pray tell, are your qualifications?"

Reggie looked as surprised as the rest. "Four years as a mess specialist in the Navy."

"Of course. Well, perhaps we are not completely without hope." Pendergast lifted his lunch plate and handed it to Reggie. "To begin with, one simply cannot get good catfish this far north. And I assume this was frozen to begin with—right?"

Reggie's expression began growing defensive. "So?"

"Well, for heaven's sake, man, we're on the ocean! Surely you have access to fresh fish—lingcod, pollack, flounder, rockfish?"

"There's the catch Wait hauled in last night," Reggie said after a long pause.

This was too much. Adderly stepped forward to intervene. He didn't want to lose his best cook. "Mr. Pendergast," he said, "is there a problem?"

"I am going to cook myself lunch. Reggie, here, is welcome to act as sous-chef."

Adderly wondered if this Pendergast was not just eccentric, but perhaps a little crazy. "I'm sorry," he said, "but we can't have customers in the kitchen, disturbing the peace—"

"The only peace that has been disturbed is that of my gastrointestinal tract. But if this will reassure you..." And the man reached into the pocket of his suit, pulled out a shield of gold and blue, and showed it to Adderly. It read federal bureau of investigation.

So Lake hadn't been kidding, after all. Adderly took a step back and Pendergast continued. "Tell me about this catch of Wait's?"

Reggie exchanged glances with Adderly. The innkeeper nodded. *Just play along,* he mouthed. Reggie nodded back, stepped over to the walk-in fridge, opened the door, then stopped abruptly.

"What is it?" asked Pendergast.

"I could've sworn I bought a dozen whole sole from Wait. But there's only ten."

"I've been meaning to talk to you all about that," Adderly said, still trying to overcome his surprise. "I've been noticing a regular shortfall on orders versus covers. I think we've got ourselves a food thief. You'd better spread the word that I'm not going to be happy about it."

While Adderly spoke, the FBI agent had stepped into the refrigerator, briefly vanishing from sight. "Aha!" He emerged a moment later, a large, gutted sole in his hands. "Not Dover sole, of course, but it will do. Now, may I have a skillet, please? Cast-iron, well-seasoned?"

Reggie produced one.

"Excellent. Ah, Reggie, what is your last name?"

"Sheraton."

"Thank you. Mr. Sheraton, how would you go about cooking this?"

"I'd fillet it first."

"Be my guest." He laid the fish down on the butcher block and watched with approval as Reggie expertly filleted it.

"Beautifully done," Pendergast said. "This fills me with hope. Now tell me: How would you cook it?"

"In lard, of course."

Pendergast shuddered. "Not clarified butter?"

"Clarified?"

There was a moment of silence. "Very well. We will confine ourselves to the simplest of preparations. Would you mind placing that skillet on a high flame?"

Reggie walked over to the commercial stove, turned up one burner, and placed the skillet on it.

"Now add some butter, please. Not too much, just enough

to coat the bottom of the pan... Wait, wait, that's more than sufficient!"

Reggie stepped back from what looked like an impossibly small tab of butter. The rest of the kitchen continued looking on in silent surprise.

Pendergast stood there, holding the fish. "Now, Mr. Sheraton, if you wouldn't mind assembling the rest of the *mise en place*—mushrooms, garlic, white wine, flour, salt, pepper, parsley, half a lemon, and cream?"

As Reggie moved around the kitchen, gathering the ingredients in increasingly resentful silence, Pendergast kept an eye on the heating pan. Adderly watched the cooking lesson with increasing amusement and curiosity.

Pendergast salted the fish on both sides and set it aside. "Chef's knife?"

Stu, the line cook, handed him one.

Pendergast examined it. "This isn't sharp enough! Don't you know a dull knife is more dangerous than a sharp one? Where's your steel?"

A sharpening steel was produced, and Pendergast whetted the knife against it with a few expert strokes. Then he turned to the mushrooms, quartering one of them in a quick, deft motion. He handed the knife to Reggie, who cut up the other mushrooms and minced a clove of garlic and some parsley as Pendergast looked on.

"You have decent knife skills," he said. "That's reassuring. Now, let's pay attention to the fish. If we are going to prepare this sole à la minute, the pan must be very hot, and the fish must cook quickly. It is now at just the right heat."

He plucked up the fish and slid it into the hot pan with a searing sound. He waited, as if counting seconds, and then said: "Now, you see? It can be turned already. And a subtle fond is developing." He slid a fish spatula beneath the sole and gently turned it, to a fresh sizzle.

"But in the Navy—" Reggie began.

"You are no longer deep-frying fish sticks for several hundred men. You are cooking for a single, discriminating customer. There—it's done!" And Pendergast slid the fish onto a clean plate. "Note that I am serving it presentation side up. Now watch, Mr. Sheraton, if you will." The FBI agent added a splash of white wine to the skillet, and as a plume of steam arose he added flour and a little more butter, deglazing the pan and whisking the ingredients together quickly. "I'm making a rudimentary beurre manié from which to build the sauce," he explained. A minute later, in went the mushrooms, then the garlic. Holding the handle of the skillet with a chef's towel, Pendergast quickly sautéed the ingredients, then added a generous dash of cream, standing directly over the stovetop and whisking constantly. After another minute he turned off the heat, picked up a spoon, tasted the sauce, corrected the seasonings, dipped the spoon again, then showed it to Reggie. "Note, Mr. Sheraton, how the sauce lightly coats the spoon. The French call that *nappe*. In future, I would ask that you make sure your sauce has been reduced to just such a consistency before serving it to me." He spooned a liberal amount of sauce over the fish, garnished it with parsley, spritzed a trace of lemon juice over it.

"Filets de Poisson Bercy aux Champignons," he declared with a small flourish. "Or, more correctly, Filets de Sole Pendergast, since under the circumstances I was forced to take several shortcuts in both ingredients and technique. Now, Mr. Sheraton: Do you think you could reproduce this preparation with the greatest exactitude, for my future dinners in this establishment?"

"It's simple enough," Reggie said shortly.

"That's the beauty of it."

"But...for every dinner?"

"For my every dinner." Pendergast reached into his pocket, extracted a hundred-dollar bill, and handed it to the cook. "This is for your trouble today."

Reggie stared at it, the look of resentment changing to surprise.

"Do you regularly work lunches as well as dinners?" Pendergast asked in a hopeful tone.

"Only twice a week," Reggie replied.

"Ah, well. Let us then content ourselves with dinner, for the time being. Filets de Sole Pendergast for the foreseeable future, if you please. You have my thanks." And with that, Pendergast scooped up the plate, turned, and left the kitchen.

Adderly turned to Reggie, laughing, and slapped him on the back. "Well, well, Reggie, it looks like we have a new item on our menu. What do you think?"

"I guess so."

"I'll add it to the chalkboard." And Adderly exited the kitchen, chuckling to himself, leaving Reggie and the rest of the staff staring at each other in openmouthed surprise long after the double doors to the restaurant had stopped flapping.

12

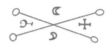

Benjamin Franklin Boyle sank the clam hoe into the muck and turned over a big, fat beauty. As he plucked it out it squirted in protest, and he tossed it into the hod, took a few steps forward—his hip waders sucking loudly in protest—sank the hoe in again and pulled open a new gash in the muck, exposing two more clams. A few more steps, another swipe with the hoe, a few more clams into the hod, and then he rested, leaning on his hoe while looking across the mudflats toward the river mouth and the sea beyond. It was slack low tide and the sun was setting behind him, purpling some thunderheads on the sea horizon. It was a lovely fall evening. Boyle inhaled the smell of the salt air, the ripe scent of the mudflats—a scent he loved—and listened to the cries of the gulls as they swept and wheeled over the Exmouth marshes.

Five years ago, at age sixty-five, Boyle had given up fishing and sold his dragger. That was hard work and the scallops just seemed to get smaller and harder to find, and in the last few years mostly what he'd pulled up were useless starfish that wrecked his nets. He was glad to have gotten rid of the boat, he got a fair price for it, and he'd saved up enough money for a penny-pinching retirement. But clamming gave him something to do, brought in a little extra money, and kept him close to the sea he loved.

Having caught his breath, he looked about the shiny flats. He could see the holes of the soft-shell clams everywhere. This was a good flat and nobody had clammed it for a while, because it was so hard to get to, with a walk through sharp marsh grass and a weary trudge across another, closer flat that had already been pretty much clammed out. Getting out wasn't so bad, really, but returning with a forty-pound hod full of clams was a bitch.

He sank his hoe into the shiny, quivering surface of mud, then pulled back, exposing more clams. He kept up the rhythm, moving a few steps forward each time, swiping, overturning, plucking, tossing, then repeating the process. As he worked, his line approached the edge of the marsh grass, and once he arrived he paused to look about for another good line. He stamped his foot on the shivering mud, and saw a bunch of squirts go off to his right. That would be a good place to dig. But as he bent down to begin his line, he glimpsed, off in the twilight, something odd: what looked like a bowling ball with hair sticking up from it. It was attached to a lumpy form, partly sunken in the murky chan-nel that snaked through the mud.

He put down the heavy hod and moved over to investigate, his waders making an unholy noise with each step. It didn't take long for Doyle to realize he was looking at a body, lodged in the muck, and a few more steps brought him up to it. It was a naked man, lying facedown, legs and arms splayed out, face and lower portion of the body buried several inches in the mud. The back of the head was partially bald, with a big shiny spot in the center of a ring of salt-encrusted hair.

A tiny green crab, sensing motion, scuttled across from one hair patch to the other and hid cowering in the comb-over.

Boyle had seen plenty of bodies drowned and washed up, and this looked like most of them did, even down to the holes piercing the flesh here and there where ravenous sea life—crabs, fish, lobsters—had begun to feast.

He stood there for a time, wondering if he knew who this person was. He couldn't recall the bald spot offhand, but a lot of people had bald spots, and without clothes he just couldn't come up with a possibility. Of course he would have to call the police, but curiosity got the better of him. He still had the rake in hand, so he bent over the corpse and slid the rake into the muck under the belly. With his other hand clutching the corpse's upper arm, he gave a pull. The body broke free of the grasping muck and flopped over with a hideous sucking-popping sound, the stiff arm smacking down hard into the mud.

Impossible to see anything; the face and torso were completely covered with black mud. Now what? He needed to rinse the mud off the face. Moving around the body, he waded into the shallows of the stream channel, cupped his hands, and began splashing water on the body. The mud ran off quickly, the stark white flesh exposed in rivulets and then sheets.

Boyle stopped, frozen. The face was pretty much eaten off—eyes, lips, nose—not so uncommon with a body immersed in salt water, as he knew. But what had stopped him was not the face, but the man's torso. He stared at it, trying to make sense of it. What he had thought at first were crude tattoos turned out to be something quite different.

Benjamin Franklin Boyle set down the clam rake, fished in his pocket under the hip waders, and removed his cell phone. He dialed in the number of the Exmouth Police Department.

When the dispatcher answered he said, "Doris? This is Ben Boyle, down in the mudflats. There's a body here, nobody local, looks like it washed out of the marshes. A real artist went to work on it. No, I can't describe it, you'll just have to see for yourself." He explained his location in more detail, and then hung up and slid the phone back into his pocket.

His brow wrinkling, Boyle considered what to do now. Even if the cops left immediately, they wouldn't get here for at least twenty minutes. There was still time to fill up his hod.

He thumped on the mud with his foot, saw where the little squirts were thickest, and began digging a line through them, building up a rhythm: two steps, sink, turn over, pluck, toss, and repeat.

13

Bradley Gavin, up to his thighs in muck, adjusted the last of the light stands and plugged the cord into the generator. With some effort he extracted his waders from the mud and stepped back onto the temporary boardwalk that ringed the site.

He'd spent the last hour hauling down planks of lumber, laying them out to the scene of the crime, wheeling out the generator, setting up the lights, taping the perimeter, and following the instructions of the Scene of Crime Officer, a big man named Malaga, who had come all the way from Lawrence with a Crime Scene Investigator and a photographer. Those three gentlemen were now waiting at the edge of the marsh for everything to be set up so they could tippy-toe out and do their work without getting muddy.

"Check the fuel gauge on that generator," said the chief, standing on the boards in shiny new waders that had not yet seen a speck of mud, arms crossed over his chest. The chief had been in a rotten mood ever since Pendergast's lunchtime visit, and the mood had only grown worse when the body was found. The reason was pretty clear to Gavin: here was something perfectly timed to create actual work, delay his retirement, and possibly compromise the low crime rate he had enjoyed during his tenure as chief. Naturally, the last of his concerns was actually solving the crime.

Gavin shrugged it off. He was used to this. Six more months and it would be over, and with any luck he'd be chief himself.

He checked the gauge. "Still almost full." He tried not to look over to where the body lay, faceup, left that way by the clammer who had turned him over. The son of a bitch had continued clamming around the body, totally screwing up anything that might have been left there. The SOCO, Malaga, was going to have a fit when he saw that.

"All right," said Mourdock, interrupting Gavin's reverie, "looks like we're set." He raised his walkie-talkie. "We're ready for the SOC guys."

Breathing hard, Gavin tried to scrape the excess mud off his waders with a stick.

"Hey, Gavin, don't let the mud get on the boardwalk."

Gavin moved to one side and kept scraping, flicking the mud off into the darkness. A chill evening had settled on the marshes, a clammy mist collecting low above the ground, adding a white pall to the scene. It looked more like some horror movie set than a real crime scene.

He heard voices and saw lights bobbing through the mist. A moment later a tall, dour-looking man walked up: Malaga. He had a shaved and remarkably polished head atop a massive neck covered with black hairs, giving him the look of a bull. A young Asian man followed him—the crime scene investigator—and behind him, grunting and shuffling, an obese man draped with camera equipment.

Malaga parked himself at the edge of the scene and spoke

in a deep, melodious voice. "Thank you, Chief Mourdock." He waved the photographer forward, who was at least a professional, taking photographs from every angle, kneeling down low, stretching up high, the silent flashes going off every few seconds as he moved about with surprising dexterity. Gavin tried to control his deep shock and maintain a professional, disinterested expression on his face. He had never actually been at the scene of a homicide before. As he glanced again at the body, splayed on its back, with those symbols carved brutally into its chest, he felt another wave of surprise and horror. He wondered who could have done such a thing, and why. It made no sense to him; no sense at all. What could possibly be the motivation for such an act? He felt anger, too—anger that his hometown had been violated by a crime like this.

As Malaga worked the crime scene, from time to time he would murmur a suggestion to the photographer, who in turn took more photos. At one point he mounted his camera on a pole and held it over the corpse, photographing almost straight down.

"All good," said the photographer at last, stepping back.

And now the CSI guy crept into the scene, his hands in latex, wearing booties and white coveralls. He laid down a satchel and removed several rolled-up felt holders, which contained a variety of things—test tubes, tweezers, small ziplock bags, pins, labels, little flags on wires, Q-tips, and a number of spray bottles of chemicals. He bent over the body, picking off hair and fibers, spritzing this and swabbing that. He scraped under the nails and taped plastic bags over the hands, and he examined the carved symbols with a penlight, picking things out and wiping Q-tips here and there, sealing them in test tubes.

All was silent. Even Malaga had nothing to say, no suggestions to offer. The last thing the CSI man did was take the dead man's fingerprints with an electronic pad. And then he was done; he packed everything up in the satchel and retreated in as cat-like a fashion as he'd arrived.

Malaga turned to Chief Mourdock. "Well, he's all yours." He gave the chief's hand a hearty shake—he seemed eager to get out of that miasmic swamp—and they turned in preparation for walking back down the boardwalk. Gavin could read pure panic on the chief's face: What now? It suddenly occurred to him that the chief hadn't investigated a homicide in the town—ever. He only assumed he had in Boston, but perhaps not, given that Boston had its own specialized homicide squad.

Gavin frowned. Shouldn't they be calling Pendergast in on this? The chief was clearly in over his head and Pendergast, odd character though he was, seemed capable. "Um," he said, "Chief, do you think we ought to tell that FBI agent? I mean, he'd probably want to know, and maybe he could even help—"

The chief turned to him with a scowl. "I don't think we need to *bother* him. After all, he's working on such an *important* case of his own." The sarcasm fairly dripped.

A velvety voice came out of the night. "My dear chief, thank you for your consideration of my other engagements, but it's no bother. Really, no bother at all." And the black-clad figure of the FBI agent emerged from the darkness, his pale face floating ghost-like in the mist.

For a moment, the chief's expression went utterly blank. Then he swallowed hard. "Agent, ah, Pendergast, we'd of course be very glad to have your input." He hesitated. "Would this be...official?"

Pendergast waved his hand. "Not at all, just some quiet help on the side. All credit to you—and, of course, the excellent Sergeant Gavin."

The chief cleared his throat, clearly uncertain of what to do next.

"Do you mind?" Pendergast said, approaching. And behind him a second figure emerged from the darkness— Constance Greene. Gavin couldn't take his eyes off her. She was dressed in old-fashioned Farmer Brown canvas overalls with high boots, her hair pulled back in a scarf. She was undeniably beautiful in an old-fashioned way—but in the artificial light of the crime scene she looked even more exotic than in daylight. She did not speak, but her eyes roved about, taking in everything.

"Who's the lady?" Malaga asked. He'd paused in his retreat at the arrival of Pendergast. "No rubberneckers."

"She," said Pendergast sharply, "is my assistant. Please extend to her every courtesy you would me."

"Of course," said Malaga, with a slightly offensive bow in her direction. He turned away and walked back down the boardwalk, vanishing in the darkness.

Pendergast slipped under the crime scene tape and approached the body, while Constance Greene hung back. Gavin wondered what was going through her head. The body was disgusting: face mostly gone, no tongue or lips, just a huge rack of yellow teeth, mouth wide open. And yet she seemed calm and unperturbed.

Pendergast knelt. "I see it is the historian. Morris McCool."

Hearing this, Gavin was shocked afresh. *The historian?*

"How do you know?" the chief asked. "The face is, um, gone and we haven't ID'd the body."

"The earlobes. You see how they are attached like that? An unusual trait; earlobes are almost as good as fingerprints. In addition, the height and weight seem about right."

"You knew the guy?" Mourdock asked.

"I had a glimpse of him at the Inn."

Pendergast adjusted the lights, then got down on his knees like the CSI before him. Arching his lean, long body over the dead man, he began picking away at the body with tweezers, popping stuff into tubes and bags that seemed to appear and disappear into his suit coat like magic. The CSI guy had been good, but watching Pendergast was like watching a ballet dancer; every move was perfect as those spidery white fingers flashed about this way and that. He spent a great deal of time probing and picking at the cuts on the chest, examining them with fanatical attention, even taking out a jeweler's loupe at one point. He poked, pried, and probed at the raw flesh that remained of the man's face. At last he rose and ducked back out.

Gavin glanced again at Constance Greene and was surprised at the lively look of interest on her face, not unlike a museumgoer enjoying a fine painting. She was considerably less shocked than he was. Was she one of those who got off on violent crime scenes? But no—somehow, she didn't strike him as that type. This was an intellectual puzzle for her—and a definite mark in her favor, he decided.

"Interesting," Pendergast murmured. "In addition to what appear to be carved inscriptions, part of the cuts also seem to form letters." He shone a small light at the markings carved into the chest, first one way and then the other. "I make it out as T-Y-B-A-N-E."

A sudden silence. Gavin stared down in even greater surprise and shock. It was true: from a certain angle, you could see a series of crude letters. TYBANE. He glanced at the chief and saw that nothing was registering on his face.

He found Pendergast looking at him curiously. "Sergeant, do you see something?"

"Nothing," he stammered. "It's just that the word…rings a distant bell."

"Interesting." Pendergast turned back to the corpse. "Most curious indeed: note how the carvings were made with a stone knife."

"A stone knife? You mean, like an Indian relic?"

"Yes, but freshly knapped and thus extremely sharp. Considerable skill was involved. The cuts were done pre-mortem, as they bled and clotted. But the precision of the work indicates the man was already unconscious when it took place; otherwise, he would have been uncooperative in the procedure. But the initial, fatal wound was made, I would say, by a long, heavy knife that went clear through the gut, perhaps a bayonet." He paused, glancing around. "The actual killing occurred farther up in the salt marshes and the body drifted here on the outgoing tide. Perhaps a study of the tidal currents might help establish a location and time of death. The body must have been in the water some time for the fish to consume the lips, eyes, nose, and tongue." He looked up at Gavin. "The clam digger who found it, is he of an unusually avaricious nature?"

"Boyd?" said Gavin. "Oh, yeah, he's famous for that. Tightfisted bastard. How did you know?"

"The fact that he continued digging clams around the body. Where does he sell his clams?"

"At the Inn. They're famous for the fried clam basket."

Pendergast gave a small shudder. "When one considers the clam is a filter feeder, a fried clam meal at the Inn over the next few days would not be far removed from cannibalism. Fortunately, there is no risk of me ever ingesting a fried clam, famous or not." He made a final inspection of the body, removed a small digital camera, and took a series of photos of the carvings.

"It looks like we got ourselves a real psycho here," said Mourdock.

Pendergast rose and pulled off his gloves. "Other than the cuts, this is a most uninformative crime scene, with the body having been stripped, transported here by water, and thoroughly washed by the tides. These cuts were done with care and skill, however, by someone who had experience carving flesh. There appears to be a purpose behind the symbols, and no doubt with the word *TYBANE* as well. Chief Mourdock, I'm afraid I have to disagree with your conclusion that this is the work of a psychopath. The person who did this was organized, purposeful, and deliberate."

14

C onstance Greene surveyed the room Pendergast had engaged on the first floor of the Inn. He'd had the bed moved out and a large pine table brought in, on which he had set up a clumsy, almost antique, reel-to-reel tape recorder, with an ungainly microphone, along with an old IBM Selectric typewriter and a Dictaphone machine.

She was amazed at how cooperative the chief had become—at least, when directly asked for assistance. That very morning, the chief had let Pendergast rifle the Exmouth PD storage room for outmoded equipment and take whatever he wanted.

"Ah, Constance. I see you are admiring my interrogation room." Pendergast stood in the doorway, cradling an old IBM PC.

"Is that what this is? An interrogation room?"

He set down the computer. "Indeed. What do you think?"

"It looks more like a museum of ancient technology."

He plugged in the PC, attached the keyboard, and booted it up. Next to it he placed an old but still-sealed box of floppy disks.

"Does that even work?"

"No."

"And what, may I ask, is wrong with your MacBook?"

"Far too pretty to be intimidating."

She glanced around again. "So this is all for show?"

"You will find, my dear Constance, that a wall of equipment, even old equipment, has a most salutary effect on a potential witness. The tape recorder does in fact work, but for convenience I have the microphone hooked up to a digital recorder hidden inside the reel-to-reel."

He began arranging everything in severe order on the table. Constance did have to admit it all formed a rather daunting façade, one that served to separate and isolate the interviewee from the interviewer.

"Please shut the door and have a seat."

Constance closed the door, swept back her dress, and seated herself. "Who are you going to interview?"

He produced a list. She scanned it, laid it down. "There are a lot of names here."

"We may not need to speak to them all. I am, as they say in these parts, *fishing*."

"In other words, you think the killing of the historian is related to the walled-up skeleton."

"Normally I put no faith in the 'gut reaction.' But in this situation, my *gut reaction* is so definite that I will make an exception: yes, they are most certainly connected."

"How?"

He tented his fingers and sat back. "I would be interested, Constance, to learn your thoughts first. You've been agitating for the freedom to investigate as you see fit, and I'm curious to hear your analysis of what we've gathered so far."

She sat forward, self-conscious under the pressure of his

steady, waiting gaze. "A few things stand out," she began. "We know the historian was investigating the disappearance of a ship along this coast in 1884. That same year, due to the eruption of Krakatoa, the whole region, including Exmouth, suffered a devastating crop failure. Between 1870 and 1890, according to the carbon dating, a man—an African American sailor—was tortured and his body walled up in the basement of the lighthouse keeper's residence. In 1886, the lighthouse keeper fell down the stairs in a drunken stupor and was killed."

A slow nod.

"If you put all that together, it seems to me the man was probably walled up in 1884 and is connected somehow to the disappearance of the ship. I wouldn't be surprised if the death of the drunken lighthouse keeper two years later was related, as well. After all, it was his basement the man was walled up in. There's a dark secret in this town—something happened here around that time. The historian found out some crucial fact which threatened to expose that secret and was murdered to keep him quiet."

"And the marks on the body?"

"I don't have an answer for that."

"What about the wine theft?"

"As you pointed out, it was a smokescreen for the removal of the sailor's skeleton. More evidence, as if we needed it, that the dark secret I mentioned is still present in Exmouth."

"And what are your recommendations on how to proceed? Prioritized, of course."

Constance paused. "One, find out what the historian discovered that caused his death. Two, find out more about the ship that disappeared, the *Pembroke Castle*. Three, find out more about that lighthouse keeper who died—

assuming that's possible. And four, identify those markings on the body."

"There are many gaps of logic in your chain of reasoning, and there is much speculation, but on the whole I am not disappointed in you, Constance."

She frowned. "I don't take kindly to being damned by faint praise. To what gaps of logic, in particular, do you refer?"

"Allow me my little joke. Your analysis, and your recommendations, are most commendable. In fact, as a result I intend to entrust you with an assignment of importance."

She shifted in her seat, trying to conceal the pleasure this gave her. "What are your own thoughts?"

"I concur with all you have said, pending more specific evidence. But I must add, the two items that I find most telling are the word *TYBANE* carved on the historian's body, along with the curious symbols ... and the ghost story."

"The ghost story?"

"The one you told me, about the lighthouse being haunted, with babies heard crying."

"You really think that's important?"

"Of the utmost."

Pendergast turned as a rap sounded on the door. "Ah, here is our first interviewee!"

He opened the door to reveal a man standing in the passage. He was in his early forties, slightly built, with thinning brown hair and a prominent Adam's apple. Constance recalled seeing him around town twice before: once in the street, watching Pendergast's arrest from a distance, and again at breakfast here in the Inn yesterday morning. On both occasions he had worn conservative, rather boring suits, contrasted almost comically—and this was why she remembered him—by hairy woolen V-neck sweaters in gaudy colors. He was wearing one today, as well: peach colored and fuzzy. *Chacun à son goût*, she thought with distaste—or, in this case, lack of *goût*.

"Ah," Pendergast said. "Dana Dunwoody, Esquire— bedecked in your usual sartorial splendor."

"Bright colors please me," the man said, shaking the prof- fered hand. "You, I assume, feel precisely the opposite."

"A hit, a very palpable hit! Please, take a seat." Pendergast waited while the man made himself comfortable. "This is my assistant, Miss Greene, who will be present at the inter- view. Constance, meet Dana Dunwoody, Exmouth's attorney at law."

Constance nodded in greeting.

"How can I be of assistance, Agent Pendergast?" Dunwoody asked.

"Just a few questions, if you don't mind."

Dunwoody waved a hand. Constance noticed the lawyer had a simple, faded tattoo of a single anchor on the back of one wrist.

Pendergast consulted a notebook. "You live on a house overlooking the salt marshes, I believe."

Dunwoody nodded.

"Were you home the night before last?"

Dunwoody nodded again.

"Did you hear or see anything unusual that evening?"

"Nothing I can recall."

Pendergast made a notation in the book. "How is the law profession here in Exmouth?"

"Adequate."

"What kind of work do you do?"

"Real estate sales. The occasional lawsuit. Some routine town legal business."

"What kind of lawsuits?"

"Various kinds. Property claims. Right-of-way disputes. Requests for zoning variances."

"I see. And your being a town selectman might be useful there."

Dunwoody plucked a loose thread from his sweater. "Agent Pendergast, I never allow my civic duties and my professional ones to overlap."

"Of course not."

Dunwoody smiled faintly. He was, Constance noted, rather sharp-witted, not easily intimidated.

"Are you married, Mr. Dunwoody?"

"Not anymore."

Constance looked at the man through narrowed eyes. He had a certain lawyerly knack for answering questions without providing any real information.

"I see. But you do have family in town."

Dunwoody nodded. "We go way back."

"How far back?"

"I couldn't tell you. It seems we Dunwoodys have always been here."

"Getting back to your current family. Your brother, Joe, is a bartender here at the Inn, is he not?"

At this, the expression of pride that had been gathering on Dunwoody's face as he spoke of his family history was replaced very briefly by a frown, before going deliberately blank. "He is."

"Do you do any criminal law, Mr. Dunwoody?" Pendergast asked.

"Very little call for it in Exmouth."

"Although the town does have its problems. The break-in at Percival Lake's, for example. And I understand from one of the cooks here in the Inn that foodstuffs go missing from the kitchen pantry on a regular basis."

"That hardly seems to constitute much of a crime."

"Have you read *The Hound of the Baskervilles*, by any chance?" Pendergast asked.

Dunwoody hesitated a second, clearly surprised by the question. "I don't see the relevance."

"Humor me. Have you read it?"

"Yes."

"Then you may recall a similar set of circumstances. Missing food, I mean. From Baskerville Hall."

As Constance watched, Dunwoody's face went even more blank. Studiously blank. He did not reply.

Pendergast slapped the notebook shut, laid it beside the typewriter. "I have no further questions. Thank you for your time."

The lawyer stood, nodded at both of them in turn, then left, shutting the door behind him.

Constance turned toward Pendergast. "*The Hound of the Baskervilles*? I hope you're not going fey on me, Aloysius."

"On the contrary. Didn't you notice his reaction—or lack of it? Most telling."

"I can't say I know what you were driving at. But he certainly seems like a guilty fellow to me."

"Indeed, Constance. All lawyers are guilty. But this one, I think, is more guilty than most." He looked at his watch. "Come on—I think we have just enough time for a cup of tea before our next guest arrives."

15

They returned from tea to find a man standing outside the closed door, baseball cap in hand. Pendergast ushered him in and he looked around with rheumy eyes, clearly intimidated by the setup. Constance had not seen this man before. As he stepped past her she caught a faint whiff of bourbon and cigar smoke.

"Make yourself comfortable, Mr. LaRue," Pendergast told him.

The man settled himself in a chair.

With precision and formality, Pendergast threaded a reel-to-reel tape onto the recorder, fussed with the controls, and then—making the final adjustments—he depressed the start button. The reels started turning. It was interesting, Constance thought, that he had not bothered taking these steps with the lawyer.

"Please speak clearly into the microphone," he said.

A nod. "Yes, sir."

"State your name and address for the record."

Gordon LaRue lived in Dill Town, he said, had lived there all his life, and had a small business cutting grass for a living.

"And how long have you cut Mr. Lake's grass?"

"Twelve years."

"On the weekend Mr. Lake was gone, and his house was broken into, you cut the grass?"

"I did. He liked me to come when he wasn't around, on account of the noise bothering him."

"And what time did you come that weekend?"

"On Sat'day, about eleven."

"Did you see anything out of the ordinary?"

"No. The grass didn't need much cutting, seeing as how it's getting into fall. Mr. Lake likes to keep a nice lawn, though, on account of the sculptures."

"Any sign that someone other than Lake had been there?"

"Didn't see anything. Didn't look like anyone had broken in. No strange cars, nothing."

"And you left at what time?"

"Twelve thirty."

"That will be all, Mr. LaRue."

As the man stood up to leave, Pendergast said casually, "Dill Town—the outlying town first settled by black whalers, correct?"

"Yes."

"Interesting. Thank you." Pendergast ushered LaRue out the door, closed it, and turned to Constance, giving her a brief smile.

"Fishing?" said Constance, wondering why they were so obviously wasting their time.

"Indeed. Let us put another fly on the water. Fetch the next fellow for me, if you will."

Constance went out and found another interviewee seated in a chair in the hallway, face red, little white hairs on his neck standing out in irritation. He rose. "I hope this isn't going to take up a lot of time," he said, looking her up and down with faded but alert blue eyes. He was about seventy, in a lumberjack shirt, suspenders, and blue work pants. A faint odor of the marshes clung to him.

"This way," she said.

He pushed through the door aggressively and refused to take the proffered chair. Pendergast once again fiddled with the equipment.

"Well?" the man asked impatiently. "I ain't gonna answer any questions, if that's what this is about."

"Just a moment, so sorry, just trying to get the equipment in order. Mr. George Washington Boyle, is it?"

"That's Benjamin Franklin Boyle," the man said. "Nice start there, Mr. Detective."

"Endless apologies." More fussing. "You are here, Mr. Boyle, in a completely voluntary capacity. So you wish to decline answering questions?"

"And if I do? You gonna get a warrant or something, make me come back?"

"No, no. I'm conducting a private investigation. I have no subpoena power. You are free to go. No hard feelings."

A grunt. "Well, as long as I'm here..." He sat down.

Constance could see that Boyle was a man of higher intelligence than his looks warranted, and that Pendergast, in feigning incompetency and giving Boyle a feeling of superiority, had managed to put the man in the right frame of mind for answering questions. A clever ploy—and in stark contrast to her own sadly underdeveloped skills with people. She recalled the long list of potential interviewees and wondered if perhaps it wouldn't have been better for her to stay back at Riverside Drive.

"Mr. Boyle, on the weekend of the wine theft, you were, I

presume, clamming on the Exmouth mudflats?"

"I went out on Saturday afternoon for a few hours."

"Whereabouts?"

"An area they call the Channel Flats."

"Can you show me on the map?" He unrolled a map of the area and placed it in front of Boyle.

"Right here." A dirty finger thumped the location.

"Ah. I see you had no view of the lighthouse at all."

"That's right. That's two miles from the light and behind the Exmouth bluffs. You can't see over the marsh grass and cattails, anyway, seeing is how they's five, six feet high in most places."

"I was hoping you might have seen something, perhaps coming or going."

"Nothing but mud and clams."

Pendergast began rolling up the map. "You must know those marshes quite well."

"Better than just about anyone."

"I imagine they have their own peculiar beauty."

"They do." Boyle said it with conviction, but also in a tone that meant he had no interest in exploring that subject further.

"And a history?"

"Oh, yes."

"But I don't suppose you have much interest in history, being a clammer."

Now the man bristled. "I was captain on a dragger, Mr. Pendergast, for forty years. I'm a seafaring man, and seafaring men have always had an interest in history."

Pendergast raised his eyebrows. "I see. But what sort of history could an uninhabited marsh have?"

"More than you might think." Boyle laughed. He was enjoying having an audience, especially someone as dim-witted as Pendergast. "All kinds of history. Stories, too. Of witches. And the Gray Reaper."

"The Gray Reaper?"

"Sometimes at night, you see a light out there in the marshes, moving around, bobbing this way and that. That's the Gray Reaper. Couple hundred years ago, they say, there was a man named Jack, and he was the meanest son of a bitch between Casco Bay and Gloucester. When he died, the devil came and got him, hauled him down to hell. But Jack was so ornery that after a while the devil couldn't stand it anymore. He tossed Jack a glowing coal and said, "You're too mean for my hell, so you take that coal and go start a hell of your own!" He roared with laughter. "He's there in the marshes, covered in the gray-black mud. That's where he got the name. Blends in, like so you can't see him. Save for the coal, of course. When you see that light bobbing out there, that's the Gray Reaper wandering around, coal in hand, looking to reap some souls and start a hell of his own."

Pendergast seemed considerably irritated by this diversion. "And the witches?"

Boyle waved his hand. "There's a story, goes back to the days of Salem. When things got hot and they started hanging the witches down there, a group of them hightailed it out of Salem in the dead of night and came north, where they settled on one of those salt marsh islands, out of the reach of civilization. Men and women both, mind you."

"Are you saying there were real witches?"

"I'm saying no such thing. The *legend* is those old Puritans hanged a lot of innocent people while the real witches got away."

"Where in the marshes did they settle?"

"Nobody knows. Inland a bit somewhere, according to

the story. But things didn't go well. A bad winter, starvation, and Indian attacks wiped them out. Later on, they say, from time to time a traveler would get lost in the marshes and come across the ruins of that witch settlement, wooden houses all rotten and collapsed. They say in the middle of this crazy settlement was a circle of flat stones with carvings on them and, in the center of that, a piece of slate with a one-word message."

"Which was?"

"T-Y-B-A-N-E."

Pendergast and Constance exchanged glances.

"What does it mean?"

"No one's ever figured it out." A knowing leer. "Until now, maybe."

"So you've heard that whoever killed the historian, McCool, carved that word on his body."

Boyle shrugged. "Can't keep no secrets in a town as small as Exmouth."

"Any speculations as to why someone would do that?"

"It's some kids, probably, tweakers from Dill Town getting their kicks, playing at raising the devil. They robbed the man to buy drugs and are dumb enough to think they'll get the cops to think witches did it."

"Why Dill Town?"

"Dill Town's got a lot of history of troubles. Crime, drinking. That sort of thing."

"Have you seen any sign of people in the salt marshes?"

"As a matter of fact, I have. I think there's a homeless guy living out there. Seen some footprints in the mud, trails through the grass. Never seen him in the flesh, but a few times I've smelled his campfire." He laughed. "Maybe he's the guy swiped Lake's wine collection. Now there's a wino's dream. Maybe he's even the Gray Reaper in person. You might want to look into that, Mr. Detective."

"I will," Pendergast said, rising. "Thank you, Mr. Boyle, for your time." He glanced at Constance. "I think we can dispense with the rest of the interviews—for now, at any rate."

Boyle got up. Then he leaned forward and asked, in a confidential tone: "How much does a guy get paid in your line of work?"

16

This was going to be interesting. More than interesting. Bradley Gavin slipped under the yellow police tape that blocked off the end of the second-floor hall at the Inn. He turned and lifted it for Constance Greene. She followed him to the closed door of Morris McCool's room. He opened the door and pushed it wide.

Agent Pendergast had made it clear that every professional courtesy was to be extended to Constance, which explained why she was being allowed once again into what was, effectively, a crime scene. He was more curious about her than about what they might find in the room, which, he suspected, was precious little. The word *intriguing* hardly began to describe this strange and beautiful woman. And this was his first chance to speak to her alone.

He turned and held out his hand. "After you, Ms. Greene," he said.

"*Miss* Greene, if you please. I find *Mizz* a disagreeable neologism."

"Oops. Sorry." Gavin watched her out of the corner of his eye as she entered, an ethereal figure in a long dress. This woman was as remote as the glaciers, and maybe that was part of what appealed to him—that, and a kind of mysterious self-possession. Gavin rather liked the old-fashioned "Miss" part. He was starting to view this *Miss* Greene as a challenge. He knew he was attractive to women; and he suspected that, as she got to know him better, he just might prove to be her type.

He followed her into the historian's room. It was done up in period furniture, like the rest of the Inn, and he took in its charming yet shabby contents: the big heavy bed in dark wood, the lace curtains, the braided rugs that were a little too worn, and the bathroom peeking through an open door, which had last seen a renovation so long ago that the tiling had come back in style and then gone out again.

"The agreement was eyes only, Miss Greene," he said. "But if you want to handle something, I don't see a problem as long as you ask me first."

"Thank you."

The SOC team had already been through the room with a fine-tooth comb, and their tags and flags could be seen festooning just about everything. They'd been looking for forensic evidence—latents, hairs, fibers, DNA, blood. He and the lady were looking for papers—specifically, evidence on what the historian might have been working on. Not that he expected that would lead to anything; he had already more or less satisfied himself that this murder was just a robbery-homicide, albeit one with some uniquely disturbing aspects.

He did a quick mental inventory. A short stack of books and papers on a rolltop desk. No computer. The maid had fixed up the room after the historian had gone downstairs for dinner, a few hours before his murder. That was too bad. Everything was very neat, but whether this was a reflection of the maid or the historian's personality was hard to say.

He walked over to the small desk where the historian had stacked the books and papers. He took out his notebook and glanced over at Constance. She was looking around the room, her violet eyes taking everything in.

He examined the books: *Storms and Shipwrecks of New England*, by Edward Rowe Snow; a photocopied document called "Registry of Missing Ships 1850–1900," from the Lloyd's archives. There were several bookmarks in each publication. As he was jotting down the titles, he heard a soft rustle and Greene materialized behind him.

"May I pick up the registry, Sergeant?"

"Sure, go ahead."

She opened it to where the bookmark was, turning from his field of view. Gavin began looking around for wallet, watch, or money. Nothing had been found with the body. He then took a closer look at the Snow book, turning to a bookmarked chapter titled, "The Mysterious Disappearance of the S.S. *Pembroke Castle*."

"May I direct your attention to this?" Constance said, handing him the registry. It, too, had a marker at a page about the *Pembroke Castle*. Gavin was vaguely familiar with the story—but he read the entry with interest anyway.

S.S. Pembroke Castle, *1884. In February 1884, enroute from London to Boston, lost in a storm along the New England coast between Cape Elizabeth (Maine) and Cape Ann (Massachusetts).*

The S.S. *Pembroke Castle* was a 300-foot (100 m) oak-hulled steamship built by Barclay Curle & Co in Whiteinch, Glasgow, Scotland, as a passenger and cargo vessel. She was launched on 12 September 1876. On 16 January 1884 the *Pembroke Castle* began her final voyage from London, England, with 140 passengers, under charter by Lady Elizabeth Hurwell of Hurwell Ossory, Warwickshire. On 18 January the ship was passed by the liner Wessex and noted in that vessel's log. On 2 February 1884, the *Pembroke Castle* was sighted at sunset by the F/V Monckton from Portland, Maine, laboring through heavy seas near Halfway Rock in outer Casco Bay. Signals were exchanged by lamp. This was the last known sighting of the ship. A northeastern storm was bearing down the coast and continued for three days. When the ship failed to reach Boston at the scheduled time, on 5 February, the U.S. Coast Guard deployed several cruisers, joined later by two Navy ships, in an unsuccessful search for survivors or debris. The ship was presumed lost in the storm somewhere along the coast between Cape Elizabeth and Cape Ann; had the ship rounded the latter cape, it would have been seen by the keeper of the Eastern Point Lighthouse, and would have been able to take refuge in Gloucester Harbor. No trace of the ship or its crew was ever found, nor has confirmed debris from the wreckage ever been identified. The insurance claim was settled by Lloyd's for £16,500 on 23 March 1885, paid to the London and Bristol Steamship Company, owner of the *Pembroke Castle*, with an additional sum of £9,500 paid 6 April 1886 to Lady Hurwell for loss of cargo.

"This must be what our historian was looking into," he said, closing the document and laying it back on the desk.

"Yes," said Greene. She had been standing close to him, reading the entry over his shoulder. There was something oddly thrilling in her proximity.

She stepped back. "Do you find it strange that no money seems to have been paid for the loss of the passengers?"

"I hadn't thought about it."

"And this 'loss of cargo'—I wonder what that was, why it was so valuable, and why it took over two years to get reimbursed for it?"

Gavin shrugged.

"Why would an English noblewoman charter a ship to begin with? And why wasn't *she* on the ship?"

Gavin looked into her face. She was really very young, no more than twenty-two or twenty-three. But there was an unusual depth in those violet eyes. He felt a most unprofessional stirring. "Well," he said, "those are interesting questions, but I doubt they're relevant."

"Why not?"

He swallowed, stung by her sharp tone. "Because I'm pretty sure some crankhead from Dill Town killed our guy for money and kicks."

"Crankhead? What's that?"

She seemed almost to be from another world—at least, a world far from Exmouth. That, too, was appealing. "Meth addict. You know, methamphetamine? *Breaking Bad*?"

A silence. "Are there many addicts in Dill Town?"

"A few years ago we busted a lab over there, and we think there might be another one operating, maybe out in the marshes."

"Why is there an addiction problem?"

"'Addiction problem' may be too strong. It's just...you know, poverty, lack of education, no opportunities...

Fishing's been in decline for decades. And fishermen, well, they're a rough bunch." He paused. "Just saying."

"I see. Thank you for that observation, Sergeant. What was found with the body?"

This segue was so unexpected it took Gavin a moment to parse it. "Um, nothing. Well, a wristwatch. The rest of the body had been stripped." She'd been there; why was she asking him this question?

"If the motive of the 'crankhead' was money, why didn't he take the watch?"

Gavin shrugged. "It was a crappy brand." He hesitated. "So what does Pendergast think?"

"About what?"

"Those markings. A red herring—or something else?"

"He hasn't said."

"And you?"

"I don't know."

There was a silence as they looked at each other. Gavin finally spoke. "I've been doing police work for a long time, and I've made one bedrock observation about crime."

"Which is?"

"That most crimes are banal. Moronic. The obvious explanation is almost always the right one. And in this case, robbery is the simplest explanation, with those crazy markings the work of drug addicts."

"If most crimes are banal and moronic, it's because most people are."

Gavin was surprised by her answer. "That's your view of human nature? That people are basically stupid?"

"Yes. There's the exception to the rule. Some people defy simple explanations. And so do some crimes. This is one of those crimes."

"*Some people defy simple explanations*," Gavin repeated. "What do you mean by that?"

"I mean that a few exceptional people stand above the common lot. For them, the rules are different. Their crimes are also different. There was nothing banal or stupid about this murder—or the criminal who committed it."

Gavin had never met a woman quite like this. He looked at her curiously, and then—most uncharacteristically—decided to take a step into the unknown. "I'm quite sure that you, Miss Greene, are one of those exceptional people."

He awaited her denial, a flare-up of anger, but it didn't come. Encouraged, he ventured further, his voice dropping just a little. "And for that reason, I would like to get to know you better."

She continued looking at him, her face unreadable. Then she said, "Are we done here?"

"We're done here."

He watched her elegant lips curve upward in a faint smile at what appeared to be some private amusement. "After you, Sergeant."

17

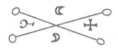

Soft late-afternoon light was filtering through the lace curtains of the would-be interview room. Motes drifted in the air. Constance watched as the FBI agent paced softly back and forth, his black-clad figure moving in and out of the light. He moved so lightly, he seemed more wraithlike than human. He'd been this way since she'd descended from McCool's room with her report. He was inscrutable, sphinxlike. His very lack of predictability was what made him so...intriguing.

"It makes no sense," he murmured.

She waited, knowing he was not speaking to her. He continued pacing.

"The ship," he went on, "was seen beating through heavy seas near Half Way Rock in Casco Bay at sunset, which on February second, 1884, was approximately four fifty pm. It was moving at ten knots, according to the log of the F/V *Monckton*. It must have rounded Cape Elizabeth around five thirty pm. High tide was at eleven twenty-five pm, and because of the nor'easter there would have been a storm surge. If the ship had sunk prior to eleven twenty-five pm, the wreckage and bodies would have been carried to shore on the surge and found. But they were not. Therefore, the ship sank *after* the tide reversed, bearing the wreckage and victims out to sea. Assuming a steady rate of speed of ten knots—likely, given this was a steamship and would have been traveling at that speed for stability—the *Pembroke Castle* would have rounded Cape Ann at eleven forty-five pm and reached the safety of Gloucester Harbor shortly thereafter."

Turn, pace, turn, pace.

"But it was not seen rounding the cape and it never made the harbor. The ship must therefore have met its end in the twenty minutes between eleven twenty-five pm and eleven forty-five pm—which would have placed the disaster right off the Exmouth shore." He shook his head. "It makes no sense."

"It makes perfect sense to me," Constance said.

Pendergast looked over at her. "Pray tell, how in the world does it make sense to you?"

"You believe the ship sank off of the Exmouth shore. That explains why the historian came back here—he deduced just what you deduced. *Quod erat demonstrandum.*"

"*Cum hoc, ergo propter hoc.*" He shook his head impatiently. "It may explain why the historian focused on this area. It does not, however, take into account a phenomenon known as the stand of the tide."

"And what, pray tell, is the 'stand of the tide'?"

"Also known as slack water. There is a period of about half an hour after high tide in which all tidal currents cease. The stand of the tide would mean that a wreck anywhere off the Exmouth shore would have been driven straight into the Exmouth bluffs and beaches."

"Why?"

"Because of the wind. This was a nor'easter—that is, wind from the northeast. The Exmouth shoreline forms a hook as it trends out toward Cape Ann. That hook is like a net: any debris from that wreck, driven southwest by the wind, could not have escaped it. The bodies and wreckage would have littered that shore."

"But what if the ship rounded Cape Ann without seeing it? What if it was already so disabled it couldn't come into Gloucester Harbor, and was eventually carried out to sea on the outgoing tide instead?"

Pendergast paused, considering. "That might appear to be a viable possibility, and I believe the rescue operation must have assumed just that, focusing attention on the very areas where the disabled ship would have been driven. Your registry mentioned that this was an oak-hulled ship. Even if it sank, there would have been a large amount of floating debris, not to mention bodies. But a thorough search found nothing."

"Then perhaps it was disabled long before reaching the Exmouth shore, wallowing in the storm until the tide turned and carried it out to sea."

Pendergast began pacing again. "The tide reverses every six hours. A wallowing ship would not go very far. Eventually *some* debris would have washed ashore." He waved his hand. "But we're going in circles. Recall this is not the only mystery here: there is another—the link to witchcraft."

"Don't tell me you believe Boyd's story of the refugee Salem witches!"

"My dear Constance, I 'believe' nothing. And I hope you will resist that impulse, as well. Let us only go where the facts take us. And the facts are pointing me into the Exmouth salt marshes and that long-depopulated colony. I will go in search of it tonight."

"At night?"

"Of course at night. It is to be a stealth reconnaissance."

"I'll go with you."

"You'll do nothing of the sort. I can move far better in the darkness alone. I may have to cross water channels, and you, unfortunately, never learned to swim. And recall the unpleasantness that ensued during our last, ah, field trip."

"You mean, the 'field trip' to the Botanic Gardens? As I recall, that particular excursion saved your life. As our friend Sergeant Gavin would put it, 'Just saying.'"

Pendergast's lips twitched in what might have been amusement or a concession of the point. "What I would like you to do, Constance, is to go to Salem tomorrow morning. I understand there are many attractions, including a 'Witch House,' a 'Witch Dungeon Museum,' and the famous Witch Trials Memorial, not to mention the 'Witch City Segway Tour.'"

"Segway Tour? Surely you're joking."

"More to the point, Salem is also home to the Integrated Wiccan Alliance." He passed her a card. "A certain Tiffani Brooks, also known as Shadow Raven, is head of the league and the leader of a coven there."

Constance took the card. "Wicca? White magic? And what am I supposed to find out?"

At this, Pendergast handed her a piece of paper with a drawing on it. Looking at it, she recognized the marks that had been cut into the historian's body, along with the crudely lettered word *TYBANE*.

"An Internet search turned this up," Pendergast said. "Recall what Boyle told us? Of an inscription that, according to legend, was found at the center of the lost witch colony that once existed inland from here?" He nodded at the sheet of paper. "That is the inscription, and those are the marks—at least, according to a long-dead archaeologist of questionable reputation."

Constance stared at the sheet. "You don't think that who-ever killed the historian, carved these markings into him, was a . . ."

"I'm not thinking anything. I simply want you to find out if those marks are genuine witchcraft, and, if so, what their meaning is. That mysterious word is also, in fact, what's at the heart of my own nocturnal journey. My dear Constance, we can't proceed until we determine whether they are genuine, or simply a killer's idea for misleading the investigation."

He stood up. "And now, adieu. I need to speak briefly with Sergeant Gavin. I recall hearing that he grew up in Exmouth."

"On what subject?"

"Just a question or two about the background of our estimable lawyer, Mr. Dunwoody. And then I've asked Mr. Lake for a tour of his sculpture garden."

She folded the sheet of paper carefully. "I thought you were going to undertake a certain reconnaissance."

"I am indeed. But for that, I require darkness."

"I see. And for myself?"

"For this evening's labor, I would like you to, ah, hang out at the Inn's bar, engage the natives in conversation, have a beer or two, and collect the gossip."

She stared at him. "I don't 'hang out' in bars."

"You will have to adjust your rules of personal conduct, as I do mine, while on an investigation. You can always drink absinthe, which, by a special miracle, they have." He leaned over, his voice lowering confidentially. "But whatever you do, *avoid the clams*."

18

T hat," said Percival Lake, gazing fondly, "was the first piece I made when I moved here with my wife thirty years ago." He patted the polished gray granite sculpture with affection before returning his arm to its prior position around Carole Hinterwasser's waist. The sculpture depicted the semiabstract form of a harpooner emerging from the stone, aiming his weapon. "I kept it for sentimental reasons, could've sold it a hundred times. It's titled *Queequeg.*"

A gust of wind blew up from the sea, ruffling the grass in the sculpture garden along the bluffs. Low clouds the color of zinc pressed in from the sea, bringing with them the smell of winter. Lake had arranged the large granite statues facing the sea, in a sort of homage to the Easter Island moai, which he had seen years ago on a journey with his late wife.

The black-clad figure of Pendergast pulled his coat collar tighter. The evening had turned a little chill, and the FBI agent was quite obviously not a person who enjoyed bracing weather.

Lake continued wandering through the sculptures, arm in arm with Carole, talking about each piece in turn, while

Pendergast followed behind them in silence. At the end of the line of statues, Lake paused and turned. "I'm curious to hear how the investigation is going," he said.

"Not well," said Pendergast.

"I see. Is it a question of a lack of evidence?"

"Just the opposite."

"Well, you've certainly caused quite a stir in town. You and the murder of that historian are all anyone is talking about." He paused, carefully choosing his words. "I have to admit, I'm feeling a little out of the loop."

"How so?"

"Well, you've been here three days. I was expecting regular reports on your progress. I heard secondhand, for example, that you've been helping the police investigate that murder. It would have been nice to hear it from you."

"My apologies."

The man was maddeningly opaque.

"Does this mean you think the historian's killing and this case are linked?" Carole asked.

"It does indeed."

A silence. Lake waited for elaboration, and when it didn't come, he asked: "Care to fill us in?"

"I do not."

Lake felt himself growing irritated. "I don't mean to be blunt, but aren't you working for me? Shouldn't I be getting regular reports?"

"I don't habitually discuss ongoing investigations with anyone unless absolutely necessary."

"So... If you're not here to tell me how things are going— why are you here? Surely it isn't just to view my sculpture."

Pendergast turned his back to the wind. "I had a few questions."

Lake shrugged. "Sure, go ahead. Although I believe I've told you everything I know."

"Is there a reason you didn't tell me of Ms. Hinterwasser's previous history?"

Lake exchanged glances with Carole. "Her history?"

"Her criminal history. She was caught shoplifting from an expensive antiques store in Cambridge."

There was a silence broken only by the wind.

"I'm not sure where this is going, Pendergast," Lake said at last, "but I am sure I don't like it."

"Why should he have told you?" Carole asked. "That was fifteen years ago. I returned the piece, made restitution. It was just an ugly little graven idol, anyway, I don't know what I saw in it. The whole story's ancient history. It has nothing to do with the burglary of our—of Perce's—house."

"Perhaps not." Pendergast returned his attention to Lake. "You were in the merchant marine, were you not?"

Lake paused a moment before answering. "I spent four years in the Navy and then three more as a mate on VLCCs."

"And I assume that's where you received the tattoo?"

"Tattoo?" Lake asked in surprise. "You mean, the whale on my right shoulder? How did you know about that?"

"It seems to be much admired in town, known from your rare appearances at the beach."

"Of course. Well, I've always loved the sea and *Moby Dick* is my favorite book—I've been rereading it every year since I was sixteen. 'Call me Ishmael' is the greatest first line in a novel ever written."

"I, myself, am not fond of animal stories."

Lake rolled his eyes. Pendergast was such an odd duck. "That's the first time I've heard *Moby Dick* dismissed as an animal story."

"Getting back to the subject at hand, Mr. Lake. Your merchant marine background was rather difficult for me to discover. Strange that, in a seaport town like Exmouth, few know of it."

"I'm a private man."

"Nor did the subject come up in your earlier recitative concerning your past. The one you gave me in the restaurant at the Inn."

Lake shrugged. "I've gotten used to not telling it. It doesn't fit in with being an artist, somehow."

"I see. I've discovered that Dana Dunwoody, before he went to law school, also worked in the merchant marine on VLCCs."

"I didn't know that."

"Did you ever happen to work on the same ship?"

"No, we did not."

"How well do you know Mr. Dunwoody?"

"Not well. He's not my cup of tea. A small-time, small-town, ethically challenged lawyer."

"Did you know he, too, has a tattoo—of an anchor, on the back of one hand?"

"That's a common enough tattoo for merchant mariners. You think Dunwoody and I are in some sort of tattoo conspiracy?"

"The other thing I found curiously hard to discover, and which you also neglected to tell me, is that you have deep roots in Exmouth. Your great-great-grandfather came up from Boston to Exmouth to marry a local woman. He was lost at sea in 1845, leaving a wife with a child. She moved back to Boston and that ended your family's connection with the town until you moved here thirty years ago."

Lake stared at Pendergast. "Is this supposed to be relevant?"

"Do you know your great-great-grandmother's maiden name?"

"No."

"Dunwoody."

"Jesus. Really? Lord, I had no idea. But there are a lot of Dunwoodys around here. Too many, in fact."

"Your last show in Boston, at Gleason Fine Art on Newbury Street, does not appear to have done well."

"In a bad economy, art is the first thing to suffer."

"And is it true, as local rumor has it, that you are presently short of commissions?"

"What are you driving at?" But Lake was, in fact, beginning to see just what the man was driving at. He felt himself losing his temper.

"Just this: Are you having financial difficulties, Mr. Lake?"

"I'm perfectly comfortable financially! I don't live the high life and I can weather a downturn in the market."

"Was the wine collection insured?"

"It was a listed asset on my homeowner's policy."

"Have you collected on the policy?"

"Not yet, but I hope to God you're not implying insurance fraud!"

"So you submitted a claim."

"Absolutely."

"For how much?"

"One hundred and ninety thousand dollars. It's all documented. I'd rather have the wine back, thank you very much. That's your job, by the way—not asking me a bunch of offensive and irrelevant questions. Digging up ancient dirt on my girlfriend, for God's sake. Are you accusing me of working in cahoots with that jackass lawyer, who happens to be my seventeenth cousin eleven times removed, to steal my own wine? Bringing you into the case just for show? Christ, don't make me sorry I hired you!"

Carole squeezed his hand. "Darling, *please*." Too late, Lake realized he was shouting.

Pendergast continued to look at them, his face the color of ice, eyes reflecting the dying light. "In any investigation, ninety-nine percent of the information gathered is irrelevant. In the search for that one percent, many offensive questions must be asked and many people aggravated. Nothing personal. Good day, Mr. Lake. Ms. Hinterwasser."

Lake, deflated, stood beside Carole and watched the dark figure of Pendergast walk down the hill toward his car.

19

A miasma hung over the marshes as A. X. L. Pendergast moved through the salt grass, a dark shape appearing and disappearing among the thick, swaying blades. At one o'clock in the morning, it was dead low tide and the mudflats were exposed, shining in the occasional patches of moonlight exposed by swift-moving clouds. The flats exhaled a sulfurous, dead-fish odor that combined with the tendrils of mist to form a stench that congealed on hair and skin. Pendergast carried with him a rolled-up map that he had hand-drafted earlier in the day, based on marine charts, USGS maps, NOAA wind and current charts, and his own observations.

The Exmouth salt marshes covered about twelve thousand acres behind the Crow Island barrier. This was where the Exmouth and the Metacomet Rivers came together on their way to the sea, creating a fantastical maze of marshes, channels, islands, and brackish pools before opening into shallow bays that extended to the sea around the northern end of Crow Island. About half of the marshlands had been designated a wildlife area. The remainder were largely inaccessible and considered wasteland, unbuildable because of environmental restrictions, plagued with greenhead flies in summer, and not interesting enough from a wildlife perspective to be included in the refuge. Their value lay solely in the clamming areas of the mudflats, exposed at low tide, but even a large portion of those were almost inaccessible by boat or on foot.

Pendergast moved with a feline grace, using the waxing moon as his only source of light. He paused now and then, to test the wind direction or smell the air. Once, briefly, he had caught the faint scent of a wood fire; whether this was from the distant houses of Dill Town, five miles northward, or from the homeless man alleged by Boyle to live in the marsh, was hard to say; nevertheless, he paused and, noting his position on the map and the direction of the wind, drew a line upwind.

Pendergast had chosen as his insertion point a section of marsh about a mile upstream from where the body of the historian had been found. This was along a channel that he guessed, given the movements of the tides and wind, was where the man might have been killed and initially dumped. It was a crude guess, but the best he could manage with the facts he had. He found nothing of interest at the spot. So he turned his attention to his ultimate destination: the isolated marsh islands in the far western reaches of the salt marsh, beyond the boundary of the refuge.

As he slipped through the grass, he did not think. Stilling the interior voice, he was like an animal, existing in the moment only as a collection of highly tuned sensory organs. Thinking would come later.

The salt grass was about five feet high and he moved through it in a straight line, parting it with gloved hands as he went along. The ground was spongy underfoot, with occasional sinks, muskrat holes, and potholes excavated by extreme high tides. The grass was sharp, but he was well swaddled in chest waders and a black Filson tin-cloth jacket.

In a half mile he came across two paths through the grass. Both were too narrow to have been made by human passage, and a minute examination of the ground revealed the hoofprints of deer in one and the paw prints of muskrats in the other.

Shortly, the salt grass gave way to a mudflat, about a quarter mile wide, through which snaked a small channel of water—all that remained at low tide.

Pendergast ventured into the mudflat, with each step sinking into the muck. In eight minutes he had made the difficult traversal to the other side, where a marsh island lay. A dilapidated sign, almost erased by time, indicated he was exiting the boundary of the wildlife preserve.

He continued on through a mixture of salt grass and mudflats. The tide was now slack and would soon be coming in. They were big tides, over ten feet vertical: he had about two hours before he would be cut off by the incoming ocean, the channels too deep and the currents too swift to wade.

Deep, deep into the marshes, in the middle of the remote island, he came across a tunnel through the grass that was not an animal trail. Now he knelt and, keeping the penlight low to the ground, turned it on and examined the earth. Almost immediately he saw the image of a human footprint, shod, made by what appeared to be a crude hobnailed boot, the hobs worn to nubs and many of them gone altogether. The footprint was fresh, perhaps no more than two or three days old.

He spread out the map and marked the location of the trail, and then he moved slowly along the tunnel-like path. It meandered about and, after a mile, ended in a mudflat at the edge of the marsh island, where any tracks had been erased by tidal currents. He could see, on the far side of the flat, where the tunnel in the grass continued.

He turned now and headed back toward the center of the island. The USGS map he had consulted indicated an area of slightly higher ground at the farther end: only three feet of vertical elevation, but three feet in a potential flood zone was significant. He struck off in another straight line through the salt grass, which was thicker and higher here, almost six feet, mingling with cattails that were beginning to lose their fluff. Where the cattails ended the land rose almost imperceptibly.

Pendergast began making a circle around the higher land, then cut across it, back and forth, in a kind of lawn mower pattern. Every few minutes he would stop, kneel in the thick grass, and examine the soft ground. At one point he smelled woodsmoke again, which he marked on his map, with another line drawn upwind.

The two lines he'd drawn intersected at a spot about two miles distant.

He resumed his search pattern, continuing for almost an hour in silence. And then, toward the center of the marsh island, Pendergast found, poking from the edge of the mud, a flat rock. He pulled it out and examined it: a worn piece of schist. Rocks did not occur naturally in mudflats. Putting it back in place, he marked its location on a handheld GPS. At that point he began moving in tighter circles, finding, here and there, additional stones. He continued punching the location of each into the GPS device. He worked as long as he dared, and then, knowing that time was running out as the tide came in, he tucked the GPS and map away and made a beeline back toward his starting point.

He had gotten no more than ten feet when he heard a noise: an unholy, ghastly, drawn-out wail that echoed over the vast marshes from a distance. Pendergast had heard that kind of scream before. It was a distinct, unique, human scream, one full of surprise and disbelief, then pain, and finally existential horror.

It was the scream of a man being killed.

20

The scream died away into a gibbering moan, which seemed to dissolve in the sighing of the night wind through the salt grass. Pendergast stood stock-still for a moment. And then he tested the wind again, knelt, removed the map, quickly unrolled it, and drew a narrow cone on it, indicating the approximate direction from where the sound had come. It seemed to be in the middle distance, carried on the wind and yet not from afar: perhaps half a mile, at most. This would put the murder—he had no doubt that was what it was—in the middle of the most inaccessible area of the entire Exmouth marshes: a riddle of channels, mudflats, and stagnant cattail swamps.

This also happened to be the area from which the scent of smoke had come.

He moved fast, like a snake, parting the grass with his arms as he went along, moving as swiftly as was consistent with silence and safety. He came across another trail, a tunnel through the grass, narrower but also human-like in origin, and shortly thereafter found himself at the edge of another mudflat. But now the tide was rising swiftly. Black water flowed inland, the trickle in what had previously been a tiny channel now a surging river twenty feet wide and still growing, carrying along foam and leaves and flotsam swept up on its rise. Clouds scudded across the gibbous moon.

He paused, considering the situation. The tide was rising swiftly, and many channels and streams still lay between him and the approximate area of the crime. Even if he could reach the spot, it would take at least an hour, and by then he would be trapped, unable to return until the far ebb of the tide—six hours at least. He lacked critical information about the victim, the killer, the local geography, and the circumstances. He was at a fatal disadvantage; it would be imprudent, even reckless, to rush blindly toward the sound.

Pendergast turned back into the sheltering grass and checked his cell phone, on the off chance that he had come into a stray field of reception. No good. He examined his map. It was imperative that he get out and report the murder as quickly as possible. In his present location, he was more than halfway across the marsh. The quickest way out would not involve retracing his steps, but would instead take him in the opposite direction, inland to a wood called the King's Mark State Forest. Through this forest, according to the map, ran a country lane that was the back road from Dill Town to Newburyport.

That would be the quickest way out—and to a phone.

Pendergast put away the map, took his bearing, and then set off, breaking from a swift walk into a steady, even jog. After a quarter mile he struck another mudflat, swiftly filling with incoming tide, and waded into it, struggling through frigid water that was now four feet deep—and would soon be double that—with steadily increasing currents. He continued in this manner, navigating by the light of the moon, until he

could see—at the far end of the lighter-colored marshlands—
a black line of trees. At last, he reached the final tidal channel, the water now churning through it. He ventured into it
and quickly found it was too deep for wading; he would have
to swim.

He retreated and unbuckled his chest-high waders; they
would have proved a death trap when filled with swiftly
moving water. Discarding the waders, he rolled the map and
other items in a piece of oilcloth, held it over his head, and
ventured into the current. This channel was thirty feet across
and, as soon as his feet lifted from the muck, the current
began to sweep him along, the opposite bank moving by fast
as he kicked with his legs and one arm. After a minute of
struggle he was able to regain a purchase with his feet and
waded the last part of it, finally arriving at a cut bank, over-
hung with dark pine trees and exposed roots. He climbed up
this and rested a moment at the edge of the woods, cleaning
the muck from his legs. According to the map, the road
skirted the marshes and went on into Dill Town, about four
miles away, a distance Pendergast could cover in a brisk
hour's walk. From Dill Town it was another quarter mile into
Exmouth proper.

He rose and started into the woods. The road would be
a few hundred yards away and impossible to miss. But the
woods themselves were dark and presented a massive tangle
of undergrowth, with patches of briar that climbed halfway up the trees, choking and killing them, leaving skeletal
branches stark against the night sky. The woods echoed
with the peeping of frogs, the trilling of night insects, and
the occasional bloodcurdling sound of a screech owl. He
continued on, skirting a patch of briars, and then coming
into a glade dappled with moonlight.

He froze. The sounds of the night wood had suddenly ceased. Perhaps it was due to his passage—or, perhaps, due to another presence in the wood. After a moment he continued on, crossing the glade as if nothing were amiss. At the far side he entered a dense stand of conifers, where, in the thickest part, he halted again. He picked up three small pebbles and tossed them, the first one ten feet ahead, and then the second, after a moment, twenty feet on, and last the third one some thirty feet, each pebble making a small noise to simulate his continued passage through the forest.

But instead of continuing, he waited in the pitch black of the trees, crouching, motionless. Soon he could hear the faint sounds of his pursuer. It was someone moving in almost virtual silence—a rare skill in a forest as dense as this. And now he could see, materializing in the shadowed glade, the figure of a man—almost a giant—sliding through the open area, shotgun in hand. As the man approached, Pendergast tensed, waiting; and then, just as the man entered the blackness of the grove, Pendergast rose up, striking the barrel of the shotgun upward while dealing him a body blow with his shoulder, low and to the side. Both barrels went off with a terrific blast as the man went down, Pendergast on top, pinning him, his Les Baer .45 pressed into the man's ear. Flower petals and berries came showering down all around them.

"FBI," said Pendergast quietly. "Do not struggle."

The man relaxed. Pendergast eased up, grasped the barrel of the shotgun, laid it aside, and got off the man.

The man rolled over, then sat up, staring at Pendergast. "Son of a bitch," he said. "FBI? Let me see your badge."

Out came the wallet and badge. "What are you doing here?"

"I'm working," the man said. "And you've just ruined

my night's work." He gestured at the flowers and berries scattered around from a burst plastic bag. "I've every right to be here. My family's been here two hundred years."

The badge vanished back into Pendergast's pocket. "Why were you following me?"

"I heard a scream, and then I see some crazy mother covered in mud, creeping through my woods, and all this two days after somebody's been murdered and cut up not five miles from here—you're damn right I'm going to follow that man and ask him his business."

Pendergast nodded, tucking away the Les Baer. "My apologies for scattering your flowers. *Atropa belladonna*, I see. Deadly nightshade. Are you intending, like the wife of Claudius, to poison someone with it?"

"I've no idea who Claudius is, or his damn wife for that matter. I supply an herbal pharmacologist with it—for tinctures, decoctions, powders. It's still compounded for gastrointestinal disorders, in case you didn't know. These woods are full of it."

"You are a botanist, then?"

"I'm a guy trying to make a living. Can I get up now?"

"Please. With my apologies."

The man stood up, brushing leaves and twigs off himself. He was at least six and a half feet tall, lean, with a keen face, dark brown skin, blade-like nose, and incongruous green eyes. Pendergast could see from the way he carried himself that he had once been in the military.

The man held out his hand. "Paul Silas."

They shook.

"I need to find a telephone," said Pendergast.

"I got one at my place. Truck's just down the road, if you want a ride."

"If you please."

Pendergast followed him through the woods until they reached the narrow road, the truck parked on the shoulder. Pendergast was displeased to be refused entry into the plush, leather-bound cab interior; instead, Silas asked him to ride in the pickup bed, like a dog. A few minutes later the pickup truck pulled into a dirt drive leading to a small log cabin in the woods, not far from the edge of the marsh about a half mile outside Dill Town.

The man led the way inside, turned on the lights. "Phone's over there."

Pendergast picked it up, dialed 911, gave a brief report to the dispatcher, and in a moment had been connected to Sergeant Gavin. He relayed the information to Gavin at length, then hung up. He glanced at his watch: almost three am.

"They won't be able to get far in those marshes now," said Silas. "At half tide those currents run ten, twelve knots."

"They'll begin searching at high tide, with motor skiffs."

"Makes sense. Are you going to join in the search?"

"I will. If I might trouble you for a ride into Exmouth?"

"No problem. But first, since we've got some time, you'd better dry out a bit." Silas opened a woodstove and chucked in two pieces of wood. As Pendergast moved to settle himself down, Silas turned. "Um, if you don't mind, not the sofa. The wooden rocking chair is plenty comfy."

Pendergast sat in the rocking chair.

"You look like you might need a shot of bourbon."

A hesitation. "What kind, pray tell?"

Silas laughed. "Discriminating, are we? Pappy Van Winkle twenty-year-old. I don't allow rotgut on the premises."

Pendergast inclined his head. "That will suffice."

Silas disappeared into the kitchen and came back out with

a bottle of bourbon and two glasses. He plunked them on the coffee table, filled one, then the other.

"I am much obliged to you, Mr. Silas," said Pendergast, taking up the glass.

Silas took a delicate sip. "So you were out there investigating the murder of that historian?"

"I was indeed."

"That scream back there was enough to make the devil himself fall to his knees, rosary in hand."

Pendergast removed his map and spread it out on a nearby table. "I would like you to indicate, if you please, where you were when you heard the scream, and from what direction you think it came."

Silas pulled the map toward him and hunched over it, his brow creased. "I was right here, in these woods, and the scream came from this direction." He drew his finger along the map.

Pendergast made some notations. Silas's finger lay over a section of the cone he'd previously drawn on the map. "This will help in the search for the body." He rolled up the map. "Have you heard any rumors of someone living in the marshes?"

"Not specifically. But if I were trying to escape the law, that's where I'd go."

Pendergast took a sip of the bourbon. "Mr. Silas, you mentioned your family had been here two hundred years. You must know a great deal of local history."

"Well, I've never much cared for genealogy and so forth. Back in the day, Dill Town was the so-called Negro end of town, mostly whaling families. But it wasn't just African American. There was a lot of South Seas blood—Tahitian, Polynesian, Maori. I'm almost half Maori myself. The Maori were the greatest harpooners who ever lived. And then some of these sea captains had South Seas wives and families, you know, brought on board during the long voyages. They'd drop them off in Dill Town before heading into Boston to their white families. When they went back out to sea, they'd just pick them back up." He shook his head.

"And so you are a descendant, then, of the original inhabitants of Dill Town?"

"Sure am. Like I said, I'm as much Maori as African. My great-granddad had some hellacious tribal tats, or so my grandma told me."

"I understand most of the African Americans abandoned Dill Town after a lynching that happened there."

Silas shook his head. "That was a terrible business. Terrible. The man was innocent, of course. But that didn't matter to the vigilante group that strung him up. After that, folks in Dill Town decided it wasn't a good place to raise their families. They had the money to get out, thanks to the whaling business, and most of them did. Some just went to New Bedford. Others as far as the Chicago slaughterhouses."

"But your family stayed."

"Well, my granddad had lost his throwing arm in a whaling accident and so he'd begun a medicinal herb business. This area's full of herbs, especially nightshade, which grows all around here. You find it especially down where Oldham used to be. He couldn't transfer that kind of skill to a big city like New Bedford. So we stayed. We just moved out of town, down the road a piece—and here we are." He spread his hands.

"You live alone?"

"I had a wife, but she left. Too lonely, she said. The loneliness suits me just fine, most of the time, although I'm always happy to meet someone different. I'm no hermit. I hit the bar at the Inn once a week, drink, eat fried clams, and play dominoes with friends."

Pendergast stood up, drink in hand, and walked to the window, staring into the darkness, southwestward toward the marshes. "If you could take me into town now, that would be much appreciated. But I do have a final question. These vigilantes you mention—who were they?"

"Nobody knows. Local folks, masked. I'll tell you this: my granddad said that in the old days, there was a bad element in Exmouth. Not just a bad element—some truly evil people. He said they were like that story of the Gray Reaper: fellows looking to start a hell of their own."

21

A re you sure it wasn't a loon?" Chief Mourdock asked.
"They've got a call that can sound human."

Sergeant Gavin, sitting in the stern of the police skiff
with his hand on the tiller, guiding it across Exmouth Bay
toward the marshes, winced. Mourdock, even in his present
smacked-down state, managed to be an ass. But Pendergast,
sitting in the bow like some strange black figurehead, rolled-
up map in hand, didn't seem to notice.

Behind them, two more skiffs followed, equipped with
radios. Because of the heavy cloud cover, a feeble gray stain
of light on the eastern horizon was all that could be seen of
sunrise. Mourdock had taken longer to assemble the party
than Gavin would have liked—the chief's skepticism about
the whole expedition was quite evident—and it was now
approaching seven in the morning as the boat chugged along
the main waterway of the Exmouth River. The temperature
had plunged overnight into the low forties, and it was even
more flesh-chilling out here in the marshes than on land. The
tide was high and the water had gone slack twenty minutes
before. That didn't give them much time before it began the

ebb, the current flowing out of the tidal marshes at an ever-increasing rate. Gavin had spent time as a teenager earning pocket money by clamming in the marshes, and he had a healthy respect for their remoteness, fearful isolation, and the confusing flow of the tidal currents, which if you weren't careful could sneak up on you. He vividly recalled being trapped on one of the marshy islands overnight because he'd lost track of the tides.

"Look out!" Pendergast called from the bow.

Gavin swerved around a partly submerged piling, then turned his eyes back forward. A group of red-winged blackbirds, disturbed by their passage, rose up in a flock from a heavy patch of cattails. A few hundred yards ahead he could see the beginning of the salt marsh mazes, where waterways and islands all came together in a confusion of channels and culs-de-sac. The mudflats were now fully covered by the high tide, but that wouldn't last long.

Pendergast had heard the scream when the tide was incoming, and he'd been able to target the general area on a map. Gavin glanced at his own map—an NOAA chart—and thought again about the currents. If the presumed killer had dumped the body into the water, the incoming tide would have carried it deeper into the marshes, where it probably would have snagged up in some backwater and they might never find it. Then again, if it hadn't gotten snagged and the tide turned, it would be carried out almost to sea, as the body of the historian had apparently been.

Really, with these crazy currents, the body could be anywhere.

"Okay," said the chief, speaking loudly into his radio over the sound of the 18-horse Evinrude, "Jack, you take the right channel, we'll take the middle, and you, Ken, take the left."

The boats separated and Gavin guided their skiff into the central channel. Soon they had lost sight of the two other boats, separated by banks of salt grass. Damn, it was cold. It was a gray, monochromatic world. He could see a chevron of Canada geese in the sky, making their way southward.

"Slow down, and keep your eyes peeled," said the chief.

Gavin throttled down the tiller. The channel had narrowed, but now, going every which way, were branching channels.

"Which way?" he asked.

Before the chief could speak, Pendergast extended a skeletal hand, pointing toward a channel, map unrolled. Gavin wondered where Constance was; he found himself wishing, rather perversely, that it was her in the bow instead of Pendergast. The man gave him the creeps.

The chief for once kept his mouth shut as they turned into the designated channel. It was narrower, and here and there tree trunks were snagged into the embankments or sunken into the muck, black branches reaching out of the water as if to impede their progress. There were a million places a body could hang up and get covered by the tide. That was assuming the body was even in the water—if it was lying in the middle of an island of salt grass, it wouldn't be found until the crows started circling.

Pendergast pointed again, and then again, never saying a word, and Gavin continued up one channel and down another. If there was a method to this madness, it wasn't evident. The chief simply sat in the middle of the boat with his hammy arms crossed, frowning, his face expressing disgust with the entire effort. He didn't even make a pretense of looking.

The minutes dragged by in silence. Gavin felt completely lost, but by the way Pendergast kept checking his map and making marks on it with a pencil, he was assured the FBI agent knew where they were.

"Um, Agent Pendergast?" he ventured.

The white face turned to him.

"The tide's turned. Just wanted you to know. Got some currents developing."

"Thank you. Continue, if you please."

If you please. That accent—he'd never heard one like it. Southern, of course, but different somehow. He wondered if the man was boning Constance.

Up one channel, down another. It only seemed to get colder. A couple of seagulls followed them for a while, crying loudly, and one dropped a jet of waste right beside the boat. Rats with wings, the lobstermen called them. Once in a while the chief would speak to the others on the radio. It seemed they were not having much luck, either, and one of the boats was apparently lost. They were trying to get a GPS reading, but without cell coverage they couldn't get a good fix.

Pendergast certainly wasn't lost. Or if he was, he was doing a good job of covering it up.

Now the current was really picking up, the water flowing out. The boat struggled against it, throttled up but not really making good time against the current. Gavin checked his watch.

"Agent Pendergast?" he repeated.

Again the white face turned.

"Tide's down about two feet. Another half hour and we better be well out of here."

"Understood." The black-clad arm pointed again, and they took yet another fork. And now Gavin could see the chief beginning to get nervous.

"Gavin's right," Mourdock said. "I think we'd better head

back out, if you don't mind me saying so."

This was ignored. They continued on.

"Stop!" came a barked order from Pendergast, his hand shooting up like a semaphore. They were passing yet another waterlogged tree, lodged in the now-exposed muck at the upper side of the embankment. Gavin throttled down, but not too much, as the current would sweep them back downstream otherwise.

"Bring the boat in to that snag," said Pendergast.

"It's too shallow," Gavin said. "We'll ground out."

"Then ground out."

"Hold on," said the chief, alarmed. "What's so damned important that we have to risk our lives?"

"Look." And Pendergast pointed.

There, just under the murky surface of the water, wagging back and forth in the current in a grotesque parody of a farewell wave, was a pale hand.

"Oh, shit," Gavin muttered.

"Toss the rope over that exposed branch and tie us up," said Pendergast.

Gavin made a loop with the rope and tossed it toward the branch, goosing the throttle to keep the boat steady. He got it on the first try, cut the engine, raised it, and then hauled the boat over to the log, tying it securely. He could feel the resistance of the mud against its bottom, the current thrumming past the hull.

"I don't think this is a good idea at all," said the chief.

But Pendergast was leaning out, hanging over the side of the boat. "Give me another rope."

Gavin passed it to him. The agent reached down, grasped the arm, and pulled it out of the water. The head now appeared, just breaking the surface. Gavin rushed over to help, overcoming his revulsion to grasp the other submerged, lolling arm.

Pendergast tied the rope around the wrist. The body was only lightly caught up on the snag and it suddenly floated free, coming to the surface and heading downstream.

"Pull!" Pendergast ordered.

Gavin pulled the rope, using the skiff's oarlock as a brake, and they hauled the body against the current and up to the side of the boat.

"For God's sake, you're not bringing that into the boat!" cried the chief.

"Move over," said Pendergast sharply, but the chief needed no urging to scramble aside as they grasped the body, preparing to haul it in. "On three."

With a great heave the two got it over the gunwale, the body flopping onto the bottom of the boat like a huge dead fish. Its clothes were torn and shredded by its journey through the currents, and it lay facedown, the back exposed. Pendergast, still grasping the lifeless arm, rolled the man over.

Gavin immediately recognized the face. When he next saw the cuts on the body, he was so shocked he was temporarily unable to speak.

Not so the chief. "It's Dana Dunwoody!" he said. He glanced at Pendergast. "You know, Brad here told me just yesterday that you had your suspicions about him. If this is what happens to your suspects, I hope you don't start suspecting *me*."

Neither Gavin nor Pendergast paid any attention. They were too busy looking at the body.

"Cut up just like that historian," Gavin finally managed to say.

"Indeed," murmured Pendergast. "The Tybane inscriptions, once again." He leaned over the body, his face so close to the gray, rubbery, glistening skin it was positively disgusting. "Curious. The cuts on Mr. McCool were done with confidence and vigor. These, or at least certain of these, appear to be different."

"Fine, fine, let the M.E. sort it out," said Mourdock. "Let's call the others and get the hell out of here."

22

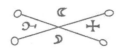

S ister, come in!"
Constance hesitated at the threshold of the shopfront in the seedy mall on the outskirts of Salem. A woman in a Victorian dress not unlike her own had risen with alacrity and swept out toward her. "Welcome to the Coven of Salem! From whence do you hail?"

Constance moved into the spacious room, which had once been some sort of store, but was now repurposed into a reception area and meeting place. There was nothing strange or sinister about it; it was, rather, a sunny, cheerful space with thick carpeting and yellow-painted walls. A dark green curtain closed off the rear of the space. She had the feeling this was the woman's residence as well as her coven.

She took another step inside.

"Shoes off!" the woman said sharply.

"I beg your pardon." Constance removed her flats.

"Come in and sit down, please."

Constance put down her bag and eased herself into a chair. It was uncomfortable and a little grimy, and she once again reflected on how much she'd rather be back at 891

Riverside Drive, playing the harpsichord or reading a book, instead of rising at the crack of dawn to take a hired car from Exmouth to Salem at Pendergast's request. The agent had returned to the Inn at four in the morning, stopping only long enough to change his clothes before running out again to rendezvous with the police. He'd looked in on her before leaving, mentioned something about an incident in the swamps, promised to give her all the details at dinner, and exhorted her to make all possible haste to Salem. *Your analysis, and your recommendations, are most necessary.* More than once, his words of praise the previous morning had echoed in her mind. He had entrusted her with this assignment; he considered it to be important—and as a result, whatever her private thoughts might be, she would do everything she could to see it through successfully.

The woman sat down opposite her. She was a solid, firm-looking figure in her forties, with a prominent bust and a pugnacious chin, thrust forward. She eyed Constance with a faintly suspicious air and spoke with stilted formality. "I am Shadow Raven, of the Salem Coven, the largest of its kind in New England." She made a strange, old-fashioned gesture with her hand, a medieval flourish of some sort.

"I am Constance Greene."

"How nice to meet you." The woman looked her up and down. "What a beautiful dress. Princess-line with a hint of mutton-leg sleeves. Where did you get it?"

"I've had it for a while."

"And what coven are you from, sister? I thought I knew all the Wiccan practitioners in New England, but I have not seen you before."

"I'm not from any coven. I'm not Wiccan."

A look of surprise. And then the woman relaxed her guard.

"I see. You have an interest in Wicca, however? Perhaps you are looking for a teacher?"

Constance considered this a moment. "Yes, I do have an interest, but not in the way you might think. I'm investigating a murder."

"And what," said Raven, her voice suddenly wary and her suspicious look returning, "could the Salem Coven possibly have to do with a murder?"

"You misunderstand. I've come not to accuse but to ask for your help."

The woman eased herself back. "I see. In that case, I would be happy to oblige. You must understand, witches have been subjected to persecution and lies for many centuries. Wicca is all about peace, harmony, and oneness with the divine. To be a white witch is to be a healer, a teacher, a seeker! It is worth pointing out that our religion predates Christianity by twenty thousand years." Her tone had become condescending. "Yes, we do perform magick, but our spells involve healing, wisdom, and love. We do not engage in satanic worship or consort with demons. Satan is a Christian creation and you can keep him, thank you!"

She folded her hands.

"I have no interest in Satan or any other demon," said Constance, trying to stem the flow and redirect the conversation. "I'm here because I'd like your opinion on a certain set of inscriptions."

"Inscriptions, you say? Let us see them."

She held out her hand. Constance withdrew the sheet of paper that Pendergast had given her and passed it over. Raven took it, glanced at it.

A sudden, ice-cold silence descended on the room. "What is your interest in these?" the woman demanded.

"As I told you, I'm investigating a murder."

Raven quickly handed them back. "Wicca has nothing to do with the Tybane Inscriptions. I can't help you."

"What, exactly, are the Tybane Inscriptions?"

"They have no relation to our coven or us. 'Harm none' is our creed. Anyone who intends harm through magick is not a Wiccan or a witch. Just to bring them in here, to soil this place of worship, is unacceptable. Now, I am a busy woman. I will ask you to remove yourself and those markings immediately."

"Do you mean to tell me," Constance said, "that you know something of these markings? And yet you refuse to tell me?"

The woman rose in a vast, indignant rustle of fabric. "The door is over there, Miss Greene."

Constance did not move. Instead, she fixed her eyes on the woman, who was staring down at her, the loose folds of skin under her chin trembling, a fat finger pointing to the door.

"Are you deaf, woman? Get out!"

At hearing this voice shouting directly into her face, Constance could feel a stirring of the terrible anger that had afflicted her in the past. She swallowed, felt herself going pale with rage. She rose to her feet, eyes locked on the woman. Raven stared back, her expression full of imperious defiance.

Constance took a step forward. Now she was so close to the woman that they were almost touching. She could smell patchouli and frankincense. The woman faltered, her eyes flickering away momentarily.

"I—" the woman said, then stopped, unable to continue.

Curiously, as if from a great distance, Constance watched as her right hand slowly rose. She took the loose wattle of skin under the woman's chin between her own thumb and first finger.

The woman stared back, unable to speak, eyes widening.

Now Constance began to squeeze, first gently, then harder. Raven staggered, made a strange gurgling deep in her throat.

In utter silence, Constance squeezed a little harder, directing her nails inward, digging into the clammy, fleshy skin.

All of a sudden, the woman found her voice. She fell backward, gasping in a huge lungful of air as Constance released her grip. "You!" she said, staring at Constance in terror. "Please...please..."

Constance lowered her hand.

"I'll help. Just don't look at me like that, *please*." Reaching behind herself, her eyes glued to Constance's, the woman found the arms of her wing chair and eased herself down, as if stricken. Red weals were already coming up on the skin of her throat.

Constance remained standing.

"What I speak of...no one can know the source."

It was a moment before the anger had receded sufficiently for Constance to trust her own voice. At last, she replied. "I will maintain total confidentiality."

"Well then...well then..." The woman reached out for a glass of water sitting on a side table, drank from it with a trembling hand, replaced it with a rattle. "No one knows precisely what the Tybane Inscriptions mean," she said, her voice hoarse. "They were found incised on a slate tablet over a century ago in the Exmouth marshes. On the site of what we believed to be the Sabbat Ground of a long-abandoned coven."

"Sabbat Ground?"

"A place where witches perform their ceremonies. But these were not Wiccans—white witches. These were black witches."

"Explain."

"Wherever there is power to do good, as in our Wiccan spells and rituals, there are also some who would turn magick the other way. The temptation for power or retribution is always present in life—through loss of a job, rivalry for affections, whatever."

"And what does *Tybane* mean?"

"*Bane* is from the Old English *bana*, meaning 'an affliction or curse.' It also refers to poison. Wolfsbane, for example, so called because it was used to kill wolves."

"And the *Ty* portion of the word?"

"A mystery."

"What, if anything, are the Tybane Inscriptions used for today?"

"There are rumors—rumors only. Some may use them to invoke dark powers, or for black rituals. The inscriptions are formidable and wicked, but only the most reckless or desperate witch would use them, because their exact purpose and meaning is so unclear. It's playing with fire."

"Have you ever used them?"

The woman hung her head.

"Where is this inscribed stone now?" Constance went on.

"It was destroyed a long time ago. But its discoverer left his notes behind."

"To what notes do you refer?"

"The papers of an amateur archaeologist named Sutter. They're here, in the Old Salem Historical Society." A pause. "Some have yielded to the temptation and made the unfortunate pilgrimage to consult those papers."

"And?"

The woman did not look up. "They have all come to regret it."

23

Constance Greene walked through the charming center of Salem on her way to the Old Salem Historical Society, which lay about a mile from the coven. She was surprised to find it to be a prosperous and imposing brick building of late nineteenth-century construction. She entered to find herself in a spacious lobby, updated with all the latest in computer catalogs and electronic equipment, and guarded by metal detectors run by a potbellied security officer.

In a moment she was through, thoroughly irradiated and wanded, much to her annoyance. A cheerful lady behind the desk was, it turned out, familiar with the Sutter papers and directed her to the third-floor department where they could be found.

A high-speed elevator whisked her up, the doors hissed open, and she found herself in a spare, formal space. An older woman with iron-gray hair pulled back in a severe bun manned a nearby desk. As Constance stepped up, the woman hung up her phone.

"Constance Greene?" she asked in a voice of alarming efficiency. "Here to see the Sutter papers?"

Constance bowed acknowledgment.

"I am Mrs. Jobe, the archival librarian. Come with me." She rose, fingering a card that hung on a lanyard around her neck. She looked at Constance with compressed lips, distaste writ large on her face.

Constance followed her down a corridor. Another door hissed open at the wave of the woman's card, and they entered a small room with a baize-covered table.

"Please don these," said the woman, producing a pair of white cotton gloves.

Constance pulled them on.

"No handling of any papers with bare hands, please. Pencil or computer use only—no pens. Have a seat while I retrieve the Sutter papers. They are certainly popular these days."

She went through another door. In less than a minute she returned, holding a plastic box with plastic folders inside. She put it on the table. "Only one folder should be removed at a time. Any questions, Ms. Greene?"

Constance sensed that, once again, she was being taken for a Wiccan. She wondered whether Pendergast, were he in her position, might be able to make use of this misapprehension. Pendergast always seemed able to pitch his approach, right from the beginning, to get the best results. He was unscrupulous in seeking advantage.

She would be, too.

"I take it that quite a few people come to see these documents?" she asked.

"They are among our most sought-after."

"Indeed? By whom?"

"Salem is a center of the Wiccan religion, as you no doubt know." She eyed Constance's dress. "We have quite a few

practitioners come to look at the papers and copy or photograph the, ah, inscriptions."

"The Tybane Inscriptions, you mean?"

"Yes." The woman turned away.

"Another question, if you don't mind."

The woman turned back and now Constance could see a
look of impatience on her face.

"Do you know much about this archaeologist, Sutter?"

"Sutter was no archaeologist. He was an amateur back at
a time when archaeology barely existed as a profession. To
be blunt, he was a crank."

"And what makes you say that?"

"You'll judge for yourself when you look at his papers."

"You've been through them?"

"It's part of my job to familiarize myself with the content
of these folders. Not to cast aspersions, but you will see
that Sutter was, at the very least, a fantasist." She waved
her hand. "If I had my way, those papers would go into the
rubbish. Their only interest is for those studying deviant
psychology. Or"—she paused significantly, once again eyeing
Constance—"those of the Wiccan persuasion."

"I see," said Constance, returning the gaze, "that you
have mistaken me for a Wiccan."

"What you are or are not is no concern of mine."

"I realize my dress is old-fashioned and my ways may
appear odd, but that's because..." She thought back to the
receptionist at the Exmouth police station. "I am Amish."

The woman showed surprise and embarrassment. "Oh.
Very well. I didn't mean to...in some way imply you were
anything but a person seeking information. We get so many
of those Wiccans in here, looking at these papers. One makes
assumptions."

"Witchcraft, the casting of spells, is an anathema in my religion. I'm here because"—here Constance did her best to choke up with emotion—"because my sister has become a Wiccan. I'm here to try to save her."

Now the surprise turned to confusion. "I'm so sorry... But how can these papers help? I mean, Wiccans may be drawn to them out of curiosity, but as I understand it Wiccans practice white magic, not black magic. And white magic has nothing to do with what Sutter documented."

"I'm trying to find her. I know she was here. Do you keep a record of those who come to look at these documents?"

"We keep records, of course, but... they're confidential."

At this Constance bowed her head and let a faint emotive noise escape her lips. "I understand. The rules must be followed. It's just that—I don't want to lose my sister to this... this Wiccan religion."

A long silence. "Well, I think we can make an exception. Let me get the files in my office."

As she left, Constance kept her head bowed for a moment, allowing a small smile to vanish from her face. The displeasure she felt at feigning an emotion she would never, in real life, reveal to another human being was overshadowed by successfully confounding this disapproving, opinionated woman. Face composed, she raised it once again, drew the plastic file toward her, and removed the first folder, labeled "New Salem."

Inside were several yellowing paper documents. She laid the first on the baize and opened it gingerly. It consisted of perhaps a dozen pages, all covered with an elaborate spidery script.

Notes Regarding the Re-Discovery of the Ancient Settlement of New Salem, the Long Lost Witches' Colony in the Exmouth Marsh Lands.

By Jeduthan Sutter, Esq.
Fellow of the Learned Society of Antiquaries of Boston, Discoverer of the Ostracon of Sinuhe
Author of Fasciculus Chemicus, and Keys of Mercy and Secrets of Wisdom.

On the third day of July 1871, I, Jeduthan Sutter, Esquire, after many weeks searching the Exmouth Marsh Lands, discovered the Witches' Settlement of New Salem in a Desert Location far from Habitation. I Elucidated the Arrangement of the Quincunx, which indicated the Ceremonial Altar of the Village where the Witchcraft Rituals and Abominations were Consummated. Wherefor, having Located the Central Altar I dug down and Recovered the Stone that was the Blasphemous Object of Worship, which contain these Devilish Revelations and Abominations. This I did with a Wise Purpose, according to the Workings of the Spirit of the Lord, who Knoweth all things, as a Warning to All. And now I, Jeduthan Sutter, prior to destroying the Foul Stone of New Salem, so that the Evil embodied in its essence, and which hath moved on from this place to Another, can no longer Harm the World, do first Finish Out the Inscriptions found on said Stone, recording for Posterity those Inscriptions as in Life, made according to the Knowledge and Understanding of the Lord God, who giveth me His Protection from the Evil they contain.

A *quincunx.* Constance was aware of that peculiar arrangement, as in the array of pips on the number five on a set of dice. The quincunx, she knew from her reading, had a mystical meaning to many religions.

She turned her attention to the next document: an oversize double-quarto sheet of paper, folded. With care she unfolded it and found a finely drawn outline of what could only have been the Tybane Stone, apparently life-size, with its inscriptions—the same five symbols she had seen carved into the body of the historian, Mr. McCool.

She took out her cell phone and began taking pictures, near and far, with and without flash, working swiftly. When she was done, she went through the rest of the papers but found little more of interest—no indication where the settlement had been found, for example, or why Sutter was looking for it in the first place. Instead, the papers consisted of numerous quotations from scripture and other religious ramblings. Sutter, as the archivist had observed, had certainly been a crank. But even cranks make interesting discoveries.

Mrs. Jobe returned with a piece of paper. "This is a list of our visitors, going back six months. We also have a security camera, concealed in that exit sign. It's confidential, of course—we don't speak of it to visitors."

"Thank you so much," Constance said, taking the list. "I'll have to look this over later. First, I must decipher these inscriptions."

"If it's any consolation," said the archivist, "I wouldn't be surprised if the inscriptions are gibberish. Poppycock. As I said, Sutter was a fantasist."

"Do you have other files on witchcraft that might help me understand these symbols—or determine if they're a sham?"

"We have transcriptions of all the Salem witch trials—on microfiche, because the originals are too fragile—as well as a fine collection of rare books on witchcraft and demonology in what we call the Cage. But I'm not sure how that will help you find your sister."

Constance looked at her with a drawn face. "I must understand them if I'm to understand why my sister would be attracted to this...filth. You see, Mrs. Jobe, whether these inscriptions are poppycock or real, it is the *intention* to do wickedness that is this world's true evil. But if they are indeed fraudulent, it could help my case with my sister...when I find her."

Two hours later, Constance sat back in her chair, blinking. The microfiche machine was a wonder of hideous 1980s technology, seemingly designed to cause blindness through prolonged use. Why computers had not been introduced here, when the Historical Society was apparently flush with money, was a mystery. Perhaps they did not wish to make it easy to review these terrible trials.

But after all that, the transcriptions of the Salem witchcraft trials had proven a dead end. All too clearly, the "witches" who were put on trial were innocent. There were, however, a few instances in which—reading between the lines—Constance got the decided impression that there *were* actual witches, both male and female, involved in the witchcraft trials: not as accused, but as accusers, judges, and witch-hunters. It made a degree of sense: What better way to sow fear and hatred in a community, while at the same time disguising one's own connection to evil?

It was time to visit the Cage.

She called for Mrs. Jobe, who led the way. The Cage was housed in the building's basement: a small vault, its floor, walls, and ceiling constructed out of steel bars, with a single locked door. Inside were two shelves of ancient books—one along each wall—and a small table and lamp in the center. The air was cool and dry, and Constance could hear the running of a forced-air system. A nearby wall sported various environmental and atmospheric monitors and dials, including a turning drum that, no doubt, registered temperature and humidity. It was a dark and sinister space that—in high anachronism—was festooned with sophisticated digital instruments.

The archivist locked her in, with another admonishment to wear gloves at all times.

There were not many books on the shelf labeled "Occult & Miscellanea"—no more than three dozen. Most she recognized from Enoch Leng's library at 891 Riverside Drive, which had a deep section on poisons and witchcraft. She began perusing the titles, taking a mental inventory: There was the famed *Malleus Maleficarum* (The Hammer of Witches); Nider's *Formicarius*; Reginald Scot's *The Discoverie of Witchcraft*; the French classic *De la Démonomanie des Sorciers*; the fabulously obscure *Lemegeton Clavicula Salomonis*; and the dreaded, shadow-haunted *Necronomicon*, bound (although no doubt Mrs. Jobe was unaware of it) in human skin. She was already familiar with the contents of these, and knew they would contain nothing to help her decipher the Tybane Inscriptions—if indeed there was a decipherment to be found.

But at the end of the shelf stood a row of extremely old, obscure, and dirty volumes. She glanced at these, finding most to be irrelevant. But the very last book on the shelf, pushed back from the others as if almost deliberately hidden, was an untitled volume that was not, she discovered, a book at all, but rather a manuscript. It was in Latin, titled

Pseudomonarchia Daemonum (The False Monarchy of Demons), dated 1563.

She laid it on the small table and carefully turned the pages, surprised by the abundance of detailed illustrations. It appeared to be a kind of grimoire or list of all the demons alleged to exist: sixty-nine in total, with their names, offices, attributes, symbols, and what they could teach the person who raised them in an unholy ceremony. The paper crackled under her gloved touch, and she had the sense no one had examined the manuscript in a very long time.

She leafed through it, looking for matches to the Tybane symbols. Most of the symbols represented the demons themselves, but a few were symbols indicating movement, travel, directions, and place.

As she paged through, her eye caught one symbol that, in fact, had a match with the Tybane Inscriptions:

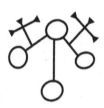

It was translated as *Obscura Peregrinatione ad Littus* (A Dark Pilgrimage to the Southern Shore).

A diligent search turned up a second Tybane symbol:

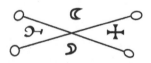

The translation was *Indevitatus*, meaning "unavoidable," "inevitable," "imminent."

With greater interest now she continued combing the text, page after page. Toward the end she hit upon two more symbols.

This first was the sign for the demon known as Forras, and she mentally translated the Latin text:

The Thirty-First Spirit is Forras. He appears in the form of a strong man in a fair human Shape. He can give the understanding to men how they may know the virtues and poisons of all herbs. He teaches the Arts of Law in all its parts. If desired he makes men to live long, and to avoid discovery of their evil. His Seal is this.

The seal was identical to a symbol in the Tybane Inscriptions.

The other symbol of interest was of another demon called Morax, and the accompanying text translated as:

Morax is a great and mighty prince of darkness, and when he puts on the shape of a man, he shows out dog's teeth, and a great head like to a deformed ape, and drags a devil's tail; he makes wonderful cunning, incites lewdness, and will lie with any woman he so desires; he has a great thirst for the blood of man and he revels in the viscera of those he kills. His Seal is this:

The Tybane Inscriptions, as she understood it—and as the body of McCool gave evidence to—comprised a series of five symbols. Four had a match in this book: the avatars, apparently, of four demons.

Near the end of the manuscript, she came across the final symbol of the Tybane Inscriptions:

The Latin inscription was *Errantem Locus*, meaning "wandering place."

Constance paused, looking up from the manuscript. There was still a lot more to decipher. But she was now sure of one thing: the Tybane Inscriptions were genuine. They were not the product of a crazy fantasist. They had been created by someone truly dedicated to Satan and the worship of the dark arts.

24

Sergeant Gavin manned the tiller again as the incoming tide bore the boat forward, deeper into the salt marshes. Once again Pendergast sat in the bow, consulting a map and moving only to point directions, leading them up a seeming infinitude of channels.

Gavin wondered what the heck Pendergast was doing again in the marshes. But he kept his mouth shut. He realized a man like Pendergast was the kind who simply did what he wanted, without explanations, apologies, or justification. Nevertheless, he was convinced this would end up a wild-goose chase. It seemed obvious that the killings of the historian and the lawyer were banal, most likely the work of drug addicts trying to cover up their robberies with symbols, which were known to at least some locals familiar with the story of the Tybane Inscriptions. Pendergast had given him some nonsense about looking for the Gray Reaper. But as he eyed the bulky metal detector lying athwart the skiff's seats, poking out of a partially zipped-up bag, he wondered: What was Pendergast going to do with that?

The hand pointed, Gavin turned. He really wished

Pendergast had not insisted that he pilot the boat. There were plenty of others who could have done it. But Pendergast had particularly asked for him, and since the autopsy on Dunwoody wasn't going to take place until the next day, the chief agreed.

This time, they were way the hell out in the marshes. They were completely surrounded; all you could see for 360 degrees around was grass and water under a gray, late-afternoon sky.

Pendergast held up his hand, and with a gesture indicated Gavin was to throttle down. Gavin did so, putting the engine into neutral. The boat continued drifting on the current.

"We seem to have taken a wrong turn, Sergeant Gavin."

Gavin shrugged. "You've got the GPS. I've been totally lost for a while."

"One moment." Pendergast spent a few minutes working the GPS and checking the map, back and forth, back and forth. "Let us backtrack."

With a suppressed sigh Gavin turned the boat around and maneuvered upcurrent at half speed. They emerged into a broader channel.

"This way," said Pendergast.

Yet another endless series of channels—and then he once again held up his hand. "This is it."

Gavin stared at the mud embankment and the sea of grass beyond, which seemed to rise into the faintest of hills. He had a sudden bad feeling.

"If you don't mind, Sergeant, please stay with the boat and wait for me."

Gavin glanced at his watch. "It's going to be dark in an hour. After that it'll be hard to navigate."

"I shall be back well before then." He grabbed the equipment bag and climbed out of the boat. In a moment he had disappeared into the grass.

Gavin shifted on the hard metal seat. The bad feeling began to deepen. Of course, he could just take off and strand Pendergast there. But if he did that, the shit would really hit the fan. You just didn't mess with a guy like Pendergast.

A. X. L. Pendergast knifed his way through the salt grass, bending it aside with one arm while slinging the equipment bag over the other shoulder. Every minute seemed to grow colder and grayer than the last, with that penetrating, barbaric cold so prevalent near the sea.

Pendergast paused several times to check his GPS. After about ten minutes, he arrived at the place where he had found the object the night before—and what, apparently, were the remains of an old settlement.

Of course, his goal was not—as he had told Sergeant Gavin—to search for the Gray Reaper, whatever that creature might or might not be.

Unrolling the map, he first oriented himself, then walked ahead until he was on top of the starting waypoint. He then assembled the metal detector, affixing the shaft onto the box, attaching the search coil, and fitting the earphones to his ears. He adjusted several dials, calibrating the device. And then, taking a careful bearing with his GPS, he began walking forward slowly, sweeping the soggy ground with the coil, back and forth, keeping his eye on the LED screen. He went about fifty feet, moved to a new line two feet parallel, then returned to the starting point, and turned again.

In about five minutes he got a squawk. Laying the machine aside, he knelt and, with a trowel, began to dig with the utmost care. The ground was spongy and soft, with no rocks or gravel, but veined with a tangle of grass roots that had to be cut by the edge of the trowel.

About a foot down, he stopped and took a small probe from his pocket, gently pushing it into the ground. Something prevented its descent. He probed around to determine an outline, withdrew the probe, dug some more with the trowel— and uncovered a peculiar disk-like object, a large coin or medallion, rudely cast in pot metal. On it was die-stamped a symbol: one he recognized immediately as belonging to the Tybane Inscriptions. According to Constance—who had emailed him a detailed report in midafternoon, along with photos, just before starting back for Exmouth—this represented the demon Forras.

He marked it on the map. With the previous discovery, he now had two outer points of the quincunx.

Carefully measuring his steps, he walked to where he estimated the third point would be, employed the metal detector, and uncovered a third pot-metal coin. This was followed by a fourth, each containing the symbols of another demon. None of them, oddly, represented Morax.

These four outer points, by their positions, betrayed the location of the central point in the quincunx: the so-called "altar" mentioned in the Sutter documents that Constance had examined. He moved to that point and knelt, pushing aside and tearing out the grass. This was where Sutter had apparently recovered the Tybane Stone itself, but there was no evidence left of that excavation, which had taken place a hundred and fifty years before.

Again Pendergast employed the metal detector; again it squawked. He cleared out an area about two feet square around the site and began to dig. Twenty minutes had passed since he'd left Gavin with the boat, which allowed him plenty of time. He worked slowly, until he had deepened the hole to about eighteen inches. With the detector, he narrowed the location of the still-buried metal object, and, with exquisite care, employed the probe.

It was perhaps another twelve inches down. Now he abandoned the trowel and began digging with his bare hands, until his fingers closed around something hard. He carefully cleared away the roots and dirt until the object was exposed, cleaned it as best he could, photographed it in situ, and then pried it from the soil.

It was a most peculiar object. The central part was made of the same pot metal—a mixture, he guessed, of lead and tin. It was in a strange, wild shape—the quasi-abstract image of a gaping, devouring mouth, full of crooked teeth, in the act of swallowing what appeared to be a coil of intestines. As Pendergast examined it, he realized it had been formed by pouring molten pot metal into water, where it had frozen into a hideous shape—accidentally, but in an uncannily demonic form. This twisted, bubbled mass of metal had been framed in a setting of silver, with the remains of something tied to it—horsehair, it seemed, and a fragment of rotten bone, preserved only by virtue of the anaerobic characteristics of the soil. And stamped into the silver was the symbol of Morax, the ape-headed demon with dog's teeth and a devil's tail.

He removed a shallow Tupperware container from the equipment bag and placed the object inside, nestling it inside Bubble Wrap he had brought for just such a purpose. Then he slipped it back into the bag along with the map and the rest of the equipment, straightened up, checked his watch, wiped his hands, and proceeded back to the boat.

He found Sergeant Gavin looking fretful and impatient.

"Find anything?" the man asked.

Pendergast took his place in the bow of the boat. "Indeed I did."

"What?"

Pendergast removed the Tupperware container from the bag, opened it, and displayed the object in its nest of Bubble Wrap.

Gavin stared, his face going white. "What the *fuck*?"

"What the fuck indeed," came the laconic reply.

25

Constance had the hired car stop in Exmouth's main street, well short of the Inn, to consider her options. It had been her intention to sit at the bar, as Pendergast had requested, and listen for useful gossip. She had not been in the mood to do so the night before. But now, she felt rather drained from her trip to Salem. Perhaps an interval in the Chart Room would prove less vexatious.

There was a rap on her window. Constance lowered it to see Carole Hinterwasser.

"Constance!" the woman said. "I thought that was you. My shop's just there. Would you care to come in for a late-afternoon tea?"

Constance hesitated. "I had rather planned on returning to the Inn."

"Just a quick cup. Come on, it would be nice to chat. I'll have the Inn send their car for you."

"Very well."

Paying off the driver, she stepped out of the car and into the teeth of the wind that whipped down the Exmouth main street, carrying with it the smell of salt air and seaweed.

A few scraps of newspaper whirled along with it, while a pair of screeching seagulls wheeled about overhead. She followed the woman into her shop, wondering what it was Hinterwasser wanted to talk to her about—as that was clearly her intention.

"Sit down, please." The shop, A Taste of Exmouth, sold mostly tourist bric-a-brac: local crafts, postcards, maps and charts, T-shirts, candles, shells, and potpourri, with tea and coffee served at three tiny tables in the back of the premises. Constance took a seat while Hinterwasser asked her shop assistant—a bright-eyed young woman with close-cropped blond hair—to make them a pot of tea. A few minutes later, the assistant brought over the tea on an antique silver tea set, with china cups, bread, butter, and marmalade. She set it down on a stand next to their table, laid out their cups and silverware.

"You're the one helping that FBI agent with the wine theft, right?" she asked with ill-concealed curiosity.

Constance nodded, a little surprised at the forward nature of the question. "I am."

"Thank you, Flavia," Carole said in polite dismissal.

The woman smiled at them both in turn, then moved away.

Constance said, "She's also a waitress at the Inn."

"Flavia Strayhorn," Hinterwasser said. "New in town. Native New Englander, but she spent the last few months hiking around northeast Asia. She's earning money for graduate school. And she seems to be picking up our small-town avidity for gossip." She laughed.

"People appear to be so curious about us."

"Well, apart from your companion being an FBI agent, your old-fashioned way of dressing has been noticed. Is there any particular reason for it?"

"No, no, it's just what I've always worn." Constance realized that—at least for the purpose of excursions such as this—she should make an effort to update her wardrobe.

"Well, your bag is new, anyway," Carole said, nodding at the saltwater crocodile bag that hung from Constance's chair. "A Hermès Birkin, isn't it?"

Constance nodded.

"Beautiful. It's probably worth more than this entire building."

Constance said nothing. Perhaps it had been a bad idea to bring the bag—a present from Pendergast on her last birthday. Really, when it came to interacting with outsiders in this modern world, she could not seem to get anything right.

"The tea's almost ready." Carole pointed to the steeping pot. "It's my special blend—Exmouth Chai. Help yourself to bread and jam."

"Thank you, this is most kind."

"Not at all—it's nice to have a chance to chat."

Constance took a slice of bread—it was fresh and homemade—then spread on some butter and marmalade. She'd had nothing to eat all day.

Hinterwasser poured out their tea, with a generous addition of milk and sugar. "I'm glad I ran into you. Did you hear about the, ah, difficult words between Mr. Pendergast and Perce yesterday?"

She took a sip. "I did."

"I want you to know how badly Perce feels about it. It's true that he's been having problems selling his work lately—you know how tastes change—and he's a little sensitive about it. He didn't mean to fly off the handle. He realizes in retrospect that an investigator has to ask questions, examine every angle, look into everyone's background. Even my past—which isn't squeaky clean, unfortunately, with a *dreadful* stain on my record. Imagine—shoplifting." She gave a laugh.

Constance had the impression the woman was hoping to be asked about that theft. She let the moment pass.

"If I was Agent Pendergast, I'd look at all the angles, too. The point is, Perce is a proud man. That's why I've taken it upon myself to ask you whether you might tell Agent Pendergast how embarrassed Perce feels about the whole thing. He would like to encourage Agent Pendergast to continue looking into the wine theft and hopefully not allow these murders, as horrible as they are, to deflect him completely from his original intention."

"I can assure you he's working hard on your case," said Constance. She did not elaborate. In his unspoken way, her guardian had made it clear that the state of the investigation was never to be discussed with anyone until he deemed the time right.

"I'm so glad. This second murder has really thrown the town into a tizzy. I've never seen anything like it. The chief is in way over his head. Luckily, we've got Sergeant Gavin to take up the slack. Anyway, I understand Pendergast heard the actual killing when he was out in the marshes."

"How did you know that?"

"Gossip spreads fast around here. The more grim or salacious, the faster it travels."

"I see."

"How horrible." Hinterwasser shuddered. "At the time, Perce and I were at the classical guitar concert at the Little Red Church. Perce loves classical guitar music and brought the musician up from Boston himself, as part of the Exmouth

Fall Concert Series. He's on the board, you know."

Constance took advantage of the stream of words to pick up a second slice of bread and slather it with butter.

"I wonder how you can keep such a trim figure," said Hinterwasser with a laugh.

Constance took a sip of tea, put down the cup. "I seem to have an overactive metabolism."

"Ah, to be a young lady again!" said Hinterwasser, refilling Constance's cup.

There was a tinkle of a bell and a figure came into the shop.

"A customer," said Hinterwasser, rising. "How rare; perhaps I ought to have him stuffed and put on display!" She went over while Constance finished her tea. The customer's sale was quickly concluded. As if on schedule, the 1936 Buick Special 8 that the Inn used as a car to ferry guests to and from town pulled up.

"Your ride," said Hinterwasser, plucking an item from a shelf and pressing it into her hand. It was a sachet of tea bags. "Here's a little something to take home—my Exmouth Chai blend."

"Thanks."

"Not at all. Thank you for stopping in." Hinterwasser pressed her hand again. "I hope you'll remember what I asked. About speaking to Agent Pendergast, I mean."

26

At ten o'clock, the Chart Room had almost emptied. Constance sat at a table in the corner, across from Pendergast, the remains of two portions of Filets de Sole Pendergast before them, prepared by Reginald Sheraton, along with an empty bottle of wine. It was a brutal night, with gusts rattling the windows and shaking the walls. The distant thunder of surf below the bluffs added a dark ostinato to the wailing of the wind about the Inn.

Constance nodded at the chalkboard that held the evening's menu. "Your sole seems to have become a restaurant favorite. I noticed it being served to at least half of the tables."

"I have always maintained Massachusetts to be a bastion of good taste." Pendergast rose. "Shall we retire upstairs? We have some important—and confidential—matters to discuss."

Constance rose and followed Pendergast past the bar, where he paused and spoke to the bartender, asking him to send up a dusty bottle of Calvados—which, by a minor miracle, he had spied on the back wall—and two snifters to his room.

She followed him up the steep, creaking stairs. Pendergast's room, which she had not yet seen, was dominated by a large Victorian four-poster bed; at the far side was a small brick fireplace, a writing table, chair, and lamp. A fire had been laid but not lit.

"Please take the chair; I'll sit on the bed," said Pendergast, going over to the fireplace and lighting the kindling. It flared up, casting a flickering yellow light about the room.

Constance produced from her bag the sachet of tea bags that Carole had given her earlier in the day. "Perhaps this would be more appropriate," she said. "You know I'm not much of a drinker. We could ask for a pot of hot water."

Pendergast took the sachet and glanced at it. "Chai?" he said, his lip curling in distaste. He tipped it into the wastebasket. "Sorry, my dear Constance—that is unfit for consumption. No: Calvados it shall be. Besides, I have little doubt that we'll be back to our cups of King's 403 oolong in the Riverside Drive mansion before much more time has passed."

A moment later, a knock came at the door and Flavia, the young waitress, brought in a tray with two snifters and the bottle of Calvados. Pendergast pressed a bill into her hand, murmured his thanks, and shut and locked the door. He poured a finger into each snifter and handed one to Constance, taking a seat on the bed.

"My apologies for the size of the room," he said. "It makes up for it in charm. I'm afraid what we must now discuss could not be mentioned in the dining room."

She took a sip of the Calvados. It went down like a tongue of warmth.

"I hope it's to your satisfaction."

She nodded. She was already feeling the pleasant effects of the wine, which she normally did not indulge in; she would have to be careful.

"Constance, I first want to tell you how pleased I am with your work. You have been both steady and reliable."

She felt herself flush at this unexpected compliment, although his emphasis on the word *steady* seemed a trifle backhanded. "Thank you."

"You have also been careful to heed my warnings not to freelance, or to wander away from the Inn after dark. I appreciate that." He paused. "This has been a peculiar investigation. We're caught in a tangle of evidence, and we've reached the point where we must stop and tease out the threads. To that end, I'd like to go over what we know so far: a recap, so to speak. And to give you the benefit of my most recent discoveries."

"Please."

"There are two balls of twine here: the skeleton in the cellar, which I feel sure is related to the disappearance of the SS *Pembroke Castle*; and the lost witches' colony. Let's start with the skeleton. A healthy, forty-year-old African European man was tortured and walled up in the lighthouse keeper's basement. Why? There can be only one reason: he had information. What information?"

He paused.

Constance spoke. "Lady Hurwell received a ninety-five-hundred-pound insurance settlement for loss of cargo. Maybe it was something to do with that."

Pendergast raised a slender finger. "Precisely! In 1884, such a sum was enormous, equivalent to millions of dollars today. The records of Lloyd's are kept as secure as Fort Knox, but one might guess the cargo was money, bullion, or valuables of some sort. That, my dear Constance, is likely why this individual was tortured: to extract the location of the valuables kept aboard the ship."

"That seems a bit of a leap."

"Not when you know who the man was: a gentleman by the name of Warriner A. Libby."

"You've learned the man's *name*?"

"I certainly have." Pendergast seemed uncharacteristically pleased with himself. "Warriner A. Libby was the captain of the *Pembroke Castle*. He was forty, born in Barbados and raised in both London and New York, of an African father and a—to use the unfortunate parlance of the time—mulatto mother. In his day, he was a respected and prosperous sea captain."

Constance stared. "That's quite remarkable."

"The man most likely to know the location of anything valuable aboard ship would be the captain. He was easily identified. I knew the age and racial characteristics of our skeleton. They matched. Quite simple." He took a sip of his Calvados. "In any case, if Libby was tortured to give up the location of the valuables carried on the ship, that tells us something crucial: the ship wasn't lost at sea. Otherwise, the valuables would have gone down with it."

"So the ship took refuge in Exmouth Harbor?"

"No. The harbor is far too shallow. This was a three-hundred-foot steamship with an eighteen-foot draft."

"So what happened to it?"

"I believe it was wrecked along the Exmouth shore, where there are many treacherous sandbars and rocks."

"Just a moment. Wrecked...*deliberately*?"

Pendergast nodded. "Yes. Deliberately."

"By whom?"

"By certain townspeople."

"But how could the townspeople contrive to wreck a ship at sea?"

"In concert with the lighthouse keeper. It's a well-known trick. Extinguish the lighthouse and build a fire on the beach, in a location calculated to guide the ship onto the rocks. Once there, the townspeople loot the ship and retrieve any cargo that washes ashore. If the ship ran aground, before it broke up the looters would likely have time not only to retrieve much cargo but also to get their hands on the money—if they knew where it was hidden. In those days, ships that carried bullion or coin always had secret spaces precisely for such safekeeping."

"So what happened to the survivors?"

"A grim question indeed."

There was a pause before Constance spoke again. "And you believe the wreck to have been deliberate, I imagine, because 1884 was the year of the Exmouth famine, when the crops failed and people were desperate. A passing ship, most likely carrying valuables, might be too great a temptation to resist for a starving town. The looters tortured the captain to get the location of the treasure on board the ship by walling him up."

"Brava, Constance."

"But why come back a hundred and thirty years later to retrieve the captain's skeleton? Was a certain party trying to cover up the old crime by removing it?"

"Unlikely. That skeleton was in no danger of being discovered."

"So why run the risk of retrieving it?"

"Why indeed?"

A brief silence settled over the room before Pendergast continued.

"McCool visited Exmouth twice. He visits, the skeleton is stolen; he returns, he is murdered. McCool must have spoken of something on his first visit—something that certain townsfolk, aware of the *Pembroke Castle* atrocity, learned of in turn. That triggered the theft of the skeleton. When McCool returned, he might have been killed to seal his lips from revealing what he'd discovered. When we deduce what McCool learned—we will know precisely why the skeleton was stolen."

Pendergast fell silent. The fire crackled. Constance could not suppress a sense of satisfaction at having helped Pendergast further his deductive work. She took another sip of the Calvados.

He continued. "Let us move on to the second tangled ball in this case: the Tybane Inscriptions. That list you gave me of those who accessed the papers at the Historical Society was most interesting."

"How so?"

"There were twenty-four names. Twenty-three of them I've verified as belonging to real people, virtually all Wiccans. Then there was a name that did not appear on the various Wiccan membership lists. It sounded fake."

"Indeed?"

"A Mr. William Johnson. Too common to be genuine, don't you think?"

"Not exactly proof, though, is it?"

"Except that when I contacted your friend Mrs. Jobe, and enlarged on your amusing story of the Amish mother looking for her daughter, I was able to discover that our William Johnson had been captured on camera. With a little gentle persuasion she emailed me the man's image."

"And?"

"He was Dana Dunwoody, our deceased lawyer."

"Good God. You have been busy." A pause. "When was his visit to the library?"

"Three weeks ago."

"He wouldn't have known of the hidden security camera," Constance said, more to herself than to Pendergast. Then she glanced toward the FBI agent. "But what's the connection between him, the historian, and this lost witch colony?"

"I cannot say. For now, Constance, let me show you this." From his portmanteau, Pendergast removed a sheaf of photographs and a map. "Come here, if you please."

Constance rose from her chair and sat next to him on the bed, looking over his shoulder. The room had become warmer and she felt a faint thrumming of blood in her neck. She caught the faintest scent of Floris No. 89, his aftershave balm. She looked at the picture.

"My God." She stared, startled. "What is that?"

"An object I retrieved from under two feet of earth in the center of the quincunx of the old witches' settlement—the one Sutter referred to as 'New Salem.'"

"How grotesque. And it bears the mark of Morax. Is it...genuine?"

"It appears to be. Certainly it was buried many centuries ago. Here it is in situ, and here's another shot of it." More shuffling. "And here is the map of the witches' colony, showing the location. I also uncovered three medallions, buried at the points of the quincunx. I've temporarily put them all in a safe-deposit box here in town, for the sake of prudence. The fourth I could not find; it seems to have washed away in the cutting of a water channel." She watched as he shuffled through the photographs. He plucked one out, which showed a warped, crudely cast medallion with a stamped mark on it.

"The mark of Forras," said Constance.

Another photo.

"The mark of Andrealphus."

179

Another photo.

"The mark of Scox. All symbols found in the Tybane Inscriptions. By the way, the Wiccan I mentioned pointed out that *bane* is, among other things, a word for 'poison.'"

"Interesting—considering that this region is known for its profuse growth of deadly nightshade." He thought a moment. "In any case, judging from your partial translation of the inscriptions, especially the part about the 'dark pilgrimage' and 'wandering place,' it suggests that the witch colony did not, as legend has it, immediately die out."

"I've come to that conclusion myself. So what could have happened to it?"

"They moved."

"Where?"

"Another good question. Southward, it would seem." He sighed. "Eventually, we'll find the common thread, although I remain certain that the witchcraft aspect will ultimately prove tangential to the central case. Thank you again, Constance. Your help has been invaluable; I'm glad you came."

A silence descended. Pendergast began putting away the photographs. Constance remained seated on the bed, her heart unaccountably accelerating. She could feel the warmth emanating from his body, feel the edge of his thigh lightly touching hers.

Pendergast finished putting away the photographs and turned to her. They looked at each other for a moment, face-to-face, the silence in the room yielding to the crackling of the fire, the distant thundering of the surf, and the moaning of the wind. And then in an easy motion Pendergast rose from the bed, grasped the bottle of Calvados from the table, picked up her glass, and turned back to her.

"A final splash before you go?"

Constance got up hastily. "No thank you, Aloysius. It's already past midnight."

"Then I shall see you at breakfast, my dear Constance." He held open the door and she glided past and into the dim hallway, continuing on to her own room without a backward glance.

27

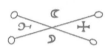

At a quarter past two in the morning, Constance awoke. Unable to go back to sleep, her mind wandering uncharacteristically down strange avenues, she lay in bed, listening to the moaning of the wind and the distant surf. After a while she got up and quietly dressed. If sleep would not come, at least she could satisfy her curiosity about something.

Picking up the small but powerful flashlight Pendergast had given her, she went to the door of her room and opened it with caution. The second-floor corridor beyond was empty and still. Stepping out and shutting the door behind her, she made her way noiselessly down the hallway, negotiating the various twists and turns until she reached the room that had belonged to the historian, Morris McCool. At one point, as she crept along, she looked over her shoulder—Constance was not given to flights of imagination, but more than once over the last several days she'd had the distinct sense she was being followed.

The end of the hallway was still covered by bands of yellow CSI tape, the room off-limits and unavailable for new guests. She had heard Walt Adderly, the owner, complaining about it in the Chart Room. Constance knew from her previous visit with Sergeant Gavin that the door was unlocked. Glancing around once more, she slipped beneath the tape, opened the door, and went inside.

Closing the door behind her, she switched on the flashlight and shone it slowly around the scuffed period furnishings. She looked at each item in turn: the hooked rugs; the bed with its oversize headboard; the small bookcase full of well-thumbed paperbacks; the dresser and rolltop desk.

In many ways, Constance was unused to this modern world: its exchange of courtliness for familiarity; its obsession with technology; its feverish embrace of the mundane and the ephemeral. One thing she did understand, however, was the keeping of secrets—a skill almost completely lost in the present age.

All her instincts told her this room possessed one.

She stepped over to the dresser, looking at but not touching it. Next, she approached the rolltop desk. Again, she looked at, but did not touch, the few books and papers arranged there.

The one time she had seen the historian in person, he had been sitting at a table in the Inn's front parlor. He'd had a worn leather notebook open in front of him, into which he was earnestly making notes, while at the same time consulting what appeared to be a rude map or diagram. At the memory, she felt a sharp pang of dismay at what must have been a frightening and brutal end.

She recalled that no notebook had been found in the room. But he kept a journal: she was certain. There was no other place it could be.

She stepped back and used the flashlight to survey the room's contents once again. As she did so, Pendergast's words echoed in her head: *When we deduce what McCool learned—we will know precisely why the skeleton was stolen.*

The old building groaned under a fresh gust of wind.

McCool was only a temporary lodger. As a result, he could not have contrived the kind of clever, elaborate, time-consuming hiding places she had become familiar with in her wanderings of the sub-basement of the Riverside Drive mansion. He could not have removed the bathroom tiles, for example; nor could he have cut away the wallpaper in search of a cavity. No matter: while he'd no doubt been possessive about his pet project, he would have no reason to believe anyone was actively trying to steal his research. If he'd secreted away any documents or other items, it would have been in a place that would resist the cursory cleaning of a maid, but nevertheless offer easy access.

She walked over to the small bookcase and, kneeling before it, pushed the books aside, one at a time. Nothing was hidden behind them. Nor was the journal hidden, "Purloined Letter"–style, among the titles.

Rising again, she let the beam of her flashlight roam much more slowly over the room, looking for any faults of con-struction, any symptoms of weathering or age, that McCool might have employed to his advantage.

In the middle of the floor, she noticed an unusually large gap between two of the boards. She knelt once again, remov-ing the antique Italian Maniago stiletto she had recently begun keeping on her person. A press of the trigger set into the mother-of-pearl handle released the small, slim blade.

A brief interval of probing at the gap made it clear the boards were securely fastened.

The bed had a skirt that fell almost to the floor. But its

lower trim was dusty and obviously undisturbed; nothing had been stored beneath.

Now Constance rose once more and went over to the rolltop desk. It had four small drawers in its top, two on each side, and four larger drawers beneath. One after the other, she pulled out the small upper drawers—full of faded Exmouth postcards and writing paper adorned with sketches of the Inn—and looked behind them. Nothing but sawdust and the traceries of spiderwebs. Next she began pulling out the larger drawers beneath the desktop, placing them on the floor one at a time, examining their contents with the flashlight, then probing the resulting cavities with her flashlight and feeling along the upper edges.

As she pulled out the lower-right drawer, a quiet thud sounded from the recesses behind. Quickly, she shone her light inside. Two items—the thin leather notebook and a periodical of some kind—had been hidden there, placed on end behind the closed drawer. She removed them, replaced the drawer, then took a seat on the bed to examine her find.

What she thought had been a periodical was, in fact, an auction catalog from Christie's of London. It dated to August of two years before, and was titled *Magnificent Jewels from a Noble Estate*. While a few entries had been indicated by bookmarks, there were no notes or jottings of any kind.

Constance frowned a moment, glancing at the cover of the catalog, thinking. Then she put it to one side, opened the worn leather journal, and began leafing through the pages of crabbed, tiny handwriting. At one page she stopped and began reading intently.

28

March 5

I spent the morning and much of the afternoon in Warwickshire, visiting Hurwell Ossory. What a time I had of it! The Hurwells are a type of ancient English family that, I'm afraid, is becoming all too common: much reduced, living like paupers in their stately home, the line weakened by inbreeding, a useless carbuncle on society. One thing they have retained, however, is their pride: they are almost fanatical in their devotion to the memory of Lady Elizabeth Hurwell and her good works. This, in fact, was initially a stumbling block, due to the way the family jealously guards their reputation (God only knows what kind of reputation they believe they have). When I told them I was planning a biography of Lady Hurwell, they were immediately suspicious. Curiosity, no doubt, compelled them to agree to my request for a visit—but when I stated my intentions in more detail they became closed-mouthed and uncooperative. This gradually changed, however, when I explained in what a good light

I viewed Lady Hurwell and how glowing a picture I planned to paint of her. I also swore them to secrecy, which (if I may offer a note of self-congratulation) was a masterstroke; it gave them the impression that there was a great deal more interest in the history of their family than, alas, there actually is.

There are only three of them left: a maiden aunt; Sir Bartleby Hurwell, Lady Hurwell's great-grandson, a sadly attenuated specimen; and his unmarried spinster daughter. They spent hours telling old family stories, showing me photo albums, and speaking of Lady Hurwell in reverent tones. Despite their admiration for the woman, they, alas, had little useful information: most of what they told me I had already learned in the course of my research. They served me a lunch of tired cucumber sandwiches and weak tea. I felt myself growing disheartened. I had held off on contacting Lady Hurwell's descendants until I was far into my research, feeling certain that a show of familiarity with their ancestor would help break the ice. However, now that the ice was broken, it seemed my efforts would yield but slender results.

Nevertheless, it was during lunch that I inquired as to the state of Lady Hurwell's papers. It turned out that the three remaining Hurwells knew nothing about any papers, but informed me that, if any existed, they would be in the attic. Naturally, I requested access. After a brief confabulation, they agreed. And so, lunch concluded, Sir B. led me along echoing galleries and up rickety back staircases to the attic, tucked up under the eaves of the mansion. There was no electric light but, luckily, I'd had the foresight to bring along a flashlight with spare batteries.

The attic went on and on. It contained a near-riot of effluvium: ancient steamer trunks; stacks of empty wooden shipping crates; tailor's dummies, bleeding stuffing; endless piles of old copies of the Times *and issues of* Punch *dating back decades, carefully tied with twine. Everything was covered in a thick layer of dust, and additional dust rose in noxious plumes with every footstep. At first, Sir B. shadowed me—perhaps he feared I might fill my pockets with some of the ancient jetsam— but in short order the dust, and the squeaking of rats, got the better of him and he excused himself.*

I spent an hour, my back aching from bending beneath the low ceiling, my eyes and nose and hands and clothes powdered with dust, and found nothing of value. Just as I was about to give up and descend back into the land of the living, however, the beam of my flashlight landed on an ancient wooden filing cabinet. Something about it piqued my curiosity: even with its veneer of dust I could see that the cabinet was of a higher quality than its neighbors. A swipe with the cuff of my jacket revealed the cabinet to be made of high-quality rosewood, with brass fittings. Luckily, it was unlocked. I opened it—and found precisely the treasure-trove I had been hoping for.

Inside the two drawers were scores of Lady Hurwell's personal documents: papers relating to the estate; various deeds; legal documents in a right-of-way dispute she'd carried on with a neighbor; an early copy of her will. But of greatest interest to me was a diary that she had kept in her teens and early twenties, and a bundle of letters, tied up in a ribbon, that was the correspondence she'd kept up with Sir Hubert Hurwell during their courtship. This was a rare find indeed—after all, Lady Hurwell had been something of a free thinker as well as a proto-feminist, and her marriage was rumored to have been a stormy one before it was cut short by her husband's premature death—and would no doubt prove fascinating. I immediately began planning my campaign to convince the remaining Hurwells to allow me to transcribe both the diary and the letters.

There was another set of intriguing documents in the cabinet, consisting of a maritime contract, an insurance document, and a list—carefully enumerated—of a series of gemstones.

I turned first to the list of gems. There were twenty-one in total, all cabochon cut rubies of the star and double-star variety, and all of the highly prized "pigeon's blood" color. The carat weights varied between 3 and 5.6. Without doubt, this was a catalogue of the famous "Pride of Africa" suite of family jewels given to Elizabeth by her husband as a wedding present. Because the stones have since been lost, I knew this detailed catalogue would prove of great interest.

The attached insurance document was of still greater interest. It was from Lloyd's of London and it verified the enumeration and evaluation of the gemstones, which had been done at Lloyd's request, and was stamped with the notation "This cargo is now certified and insured."

Next I examined the maritime contract. It was dated November of 1883 and was made between Lady Hurwell and one Warriner A. Libby, a licensed sea captain. According to the stipulations of the contract, Libby was to take command of the London and Bristol steamship SS Pembroke Castle *and, on behalf of Lady Hurwell, deliver its "most precious and unusual cargo" to Boston with all haste. The contract contained several very specific certifications related to the "twenty-one gemstones enumerated in the attached insurance document." Libby was to carry the gemstones in a leather pouch, which would be sewn tightly shut and affixed to a belt. The belt was to be worn on his person at all times, even at night. He was not to cut open or otherwise interfere with the pouch or its contents, nor was he to speak of it to anyone. Upon making landfall in Boston, he was to immediately deliver the belt and the attached pouch to Oliver Westlake, Esq., of Westlake & Hervey, Solicitors, Beacon Street.*

"Most precious and unusual cargo." If this is what I believe it to be, the document may well shed light on what I've found to be a rather obscure episode in Lady Hurwell's life—an episode that ended with her receiving a large insurance settlement from Lloyd's. It would also shed some light on a persistent maritime mystery connected with Lady Elizabeth and the loss of the "Pride of Africa" jewels. I knew that my first job was to convince the remaining members of the family to give me further time to study these papers...although I took the precaution of using my phone camera to photograph them by the glow of the flashlight, just in case. My next job would be of a rather more extended nature, and might in fact ultimately entail a journey—a journey all the way from that dark and dusty attic to the shores of North America, in search of the final resting place of the SS Pembroke Castle.

29

Lake climbed the final narrow, curved steps, then moved to one side, puffing from the exertion, to afford the others room to join him. Normally, the lighthouse top was a favorite spot of his: the view from the generous, 360-degree windows was remarkable, the solitude much appreciated. Today, however, the view was marred by a dirty, swollen sky. And with four people crowding the small space, solitude was in short supply.

He looked on as his companions arranged themselves around the tower: Carole; Constance, distant and elegant as usual; and Pendergast. The FBI agent was wearing a black cashmere coat, which served only to make his alabaster skin look that much paler.

Lake shifted uneasily. Despite himself, he could not help but feel a trickle of resentment lingering from his last meeting with Pendergast. "I assume," he said, "you didn't ask us up here to enjoy the view."

"That assumption is correct," Pendergast said in his bourbon-and-buttermilk voice. "I would like to bring you up to date on the status of our investigation."

"So you've reconsidered," Lake said. "Keeping me in the loop, I mean."

"The fact is, we have reached a point in this affair where it seemed prudent to share our findings."

Something in Pendergast's voice silenced Lake's gathering reply.

"A hundred and thirty years ago, on the night of February third, a desperate group of Exmouth natives—I am not certain how many, but I'd imagine the number was fairly small—led Meade Slocum, the lighthouse keeper, up here and forced him to extinguish the light. It's possible, of course, that Slocum was a willing conspirator, but his ultimate fate—a broken neck, and the obvious guilt he felt, with his drunken talk of the lighthouse being haunted and the crying of babies—suggests otherwise."

"Extinguish the light?" Lake asked despite himself. "Why?"

"Because another light was being substituted for it. Out *there*." And Pendergast pointed a mile to the south, down the shoreline, where a finger of nasty, jagged boulders known as Skullcrusher Rocks stretched out into the ocean, boiling with surf. "A bonfire."

"I don't understand," said Carole.

"This was following the 'lean winter' of 1883, the year Krakatoa erupted. The next summer, crops failed in many places around the world, New England included. Exmouth was starving. The intent of this group was to lure a ship onto the rocks and then plunder it. In one sense, they were successful: the British vessel *Pembroke Castle* was, I believe, deceived by the false light and foundered upon those rocks. In a larger sense, however, the group failed. Instead of rich cargo, the *Pembroke Castle*'s manifest consisted of passengers: so-called fallen women from the slums of London, some pregnant, others with small children, bound for a fresh start in Boston at an as-yet-unbuilt home for unwed mothers."

"The historian," Lake blurted out. "McCool. That's what he was researching."

Pendergast continued. "I do not know what happened to the passengers, though I greatly fear the worst. What I do know is that the captain of the vessel was walled up in your basement, no doubt in an attempt to torture him to disclose the location of the ship's valuables."

"My God," Carole murmured.

"I don't get it," said Lake. "Why dig up and remove the skeleton after all these years?"

"Because the captain never disclosed the location of those valuables." Pendergast paused, looking past Lake toward the cruel rocks and the ceaseless, roaring surf. "Unbeknownst to the marauders, the ship and its mission had been financed by an English noblewoman, Lady Elizabeth Hurwell. She paid for the venture. And to finance the women's home she intended to establish in Boston, she sent along the so-called Pride of Africa, a fabulously valuable set of rubies, which would be worth several million dollars today. She entrusted their care to the captain. After the wreck, the captain—no doubt seeing the mob on the beach and comprehending that his ship had been deliberately lured onto the rocks—would have done the only thing possible. There was no time to bury the jewels. And so he hid them in the safest place he could."

There was a pause.

"And where was that?" Lake asked.

"He swallowed them," Pendergast replied.

"What?" Lake exclaimed.

"Even under torture, the captain never divulged the secret," Pendergast went on. "His torturers suspected there was treasure on the ship, but they never learned it consisted of rubies—stones that were not much larger than pills. His remains, and their concealed fortune, slumbered in your basement for more than a century, the body's location known to no one—*save for the descendants of the original atrocity.* And then, one day, a historian came to Exmouth looking for information on the *Pembroke Castle*. In researching a biography of Lady Hurwell, he'd learned that the 'Pride of Africa' gemstones were on that ship. And he must have mentioned it...to the wrong people, who in turn put two and two together."

"Two and two..." said Lake slowly. "Good Lord...I think I see where this is going."

"That's why your wine cellar was ransacked. The descendants of the *Pembroke Castle* looters learned about the jewels from McCool and deduced they must have been swallowed by the captain. If so, they would still be in the niche with his skeleton, ready for the taking. And they took not only the jewels, but the skeleton as well—the less evidence left behind, the less chance of linking them to crimes both old and new. Unfortunately for them, they missed a single bone."

Lake took a ragged breath. He felt shocked; horrified; and yet in a strange way thrilled. A fortune in gemstones, in his basement all these years...but, as he considered the story in totality, it began to seem more than a little far-fetched. "This is pretty fancy speculation, Mr. Pendergast. I'm no detective, but do you have any actual physical evidence to support your theory that a ship was deliberately lured and wrecked on our shore, or that its captain swallowed a fortune in gems?"

"I do not."

"So why this bit of theater? Why bring us up here to show us the coastline—rather a long coastline, I might point out—

where this ship *might* have been wrecked deliberately—when all this is speculation?"

A brief pause, then Pendergast answered. "To keep you—as you yourself requested—'in the loop.'"

Lake sighed. "Well, all right, fair enough. Thank you."

The pause that followed this was longer. Lake, wondering if perhaps he'd spoken too bluntly, took another tack. "And you think these same people who ransacked my cellar killed the historian?"

"Yes."

"What about the other murder—Dana Dunwoody?"

"That is less clear. There is much that remains to be done. First, as you so helpfully pointed out, we must find hard evidence of the *Pembroke Castle*'s fate. And then we must determine why the killers carved the so-called Tybane Inscriptions into their victims' corpses."

Lake nodded. "There's a lot of disagreement around town about that. Half think the murders are the work of a group of idiots playing at witchcraft. The rest insist the inscription business is a red herring to mislead the police."

"That is precisely the dilemma we must solve."

"But you don't think it might be people seriously practicing witchcraft?" Carole asked.

"That is an open question."

"Come now!" said Lake with a laugh. "Those witch legends are just that—legends!"

This time it was Constance who spoke up. "I'm afraid not," she said. "I've learned that a coven of witches did indeed settle in the marshes in the late seventeenth century after fleeing Salem. And the colony did not die out. It relocated, somewhere to the south."

Lake looked at Carole. Her face was pale and frightened.

195

He could well understand it—the thought that the people who had ransacked their basement were not only thieves but murderers was disturbing indeed. But witches? That was truly ridiculous.

"And now, Mr. Lake, you are fully apprised of the state of the investigation. If you'll excuse us, we'll get back to the business at hand." And with that, Pendergast led the way down the circular stairway from the lighthouse tower in silence, Lake bringing up the rear, descending slowly and thoughtfully.

30

It was half past two when Pendergast parked the Porsche Spyder at the end of Dune Road. He got out of the car and Constance did the same, watching as he opened the trunk and extracted a metal detector and a canvas satchel full of equipment. He was wrapped up against the weather in a sou'wester and heavy oilskin coat. The day had grown grayer still, the air so humid it seemed composed of tiny droplets of salt water. Yet there was no fog, and the visibility was good: she could see the Exmouth lighthouse, where they had spent part of the morning talking to Lake, about a mile to the north.

She followed Pendergast along a narrow, sandy path toward the water. Where the path rose to a height of land he paused, gazing eastward, his head moving almost imperceptibly as he scrutinized the coastline. The afternoon had grown chill as well as gray, and Constance's concession to it had been to dress in a Fair Isle sweater and midcalf skirt of muted tweed.

Constance was familiar with Pendergast's silences, and she was comfortable spending time with her own thoughts, but after fifteen minutes she felt impatience getting the better of her. "I know you don't like to be asked prying questions, but what are we doing here?"

For a moment, Pendergast did not reply. Then he broke off his scrutiny to turn toward her. "I fear our sculptor friend has a point. My theory about the shipwreck remains a figment of my cerebrum. We are here to gain proof."

"But the *Pembroke Castle* was lost a hundred and thirty years ago. What kind of proof can we find after all these years?"

"Recall what I told you before." And he pointed south toward a distant section of the coast that angled sharply outward into the sea. "That hook of the shoreline would act as a net. If a ship had foundered on it, there would have been debris."

Constance glanced in the indicated direction. "How can you make such a deduction from the current topography? Surely thirteen decades of storms would have altered the shoreline."

"Were we on Cape Cod, I might agree with you. But the coastline here is sand interspersed with rocky areas that act like a series of natural breakwaters, preserving its shape."

He fell silent again, making another survey of the windswept scene. Then he reshouldered the satchel. "Shall we?"

Constance followed him down the bluff toward the shoreline. This section was studded with cruel-looking boulders as big as automobiles. Even at this distance she could see that their flanks were covered with razor-sharp barnacles. The surf thundered among them, sending up huge spumes that lingered in the heavy air. Spindrift blew off the angry combers that rolled in ceaselessly toward land.

Pendergast stopped well short of the rocks. He laid the metal detector on the ground, then removed a GPS unit, binoculars, digital camera, and a mysterious device, which he placed on the ground as well. Next, he drew out a map and unfolded it, holding down the corners with stones. Constance saw that it was a large-scale topographical map of the Exmouth region, with a ratio of 1:24,000, heavily notated in Pendergast's neat script. He examined the map for several minutes, frequently looking up from it to scrutinize some point along the coastline. Then he folded it back up and replaced it in the satchel.

"Eleven thirty pm," he said, more to himself than to Constance. "The wind would have been blowing from that direction." He looked northeast, toward the lighthouse. "And the light would have been extinguished."

He picked up the GPS and the strange device and began walking southwestward, moving tangentially to the shoreline. Constance followed, waiting as he paused now and then to consult the GPS. He stopped at a point that placed them between the lighthouse and a nasty line of jagged rocks that stretched out into the sea.

"The bonfire would have been built well back on shore, and on a high point, perhaps the crest of a dune," he murmured. "It would not have been a large fire—maintaining an illusion of distance being important—but it would have burned hot and bright."

More pacing back and forth; more consulting with the GPS unit. Then, taking the sou'wester from his head and stuffing it into a pocket of his coat, Pendergast lifted the unknown device and pointed it in various directions, sighting along it as a surveyor might sight along a theodolite.

"What is that?" Constance asked.

"Laser range finder." Pendergast took a number of measurements, comparing them to the GPS readout. After each measurement, he moved to a new location. Each move was progressively smaller.

"Here," he said at last.

"Here what?" she said, half exasperated with Pendergast's inscrutability.

"Here would have been the ideal place to situate the bonfire." He nodded south, toward the fang-like series of rocks surrounded by blistering surf. "That reef is known as Skullcrusher Rocks. You will note that our location lies on a line with the Exmouth lighthouse, but in such a fashion as to place Skullcrusher Rocks, there, *between* the lighthouse and a passing ship. A ship on a southerly course, keeping near the shelter of the coast because of the storm, would have used the Exmouth Light to guide it around the northern shore of Cape Ann. If you move the light a mile south, the ship, using the false light as its bearing, would steam right into those rocks—which on a dirty night would be invisible."

Constance looked at the ground around them. They were standing on a shingle beach, covered in small, even pebbles. It stretched away to both the north and the south.

Pendergast went on. "With a high-tide storm surge and a northeast wind, the debris would have washed in all around us."

"So where is it? Or was it? The reports said no debris was ever found. A three-hundred-foot ship can't just vanish."

Pendergast continued staring out toward the rocks, his eyes narrowed, the wind stirring the blond-white hair back from his forehead. If he was disappointed, he showed no sign. Finally he turned and looked north.

Something in his stance and expression stopped her. "What is it?" she asked.

"I want you to turn around slowly—do it casually, don't

excite attention or suspicion—and look at the rise of dunes to the north, toward Exmouth."

Constance ran a hand through her hair, stretched with feigned leisureliness, and swiveled around. But there was nothing—just a bare line of dunes covered with a thin mantle of sea grass, whipping in the wind.

"I don't see anything," she said.

"There was a figure," Pendergast said after a moment. "A dark figure. As you turned, he disappeared back behind the dunes."

"Shall we investigate?"

"By the time we get there, I'm sure he'll be long gone."

"Why are you concerned? We've seen other people wandering these beaches."

Pendergast continued gazing northward, saying nothing, a troubled expression on his face. Then he shook his head, as if to throw off whatever speculations were running through his mind.

"Constance," he said in a low voice, "I am going to ask you to do something."

"Fine, so long as it doesn't involve swimming."

"Would you have any objection if we were to remain here for some time?"

"No. But why?"

"I am going to undertake a Chongg Ran session."

"Here?"

"Yes, here. I would appreciate it if you could ensure that I remain undisturbed, save on one condition—if the figure, *any* figure, were to reappear again, atop that line of dunes."

Constance hesitated only a moment. "Very well."

"Thank you." Pendergast looked around once more, his gaze bright and penetrating, as if committing every last detail to memory. He knelt. Then—smoothing away some pebbles and making a small depression in the sand for his head—he lay down on the beach. He tightened the belt of his oilskin coat, pulled the sou'wester from his pocket, and arranged it beneath his head as an improvised pillow. Then he folded his arms across his chest, one over the other, like a corpse, and closed his eyes.

Constance studied him for a long moment. Then she glanced around, noticed a large piece of driftwood rearing out of the sand about ten feet away, walked over to it and took a seat, her back rigid, carriage erect. The beach was utterly deserted, but had there in fact still been an observer hovering nearby, something in Constance's demeanor might have suggested to him a lioness, watching over her pride. She became as motionless as Pendergast: two still figures, set against a dark and lowering sky.

31

Special Agent Pendergast lay, without moving, on the shingle beach. Although his eyes were closed, he was intensely aware of his surroundings: the cadence of the surf; the smell of the salt air; the feel of the pebbles under his back. His first job was to shut down the external world and redirect that intensity inward.

With a conscious effort born of long practice, he slowed his respiration and heartbeat to half their normal rates. He lay in stasis for perhaps ten minutes, going through the series of complex mental exercises necessary to attain the meditative state of *th'an shin gha*—the Doorstep to Perfect Emptiness— and preparing himself for what lay ahead. And then, very methodically, he began removing the items that made up the world around him. The town of Exmouth disappeared, along with all its inhabitants. The leaden sky vanished. The chill breeze no longer rustled through his hair. The ocean, with its sound and smell, disappeared. Last of all went Constance and the surrounding beach.

All was blackness. He had reached *stong pa nyid*—the State of Pure Emptiness.

He allowed himself to remain in this state, floating, alone in the void, for what in the heightened state of Chongg Ran seemed like an eternity, but was in fact no longer than a quarter of an hour. And then, in his mind, with exquisite deliberation, he began to reassemble the world in the reverse order from which he'd deconstructed it. First, the shingle beach unrolled itself in all directions. Next, the firmament arched overhead. And then came the sea breeze—save that it was no longer a breeze, but a howling midnight gale, full of lashing rain that stung as it pelted the skin. The sea came next, thundering in with great violence. Last, Pendergast placed himself on the Exmouth beach.

It was not, however, the beach of today. Through intense intellectual focus, Pendergast had re-created, in his mind, the Exmouth of long ago—specifically, the night of February 3, 1884.

Now, as he allowed all his senses to return, he became fully aware of his surroundings. In addition to the raging storm, he noticed an absence: a mile to the north, there was nothing but darkness. The lighthouse did not blink; it had vanished in the murk. But then, in a brief flash, it stood revealed when a tongue of lightning split the sky: a pale finger of stone rising into the angry night.

Directly before him, however, was a very different source of light. A teepee-shaped pyramid of sticks, twigs, and bracken had been built on a dune above the beach and was burning fiercely. Less than a dozen figures clustered around it, huddled in greatcoats. Even though he was there in mind only, Pendergast retreated from the light of the fire into the reassuring safety of darkness. The men's features, backlit by the flames, were barely distinguishable, but they all shared the same look: hardness, desperation, and a cruel anticipation. Two of the men were holding a thick blanket, and they were standing between the ocean and the bonfire. A third man, apparently the ringleader, and whose heavy, brutish features seemed somehow familiar in the firelight, held an ancient stopwatch in one hand and a lantern in the other. He was loudly counting off the seconds, from one to nine, and then starting over again. For two seconds out of each nine, the men holding the blanket shifted it to one side, exposing the light of the bonfire briefly, before blocking it again. This, Pendergast knew, was to simulate the nine-second periodicity of the Exmouth Light.

To the south, the indistinct shapes of the Skullcrusher Rocks were visible only as smudges of creamy, storm-tossed waves.

Skullcrusher Rocks. Walden Point, on which the Exmouth Light was situated, was too close to town; a wreck there would have been noticed. But a wreck on Skullcrusher Rocks...south of town, out of sight—and the wreckage would have been swept directly into this stretch of beach, concentrated in a small area.

Except for the man with the stopwatch, the group near the bonfire spoke little, their gleaming, rapacious eyes staring out to sea, probing the murk. The wind howled in from the northeast, and the rain was driving almost horizontally.

And then a shout went up: someone had spied an evanescent gleam in the darkness, out to sea. The group crowded forward, peering. One pulled a spyglass from out of his greatcoat and peered to the northeast. There was an anxious period of silence as he stared through the howling dark.

Then, the call: "It's a steamer, boys!"

Another shout went up, this one quickly hushed by the leader, who continued to count with his stopwatch, ensuring that the flame of the bonfire maintained the precise periodicity of the Exmouth Light. Now the lights of the ship became more visible, appearing and disappearing as the vessel rose and fell on the heavy seas. An electric shiver went through the group: the ship was clearly steering by the fake light, and was on a heading directly for Skullcrusher Rocks.

Rifles, muskets, pistols, cudgels, and scythes were produced from beneath the greatcoats.

Now a cloak of obscurity fell, and the scene on the beach dissolved. When the dark lifted, Pendergast found himself on the bridge of a vessel: the steamship *Pembroke Castle*. A man clad in a captain's uniform stood next to him, staring fixedly with his spyglass at a light onshore. To his right stood the navigator, chart spread out under the dim red glow of a navigational lantern. His tools were laid upon the chart—parallel bars, dividers, pencil. Beside him, the binnacle was only a quarter open, just a gleam emanating from it—the bridge being kept as dark as possible in order for all to maintain their keenest night vision. The helmsman stood to the other side of the captain, wrestling the wheel through the heavy seas.

The air on the bridge was tense, but the captain—through his economical movements and his terse, efficient orders—radiated calm and command. There was no sense of the impending disaster.

In his mind's eye, retreating into a far corner of the bridge, Pendergast noted that a following sea was bursting over the stern of the ship, black water sweeping fore, the vessel rolling heavily with each swell. A mate came forward, drenched to the skin. In response to the captain's inquiry, he reported that the steam engines were working efficiently, the oak hull was holding: leaks had been reported, but it was nothing that the bilge pumps couldn't handle.

Now Captain Libby lowered the spyglass long enough to hear the reports of the first and second mates. The first mate noted that the taffrail log gave the ship's speed as nine knots; the heading was south-southwest, 190 degrees true. The second mate reported the depth of water, via the drop of the sounding line. "Twelve fathoms," he cried over the storm. "Shelly bottom."

Captain Libby did not reply, but his face grew troubled. He raised his glass once again toward what appeared to be the Exmouth Light. "Keep your soundings continuous." He turned to the navigator. "Keep the light hard a-starboard."

Pendergast knew enough of maritime navigation to be aware that, because the ship was close to shore and in great danger from the storm, the depth soundings were critically important.

A few minutes later, the second mate returned with another depth report. "Ten fathoms," he said. "Rocky bottom."

The captain lowered his spyglass, frowning. "Check again," he said.

The second mate briefly disappeared again into the storm. "Nine fathoms, rocky bottom."

All men on the bridge knew that the *Pembroke Castle* drew three fathoms, or eighteen feet, beneath the waterline. Captain Libby turned to the navigator for an explanation.

"It makes no sense, sir!" the man yelled over the wind. "According to the chart, we should be holding steady at sixteen fathoms, sandy bottom."

"A rocky bottom means shoaling water," the captain rapped back. "Either the chart is wrong, or we're off course."

The navigator, working behind the pelorus—a kind of dummy compass—took a bearing off the light and then worked furiously with his charts. "It can't be," he said, more to himself than to anyone else. "It just can't be." He took another bearing off the light.

"Six fathoms," the voice of the second mate droned. "Rocky bottom."

The captain stepped over to the pelorus and took his own heading. "Bloody hell," he said, raising his spyglass again, peering ferociously into the lashing storm, but now nothing was visible—not even the light.

"Hard to port," the captain abruptly ordered the helmsman in a stentorian voice. "Set new heading 90 degrees true."

"But Captain," the first mate protested, "that will put the sea directly on our beam."

"So be it," said Libby. "Carry on!" But the helmsman was already swinging the wheel, making the course change, the ship shuddering into a turn.

Even as the *Pembroke Castle* turned, however, a cry came up from the watch at the bridge wing: "Surf ahead!"

The captain wheeled about, staring through his spyglass. Silently, Pendergast crept up behind. There, ahead, the faintest smudge of white seemed to float on the darkness of the waves.

"Hard right rudder!" Libby roared. "Reverse engines, full astern!"

The order was transmitted to the engine room while the helmsman leapt to obey the wheel order, but the ship was heavy, it was long, and it was fighting a beam sea. The white smudge grew brighter, and a sudden tongue of lightning revealed them for what they were: the Skullcrusher Rocks.

"It's impossible we're so far off course!" the navigator cried.

"Full astern!" the captain shouted again, even as the laboring rumble from the engines vibrated the deck. But the crew of the bridge, and Pendergast, could see it was far too late: the horrid rocks loomed up out of the driving rain, surrounded by exploding surf…

…And then there came a shuddering crash as the bow of the ship was thrust violently upward onto the rocks. A massive sea broke over the port rail, bashing through the bridge windows and carrying the first mate and navigator overboard with it.

"Abandon ship!" Captain Libby called out to the second mate. "Crew to stations, lifeboats away, women and children first!"

"Abandon ship! Crew to stations!" The orders went echoing down the line of command as the crew leapt to obey.

Once again the scene dissolved in a second cloak of darkness, Pendergast's mental point of view returning to the party on the beach. The men were standing, horrified and silent, at the spectacle of the great ship, barely a hundred yards away, as it was thrust up and over the rocks, pounded by the thunderous sea, its back breaking, the stacks coming down, muffled explosions coming from the boilers as seawater rushed in through the breached hull. The violence of the ocean, the distant cries and screams, seemed almost beyond comprehension. The men were struck dumb, aghast at what they had wrought.

There was an effort to lower lifeboats, but the ship was violently careened on the rocks, swung back and forth by the sea, and the effort was almost impossible, the lifeboats bashed to pieces on the rocks or driven into the ship's hull, spilling their passengers into the sea.

Within minutes, the driving wind and storm surge began carrying wreckage ashore—spars, planks, barrels…and then survivors. A ripple of surprise went through the group standing on the beach. Instead of well-dressed officers, what appeared out of the dark and the storm were young women—some grasping babies or toddlers, still others clinging to debris. They struggled through the surf and onto the beach, crying piteously for help, soaked to the skin, bleeding from scrapes and cuts. Other bodies, already drowned, were washed up the strand and deposited in grotesque, wanton poses. Among them were the bodies of men in dungarees—crew.

Pendergast turned his attention from the wreck to two of the men onshore, so alike they must have been brothers—the one with the stopwatch, the other with the spyglass. Their faces registered confusion and surprise. They clearly had not expected the ship to be laden with so many passengers—especially not women and children. The other men were shocked as well. For a moment, all were paralyzed, unable to act. Then, on impulse, one broke for the water, preparing to help a woman and baby ashore. As he ran past the man with the stopwatch, the leader angrily seized him and threw him to the ground. Then he turned to the others. "These are witnesses!" he cried, addressing the crowd. "Do you understand? *Witnesses!* Do you all want to swing for this?"

The only answer was the howl of the storm and the piteous sounds of drowning and desperate women and children, struggling up through the surf.

And then, coming in through the waves, Pendergast beheld a remarkable sight: a large dory, crammed with women and children. A lifeboat had managed to survive. Captain Libby stood at the bow, holding a lantern and giving orders, two crewmen at the oars. As the group onshore watched, Libby brought the boat expertly through the surf, and the women and children poured out onto the beach even as the captain jumped back into the boat and ordered the men back to the wreck in a heroic effort to save more. The survivors swarmed toward the guttering bonfire, believing themselves saved.

The leader of the mob was enraged at this development. "That'll be the captain!" he said, pointing with a shaking finger. "That's the man we want! He knows where the loot is! Get him—now!"

The mob, galvanized, rushed forward with a roar, brandishing guns, knives, and scythes. As the boat returned with more survivors, it was overtaken. The two crew members were quickly dispatched. Libby drew his sword but was overcome by numbers, dragged out, and hauled before the leader.

The captain, his features distorted by gashes across his forehead and left cheek, looked at the leader with anger and disgust. "You did this!" he said. "You lured us in. Murderer!"

In response, the leader put a gun to the captain's head. "Tell us where the money is."

The captain remained motionless, saying nothing. The leader cracked his pistol across Libby's face. The captain sank to his knees, temporarily stunned. At the leader's order, the captain was hauled roughly back to his feet, blood now streaming from a broken nose. He was searched, but no valuables were found. The leader, further enraged, dealt him a stinging backhanded blow. "Haul him off to the lighthouse," he ordered the men.

Two of the men grabbed the captain by the upper arms and began half pushing, half dragging him northward along the beach. Rousing himself, the captain cried: "What are you going to do with the women and children?"

In answer, the leader spat into the sand—but not before glancing over his shoulder at the dunes beyond the shingle beach. Then he turned back to his men. "Take that dory out to the ship," he said. "Search it, starting with the captain's quarters! Find the loot before the ship breaks up!"

The men, though still in shock, were now united. The utter barbarism of the atrocity they'd committed had bound them together, made them resolved to see it through to the end, no matter what. The mob went lumbering down the beach and launched the dory into the water, manning the double sets of oars and driving it through the surf until they reached the broken back of the ship, wedged on the reef, battered and being driven into pieces by the sea. Converging on a gaping rend in the center of the hull, they disappeared inside, the torches winking out one by one as they were swallowed by the hulk's interior.

Pendergast watched them from his position at the rear of the beach. Then he turned his attention to the pathetic, bedraggled groups of women, young children, and babies, huddled together in threes and fours, crying and pleading for help.

Another man was staring at them, too: the leader of the mob. In one hand was his pistol; in the other, a heavy, cruel-looking cudgel. And the expression on his face was so harrowing that, in an instant, the memory crossing was cut violently short and Pendergast found himself once again in the present, lying upon the stony beach, Constance Greene nearby, a statue standing guard over the deserted scene.

32

Carole Hinterwasser stepped up to the front door of her shop, A Taste of Exmouth, and peered out the window through a slit in the gauzy drapes. It was four thirty, half an hour before the regular closing time, but a closed sign had already hung on the door for the past ninety minutes. She looked left, then right. Main Street was quiet, with only a few pedestrians moving purposefully along.

Soft footsteps approached from the rear of the shop, and then she became aware of the presence of Bradley Gavin behind her. She felt his body touch hers, felt his warm breath on her neck as he, too, peered through the window.

"Anything?" he asked.

"No." She took a step back. "Careful. Somebody might see you."

"Who's to say I'm not just browsing?"

"In a closed store?" Even though they were alone, she found herself whispering.

"I meant to ask—where's that girl, Flavia, been all this time?"

"Down in the basement, doing inventory. She hasn't heard a thing—I made sure of that."

"Do you think they suspect?"

"I don't know," she replied. "We've always been discreet, but Exmouth's a small place." She walked over to the bank of lights, snapped them all off. Immediately, the room grew dim, illuminated only by the glow of a sunless sky.

There was a brief pause, then Gavin said, "You're right. And all these recent events—the theft of Lake's wine, Agent Pendergast snooping around, the murders, and the Tybane markings—it's never been so bad. It's like living under a microscope. My grandfather liked to say: 'If you throw out a big enough net, there's no telling what you might drag in.' As you said, it's a small town. These murders have nothing to do with us, but with all this investigation, someone might find out, anyway... by accident."

Carole nodded. "So—we're in agreement. Right?"

"Right. Things can't go on like this any longer. It's got to be done, as soon as possible. It's for the best."

In the half-light, she took his hand in hers.

Gavin had been looking at the ground as he spoke. Now he raised his head, held her gaze. "It's not going to be easy for us, you know."

"I know."

They stood there, motionless, for a long moment. Then Carole gave his hand a squeeze.

"You go first," she said. "I'll wait a few minutes, then go myself. I told Flavia to lock up when she's finished downstairs."

He nodded, waited for her to open the door, and then—glancing quickly up and down the street—slipped out.

From behind the gauze curtains, concealed from view,

Carole watched him stride down Main Street. Motionless, she let five minutes pass, then ten. And then she, too, exited the shop, closed the door behind her, and began making her way in the direction of the lighthouse.

33

C onstance's first indication that Pendergast had returned from his memory crossing was the movement of his limbs on the shingle beach. Then his eyes opened. Despite the length of time he had lain motionless, more still than any sleeper, those eyes retained the bright glitter of the most intense concentration.

"What time is it, Constance?" he asked.

"Half past four."

He got up, brushed the traces of sand from his coat, and picked up the satchel and metal detector. He spent a moment looking around, as if getting his bearings. And then, motioning her to follow him, he began walking inland from the shingle beach, northwestward, tangential to the line of the Skullcrusher Rocks that lay to their right. He moved with quick, purposeful strides. She noticed that he no longer bothered checking the map or GPS.

Together, they continued to a spot where the beach ended at a rise of land covered with grass and the occasional scrub pine. They climbed to the top, where Pendergast paused to look around. Beyond lay a field of dunes, anchored with grass and low bushes, forming a series of broad, sandy hollows, perhaps fifty feet across. In a moment he descended into the closest hollow. At its bottom, he set down the satchel.

"What are we doing here?" Constance asked.

"If someone on the shore wanted to bury something, this would be the place to do it." Reaching into the satchel, he pulled out a slender, telescoped rod of flexible steel, which he opened to its full, six-foot extent. He began probing the sand at the bottom of the hollow, sinking the steel rod down at various points as he moved in a steady pattern from one side of the depression to the other. After a few minutes, something stopped the probe. Pendergast knelt and probed in a tighter pattern, sinking the steel tip into the sand in half a dozen locations. Then, rising once again, he took from the satchel a small, collapsible shovel.

"I assume, with all this activity, that your memory crossing was successful," she said dryly.

"We shall know in a moment."

Sinking the shovel into the spot of his most recent probe, he began to dig, placing the sand carefully to one side as he did so. He continued digging, making a hole approximately five feet in diameter, to a uniform depth of two feet. Once this circular pit was complete, he began to dig deeper. The sand was damp and loose, making for easy digging. A few moments later, the blade of the shovel hit something with a dull clang.

Quickly, Pendergast put the shovel aside and knelt within the hole. Using his fingers, he swept away the sand, exposing some rusted pieces of metal.

"Iron hull fasteners," he explained.

"From the *Pembroke Castle*?"

"I'm afraid so." He glanced around. "The site seems obvious in retrospect, doesn't it?"

"How did those fasteners get back here in the dunes? Did the sea wash them in?"

"No. The wreckage of the ship was deliberately carried back here and buried. At least, all that washed in. The turn of the tide would have eventually taken what didn't wash up here out to sea."

He dug some more, pulling pieces of iron from the sand, shaking them clean, and placing them to one side. The shovel revealed more pieces of metal, which he also placed aside, some still attached to rotting pieces of wood that had once been hull planking. And then, as the shovel bit deeper into the moist sand, it hit something else: something that made a very different, hollow sound.

Pendergast knelt again. Constance joined him. Together, they carefully brushed away the sand from the point of impact. Slowly, a skull was revealed: small, pale brown. One temple was caved in.

"Good God," Constance murmured.

"Not more than a year old," Pendergast said. His tone was cold, remote.

Together, they continued sweeping away the sand with the flats of their palms. More small bones were revealed: ribs, hips, long bones. Crowded alongside, additional skulls came to light: some small, some adult. All showed signs of blunt trauma.

"We must leave everything in place," Pendergast said. "This is a crime scene."

Constance nodded. Now the bones became so numerous that they formed an almost solid layer embedded in the damp sand. Evidently the people had been killed and buried first, with the ship's wreckage dumped on top. Pendergast took out a small whisk from the bag and swept the sand away, exposing additional bones. The little ones had evidently been piled helter-skelter on top of one another, seemingly tossed in heaps, while the adults were laid in parallel.

Finally it was too much. Constance stood up and, without a word to Pendergast, walked out and climbed to the top of the hollow, where, breathing deeply, she looked eastward over the cold, unfeeling, alien ocean.

34

Sergeant Gavin tried to tell himself this was just another murder scene—like that of the historian, McCool, and Dana Dunwoody. And yet at the same time it was so very different. There were the usual pitiless floodlights turning night to day; the purring generators; the police-tape perimeter; the SOC people and the CSI people and the forensics experts and the photographers. Here was the SOCO, Malaga, from Lawrence, a giant of a man, moving about with deliberate grace. The atmosphere was quite unlike what Gavin had observed at the previous murder scenes—everyone went about their business slowly, almost haltingly, without the usual urgency of a murder that needed to be solved. And there was something else—a team of serious-looking men and women, up from Harvard's Department of Anthropology, who had gridded off the entire site with a crosshatch of staked lines of string, stretched taut, so that the hollow resembled nothing so much as a giant bingo board. They were led by a Dr. Fosswright, a small, neat, dour-looking gentleman with short white hair and a carefully trimmed beard. The forensics people were shuttling back and forth to consult with him, almost as if he were in charge of the scene. Perhaps, in some ways, he was: it was his people who were undertaking the excavation of the site—with little brooms, dental tools, and small paintbrushes—and taking notes on laptops and tablets and shooting innumerable photographs.

Off to one side stood Chief Mourdock, hammy arms hanging by his sides, doing absolutely nothing. Sergeant Gavin shot a private glance at him. The chief looked dazed, like a deer in the headlights. It was remarkable, the change that had come over him. A week ago, he'd been swaggering around, full of himself, acting like the big-city-cop-in-a-small-town. Now he looked pale, unsure, even unnerved; his comfortable little fiefdom, his rapidly approaching retirement, had all been thrown into a state of uncertainty.

And now Gavin saw the architect of that change approaching—Special Agent Pendergast. He had been off to one side, talking to the lone reporter who'd appeared on scene—a young woman from the *Boston Globe*. It surprised Gavin that the tabloid *Herald* wasn't also covering the story. But then again, it was more archaeology than a sensational contemporary murder story. The story would probably appear on some inside page of the *Globe*, perhaps be picked up by the *New York Times* and the *Washington Post* and then soon be forgotten, except for historians...and the locals.

Gavin found it curious that Pendergast would be talking so freely to a reporter. He was usually as close-lipped as an oyster. If it had been anybody else, Gavin might have thought he was staking out bragging rights. But that wasn't Pendergast's style. Gavin wondered what he was up to.

He had to admit that he, personally, felt stunned by this discovery. It was almost impossible to believe that members of his own community, the community of his father and his grandfather and his ancestors going back a dozen generations, had cold-bloodedly lured a ship onto the rocks and—finding it full of women and children instead of gold— had butchered them and buried them in a mass grave. It was equally shocking to think that some of his Exmouth contemporaries, descendants of that murderous mob, had passed down that dreadful knowledge—and had then used it to perpetrate the break-in at Percival Lake's house. But Pendergast's logic, which he'd laid out in a briefing for Gavin and the chief earlier that evening, was unavoidable. And the proof lay before him: in ever-deepening holes between the grids of string, in the evidence bags full of bones and crumbling, pathetic possessions. What really got to him was when the diggers had uncovered a beautiful, painted porcelain doll found mingled with the heap of small children.

One thing Gavin was absolutely sure of: none of his own antecedents had participated in this atrocity.

He felt a strange mixture of emotions—shock, repulsion, worry, anger...and embarrassment. This was not the way he wanted outsiders to think of Exmouth. The very last thing he wanted was more attention focused on the town. By now, all of Exmouth probably knew the story of the mass murder. His fellow townsfolk would surely feel, as he did, horror for the stain it cast on their village and its history. There would be gossip about whose ancestors were responsible. The whole town would be convulsed with suspicion, scandal, and shame. Ugly and even dangerous times were ahead.

Pendergast approached Gavin. "I am sorry, Sergeant. I can imagine how mortifying this is."

Gavin nodded. "How did you...?" he began, then stopped. It was a question he'd been asking himself ever since Pendergast briefed him on the atrocity—but even now he could not quite bring himself to ask for more information.

"How did I make this discovery? Suffice it to say, McCool did the historical legwork." He waved one hand at the ant farm of activity going on in the hollow before them. "The key fact is this: one or more present-day descendants of those killers of yore know of the massacre. They also knew about the tortured and walled-up captain. Among those individuals we will find our modern-day killer. The only step remaining now is to identify him...or her."

As Pendergast spoke, Malaga, the head of the SOC team, came up. He fixed the FBI agent with his usual frowning expression. "Well, Agent Pendergast, thanks to you we've really got our hands full."

"So it would seem."

Malaga ran a hand over his shaved head. "There's one thing I'm curious about. When I got here, two dozen skeletons had been exposed from the grave site. Once you realized it was a crime scene, why did you continue to uncover the remains?"

"I needed to confirm my theory—that not just murder, but mass murder, had occurred here. But if it's a crime scene you want, it would appear there are many additional souls yet to be recovered. Poor Dr. Fosswright looks a bit overwhelmed and might welcome the assistance of you and your men." And with this he nodded at Malaga and Gavin in turn, pulled his coat more tightly around his shoulders, turned, and began making his way through the dune fields back toward the lights of town.

35

The Essex County Coroner's Office, Northern Division, was situated in a separate two-story wing of the Newburyport Medical Center. As Agent Pendergast entered the inner office, the M.E., Henry Kornhill, stood up from behind his desk. He was some sixty years old, tall, round about the middle, with sandy tufts of hair above each ear. He was wearing a white lab coat that—judging by its crispness and the early hour—had not yet seen duty that day.

"Dr. Kornhill," said Pendergast. "Thank you for seeing me."

"Of course." The coroner indicated a chair on the far side of his desk and Pendergast took a seat. "I understand you're here about Dana Dunwoody."

"Yes."

"Do you wish to see the body?"

"That won't be necessary; evidence photos will suffice. I would, however, like to hear your thoughts about the cause of death."

The M.E. frowned. "That was logged in my official report."

"Indeed. But I'm not interested in your *official* opinion.

I'm interested, informally, in anything you might have—in your long experience—found interesting or unusual about the condition of the body, or concerning the cause of death."

"Informally," Kornhill repeated. "We scientists don't normally indulge in speculation, but in fact there were some aspects of this homicide that intrigued me."

Pendergast waited as Kornhill opened a folder that lay on his desk, perused it, and took a moment to form his thoughts. "I found it to be, for want of a better term, a messy killing. Judging by the bruising to the knuckles and forearms, Dunwoody tried to defend himself." A pause. "And if I had to guess, I'd say the victim knew his attacker."

"Why do you say that?"

"Because all the wounds were anterior. Dunwoody was facing his killer. The first blow seems to have been to his right cheek, above the zygomatic arch. A fight took place. Death was caused by blunt force trauma, partially collapsing the frontal bone and the parietal bone along the coronal suture."

"And the stab wounds?"

"Same thing. There were a total of seven, once again all to the anterior. The, ah, carvings were to the posterior."

"They weren't the cause of death?"

"Although a few of the stab wounds may have been ante-mortem, based on hemorrhaging, the great majority were done postmortem. And the carvings were all done postmortem. And all of them were too shallow to have caused dramatic exsanguination. The cuts were feeble, almost tentative. This was not an overkill situation."

"Let's turn for a moment, if we could, to the other recent murder—that of the historian, Morris McCool."

Kornhill reached across his desk, pulled a second folder closer. "Very well."

"His cause of death was quite different—a long, heavy blade that pierced the body laterally, from one side to the other."

"Correct."

"Would you say that, in your opinion, McCool also knew his killer?"

The coroner paused a moment, as if wondering whether this was a trick question. "No."

"And why not?"

"Because the nature of the fatal wound would lead me to believe—again, speaking informally—that he was ambushed."

"I see." Pendergast leaned back in his chair, tented his fingers. "I find it interesting, Doctor, that these two killings have so many points of both commonality and divergence."

Kornhill rubbed his forehead. "How so?"

"One murder was premeditated: an ambush. The other was spontaneous, not preplanned: arising from an argument. One killing was done decisively with a heavy knife. On the other, the stab wounds were more hesitant. And yet in both cases certain markings were carved into the skin."

Kornhill continued rubbing. "That's correct."

"With McCool, the carvings were perimortem. In the case of Dunwoody, the carvings were postmortem. Interesting, don't you think?"

"The transition from perimortem to postmortem is not a bright line, but I would not disagree with your conclusion. Really, Mr. Pendergast, it's not my place to speculate on why these murders were committed."

"Ah, but it is mine, Doctor." Pendergast paused. "You have autopsy photographs of the markings inflicted on both McCool and Dunwoody?"

Kornhill nodded.

"May I trouble you to lay them on the desk for comparison?"

The M.E. rose, opened a filing cabinet set against the rear wall of the office, pulled out some additional files, and then laid a series of photos on the desk, facing Pendergast.

The special agent examined them with interest. "From an, ah, *artistic* standpoint, it would appear these symbols were carved by the same person—don't you agree?"

Kornhill shuddered. "I suppose so."

"And would you also agree that the same weapon was used?"

"That's a strong possibility. It was an unusual weapon in both cases, a blade wide, jagged, irregular, but very sharp."

"So far, we once again have commonality. But I would ask you to indulge me, Doctor—please take a close look at the precise *nature* of the cuts."

The M.E. glanced at Pendergast a moment. Then he turned the photographs around, one after the other, and examined each one closely in turn. At last he raised his eyes in mute inquiry.

"Do they appear to be similar?" Pendergast asked.

"No."

"Could you describe the difference, please?"

"It's a question of contour. In the case of McCool, the cuts are irregular, even dog-eared in places. But the markings, ah, carved into Dunwoody have a much more regular contour. They are also of a shallower nature."

"One last question, Doctor, and I'll leave you to your work. If you had to speculate—once again, I ask informally—what would account for the difference between the way McCool's body was carved, and the way Dunwoody's was?"

Once again, the M.E. paused to consider. "The cuts on McCool were deeper, more violent. Those on Dunwoody, on the other hand, seem almost...hesitant."

"I believed you used the terms 'feeble,' 'tentative.'"

"I did."

"Excellent. Thank you. You've confirmed my own suspicions." Pendergast stood up, extending his hand.

Kornhill rose as well, shook the hand. "I'm confused. All the similarities, all the differences... What are you implying? That these two were killed by different murderers?"

"Quite the opposite: same murderer, different motives. And what is most significant—a different relationship between victim and killer. Good day." And with this, Pendergast turned and left the office.

36

The Chart Room restaurant was dimly lit as always, but Gavin quickly spied Agent Pendergast at the far end of the bar. The guy's funereal style of dress and the paleness of his face made him easy to spot.

Pendergast noticed him, nodded slightly, and Gavin approached the bar.

He felt more exhausted than he ever had in his life. Yet it was not a physical kind of exhaustion—it was more emotional than anything else. He'd spent half the previous night, and much of the current day, out at the site of the mass grave. It wasn't like he had that much to do there—a different kind of expertise than his was required for the job—yet it was his duty to attend. He'd had to watch as, one by one, the bones, some large, many small, were teased out of the sand, cleaned, tagged, photographed, and tucked away in large plastic evidence lockers.

Despite the exhaustion, however, he was curious. Pendergast had left a message at police headquarters, asking Gavin to meet at the Chart Room bar at seven. He had no idea what Pendergast wanted, but he suspected it would be unusual, since everything Pendergast did seemed out of the ordinary.

"Sergeant," Pendergast said. "Have a seat." And he waved at the stool beside his own.

Gavin settled onto it.

The bartender, Joe Dunwoody, who was washing glasses nearby, glanced over. "What'll you have, Brad?"

"Dewar's on the rocks." He watched as Dunwoody prepared the drink. The bartender, who'd been at work here when his brother Dana was killed, had—as far as Gavin knew—taken only one day off work as a result of the tragedy. But the brothers had never been close. Joe did look glum; but then he always looked a little glum.

Glum, in fact, was a good word to describe the Chart Room as a whole. Only half of the tables were filled, and the people sitting around them appeared shell-shocked, speaking in hushed tones if at all. News of the mass grave and the intentional sinking of the steamship, apparently by locals—coming as it did on the heels of the two recent murders—had hit Exmouth hard.

The only exception, it seemed, was Pendergast himself. If not exactly cheerful, he radiated a kind of restless energy, even excitement. Gavin watched as the man prepared some kind of ridiculously complex drink: he'd balanced a spoon atop a glass, a sugar cube nestled in the spoon, and he was meticulously dribbling a stream of water over it. As the sugared water hit the pale liquid in the glass, it blossomed into a milky cloud.

"Thank you for coming." He laid the spoon aside, took a sip of his drink. "I imagine you were out on the beach for much of the day?"

Gavin nodded as he tasted his own drink.

"That can't have been pleasant."

"Not at all."

Pendergast studied the opalescent liquid in his glass. "Sergeant, I've asked you here because you've been most helpful during my time at Exmouth. You've tolerated my presence, worked hard, answered my questions, and volunteered information. You've taken me on excursions into the tidal swamps when, no doubt, there were other things you would have preferred to do. It has often been my experience that local law enforcement does not appreciate the presence of federal officers, especially those that appear to be, ah, moonlighting. I found you a welcoming presence rather than a hostile one. I appreciate that. And that is why I've chosen you as the first person I'm going to share some interesting news with."

Gavin nodded for him to continue, trying not to blush from the praise. His curiosity had vastly increased.

"Do you recall how, last night, I told you that only one step remained: to identify the killer or killers?"

"Sure." Gavin drained his scotch—the drinks they poured in the Chart Room were infamous for being miserly.

"I have now made that identification. There is a single killer: and I know who it is."

"You—" Gavin began, then stopped. Two thoughts flashed through Gavin's mind in quick succession. The first was one of overwhelming relief. *It's almost over*, he told himself. *This nightmare's about to end.* The second was the observation that Pendergast had made a point of telling him first. He hadn't told Chief Mourdock. This was interesting. Pendergast knew Mourdock was retiring; this was Pendergast's way of helping Gavin out with his own aspirations. If properly handled, this could be a real feather in his cap and almost guarantee his appointment to chief.

Joe Dunwoody, halfway down the bar, pointed at Gavin's empty glass. Gavin nodded for a refill.

"Not only have I discovered the identity of the killer," Pendergast continued, lowering his voice somewhat, "but just today I found the location of his hideout, deep in the swamp."

"What are we waiting for?" Gavin asked, half sliding off his stool. *Forget the damn drink*, he thought; eagerness had taken the place of exhaustion. "Let's go."

Pendergast shook his head. "Going out there now, in the dark, would be unwise. Our man clearly knows that region of the swamp better than I, and probably better than you. If we aren't careful, we'll spook him and cause him to flee. No—we'll head in at first light, approach with stealth, and surprise him. You, of course, will make the actual arrest."

This image was most gratifying to Gavin. "What about the chief?" he asked as the fresh drink arrived. "We're talking about a murderer, after all. We might need backup." *And not telling him would piss him off royally*, he thought. Retirement or no retirement, it wouldn't pay to get on Mourdock's bad side.

"I fear Chief Mourdock would be a hindrance. However, it's a prudent suggestion nevertheless, and he should be there—if only for reasons of protocol. Why don't you brief him over the phone once you get home?"

"I'll do that."

"Very good. And now, if you don't mind, I'll retire to my room. I have preparations to make for tomorrow. Shall we meet at police headquarters at five am?"

"We'll be there."

"Excellent. Until the morning, then." And with that, Pendergast drained his glass, shook Gavin's hand, and slipped out of the Chart Room, heading for the stairway that led to the rooms upstairs.

37

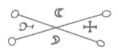

The figure moved quietly through the tall salt grass, barely more than a passing shadow in the near-moonless night. Although the wildlife preserve west of Exmouth was invariably deserted, and the man was in a great hurry, he was nevertheless careful to be as quiet as possible: the only sounds were the swish of the dry grass as he passed and the faint sucking sounds when he traversed one of the frequent mudflats.

The trek was a long one—an hour and a half—but he had made it many times before and was used to the journey. He did not mind the darkness; in fact, he welcomed it.

At the boundary of the wildlife preserve he paused to shift his pack from one shoulder to another and look around. The tide was ebbing fast, and his night-accustomed vision could see that the receding water had exposed a labyrinth of pools, flats, marshy islands, and low swamplands. The land seemed cloaked in a watchful silence, although a steady wind was starting to pick up. He hurried on, more quickly than before—he'd have to be on his way back before the turn of the tide if he didn't want to be marooned in these wastes.

Deep in the swamps, the tall grass grew denser until it

seemed more jungle than marsh. But here, too, the figure knew his way. He was now following the faintest of paths, recognizable as a trail only to the most experienced eye. He'd given nicknames to many of the various landmarks he passed: an irregularly shaped tidal pool was the Oilstain; a heavily twisted clump of salt grass, dried-out and dead, was Hurricane. These landmarks helped him navigate. At Hurricane, he turned sharp left, still following the secret, near-invisible trail. He was almost there. The wind was now driving hard, filling the air with the dry rattle of stalks.

Ahead in the darkness, the grass became a wall he almost had to push his way through. And then, suddenly, he came into a small clearing, less than fifty feet in diameter. In the faint light of the obscured moon, he glanced around. The clearing was a riot of disorder. To one side was a huge trash heap, from which led a trail of garbage: chicken and fish bones, empty food cans, turnip tops. In the middle of the clearing were the smoldering coals of a fire. And across from the trash heap was an ancient canvas tent, torn and filthy with dirt and grease. Utensils and a few provisions were scattered around it: a frying pan, jugs of fresh water. Behind the tent, he could smell, rather than see, a steaming pile of dung. The camp was deserted—by all signs, very recently.

The man glanced around again. Then he called out quietly: "Dunkan? Dunkan?"

For a moment, all was still. And then a man emerged from the wall of salt grass on the far side of the camp. Joe was used to the sight, but even so it always sent an electric tickle of anxiety through him. The man was dressed in tatters: apparently a dozen or so rotting garments, their original use now unguessable, fashioned together and carefully gathered around his limbs almost like a sarong. He had wiry red hair and a monobrow, and a long, greasy beard was twisted into three points with strange fastidiousness. He was all hair and sinew, and he looked at Joe with wild eyes that nevertheless glinted with cunning and intelligence. A flint knife was in one hand; a long, rusted bayonet in the other. Clearly, he had heard Joe's approach and had taken refuge in the grasses.

"What is it?" the man named Dunkan said in a voice hoarse from little use. "You aren't supposed to come tonight."

Joe let the pack drop from his shoulder to the ground. "You have to leave," he said. "Right now."

At these words, deep suspicion overcame Dunkan's expression. "Yeah? Why?"

"That FBI man I told you about. He knows about you, he's discovered your camp. I don't know how, but he did. I heard him say so in the bar tonight. He's coming here in the morning with the police."

"I don't believe it," Dunkan said.

"Goddamn it, Dunkan, you have to believe it! It's your fault. If you hadn't killed Dana, none of this would have happened!"

Dunkan took a step forward, and Joe backed away. One of his hands slipped into his pants pocket and closed around the grip of a .22 pistol. Dunkan saw the gesture and stopped.

"Our brother had to die," he said, eyes flashing. "He was trying to cheat me."

"No, he wasn't. How many times do I have to explain it? He put the jewels in a safe-deposit box until we could sell them. Nobody's going to get cheated. There was no reason to get mad like that and kill him."

"He's cheated me all our lives. You have, too. I wanted my share, and he wouldn't give it to me. I did all the work. I took the risks. I killed that Englishman, didn't I?"

"*You* did all the work?" Joe said. He was angry now, too,

but also extremely wary of his brother. "How about Dana or me taking turns, coming out here every week with your food and water? And what the hell are you going to do with a packet of gemstones? We've got to turn them into money. *Then* you'll get your share."

"I did all the work," Dunkan insisted. "I wanted my jewels then, and I want them now. You've got them. I know you have." Gun or no gun, he took another step forward. "Give me my share."

Another spike of anxiety coursed through Joe. He'd seen his brother like this before; he knew his violent temper, what he was capable of. "Okay, listen. You'll get your share. I promise you. With Dana gone, we can now split it fifty-fifty. But those jewels won't do you any good. They're safe in the bank vault at Exmouth. We can't sell them, not yet. But the main thing is that the FBI agent is going to be here at first light." Keeping an eye on Dunkan, Joe knelt, reached into the pack, pulled out a thick wad of cash. "Here's two thousand dollars—my whole stash. Consider it earnest money until we can fence the rubies. And there's some food and water in the pack, too—enough for another week. But you have to go, *now*. Otherwise they'll catch you, send you to prison. They'll send me to prison, too, as an accessory."

"It was Dana's idea to kill that Englishman. Kill him, and mark him up like that. I did what he asked. I'm innocent."

"Dana's dead now, and that's not the way the law works. You did the killings. It's on you—and on me. Okay? We're in this together—right?" He tried to modulate his voice, sound reasonable, not further piss off his crazy brother.

It was working. The hostile expression on Dunkan's face had abated. He took the bundle of cash Joe offered him, flipped through it with a greasy thumb.

"Go to the other place," Joe said. "You know the one—the old roundhouse at the abandoned switching yard. I'll meet you there a week from now. Once they find this place is empty, they'll think you've run for good. They'll watch it for a couple of days, but when they give up, I'll know. And once it's safe to come back, I'll tell you. In a little while, I'll be able to sell the jewels. Until then, you just hold on to that cash and stay low."

There was a long silence. Finally, Dunkan nodded. As Joe waited, the man turned back toward the tent and began gathering up his few pathetic things. Collecting them in a ragged sheet, he bundled it up, then turned back toward his brother. As he did so, his gaze went over Joe's shoulder, and his face abruptly contorted with feral rage.

"Traitor!" he cried, raising the stone knife. "Judas!"

A shot rang out, the round singing past Joe's ear. Dunkan cried out as the knife was knocked out of his hand with the sound of a ricocheting bullet. With a roar he turned and sprinted toward the wall of dry salt grass, vanishing into it in an instant. As Joe pulled his gun and spun around to confront their attacker, he felt a blow to the side of his head; the gun was torn from his hand; and a knee impacted the small of his back. In a second he was pinned to the ground, his wrists held in an iron grip. They were pulled behind him and the cold steel went on with a click. Next, he felt his legs being securely bound. Writhing on the ground, he finally saw who his attacker was.

"Pendergast!"

The FBI agent was wearing gray-and-black camos.

"I thought you were coming in the morning!" Joe said.

"That's what you were supposed to think." Pendergast got up, fetched the .22, shoved it into a pocket, and then vanished into the grass in the direction Dunkan had fled.

38

Pendergast pushed his way through the salt grass. Dunkan, the feral brother, had a head start, and Pendergast could tell from the distant crashing noises that he was moving with the speed and sureness of someone with knowledge of the marshlands. But Pendergast was an expert tracker; he had hunted lion and Cape buffalo in East Africa; and he undertook this pursuit with the same assurance and strategy he would employ in pursuing big game. It was very dark, but he used his flashlight as little as possible, hooding it with one hand to keep its glow from being observed.

He moved along the disturbed trail of grass made by Dunkan's headlong passage. It was exceedingly hard to follow, but having been in the marshlands several times before, he knew now what to look for. As he ran, he considered his prey's options. The man's appearance was too bizarre for him to chance being spotted in daylight. Nor would he make for the "old roundhouse" now. Chances were that, for the time being at least, he would go to ground in the place he knew best: these very marshlands. He could hide out here for a while, formulating a plan, until the search parties and tracker dogs arrived.

Of course, if he managed to kill Pendergast, he might not have to leave at all. That seemed his most likely choice.

Ahead, the sounds of movement had ceased, masked by the wind. The path, too, became more difficult to follow, as it appeared Dunkan had slowed down and was now moving with greater care, following a faint animal trail. The breeze was from the southwest, however, and Pendergast could detect the man's stink: a mixture of sweat, dirt, and urine. That put him upwind, to Pendergast's left. The FBI agent corrected course, now moving stealthily as well.

A lion hunt was, in fact, an excellent metaphor. Pendergast could not hope to outsmart or outtrack Dunkan: the man was in his element. Pendergast would have to rely on his instincts and his acute senses.

A few stalks of freshly broken grass showed Pendergast that the man had deserted the animal path. He followed Dunkan's trail, allowing himself just enough flashes from his light to keep on it. The track burrowed deeper and deeper into the heavy, tall grasses of the marsh. They were on a medium-size marsh island and eventually they would reach a mudflat and tidal channel.

After five minutes of silence, save for rattling gusts of the wind, there came a sound to his right—a sharp snap. Immediately, Pendergast stopped in place, sniffing the air. The raw human stink was no longer detectable. That meant only one thing: Dunkan was no longer ahead of him, no longer upwind.

But where was he? In an instant, Pendergast understood that the feral brother, unable to shake Pendergast, had decided to circle back and come up on him from behind.

Allowing himself another brief wink of the light, Pendergast veered southwest and pushed his way through the grass. After making a slow arc of about a hundred yards, he stopped. With any luck, he was either behind Dunkan now or—even better—perpendicular to his path. Keeping intensely still, gun and flashlight at the ready, he listened for any sound—an intake of breath, the faint snap of a twig— that would signal Dunkan's approach.

Nothing.

Five minutes passed in which Pendergast remained in position, unmoving. And then he noticed it: Dunkan's stink, drifting toward him once again from the southwest.

What had happened? After brief consideration, he realized that Dunkan had probably heard him and was abandoning his double-back. The stench that briefly reached his nostrils was fainter: Dunkan had used the time to put significant distance between them. Maybe he was trying to escape him, after all.

Rising from his place of concealment, Pendergast moved quickly upwind, in the direction of the odor, using his flash- light more often now in search of signs, more focused on speed than silence. Several minutes of running and pushing through the dense grass brought him to the edge of a mudflat. On the far side of the flat lay a wide tidal channel. The tide was coming in strongly: ripples of black water were moving inland with dangerous rapidity, filling in the labyrinth of tidal islands.

His flashlight made out a set of nearby footprints. They led out of the salt grass and went straight down to the water. Pendergast let his light play out over the channel. And there was Dunkan, head bobbing as he struggled across the water toward the mudflats on the far side.

Pendergast did not hesitate; stuffing his flashlight into the pocket of his camos, he ran down to the water's edge and plunged in. The water was as cold as ice, with at least a ten-knot current and a vicious undertow, which threatened to drag him down and carry him away. He swam hard, stroking his way across, fighting against the cold and the tug of the salt water. As his head came up from above the waterline he could again make out Dunkan, now out of the water, upstream from him, struggling through the mud on the far side.

It was the work of three desperate minutes to get across, while being swept along for at least a hundred yards. At last, Pendergast found his footing on the other side and heaved himself out of the water, nearly frozen, and began to half wade, half crawl through the knee-deep muck of the island. The moon came out from beneath scudding clouds just long enough for him to catch a glimpse of Dunkan. He was standing at the edge of the wall of high grass, a hundred yards away, bayonet in hand. Covered head to toe in mud, only the whites of his eyes showed—and they stared at Pendergast with wild fury.

And then he turned and disappeared into the grass.

Pendergast struggled across the expanse of mud until he reached the point where Dunkan had disappeared. He noticed that the dried grass had been mashed and broken into such wild and random tangles it was nearly impossible to tell which broken stalks might have been the work of a passing man and which the result of wind and storms. But Dunkan had left traces of his passage in faint smears of mud.

As Pendergast forced his way inward, the grass became even thicker. Initially, smears of mud guided him through the dry grass, but soon those traces vanished and he lost the trail. The moon was once again obscured and there was near-zero visibility; even his flashlight was of little use in the dense grass. Dunkan was no longer upwind; he could be anywhere.

After several more minutes of fighting his way through the grass and dry reeds, Pendergast once again stopped to listen, Les Baer .45 in hand. Silence. Dunkan, it seemed, had the uncanny ability to move with a minimum of sound, without disturbing the grass—a feat that Pendergast knew he could not reproduce.

As he stood motionless in the dense thicket, Pendergast realized that, in his zeal of pursuit, he had made a serious tactical error. He was, to all effects and purposes, blinded on all sides by the walls of tall grass. Even though he was armed, he was at Dunkan's mercy. For all he knew, Dunkan was aware of his position and was at that very moment preparing an attack. The wind had picked up and was masking the sound of Dunkan's movements.

He became quite sure Dunkan was going to strike at him, sooner rather than later.

He thought fast, turning in a rapid circle, senses on high alert. It might be just a matter of moments. He tensed, every muscle at the ready.

And then, with the faintest flicker of grass, the bayonet flashed out from the darkness, gripped by a muddy hand, the cold steel plunging directly toward Pendergast's heart.

39

At the last moment, Pendergast—from long-honed instinct—twisted away from the blade with such speed that he was briefly airborne. As he came crashing down, Dunkan burst from the grass, bayonet in hand, slashing at Pendergast and cutting a long slice across the fabric of his sleeve, sending the flashlight spinning. Flipping over and leaping to his feet, Pendergast got off a shot from his Les Baer. But the feral man had vanished back into the jungle of salt grass. Pendergast fired again in the direction he had disappeared—once, twice—then stopped to listen. He was just wasting ammunition. The man was certainly maneuvering back around for another attack.

Pendergast knelt to retrieve his flashlight, feeling around in the dark, but found it broken. He was now totally blind, in unfamiliar territory. The next attack could come at any time, from any direction. The tide had now come in to such an extent that he was trapped on this grass island with Dunkan. Neither could escape the other. But despite his firearms, he was the one at a severe disadvantage. With this dense grass and rattling wind, Dunkan could once again literally creep to within a few feet of him unobserved. If he stayed there and waited for the attack, he would lose.

The question was how to turn the odds in his favor. There was a possible solution. It was extreme—but it might work.

Even as he worked out the solution, he realized Dunkan must be edging in for the next attack, and this time he might not be so lucky as to avoid it. One thing he was sure of: Dunkan would approach upwind, so as not to betray his presence by his stench.

Upwind. That was crucial.

He seized a bunch of dry grass, bundled it together, pulled out his pocket lighter, and lit it on fire. It flared up in the wind, crackling loudly; he thrust the burning bundle into the dense vegetation, sweeping it along, instantly igniting the dry stalks into loud, crackling flames. The gusts drove the fire fast downwind, as Pendergast backed himself upwind, moving diagonally away from the propagating fire. He then thrust the improvised torch into the dry grass again and again, each new fire leaping up and combining with the rest.

In less than a minute, a veritable wall of fire was advancing across the island, crackling and roaring like mad, sparks and flames leaping upward. Pendergast continued to move upwind, through the unburnt grass, until he reached the point where the mudflats that ringed the island began. The clouds were a little thinner now, and the tide was still rushing in. The whole scene was lit up in the ghastly light of the fire, which reflected off the shiny mudflats, turning them the color of blood.

Pendergast watched the conflagration carefully. As he had anticipated, the fire—guided by the rising wind—moved in an arc, like a hinge closing in on itself. The blaze now became an inferno, the surrounding air increasingly hot. Minute by minute, the area of unaffected grassland dwindled. Les Baer at the ready, Pendergast began to circle the island, keeping to the very edge of the grass, moving swiftly and silently.

Finally—over the roar of the flame—Pendergast heard a cry: a howl of rage and desperation. He moved along the edge of the grass in its direction. Soon after, it was followed by the sound of crashing footsteps: Dunkan had been flushed out and was running in a panic from the flames.

Fast as a striking snake, Pendergast darted into the grass. The terrified figure was running on a path tangential to his own, his retreating shoulders backlit by the flames. Pendergast raced after him, leapt upon his back, stunning him with a blow from the butt of his gun; as they crashed to the ground he ripped the bayonet from Dunkan's hand and threw it into the oncoming flames. Cuffing Dunkan's wrists behind him, he rose and half dragged, half carried the semiconscious man away from the oncoming fire and out onto the flats. There, he let him flop down in the mud.

While waiting for the man to recover his senses, Pendergast cleaned as much soot and dried mud from his own arms and legs as possible. Soon, he saw Dunkan's eyes flutter open, grotesquely white within their coating of mud. They fastened on him in mute fury.

"Save your energy," said Pendergast. "We're going to have to wait awhile for the turn of the tide. And then I'll take you to your brother."

40

The storm that had been lingering over Exmouth the past few days had blown away on the previous night's wind, and the morning had dawned bright and warmer. Now the noon sun shone benevolently over the main street, gilding the shopfronts and window displays, and throwing the large crowd gathered before the police station into sharp relief. Percival Lake stood back from the crowd, Carole at his side, on the doorstep of her shop. He clutched a shopping bag in one hand, and held Carole's hand with the other.

It was, he thought, an almost painfully typical New England small-town event. A microphone and podium had been set up on the steps of the police station, and over the last hour almost everybody who was anybody in town had taken their turn before it. It had started with the first selectman, an elderly and reclusive man of ancient New England stock, who, despite his position, rarely appeared in public anymore. He had been followed by the town's other remaining select-man, Dana Dunwoody of course being unable to attend. Next came notables such as the director of the library and that tiresome ex-thespian, Worley. And now, finally, Chief

Mourdock was taking his turn before the microphone, his portly figure angled so that the smattering of press photographers could snap his profile. He'd already cataloged in detail his critical role in cracking the case. Now, he was expressing relief that this "shameful taint"—meaning the Dunwoody clan and their contemporary, as well as ancient, crimes—had at last been scrubbed from the town. To one side stood his deputy, Gavin, looking distinctly uncomfortable at all the attention. On Mourdock's other side was a sealed glass case, containing the twenty-one blood-red rubies that made up the "Pride of Africa," dazzling in the sunlight. They were being watched over by a stuffy representative of Lloyd's of London, who—Lake knew—was not only guarding them, but would shortly take possession. Lloyd's had, after all, paid out the claim on the gemstones over a century ago and owned them as a result.

Lake still couldn't get over the fact that those jewels—and the body that had once contained them—had lain behind the wall of his cellar all these years.

The last few days had been such a series of shocks— one revelation after another, each more bizarre than the last—that Lake felt quite exhausted. As no doubt did many residents. And yet they had turned out, almost every single one. A sea of heads, hundreds and hundreds, stretched away from the police station steps for at least a block, all sharply defined by the brilliant sun. His gaze roamed over them, picking out familiar faces. Mark and Sarah Lillie—wearing matching outfits; old Ben Boyle; Walt Adderly, proprietor of the Inn. Somehow—despite the inflated words of Mourdock, despite the pompous speechifying and small-town politics— the ritual was, undoubtedly, a benediction. Mourdock, in his own obnoxious way, was right. A horror that had been festering in Exmouth for over a century had been identified, named, and rooted out. Now, after all that had happened, the town could heal.

The chief finally went into a rousing We-Are-the-Salt-of-the-Earth, America-Is-Great, God-Bless-Us-All finish. There was applause and cheers. And then it was over. Accompanied by the snapping of press photographs, the crowd began to disperse.

Lake caught sight of Agent Pendergast, standing on a far corner, in his usual black suit. Constance Greene was at his side, a thin, lovely specter in an old-fashioned lace dress. Her only concession to the modern world was a pair of classic Ray-Bans as protection from the sun.

"What a perfect small-town spectacle," said Lake.

Carole laughed. "That's what I love about this place."

Squeezing Carole's hand, Lake stepped away from the shopfront and made his way across the street, threading through the crowds until he reached Pendergast. The agent, who had been looking this way and that, scrutinizing the crowd with great care, fixed his eyes on him as he approached.

"You think Mourdock might have mentioned your name, if only once," Lake said. "After all, it was you, not him, out there in the dark last night."

"I dislike publicity," Pendergast said. "Let the chief have his moment in the sun—literally."

"It still seems like a miracle to me—that Dana and Joe had a brother, hiding out in the marshes all these years."

"The Dunwoody brothers came from a dysfunctional family, going way back. The youngest brother, Dunkan, was born mentally and emotionally disadvantaged. He was not only unloved—he was his parents' shame. They kept his birth a secret, never sent him to school. From what I can tell, he returned his parents' dislike. As soon as he was old enough, he ran away. In time, he returned 'home'—in a manner of speaking. He had been living in those marshes for many years, grudgingly helped by his brothers...who then ultimately found a use for him—as a killer."

"How in the world did you discover his identity?"

Pendergast shrugged. "A process of elimination. I'd written off every suspect in town—including you."

"Me?"

"It's not uncommon to stage a crime in your own home and then feign interest in the investigation in order to put yourself above suspicion. But your reactions during our stroll in your sculpture garden—and, more particularly, in our later talk in the lighthouse—convinced me you truly had nothing to do with the theft. Besides, despite your pedigree you're not an Exmouth native. Only a local could know about the old crimes, and thus have perpetrated the new one. But in looking around the town, all my suspects were eliminated. That left an unknown third party—someone like Dunkan. The Dunwoodys had already attracted my interest. In the days before Dana's death, I'd noticed a small piece of bright-colored sweater material, similar to the garish outfits he favored, clinging to a shrub far out in the marsh. And when I made a reference to *The Hound of the Baskervilles* and the food missing from the Inn's kitchen, his reaction was telling. His murder, of course, was a temporary setback. But then, I noticed his brother Joe's tense demeanor—although he had an ironclad alibi and didn't seem capable of fratricide in any case. The Dunwoody family had deep roots in the town, and indeed in the nineteenth century there were many more of them. But again, it was the regularly pilfered food from the Chart Room kitchen that sealed my interest. So I laid a trap for Joe last night at the bar...and he took the bait."

"A feral brother. He must have been behind all those local legends of a Gray Reaper." Lake shook his head. "Well, all I can say is that when I came to see you about the theft of my wine, I never expected it would lead to all this." He handed over the shopping bag. "By the way, here's that bottle of the Haut-Braquilanges. I recall saying you could have your pick of the case—and you still can, if you'd like—but this one seemed to be the best-preserved."

Pendergast took the bag. "I'm sure it will be more than satisfactory, thank you very much."

Lake hesitated just a moment. "Who actually carried out the theft? From my cellar, I mean."

"Joe and Dana."

"You've interrogated Joe, I take it?"

"Yes. He's talking quite freely now."

Lake was almost afraid to ask the next question. "Do you know what...what he did with all the wine?"

"I'm afraid he took it out to sea in his boat and dumped it overboard."

Lake clapped a hand over his mouth.

"It took him three trips, late at night, to dispose of it all."

"Oh, my God," Lake said in a strangled voice.

"I know," Pendergast replied grimly.

Now Constance spoke for the first time. "I have observed," she said in a low and even voice, "that there are some crimes for which the death penalty does not seem a sufficiently severe sentence."

41

In typical New England fashion, the day, which had dawned warm and sunny, soon darkened in the hours following the ceremony, and a fresh storm rolled in. Glancing out the windows of Pendergast's room at the Inn, Constance could see the branches of nearby trees twisting in the wind. Although it was the night of a full moon, it was hidden behind layers of massive storm clouds that were even now throwing fat droplets against the panes of glass.

"A classic nor'easter," said Pendergast.

Constance turned back toward him. The small crowd of reporters that had come to cover the ghoulish story were gone, and the atmosphere of the town had fallen into a hum of excited relief. Following dinner, Pendergast had invited her up to his room to share the bottle of Haut-Braquilanges. Constance was of two minds: On the one hand, she was flattered that he would share such a princely bottle with her. But she also remembered the effects that the glass of Calvados had had on her the last time she was in his room, and she did not want to lose control like that again.

"Are you sure you want to drink it now?" she asked.

"Carpe diem. Who knows what tomorrow might bring? And what a fine setting we have: the storm outside, the fire within, and our own good company."

Handling the bottle with care, Pendergast removed the capsule, withdrew the cork, set it aside, and, using a candle to see through the wine, decanted it. He immediately poured a tiny taste, swirled, and downed it. The expression on his face, eyes closed, head back, was one Constance had never seen before—pure sensual pleasure.

"What about me?" she asked after a moment.

His eyes sprang open. "Ah, Constance, I was just making sure it hadn't turned to vinegar. To spare you a shock. I'm happy to say it has not."

He set his glass down and poured one for her, refilling his. "We must drink it quickly."

"Shouldn't it air?"

"A wine of this age and complexity turns fast. *Apres toi.*" He picked up his glass. She took the other.

"I'm not sure what to do," said Constance with a nervous laugh. "I've drunk wine before, of course, but not one like this."

"First, we touch glasses."

They touched glasses. Their eyes met. Nothing was said.

"And now, we drink. Just follow my lead. A great deal of unnecessary pomp surrounds the drinking of wine. All you really need to do is swirl it about, inhale, and then sip— like this."

Pendergast swirled, inhaled once, twice, swirled again, then took a sip. He drew a little air in, took another sip.

Constance did the same. It tasted to her like…wine, nothing more, nothing less. She colored, thinking how he was wasting it on her.

"Don't worry, my dear Constance, if you don't immediately taste what I taste, or enjoy it as deeply as I do. Wine is like many of the finer things in life, which take time and experience to extract their full pleasure and meaning."

He described to her again how to swirl, and smell, and then sip, drawing in air.

"The vocabulary of wine drinking is rather recherché," he said. "It's an expression of the inadequacy of words to describe taste and smell."

"So what does it taste like to you?"

"I would say this wine enters the palate like silk wrapped in a velvet texture. That is because of its age—almost all the fruit and tannins have been transformed." He sipped again. "I note spice, cigar-box, truffles, faded flowers, autumn leaves, earth, and leather flavors."

Constance sipped once again, but couldn't even begin to find those tastes in the wine.

"This wine is austere, structured, with great finesse, and a long, lingering finish."

"What, exactly, makes it so good?"

"Everything. Each sip brings out another flavor, another characteristic." He sipped again. "It is just so marvelously complex, so balanced, with each flavor coming forward in its turn. Most important, it has that *goût de terroir*, the special taste of the earth from which the grapes emerged. It contains the very soul of that famous and long-gone two-acre hillside, ruined by mustard gas during World War I."

Pendergast poured them each a second glass and Constance tasted it carefully. It was softer than most wines she remembered drinking, and it had a perfumed delicacy to it that was pleasing. Perhaps she could learn to enjoy wine in the way Pendergast did. As she sipped, she was aware of the slightest numbness of her lips and a pleasant, tingling warmth that seemed to radiate from her very core. She thought she might be detecting notes of truffles and leather in the wine, after all.

Pendergast rose from his seat beside her on the bed and began to stroll about the room thoughtfully, glass in hand. Obtaining, and drinking, the exquisite wine had put him in rare spirits, and he was uncharacteristically voluble. "Even more than with most criminal investigations, Constance, this one is heavy with irony. We have the historian, McCool, arriving with knowledge of the jewels, but not the location of the *Pembroke Castle*'s destruction—while at the same time we have the Dunwoody brothers, knowing exactly where the ship ran aground but ignorant of the existence of the jewels. When the two came together, voilà! The crime was born. The brothers needed time to stage their sham wine theft, which explains the several weeks gap after the historian left. The brothers also knew there was a good chance the historian might return, and they wanted to be ready for him—hence Dana Dunwoody's idea of looking up the Tybane symbols. After the killing, Joe, the bartender, was in an excellent position to spread rumors of the inscriptions carved into McCool's body, and the implication that witches were involved—something that Exmouth natives, who had all grown up hearing such legends, would enthusiastically adopt. A perfect red herring, really."

"But how did you know of the third brother? Your explanation to Lake this morning seemed intentionally vague."

"It was. It was clear, from my investigations, that somebody was living in the marshlands. The missing food, the trails I had come across, the smell of a campfire, the sense I had of being shadowed in my excursions into the salt grass, pointed to only one thing. And they also suggested Joe Dunwoody as a suspect. The thread of cloth I found from Dana Dunwoody's clothing, and his visit to the Salem library to look at the inscriptions, made the brotherly angle even more likely. But it was my visit to the medical examiner that clinched it. Dana's killing was a sudden, unexpected act of rage—not like the premeditated murder of McCool." He seated himself once again on the bed next to Constance. "And while Dunkan tried to cover his tracks by carving up his brother as he'd carved up the historian, he didn't have much stomach for the task—hence the hesitant nature of the cuts."

Constance took another sip of wine. The howl of the wind and drumming of rain was pleasant here in this cozy room, with its dim lighting and its crackling fire. She could feel the warmth of Pendergast's body next to hers.

She noticed that Pendergast was looking at her. Was that look quizzical—or was it expectant?

"Yes, Constance?" he asked mildly. "I sense you have other questions about the case."

"It's just..." she began after a long moment, trying to marshal her distracted thoughts. "It's just that something seems to be missing." She said this more to fill an increasingly dangerous silence than anything else.

"How so?"

"Those tracts I read in the Salem library. About the 'wandering place,' the 'dark pilgrimage to a southern shore.' We proved that the witches did not die out, as everyone had thought, but that they had moved—to the south."

"It's a curious side story, without a doubt." Pendergast took another sip of wine, then refilled both of their glasses. He once again sat down on the bed. The decanter was now almost empty.

Constance put her glass on the table. "Then where did

they go—and what happened to them? The only place south of the site you discovered in the marshes is Oldham."

"But Oldham wasn't a witches' settlement. It was a working fishing village—that was depopulated, I might add, some eighty years ago, following the hurricane of '38. And it was not witches who carved those inscriptions into the bodies of McCool and Dana Dunwoody—we already have statements from the real 'engraver,' who is anything but a witch. And wasn't it you who, not so long ago, was deriding any possible link to witchcraft in this case?" A pause. "You can't take such things too literally, my dear Constance. I know of your penchant for the bizarre and unusual—all those years of reading outré books in the sub-basement of Eight Ninety-One Riverside Drive, after all, must have had their effect—but even if the story is true, 'south' could have meant anything or anyplace. It could have meant Gloucester or even Boston. And by now, those witches—assuming they were witches—are but a distant memory."

Constance fell silent. Pendergast put his hand over hers. "Trust me—you have to let it go. I have yet to work a case in which every strand braids together perfectly."

Still Constance said nothing; she was now hardly listening. She felt her heart accelerate and her chest grow tight. A tingling sensation spread over her body. Pendergast's hand, still lying over hers, felt like a burning thing. The storm of emotions within her seemed to break. Almost without knowing what she was doing—as if someone else was controlling her actions—she slipped her hand out from beneath Pendergast's, then placed it over his. Slowly, deliberately, she raised his hand from the quilt and placed it on her knee.

Pendergast went rigid. His eyes looked into hers, the firelight reflecting in flashing, silvery shards.

Equally slowly, equally deliberately, she began guiding his hand upward under her dress.

There was a moment of stillness. And then, he turned toward her with such suddenness that his wineglass dashed against the floor, shattering into a thousand pieces. One hand tightened on the inside of her thigh, while the other hand grasped the front of her dress with nearly enough force to tear buttons away. His lips crushed hers...and then, just as abruptly, he drew back. Almost before she could comprehend what was happening, he had risen from the bed in a smooth motion. Now, inexplicably, he began retrieving the fragments of his wineglass and dropping them into the wastebasket with hands that shook ever so slightly. Constance simply watched him, not moving, stunned and unable to think.

"I am terribly sorry, Constance," she could hear him saying. "I believe I may have damaged your dress."

Still, she couldn't find any words.

"You must understand. I am a man, you are a woman...I have greater affection for you than for any other living soul..." He continued picking up the glass as he spoke.

She found her voice. "Stop fussing."

He paused, standing between the table and the dying fire. His face was flushed. "I feel that the peculiar nature of our relationship precludes our acting on any feelings that we might..."

"Do shut up."

He fell silent. He remained standing, looking at her.

Constance rose. She felt confusion first, then embarrassment, and finally humiliation and anger. She stared at him, her body trembling.

"Constance?"

With a sudden, violent, backhanded movement, she

dashed the other glass from the table, shattering it against the hearth. "Pick *that* up, too, why don't you?"

Then she turned, strode toward the door, and flung it wide.

"Wait!" Pendergast cried after her. "Don't leave—"

But the rest of the sentence was cut off as she slammed the door and ran downstairs toward her own room.

42

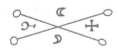

Percival Lake returned from the window that looked out over the bluffs to the raging Atlantic below. It was turning out to be quite the storm. Every sweep of the lighthouse's beam cast a fleeting radiance across the distant dunes and ocean, illuminating the line of white rollers marching in and thundering up the beach. The lights of the house were out, but the lighthouse had its own emergency generator, supplied by the Coast Guard, which kept it going no matter what the weather.

He turned from the window and watched Carole lighting the last of the candles, which flickered along the mantelpiece and on tables in the living room. That, combined with the warm glow from the fire in the massive stone fireplace, gave the room a delicious atmosphere. Blackouts were common out where they were, at the very end of the line. Lake enjoyed them . . . as long as they didn't go on too long.

Carole straightened up. She had seemed nervous and overwrought the last few days, but now was back to her splendid self. "I just love candlelight," she said.

Lake came over and put his arm around her. "I have an idea. A very special idea."

"I know what your 'special ideas' are all about," she said, giving him an elbow.

"Well, this one is different. Come with me." He plucked up a candle in a holder and, leading her by the arm, went to the cellar door. "Come."

He led her down the narrow stairs. At the bottom, the sound of the storm was muffled, the creaking of the joists in the old house louder.

"What do you have in mind?" she asked.

"You'll see."

He went down the basement corridor, past his sculpture studio, and into the oldest section of the basement. It was still a wreck from the theft, the shelves that had held the bottles lying on the floor, surrounded by broken glass and the smell of wine. The niche Pendergast had discovered still stood open, gaping, the rusted chains hanging within. To think that all those precious bottles were at the bottom of the ocean! He bypassed the empty shelves and went to the wooden case of Chateau Haute-Braquilanges.

"Hold this." He gave her the candle as he bent down and removed the top. The bottles were nestled in their wooden holders. One holder was empty: the bottle he had given to Pendergast. Reaching in, he grasped another and held it up.

"Since I've broken the case, let's drink another."

"Really? Isn't it worth, like, ten thousand dollars?"

"Much, much more. But we're not getting any younger—and what is wine for if not to drink?"

"Maybe you're not getting any younger," she said, laughing. "Anyway, even after all this time I don't know a thing about wine. You'd be throwing it away on me."

He put his arm around her. "That's where you're wrong. My dear, you and I are going to rebuild this collection. We're going to travel to Italy, France, and California, tasting and buying wine and shipping it back. You need to educate your palate. And what better way to do it than to begin with the greatest wine ever made?" He gave her a squeeze.

"That sounds lovely. Okay, you've convinced me."

"That was easy."

They turned to go. As they passed the open niche, Lake paused. "To think a fortune in jewels was sitting right there, under our noses. Too bad we didn't find it ourselves."

He felt Carole give a shudder. "I'm glad we didn't. Think of all those mothers and babies, butchered. Talk about blood gemstones. Bad juju for sure."

"True."

Cradling the bottle, careful not to disturb its sediments, he brought it up the stairs and into the living room, setting it down with exquisite care on the table in front of the fire. He removed the lead capsule and wiped off the neck of the bottle with a damp cloth. The cork looked good, no signs of leakage or mold. Then, again with care, he inserted the tip of a corkscrew into the center of the cork and slowly twisted it in, hooked the edge of the lever against the side of the bottle, and—with bated breath—eased it out.

This was the moment of truth. He hadn't mentioned it to Carole, but the chances were good that a wine this old had already turned to vinegar, or at the very least had become corked. But as he inhaled the scent, he took in a rich variety of aromas that not only indicated the wine was fine, but were of staggering nuance and complexity. He took another sniff, marveling at the layering of characteristics.

"Well, well," he murmured.

"Is it good?"

He nodded, bringing over a decanter. As if handling a

baby, he carefully decanted the wine, leaving an inch left around the punt. He then poured out two glasses. They both took a good drink. The wind shuddered the house, rattling the windows. The lighthouse beam swept across the sea, then swept again.

In silence, they enjoyed the wine, without the usual wine chatter about this taste or that smell. Lake liked that. There was way too much talk about wine drinking. It was like those people who talked incessantly in museums; God forbid they should simply *look*, for a change.

He was delighted to see how much Carole was enjoying the wine. Yes, she could learn. They would travel and taste and buy. It would give them something to bond over, which, if truth be told, he'd found rather lacking in their relationship. It would be a wonderful experience...and it would help him finally accept the loss of his wife. This would be the way he would at long last overcome that hole in his heart, that seemingly permanent feeling of loss.

They continued sipping.

"What was that?" Carole asked.

He paused. There had been a thump. A gust of rain lashed the windows as they listened. Then came a second, louder thump. It appeared to come from the porch.

"I think the wind just blew over one of the rocking chairs." He turned back to the wine.

Another shuddering thump sounded on the porch, almost like a stamping foot.

"That was no rocking chair," Carole said.

"Let me check." He rose, picked up a flashlight from the table, and went out of the living room and into the front hall. As he reached the door he heard something strike it, like a clumsy knock. Suddenly uneasy, he went to the vertical row of sidelights beside the door and shone the light out onto the porch to see if someone was there.

There were muddy, indistinct footprints leading across the rain-swept porch, but he couldn't see who was at the door. Good God, he thought, who in the world would be out in that storm? But whoever it was, he was standing too close to the front door to be seen. The antique door had no peephole.

"Who's there?" Lake called out over the sound of the storm.

This was answered with another fumbling knock, and then the rattle of the doorknob. The door, thank God, was locked.

"Look, if you're in trouble, I'll help you—but you've got to talk to me first!"

Carole appeared in the hallway. "What's going on?"

"Some crazy person at the door." He turned back. "*Who is it?*"

Now came the sound of a heavy body pressing itself against the door, which groaned with the pressure.

"Who the hell's there?" Lake yelled.

This time the body slammed against the door, rattling the hardware. Carole gave a short scream and jumped back.

"Carole, get me the baseball bat!"

She disappeared into the darkness of the kitchen. A moment later, she returned with the birch Louisville Slugger they kept in the broom closet.

Another body-slam against the door, more powerful this time. The wood cracked around the frame.

"You son of a bitch, you come in here and I'll kill you!" Lake cried. It was dark and he could hardly see. "Carole, shine this flashlight over here!"

He stood back, cocking the bat, while she stood behind him, holding the flashlight with shaking hands.

Another powerful slam, more cracking of wood. The lock plate jarred loose with a rattle.

"Stop it!" he screamed. "I've got a gun! I'll shoot you, God help me if I won't!" He wished to hell he did have a gun.

Another crash and the door flew open, splinters of wood scattering. A figure burst in and Lake swung the bat hard, but the figure, leaping over the shattered remains of the door, moved so fast that he got in only a glancing blow to its shoulder as it blew past him, filling his nostrils with a sudden overwhelming stench. He turned around and drew back the bat just as Carole let out a bloodcurdling scream, the flashlight dropping to the floor and plunging the room into gloom. At the same time there was a wet sound, like a water balloon bursting. In the dimness, Lake saw the dark shape drop down to its knees and hunch over Carole, lying splayed on the Persian rug. He could hear the sodden sounds of mastication. With a roar he rushed over and swung the bat at the shape, but it rotated upward, two blunt hands rising to catch the bat; it was twisted out of his hands with horrific force; and then he felt a gigantic ripping jerk to his midriff, heard the sound of something wet and heavy hitting the ground, before he himself fell backward, screaming, into a bottomless pit of pain and horror.

43

I told you we were out of candles," Mark Lillie said, opening and slamming drawers, his voice raised over the banging of a loose shutter in the wind. "Two weeks ago when we had the last blackout, I told you we needed candles."

"You only imagine you told me that," said Sarah. "What about the shutters I've been telling you to fix for the past year?"

As if to underscore her comment, the shutter banged again. He pulled a flashlight out of a drawer, cursing.

"What's wrong with that?" Sarah asked.

Mark turned it on, shining it in her face. "A flashlight doesn't exactly light up a room."

"Get that out of my eyes."

"I'm just making a point. This is like the fifth blackout this year. You'd think that you—of all people—would have a good supply of candles."

"No one's stopping you from buying candles when you're in town—which you are every day."

"I assumed you'd taken care of it. There's this thing called a division of labor."

"You never mentioned we were out of candles."

"I did. You just forgot." He threw himself down on the sofa in disgust. This was what their life was like, fighting every damn day over the stupidest of things. He wondered what he'd ever seen in this woman. They didn't have kids. No reason they couldn't end it now. But there were complications, financial entanglements...

The shutter slammed into the side of the house again, and a strong gust rattled the windows in their frames. The shutter slammed yet again, harder, and this time a windowpane broke with a tinkling of glass. A howl of wind came in, accompanied by a gust of rain, knocking over a photo frame standing on the sill.

"There!" Sarah cried triumphantly. "Now look at what's happened!"

The wind gusted again, a splatter of raindrops spotting the table—and carried along with it the howl of an animal outside.

"What was that?" Mark asked.

Sarah stood where she was, not saying anything, straining to look into the darkness. "That was really close to the house."

"Somebody's stupid dog, left out in the rain."

"It didn't sound like a dog."

"Of course it's a dog. What else could it be?"

Another howl, this time from the darkness right before the window.

"Go take a look," said Sarah.

He took the flashlight and went into the front hall, shining the light out through the door window.

"*Ahh!*" he screamed, falling back just as the door burst open with a crash. A dark shape out of a nightmare bounded in, cloaked in nothing but a vile stench. Lillie wildly flailed his arms in disbelief and terror, trying to fend the beast off, but with a terrible inchoate roar it swung two stringy arms around him, grasping his midriff with its clawed hands.

"No, no!" he screamed, trying to twist away as he felt the long, sharp nails digging into his gut.

"Stop it! *No!*" He could vaguely hear his wife in the background, screaming.

A sudden popping sound, like fat being pulled off of meat, and the hands opened him up like drawing back a pair of curtains. All was dark, the flashlight was gone, and he was only able to feel—and what he felt was a blast of cold air inside his very body cavity that, for just a moment, overwhelmed even the sudden agony. He fell back with a scream of horror and pain beyond description, and even as he did he could feel something reaming him out from the inside, accompanied by the loud, wet, busy sound of chewing.

44

C onstance Greene was soaked to the bone, her sodden
dress clinging heavily to her body, the hem bedraggled
with sand and mud. But she did not feel the cold: her homeless childhood on the docks of New York City seemed to
have made her permanently immune to chill. The wind
thrashed the salt grass and cattails, which swayed crazily
as she pushed her way through, her low boots squishing
along the marshy ground, the flashlight beam playing into
the murk, illuminating the slashing drops of rain. She moved
swiftly, her mind an angry, embarrassed, humiliated blank.

At first, her instinct had been simply to get away—get
away before she did something so violent and permanent she
would regret it forever. But as she ran from the Inn, south
toward the dunes and the salt grass, the faintest of plans
began to form.

Somewhere in the back of her mind, she knew that what
she was doing wasn't simply defying Pendergast, but was
also irrational and perhaps dangerous. She didn't care. She
also knew that her guardian, for once, was wrong: there was
something else going on in the town of Exmouth, something

dark, strange, beyond ratiocination—and still unsolved. She knew more than he did about such documents as the Sutter manuscript; she knew there was often more to them than was commonly believed. *Obscura Peregrinatione ad Littus* (A Dark Pilgrimage to the Southern Shore): there was a mystery here still to be uncovered, and the answer to that mystery lay to the south, in the ruins of Oldham—she was sure of it. What that answer was she could not begin to guess. But she would prove to Pendergast that she was right. She would prove it—and then she would shut herself away in certain sub-basement chambers of the Riverside Drive mansion known only to her until she felt in the mood to see the sun again.

As the land rose, the salt grass gave way to scrub oaks and twisted Scotch pines. She had passed Skullcrusher Rocks and the hook of land beyond, crossed a mudflat and channel—it was low tide—and reached Crow Island, at the far edge of the wildlife refuge. The ocean lay eastward, to her left, beyond the long, narrow barrier island. She paused to listen, but the wind was so loud that she could not hear the surf. The only thing visible in the swirling blackness was the faint blinking of the Exmouth lighthouse behind her, the beam sweeping by every nine seconds. It was this light that she navigated by, the beacon showing her the way to Oldham.

The scrubby trees began to thin, and dunes anchored by dune grass made their appearance. Now she could finally hear the thundering of the unseen ocean—or rather feel it beneath her feet, the shaking of the ground caused by the huge Atlantic rollers pounding the beach. She angled across the island, once again checking her position with the lighthouse. The deserted town could be no more than another mile or two. She would be there very soon.

A good nor'easter didn't frighten Bud Olsen. On the contrary, he liked it. It filled him with vigor. And it didn't bother Aubrey, his golden retriever. After retiring from fishing ten years before, Olsen had moved into town and now lived in a small house at the end of Main Street, where he could walk everywhere—especially to his Tuesday lunch club and to the library, where he was a vigorous borrower of books, preferring the maritime adventure stories of Patrick O'Brian, John Masefield, and C. S. Forester.

At nine o'clock, with the wind rattling the casements, Aubrey began whining at the door and wagging his tail. Olsen laid aside his book and rose from the chair with a grunt. He turned off the kerosene lantern and walked to the door.

"You want to go out, boy?"

Aubrey wagged his tail more vigorously.

"Well then, let's have ourselves a little walk." More by feel than by sight, he donned his oilskin and sou'wester, pulled on a pair of boots, fished the flashlight out of the hall drawer, and snapped the leash on Aubrey. He pushed the door open against the wind, then walked down the porch stairs and out into the street. The town was mostly dark because of the blackout, but the police station at the far end of town was lit up by an emergency generator. The wind whipped across the water of the bay, the rain lashing almost horizontally. Bud lowered his head, the wind tugging at the sou'wester, which was securely tied around his chin.

They turned left and headed down Main Street toward the center of town. As they passed the various houses he could see the soft shadows, backlit in orange, of people moving about with candles or lanterns in hand, giving the town a cozy, old-fashioned, Currier and Ives sort of feeling.

This was how it had been in Exmouth a hundred years ago, Bud thought, before electricity. It wasn't so bad. Electricity had brought nothing but trouble, when you thought about it—glaring light, pollution, computers and iPads and all that nonsense that he saw every day, as everyone—and not just kids—walked around town staring like zombies into little bright rectangles instead of greeting one another, instead of smelling the salt air and observing the scarlet maples in their autumnal glory...

His reverie was interrupted by a growl. Aubrey had stopped, staring ahead into the darkness, his hair bristling.

"What is it, boy?"

Another low growl.

This was unusual. Aubrey was probably the friendliest dog in town, who posed a danger to burglars only by virtue of tripping them in the dark. He would greet the grim reaper himself with a wagging tail.

Aubrey took a step back, stiff with fear, the growl turning into a whine.

"Easy now, there's nothing there." Bud shone the light around, but it didn't penetrate far into the swirling murk.

Now the dog was shaking and cringing, the whine increasing in intensity. Suddenly Bud smelled a dreadful odor—the stench of shit and blood—and with a yelp the dog pulled back abruptly, a puddle of urine appearing on the ground beneath it.

"What the hell?" Bud backed up as well. "What's that?" he called into the darkness.

With a screech of terror Aubrey jerked back on the leash, pulling it out of his hands and hightailing it down the street, leash dragging behind him.

"Hey, boy!" Bud watched the dog tear off into the darkness. This was the craziest thing. He heard a noise behind him and turned back to see something that at first he could barely comprehend: a stringy, naked, oddly elongated figure emerging from the darkness.

"What the *hell*—?"

The figure lunged forward and Bud felt the hot, gurgling breath of it, the stench of the slaughterhouse, and with a muffled shriek of terror he turned to flee when a pain he could never have imagined suddenly tore through his vitals; he looked down with surprise and horror to see a glabrous pate buried in his gut, streaming red with blood, muscled jaws working, apparently *eating* him to death...

Constance emerged from the last line of dunes, skirted a half-buried sand fence, and came out on the beach. The surf was tremendous, massive curlers collapsing far offshore, driving in as a line of boiling water and breaking a second time and thundering up the beach to the foot of the dunes. Until this trip to Exmouth, Constance had never seen such an angry ocean, and—with her inability to swim—she found the sight unsettling. It was easy to see how a ship would be pounded to flotsam in a sea like this in very little time. Her flashlight beam barely penetrated ten feet into the murk.

She looked back. The Exmouth Light was just visible, blinking away steadily despite the blackout. She recalled the old maps she had looked at in the Historical Society. The ruins of Oldham couldn't be much farther to the south. Sure enough, as she continued on, she at last made out the stubs of pilings poking out of the sand as the shore curved into the estuary that formed the end of Crow Island and the former Oldham Harbor. A few more minutes brought her to a granite seawall, built of huge blocks that had once protected the opening to the harbor.

She skirted the seawall and walked inland. The dune area gave way to hard ground, scrubby pines, and stunted oaks. And there were house foundations here: cellar holes of stacked granite stone, full of oak leaves and drifted sand. It wasn't hard to make out where the single street had passed through town, cellar holes on either side, along with the odd piling or rotten wooden beam.

A map of Oldham she'd examined at the Historical Society had indicated the town's only church stood at the far end, where the street divided, so to be visible the length of town in a traditional New England arrangement. And sure enough, as she moved along the long-abandoned road, she found a larger, deeper foundation at the far end, in somewhat better condition than the other ruins, consisting once again of hand-cut and stacked granite blocks. A stone staircase led down into the remains of a basement.

Constance stood at the top of the stairs and looked down. There was nothing visible but sand and rubble. What was she expecting to find here? The futility of her plan struck her. Despite the remoteness and the desolation, these ruins had no doubt been picked over by beachcombers and other people in the many decades since Oldham was abandoned. What could she possibly find—especially when she didn't know what, precisely, she was looking for?

She felt another surge of humiliation, chagrin, and anger. Against her better judgment she walked down the granite steps and into the open cellar. Here, within the shelter of the hole, the wind subsided. She shone her light around. The cellar was about thirty feet by forty, with a central stone structure that supported the remains of two fireplaces on the first floor. Those fireplaces could still be seen, of mortared stone, falling apart, a partial chimney sticking up like a hollow stub. The wooden part of the church was mostly gone, with only a few heavy, worm-eaten beams lying here and there, as soft as punk. Oak leaves lay piled up in the corners and against the back part of the central chimney. Bayberry bushes grew thickly along the north-facing stone wall, and a large stained canvas—it looked like an old sailcloth—lay rotting against it.

Constance finished a circuit of the cellar. If there was some dark secret hidden in this town, it would probably be here, in the church. But what? She brushed aside the leaves here and there, uncovering only broken glass, rusted nails, and bits of crockery. The wind picked up and she moved into the shelter of one of the walls. The sailcloth she had noticed was sprawled in the dead weeds. She grasped one end of it and pulled, dragging it back. A foul smell arose, like that of a dead animal, and instinctively she let the canvas fall back. She hesitated, grasped it again, and this time dragged it out of the way, back from the wall. The stench rose again. Shining her light, she saw that the sailcloth had been concealing a small, four-foot-square iron plate in the stone of the rear wall. The plate appeared to be covering a niche. The smell was awful, but no dead animal could be seen—in fact, the smell seemed to be coming from behind the plate.

She knelt and, breathing through her mouth, looked closely at the plate. It was rusted but not, it seemed, as rusted as it should have been. It looked like the entrance to a root cellar. The plate was hinged, the hinges oiled and suspiciously operable.

Her heart beat faster. There was something behind here; she was sure of it.

She shone the flashlight around the space, checked to make sure her stiletto was still tucked into the folds of her dress. Then, quietly and carefully, she lifted the iron plate—which moved easily on its hinges—revealing not a root cellar but a low tunnel, a descending stone staircase. A horrible smell came drifting up: a mingling of feces, urine, and rotting meat. She ducked through the opening and began descending the stairs into darkness.

At the bottom she paused, listening. The storm above was now greatly muffled, and she could hear a faint, intermittent sound ahead: the sound of childlike weeping.

45

Gavin sat in the back room of the station house, staring glumly at the checkerboard. Once again the chief was winning, and it galled him no end to be beaten in checkers by a person who was in every way his intellectual inferior. How did Mourdock do it? He'd probably read a book and learned some cheap tricks, like those guys who played ten-second chess for money in Boston Common.

He finally made his move.

"King me," the chief said, his plump fingers moving a piece into the back row.

With ill-disguised annoyance Gavin stacked on a second chip. He was going to lose this one, too.

What made it worse was that the chief, insufferable at the best of times, had become puffed up like a toad since his triumph that afternoon, where he'd basically hogged all the credit for solving the case, when it was Pendergast and Constance Greene who had done all the work. Gavin couldn't understand why Pendergast had just stood at a distance during the press conference while the chief monopolized the limelight. At least, he thought, the case was over. He couldn't get out of his memory those two corpses, obscenely carved up with the Tybane Inscriptions, and it had been a tremendous relief to learn it was just those dumbass Dunwoody brothers trying to divert suspicion from their own criminal bullshit. It was like he'd been telling everyone from the very beginning: The carvings were only a red herring. No witches or witchcraft was involved at all—a ridiculous false alarm.

"Your move," Mourdock said, intruding on his thoughts.

The chief had moved his king into a clever position in which Gavin saw he was inevitably going to lose two pieces and, with them, the game. There was nothing he could do. He moved a piece, and the chief quickly double-jumped his men, smacking the pieces down with excessive force as he did so. Fucking jackass.

"I resign," Gavin said immediately.

"Come on, don't give in so early," said the chief, almost at a whine. "You might still win."

As Gavin was shaking his head he heard a sudden crash in the outer office—the front doors had been flung open. This was followed by a half-bellowed scream for help.

Gavin and the chief leapt up, the board and its pieces scattering. A woman—Rose Buffum, Gavin instantly recognized—stood in the doorway, streaming wet, her sodden clothes clinging to her heavy body, her long gray hair plastered against her head, her eyes wide in terror.

"God help me!" she screeched, choking. "Help me!" She staggered toward Gavin.

"What is it?" Gavin grabbed one arm and the chief took the other. She was shaking violently. "Are you hurt?"

"My God, *my God!*" she wailed.

They eased her down in a chair. Gavin rushed to get her a cup of coffee.

"Call nine-one-one, get an ambulance," said the chief. "There's blood here."

Buffum lay back in the chair, half swooning, eyes rolling in her head. Gavin put down the coffee and grabbed his radio. He quickly got the dispatcher in Newburyport and called in the 911. Meanwhile, the chief was wiping down Buffum's face with a paper towel, dabbing here and there.

"Where are you hurt?" he asked.

The woman gasped. "It isn't my blood!"

"Okay," said the chief. "Have a sip of coffee and tell us what's going on."

Buffum ignored the coffee, let out another gasped wail. "The monster!"

"*Monster?*" Mourdock repeated in a skeptical tone.

"It won't stop killing." And then, as if seized with a sudden thought: "Oh, dear God, lock the doors!"

"We don't lock the station doors," said the chief.

"Get us in a cell, then. It's coming!"

"What's coming?"

"It's a demon from hell, ripping people apart!"

Listening, Gavin felt a sudden freezing in his vitals. *The monster.* No. Impossible.

"Ripping people apart, and...!" At this the woman doubled over and, with a retching sound, lost her dinner all over the floor of the station.

The chief backed away with a disgusted expression. "We have an ambulance coming, Rose. Just hang in there." He looked at Gavin. "What should we do?"

Gavin stared at him. There was no doubting the woman's sincerity. Rose Buffum had all the imagination of a fence-post—she wasn't the kind of person to be seeing things.

The chief knew this, too. The skepticism was quickly draining from his face.

"We holster our service pieces and go out there," Gavin answered.

"Don't leave me!" Rose cried.

"Go out there?" Mourdock said uncertainly. "The two of us?"

"We've got to find out what's going on." Gavin had to see. It couldn't be true…

"Put me in a cell, then," Rose screamed. "Lock the door!"

"If that'll make you feel better." The chief escorted her into an adjacent cell and locked her in, giving her the keys. Then he turned. "All right, let's see what's going on."

Gavin fetched his Glock and his holster, buckled it on.

"Check your flashlight," the chief said.

Gavin checked the big flashlight hanging on his belt. Then he followed the chief out into the darkness and looked down Main Street. In the dim light of the houses, he could see two shapes lying in the street.

Bodies. So it was true. He felt a sickening lurch. And now he could hear, over the roar of the storm, a faint scream from halfway down the street; a sudden flare in a house window, the curtains leaping into flame, the glass shattering, the screams from within suddenly louder—and then abruptly cut off in a loud gargle.

"Oh, Christ Jesus," the chief said, staring.

And now from out of the burning house leapt a figure, silhouetted in the firelight: a tall, pale, stringy thing with a massive overhanging jaw—and a *tail.*

46

Walt Adderly, proprietor of the Captain Hull Inn, sat at the bar of the Chart Room, listening to Benjamin Franklin Boyle regale the regulars—yet again—with the story of how he found the corpse of the historian. The normally taciturn Boyle was in an expansive mood, rolling his eyes theatrically, gesturing with his mug of beer, and in general putting on a good show. He'd had more than his usual pint, his skinflint habits thrown to the wind on this special day. Like many seafaring men, Boyle was an accomplished storyteller, and it seemed the crowd just couldn't get enough. The power had gone out an hour before, which somehow only added to the festive mood. Candles had been brought out and set up along the bar, the patrons drinking and celebrating the bizarre end to the murder mystery. As the drinks and conversation flowed, there was a general feeling of relief that Exmouth had returned to normal. Naturally, most were shocked by the involvement of the Dunwoodys, although there was a minority that opined as to how they'd "never trusted that family." Adderly himself had never had a problem with his longtime bartender, Joe Dunwoody, aside from the stealing of food. He even felt sorry for him in a way.

Boyle had just gotten to the point in the story where he was about to turn over the corpse with his clam rake when the front door to the Inn slammed, hard.

Adderly looked toward the sound as Boyle fell silent. He leaned back in his chair, then called out down the dark hall to the front parlor. "Come in, friend, and get yourself out of that filthy weather!"

Boyle returned to the story. He was flush with the attention and the beer.

But no one appeared from the direction of the front parlor. Adderly held up his hand for silence. He looked back down the hall. "Come on in, don't be shy!" And then, in a sudden impulse of generosity, he added: "Round's on the house!"

This announcement was greeted with a murmur of approval all around. Boyle turned to the bartender and twirled a finger. "Fill 'er up!" He suspended the story while Pete, the backup bartender, began refilling everyone's mugs.

A loud crash came from the dark hallway. It sounded to Adderly like someone falling down. Apparently their new visitor, whoever it was, already had a head start on the celebrations.

"Hey, Andy, that guy out in the hall needs a little help," Adderly said to the man perched on the stool closest to the door.

Andy Gorman got off his stool, picking up one of the candles. "Don't resume till I get back."

"No problem," said Boyle, burying his lips in the frosty brew.

Shielding the candle, Gorman walked out of the bar and down the hall, a wavering point of light in the darkness.

A moment of silence—and then a piercing scream came from the hall. Adderly almost dropped his own mug in surprise and swung around, staring down the black corridor. Everyone rose at once. Gorman's candle seemed to have gone out: the hall was black. The storm shook and rattled the old structure.

People exchanged glances. "What the hell?" someone said after a moment.

"Andy? *Andy!*"

At that moment, a smell rolled out of the hall: a stench of death and rot and fecal matter that overwhelmed Adderly's nostrils. All was silent; no one moved. And out of that silence, over the rattle of the storm, Adderly heard the rapid, breathy sound of animal panting.

In his room on the top floor of the Inn, Pendergast sat up in bed. He listened intently, but the scream from downstairs had abruptly cut off and he heard nothing more save for the storm. The celebratory noise from the bar had also ceased.

He slipped out of bed, swiftly donned his clothes, grabbed a flashlight, and strapped on his Les Baer. He ran down the hall, descended one flight, and then—after the briefest of pauses—grasped the doorknob to Constance's room. When he found it locked, he rapped on it.

"Constance," he said. "Please open this door."

No response.

"Constance," he repeated. "I'm very sorry for what happened, but this is no time for melodramatic gestures. Something is—"

Even as he spoke, he heard a sudden chorus of cries erupt from downstairs, a cacophony of shrieks mingling with the sounds of a ferocious stampede, the crashing sound of chairs being overturned, glassware breaking, and feet thundering on the wooden floor.

Without waiting any longer, he turned his shoulder to the door and, in one blow, broke it down.

The room was empty, the bed still made. There was no sign anywhere of the flashlight he had given her.

Pandemonium had broken out downstairs. He scrambled down the stairs, pulling out his weapon as he did so, to arrive in the front hall. His flashlight revealed the front door yawning wide and swinging in the howling wind. A body lay sprawled over the threshold.

He turned and ran down the hall into the bar, where a scene of extreme violence greeted his eye: a second eviscerated figure lay on the floor, while half a dozen others were crouching, terrified but unhurt, behind the bar.

"What was it?" Pendergast rapped out.

"God help us, help us!" a man shrieked, triggering a storm of wild importuning from the huddled group, with the words *monster* and *demon* and *ape* and *hound* mingling unintelligibly with the cries of the terrified patrons.

"Where did it go?" Pendergast said.

A man pointed out the door.

Pendergast turned and raced back down the hall and out into the storm, leaving the patrons crying futilely after him for protection. He could see bare footprints crossing the porch and the sandy walk beyond, already being erased by the rain. He hesitated, peering into the storm in the direction the creature had gone: southeastward, into the salt marshes. Whatever it was, it had wreaked havoc and then escaped.

His mind shifted. Constance was missing. She hadn't retired—she must have left the Inn some time ago, perhaps immediately after the abrupt conclusion of their conversation. He passed a hand across his forehead.

Where did they go? she had asked. *What happened to them? The only place south of the site you discovered in the marshes is Oldham.*

That, Pendergast felt certain, was where she had gone: Oldham, the long-abandoned town that, for reasons he could not fathom, she had focused on. Not two hours before, she had all but implied that the heart of the mystery remained unsolved. Even as he considered this, he felt a twinge that perhaps he had dismissed her concerns too readily—that her intuition had told her something that his own cold analysis had overlooked.

The killer was barefooted, in a storm, with the temperature dropping into the forties. That fact, more than any other, profoundly disturbed him, as it indicated there was something about the case he had missed completely—something fundamental—just as Constance had insisted. And yet, even as he pondered the mystery of the bare footprints, he couldn't find even the glimmer of a solution.

With a burning sense of chagrin, he set off into the storm, following the faint and quickly disappearing marks in the sand.

47

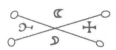

The house burned brightly as Gavin stared down Main Street. This couldn't be happening. He could see, in the light of the fire, the bodies in the street: people he knew, friends and neighbors. The door to another house stood open...and he had a terrible feeling there would be another body inside it, as well.

That...*demon* had rampaged through town in minutes and had then seemingly vanished, leaving behind a scene of mayhem. How could this have happened?

He heard the chief calling the Lawrence PD on his radio, requesting a massive SWAT team presence. His voice was almost hysterical. "We've got a maniac on the loose here, multiple fatalities, I can see at least two bodies from where I'm standing... Yes, ma'am, damn it, I said two bodies! We've got a house on fire... Send me everything you've got, everything, you hear? The whole 10-33 arsenal!"

Gavin tried to get a grip. He had to think, *think*. This was unbelievable, a horror beyond all horrors...

"Gavin!"

He turned. The chief was staring at him, face red and

perspiring despite the cold. "It's going to be an hour before Lawrence can get choppers in the air. The first responders will arrive by vehicle... Are you *following* me?"

"Yes, yes, Chief."

"We need to split up. I'm going to take the squad car and wait for them by the bridge, guide them into town. I want you to head down Main, search the houses. Starting with that one with the open door."

"Without backup?"

"The killer's gone, for chrissakes! We've got local Fire and Rescue coming in ten minutes, we got SWAT teams in twenty, choppers in an hour. You're going to have plenty of backup. Just reconnoiter, provide first aid to the injured, secure the crime scene."

Gavin didn't have the ability to argue. The chief, the son of a bitch, the coward, was going to wait at the bridge, locked in his car where he would be safe, while asking his sergeant to put his ass on the line, going alone and blind into those houses.

As he opened his mouth to protest, he had a further thought: splitting up might actually be a good thing. Gavin realized he had something a lot more important to do than tally up bodies, and in order to do it he needed to ditch the chief.

"Right, Chief. I'm on it."

"Good man." The chief turned and headed back toward the station house, while Gavin made a show of walking down Main Street, taking stock. Even as he did, he could hear the Search and Rescue sirens going off, calling in volunteers. They would be on the scene in minutes... and if he was still around, he'd never get the chance to try to figure out what had happened and get things back on track.

Glancing behind, he saw that the chief had disappeared

into the station house. He turned and ducked between two houses, into the concealing darkness. Pulling out his flashlight, he broke into a run. Oldham was maybe five miles away. It was, he told himself, no more distance than what he habitually jogged in the morning. Giving allowance for crossing a nasty section of marsh and tidal flats on Crow Island—thank God it was low tide—he could be there in no time.

48

Chief Mourdock slid his bulk into the squad car and exited the station garage, lights flashing, siren wailing. He had a vague idea that the sight of the squad car in full siren would be a comfort to the people cowering in their houses.

He felt completely flummoxed by what he had seen. Rose Buffum had spoken of a demon, a monster, but of course that was crazy. It had to be a Jack the Ripper type, a homicidal lunatic, who had come into Exmouth and gone on a rampage. Things like that happened in the unlikeliest places. It was just some random horror.

And yet those splayed, torn bodies...

At this thought he felt a cold, paralyzing fear, so powerful he gasped aloud. Six months from retirement...and now this, on top of the Dunwoody murders?

Fuck it. He would get to the bridge, park, lock the squad car, and wait for the SWAT teams and backup to arrive from Lawrence. At this time of night, in the storm, the roads would be free of traffic. They'd be here in no time.

...But what if there were downed trees? What if the roads were blocked? What if the power failure delayed them?

The fear stabbed like an icicle probing his guts. He reassured himself that all he had to do was wait for the SWAT teams to arrive and take over. They would push him aside, relieve him of all responsibility and decision making. Then, whatever happened, it wouldn't be on him.

The Metacomet Bridge loomed ahead, the row of sodium lights that normally illuminated it dark. He eased onto the bridge, the rain lashing his windshield, the wipers slapping back and forth. He drove halfway across and put the vehicle in park, keeping the engine running, making sure the doors were locked. When he satisfied himself that he was safe, he pulled out the mike and called the Lawrence dispatcher. He was assured that a massive response was on its way, all the 10-33 equipment Lawrence had accumulated since 9/11 being put into service—MRAPs, BearCats, heavy weaponry, stun grenades, tear gas, and two M2 Browning .50-caliber machine guns. The convoy would arrive in Exmouth in less than ten minutes.

Until that time, Mourdock told himself, he could do nothing.

But now he wondered if maybe it had been a mistake sending Gavin into town alone. It would look really bad if his deputy were killed, with him sitting here doing nothing. But Gavin would be safe; the killer had gone. Surely the killer was gone.

Mother of God, he was looking forward to his retirement, his pension, his sofa, and a cold six-pack in front of the ball game.

But the more he thought of it, the more he realized that, whether or not Gavin was killed, it *would* look bad—him, sitting out here in his locked patrol car, away from the town that he had been hired to protect. It wouldn't go unnoticed by the first responders...

Suddenly he had an idea. He could turn around, take Dune

Road toward the ocean, avoiding downtown and its chaos. There was a turnout south of town, not far from the light-house, where he could wait. If he turned off his headlights, nobody would see him, nobody would know. Then, when he heard the sirens and saw the lights of the approaching cavalry, he could rush back into town as if he'd been on the scene the whole time.

The vise of fear that had clamped around his chest eased ever so slightly. Cowardly? No—just looking after number one. After all, he'd put in his twenty...almost. And there was that sofa and that cold six-pack to protect.

Throwing the vehicle into gear, he did a three-point turn, drove off the bridge, then took a right off Main onto Dune Road. To his left, he could just make out the faint glow of the burning house. Then came the lighthouse beam, winking through the storm.

Past the lighthouse, he reached the turnout, maneuvered the patrol car around in readiness to scoot back into town, killed the lights but left the engine running. He glanced at his watch. Five minutes for the convoy. Just five more minutes and his ordeal would be over...

A sudden blow rocked his car. He gave a shout, staring wildly out into the darkness.

Something had slammed into the rear door on the driver's side—a branch blown on the wind, maybe. As he fumbled to turn on the exterior searchlight, another massive blow hit the door, turning the window into a dense spiderweb of cracks.

Abandoning the searchlight, his breath coming hot and fast, Mourdock extracted his flashlight and turned it on. Something was prodding at the fractured, rubbery window, pushing it in. A hand broke through—a bloody hand with horrible, blunt brown nails that were an inch too long.

Mourdock screamed, dropping the flashlight and scrabbling for his weapon.

A second hand—sinewy, pale—punched through the window and ripped out the loose glass. Then a hideous bald head, encrusted with blood and gore, pushed in while one arm simultaneously reached around, fumbling at the door with a curiously infantile gesture.

"Noooo!"

The chief finally got his Glock out and pointed it, firing wildly, but now the door flew open and the maniac lunged into the backseat. Oh, God, it *was* a monster: a hideous, naked, emaciated monster with a pit bull's face and projecting snout, a huge rack of blunt teeth, a pink tongue, and brown eyes that glittered with homicidal malice.

Still firing wildly, Mourdock fumbled with the gearshift, trying to maneuver it into drive...but just then a hand snaked out, plastering itself onto his face, those blunt nails curling around his cheekbones and spastically tightening.

"Ahh*mmmmmm!*" Mourdock, feeling the foul-smelling palm pressed against his nose and mouth, the nails sinking deep into his flesh, tried to scream and pull away; there was an agonizing wet jerk and his voice was released in a spray of blood as his flesh parted from his skull, and then he heard a hoarse gasping sound so close he wondered where it could have come from, until he realized it had come from himself.

Agent Pendergast had lost the trail of the killer just south of town, but he sensed, from the purposeful beeline, that it was headed for Crow Island. And now, as he crossed the road that traversed the marshes and led to the beach, he saw a police car—the chief's squad car. The headlights were off, but the engine was running. Through the gusting rain he detected movement.

Suddenly, a figure leapt up onto the hood, then scurried crab-like down the front grille just as a flash of lightning brilliantly illuminated the vehicle. In a moment, it was dark again. But in that moment, Pendergast saw something freakish and bizarre, something so far out of his experience as to be inexplicable: a tall, bony, emaciated man, completely naked, covered with countless cuts and scars, with a bald head, a dog's face, and a long, forked tail with a hairy knob at the end.

And then it was gone.

Pulling out his Les Baer, Pendergast raced toward the patrol car. He saw the creature moving away at the speed of a running dog, then loping off the road—heading toward the wildlife refuge and Crow Island.

He turned his attention to the squad car. The windshield was opaque, coated with blood from the inside. The back door, however, was open, its window broken and missing. Grasping the frame, he leaned in. His flashlight beam revealed Chief Mourdock. The man was sprawled across the front seat. He was all too obviously dead.

Pendergast withdrew from the car and jogged to the spot where the unearthly creature had left the road. Gun at the ready, he followed the tracks through the sand to the fence edging the wildlife preserve, which the creature had evidently leapt over. On the far side the tracks continued, straight as a compass line. Pendergast paused long enough to mentally visualize a map of the area, quickly realizing that the straight line ended at Oldham.

Constance was at Oldham.

He broke into a run, acutely aware that the creature was twice as fast as he was.

49

Constance moved cautiously through the labyrinth of tunnels. While dirty, stinking, and encrusted with niter, she could tell that these passageways had not been abandoned. Quite the opposite: they had been kept up with fresh mortar and braced with wooden beams at various weak points. Some of the bracing was so recent that the wood was still oozing pine sap. While the entrance had been carefully left looking derelict and deserted, these underground tunnels themselves were clearly well-used.

What were they for? And who were the people using them? She had ideas about that.

In attempting to follow the sound of the crying child, she had managed to lose it in the winding passageways. The tunnels, and the movement of air through them, did deceiving things to sound, magnifying it in one place and canceling it in another. As her light flashed over the walls, she saw—sometimes scratched into the niter, other times written in chalk or paint—symbols not unlike the Tybane Inscriptions: witchcraft symbols she recognized from the *Pseudomonarchia Daemonum*, but of an even more complex and sophisticated nature. What before had been merely suspicion now hardened into conviction: these tunnels, she realized, must be in use by a cult, not Wiccans but real witches—*black* witches.

She paused, considering the cruel irony. The rumors and legends, dismissed by almost everyone, had a basis in truth: witches had indeed fled from Salem during the trials, established a colony in the marshes, and then moved here, to Oldham, when the marsh colony proved unsafe. The entrance to these tunnels lay underneath the pseudo-church—what better way to cover up their Sunday rituals from prying eyes?

The residents of Oldham, she knew, had moved to Dill Town seventy-five years before, and many had migrated from there into Exmouth proper—where they undoubtedly remained even now, living apparently normal lives, but retreating here for their dark rituals. Constance wondered which of the numerous townsfolk she had met since arriving here were secretly part of this coven.

Now she paused to examine her own emotions. She was aware of feeling, rather than fear, a kind of curiosity. These dark tunnels, which in the average person would elicit great anxiety, were not that different from some of the passages that ran beneath the old mansion on Riverside Drive—save for the vile stench and the unsettling symbols that covered the walls.

She listened intently. She could hear the crying again now, the faint echoes strangely distorted by the underground twists and turns. She moved slowly in their direction. The sounds slowly grew clearer, and now she could hear a second voice: hoarse, ragged, but somehow motherly.

The tunnel made a sharp turn and passed beneath a low arch—and then Constance found herself in a long corridor, broad and high-ceilinged, with a ceremonial feeling to it. The walls had been plastered and were excised with demonic symbols, every square inch carved in precise, maniacal detail with symbols the likes of which she had never seen, even in the *Daemonum* or the numerous other occult books into which she had delved. An even fouler smell hung in the air here, of filth and feces and suppurating flesh. Along the walls stood small stone reservoirs, brimming with oil, each with a floating wick. Clearly this was used for some kind of processional. But a processional to where? The corridor ended in a stone wall.

She heard a girl's cry, much louder and closer. She turned toward it, startled. The sound had come from behind her, past a low archway leading from the long corridor. She slowly approached the archway and shone her light down the passage beyond. It was short and ended in a stone cell, barred with rusty iron and locked with a shiny brass padlock. Inside the cell huddled what at first glance looked like two heaps of filthy rags, topped by brushy, tangled hair. As she stepped closer, staring in horrified fascination, Constance realized she was looking at human beings—an old woman and a girl. Mother and daughter? The way they were huddled together in the chilly cell made it appear so. They stared at her, suddenly hushed, their hands raised against her light, smudged eyes wide with fear. Their faces were so dirty, Constance could not make out the features or even discern what color their skin was.

She lowered her light and approached. "Who are you?"

No answer; two silent stares.

She seized the padlock and gave it a shake. "Where is the key?"

This question, instead of receiving an answer, triggered an unintelligible wailing and sobbing from the girl, who stretched a hand out through the bars. Constance stepped forward to grasp it, the filth causing her to hesitate for just a moment. With a cry the girl seized the proffered hand and grasped it with tremendous strength, as if it were her only lifeline, and began babbling. It was not a language Constance understood, and after a moment she realized that, in fact, it wasn't a language at all—just an outpouring of quasi-human vocalizations.

The older woman remained eerily silent and passive, her face expressionless.

"I can't free you until you let go of my hand," Constance said.

As she pulled away, the girl kept up a frantic wailing. Exploring with the flashlight, Constance looked everywhere for a key—walls, ceiling, floor—nothing. Apparently, the jailers kept the key with them.

Constance turned back to the cell, where the girl was still mumbling and weeping.

"Stop that noise," she said. "I'm going to get help."

More moaning. But the mother seemed to understand, and she placed a restraining hand on the girl, who fell silent.

"Who are you?" Constance asked the mother. She spoke slowly, enunciating the words. "Why are you here?"

A voice spoke from the darkness behind her. "I can answer that question."

turned and walked back into the long central hallway, heading toward the cul-de-sac at the end. He was aware, with a tingling glow in his chest, that Constance was indeed following him. He paused at the far wall, pushed three loose bricks in, and slid wide the secret door and fastened it open. With a lighter he quickly circled the room, lighting the candles in each of the four sets of candelabras.

Then he turned with a smile to face Constance.

She did not run. She did not erupt in anger or become hysterical. She simply stared.

Even though he had been there hundreds of times, he knew it was an impressive sight. In the center stood the altar, an ancient block of granite, dating back to the eleventh century, hidden behind a gauzy, hanging shroud; this altar, created in France, had been carried to England, and thence across the seas, hidden, transported from place to place, until it ended up here. Along its sides were Romanesque carvings of devils, polished by a thousand years of use. To one side sat a fantastically carven table, half as long as the altar. On its top were arranged a large silver cup set upon a linen cloth, along with lancets, scarificators, and other bloodletting tools.

Illuminated in the wavering candlelight were the frescoed vaults of a pentagonal room, again depicting devils, gargoyles, ouroboros, Barbary apes, men and women, all cavorting in a kind of paradise of sin: a truly Boschian scene. Thick tapestries hung on the walls, decorated with forest images, flowers, and unicorns, also dating back to Romanesque times; and along the columns holding up the barrel ceiling were elaborately decorated alchemical symbols. The ceiling itself was hung with dozens of fine constructions made out of whittled bones bound up in twine, reminiscent of animals, birds, and beasts. Even in the still air they managed to endlessly sway and turn, as if alive and agitated, throwing raking shadows in the indirect candlelight. Ancient benches, polished by use, stood in serried ranks along the pentagonal walls of the room, and the floor was thick with layers of Persian rugs, some dating back three hundred years.

Gavin watched Constance carefully. As he hoped, she was calmly taking it all in with those intense violet eyes, without hysteria or perturbation. He felt a swell of confidence that what was happening here was, in a way, ordained. This was one remarkable woman.

He smiled. "Welcome."

"Welcome to what?" she asked in an even voice.

"Before I go into that, may I ask how you got here?"

No answer.

"Let me guess, then: you're here because you figured out the abandoned witches' colony had not vanished, but moved to this spot. And you came to investigate. Am I right?"

She did not react. God, it was hard to read her face, beyond those strangely quiet but intense eyes.

"And now you've arrived at all this." He spread his hands. "It must be very confusing."

Still she said nothing.

"How to begin?" He gave a nervous laugh. This girl made him feel like a teenager again. "I don't know how you did it, exactly, but your coming here is...a sign. It is without doubt a sign."

"A sign of what?"

He looked at her beautiful, oddly impassive face. He sensed this woman was even deeper than he had believed. So much the better.

"This, Constance, is our chamber of worship."

"Our chamber."

"Yes. *Our* chamber. And this is our altar."

"May I ask what religion?"

"You may. We practice the oldest surviving religion on earth. The *original* religion. As you've no doubt guessed, we are witches." He observed her face closely, but could not quite interpret the look that briefly crossed her face. "Real witches. Our worship goes back twenty thousand years."

"And those women you've brutalized?"

"Not brutalized. Not at all. Please, give me a chance to explain before you judge. Constance, I'm sure you must realize that your coming here—and my arrival at the same time—is not an accident. Nor is it an accident that Carole failed to poison you with that chai tea of hers. She's a jealous woman—but we're off the subject."

Constance did not reply.

"From the very beginning, I saw that you were one of those exceptional people you spoke of back at the Inn. Do you recall that conversation?"

"Very well."

"I knew then that you could be one of us. We haven't taken a new member into our family in two hundred years. It takes a very special person to understand who we are. You're that person. There's a rebellion in you, a yearning for freedom. I see in you the desire to live by your own rules."

"Indeed."

Gavin was amazed at how easy this was, how natural it felt. "And there's a darkness in you."

"Darkness?"

This was more than encouraging. "Yes, but a good kind of darkness. The darkness that brings light."

"Who are you?"

"I'm a witch. My parents were witches, my grandparents,

going back half a dozen generations in Exmouth, and before that Oldham, the New Salem Marsh Colony, Salem, the British Isles, and so forth into the mists of time. I was born into this tradition just as naturally as Christians are born into their faith. Our practices may seem a little startling to an outsider, but so would a church service to someone who knew nothing of Christianity. I hasten to add that we're not in opposition to Christianity. We believe in live and let live. We aren't cruel people. For example, we never would have participated in that horrible mass murder of women and children on board that ship. That was done by so-called Christians."

Gavin paused, looking at her with curiosity, trying to peer into her mind. "Look at the beauty of this chamber, the ancient things in here, the sense of history and purpose. The corridors leading here, I know, can be off-putting—the blood and the smell and the rest. But you see, Constance, our Sabbat ceremony is free of euphemism. It involves real blood and real flesh in *real* sacrifice. And, I might add... real sensuality."

Again, her face betrayed nothing of her thoughts.

He reached out to take her hand, and she allowed it. Her hand was cold and clammy, but he pressed it anyway.

"I don't want to force our beliefs on you. But let me tell you a little of our history and origin. I'm sure you know much of the story already: for seeking his freedom, Lucifer and his followers were cast out of heaven. But not into hell. They ended up right here on earth—and we are the *Maleficarum*, their spiritual descendants. Lucifer, the rebel angel, gives us the freedom to be and do what we wish."

"And you wish to convert me to these beliefs."

Gavin laughed, blushing despite himself. "You didn't end up here, this night of all nights, by accident. You and I were guided here by forces greater than ourselves; forces we ignore at our peril."

"What kind of forces?"

"Earlier tonight, two members of our community were supposed to have conducted a rare and extremely important sacrifice. However, it didn't go as planned."

"What kind of sacrifice, exactly?"

"We worship Lucifer, but we breed a mortal devil as the focus of our worship. He's part demon, part human. His name is Morax and he has lived here, in these tunnels, for many years. He is a symbol, a spiritual gateway, a...a medium to help us communicate with the unseen world. But now, we're in troublous times. Your friend Pendergast discovered and defiled our ancient settlement, removing important artifacts. That was a shock to the Daemonium, to our protectors. And Carole tells me you figured out that the witches' colony didn't die out as everyone believed, but instead moved south. Here, as a matter of fact. As a result, our community has been thrown into its worst crisis since 1692. Secrecy is the only way we can survive. We've always perpetuated the idea that the witches, the *real* witches, who fled Salem died out centuries ago. But with all that's happened in Exmouth recently—the killings and the subsequent attention—our coven was in danger of being exposed. Worse, the blasphemous use of the sacred Tybane Inscriptions by the Dunwoodys, trying to cover their murderous family history, surely angered the Daemonium. This forced us to do what we've only had to do a few times in the past: sacrifice our living demon to appease the powers of darkness. The last time we sacrificed our demon was during the hurricane of 1938. As a result, we were without doubt saved from extinction. And so just yesterday the coven leadership decided that we once again had to sacrifice our demon, Morax, to Lucifer in order to gain his intercession; to keep our worship a secret. It was supposed to happen earlier this evening—on the first night of the full moon."

"And it didn't go as planned?"

"Not *yet*. The demon escaped before the ritual could be completed. Nevertheless, he must be sacrificed. That's why I'm here—to finish the job my brethren failed to do. Morax is in Exmouth now, free for the first time in his life, satisfying his bloodlust. But he will come back here when he's sated. It's the only home he knows. And when he does, I'll be ready."

"And after you sacrifice him? What then?"

"Lucifer works in mysterious ways. We'll be protected— I don't know how precisely. And we will eventually breed another demon from the same genetic line." He nodded toward the archway that led to the women's cell. "Those two, a mother and a daughter, are in fact our breeders. They carry the gene, which came to us with whalers from the South Pacific back in the eighteenth century, when a family of remote islanders joined our order. A certain defect was common among these islanders—some were born with a tail. These were true tails, Constance, not vestigial tails: caudal appendages with fully formed vertebrae, an extension of the coccyx. When my ancestors saw the women of this family give birth to such a creature—well, you can imagine their excitement. This was Morax, reborn—Morax in the flesh, just as he had been described and depicted in the ancient texts. It was a gift to us from Lucifer. And it immediately became a central element of our worship ceremony. And so it, and its descendants, have remained to this day." He nodded out the archway again. "The mother bred the current Morax; the daughter will breed the next one."

"This is highly illuminating," said Constance.

He beamed at her. "A deep and powerful philosophy, Constance, and it can't be understood all at once. You have to live and breathe it, as we have these many millennia. We bother no one. Once a month we anoint the altar with the blood of Morax, which we regularly draw. Real blood is important in our ritual. Otherwise we live our lives in the most ordinary ways, like everyone else. We pray, we ask for help, and we communicate with the unseen Daemonium— the ranks of demons and devils, equivalent to the Christian saints. But we don't stir pots and toss in eyes of newt or jab pins into dolls. Ours is a libertarian philosophy. And I might add, in our group, women and men are absolutely equal."

"And you want me to join you."

"Yes. But it's more than that. Carole Hinterwasser and Mark Lillie, our former leaders, are dead by the demon's hand—which elevates me to the leadership of the community. I need a partner. I want you to be that partner."

He still could not read her face. He took a step toward her. "I sense in you, not just a depth of understanding, but also a burning sensuality, white hot—and yet beautifully controlled."

She continued to look at him, without moving, and without betraying her thoughts. He had never met a human being with that much self-possession. It only reinforced his feeling that she was destined to join with him.

He plunged ahead. "Sensual pleasure is at the very core of our religion. That's how we celebrate the gift of life, through our physicality, our flesh and blood and organs of pleasure. That's how Lucifer asks us to worship him: by celebrating the sensual pleasures of the body."

"In other words," Constance said, "you worship carnally."

"We call it Sexual Discourse."

"In public?"

"As with all worship, we celebrate together. To celebrate Sexual Discourse in front of all increases the excitement, the pleasure. We observe the Sabbat rites here, in this room, on that altar."

"So you copulate on the altar, in front of a crowd?"

"Crudely put, yes. Two select individuals—not married, who have not had previous congress with each other—take their first, fresh sexual pleasure with one another on the altar, anointed with the blood of Morax. I can assure you it will be a sexual experience like none you've ever had in your entire life."

"Like nothing *I've* ever had?" asked Constance.

"It would be my honor to initiate you into the faith."

"Right now?"

"I hadn't planned it that way. Normally it's done in front of the group. But we're in an emergency situation, and the forces have arranged for you and me to meet, here, tonight. So…yes. For anyone who wishes to join with us, the act is obligatory."

"And if I wish not?"

Gavin was surprised by this reply. She had followed his words this far, she was clearly sympathetic to what he was saying… "Look, why speculate? You're going to join us, I just know it."

"I am?"

He felt a flicker of concern, even panic. He wondered what to say, how to seal the inevitable.

"Why wouldn't you join us? You're perfect. You're every-thing we look for. I've no doubt you'll be a great leader."

"And if I do not?"

"Please, Constance, consider my proposal carefully, because this is your first, last, and only chance. I *know* you have the wild yearning for freedom in your blood. We'll unleash that freedom together, and it'll be beautiful."

"Beautiful."

The word, heavy with sarcasm, hung in the air. Gavin began to feel a crushing sense of disappointment, mingling with anger; maybe, after everything he'd shared with her, after the many signs he'd seen of their compatibility, she was going to say no, dashing all his hopes. He put his hand on the grip of his sidearm. She couldn't be allowed to walk out of there. That would be the end of everything.

"Constance, think *very* carefully."

But now he could see that her apparent interest was not acceptance; her calmness was not a sign of acquiescence; and her questions had only drawn out from him information that could be used against him.

"Oh, Constance, Constance, please don't do this."

More silence. So be it. Gavin knew that this woman would be an unshakable friend, but also a most dangerous opponent. He felt he'd been tricked. One of the things he'd learned as a kid was always to throw the first punch—and do it early, before your opponent realized a fight was coming.

So he punched first. He lunged forward, knocking the stiletto from her grasp, wrapping one arm around her neck and jamming the gun into her ear. Shoving her back against the nearest wall and pinning her there, he slapped his set of handcuffs around her wrists.

It was over before it had begun. He had completely caught her by surprise. He released her and stepped back, gun pointed. "It doesn't have to be this way," he said.

She stared at him and he was truly taken aback by the look in those eyes.

"I'm sorry I had to do that, but I need your decision now."

Silence. She drilled him with that baleful stare.

He wagged the gun. "This is the moment of truth."

In response, she knelt, and—with her cuffed hands—picked up the stiletto he had knocked to the ground. There was a *snick* as she exposed its blade.

Surprised, he took a few cautious steps back, wondering if she knew how to throw it. But then he remembered that her wrists were still cuffed and her handling of the knife looked inept.

"What exactly are you going to do with that?" he asked.

She reached up and touched the tip of the knife to her own throat, just above the jugular vein. "I'm going to deprive you of the satisfaction of raping and killing me."

As she spoke, she pressed the point into her skin. After a dimple of resistance it cut into the flesh, a rivulet of blood running down.

Gavin felt an electric shock; despite himself, he was overcome with admiration. This was an amazing woman. My God, she would have made a magnificent partner. He felt a stirring in his loins. But he also realized she'd never join with them. His excitement mingled with a terrible feeling of failure.

Fuck it. She'd been offered the chance of a lifetime and refused it.

He stared as she pressed the knife a shade deeper. He could tell this was no bluff—she was willing to kill herself rather than submit to him. She *was* going to kill herself. His dismay at not joining with her gave way to an excitement of a very different sort.

"Go ahead," he said, breathless with anticipation.

He watched as she steeled herself. The knife bit deeper. He was transfixed; he had never seen anything so erotic in his life. Watching her ease the knife into that delicate white throat, seeing the ruby blood running down her pale skin, he felt a powerful shudder ripple through his body.

And then the look in her eyes changed ever so slightly. She paused.

"Don't stop," he said hoarsely, the blood pounding eagerly in his ears. "Do it. *Do it now.*"

Now the knife blade slipped back out. Blood was running freely, but it was only a superficial cut.

Disappointment and anger surged within him, and he raised the gun. "I was sure you had the guts," he said. "I was wrong."

Constance's eyes had been fixed steadily on his own, but now they flickered to one side; with a sudden, terrifying realization, he whirled around just in time to see that she'd fatally distracted him; a grimacing, dog-faced creature took a final hop toward him and he felt a hand with blunt nails seize his arm in a grip of iron.

51

This was Juan Rivera's second time in Exmouth, and as he looked down what had once been a quaint village street, he saw it was now more reminiscent of Dante's *Inferno*. The SWAT team he was leading had dismounted from their vehicles to approach on foot, their first job to secure the area so paramedics could retrieve the dead and injured. A temporary command station was being set up behind them, radios blaring, sirens going, searchlights blazing. Two MRAPs idled, each with .50-caliber machine guns, ready to move into action if the killer or killers reappeared.

But it looked like the killers were gone. The town was silent—deathly silent. From where he was standing, he could see two bodies in the middle of the street. But even as he squinted into the darkness, he thought he could see at least one other, more distant but equally disquieting shape in the distance. The storm, a swift-moving nor'easter, was starting to pass; the rain squalls were coming less frequently and the wind was dropping. The streetlights were out and the houses dark from a power failure. The scene was lit, instead, by a single house halfway down the street, which was in the last stages of burning, casting a garish glow across the nightmarish scene.

The horror his forward recon team had discovered on Dune Road—the police chief savaged inside his own squad car—had deeply unnerved him. The reports they'd received as they were on their way had been fragmentary: crazy stories of monsters, demons, anarchy, and mass killing. The sergeant—Gavin was his name—was nowhere to be found and hadn't responded on any police hailing frequencies. Rivera wondered if he, too, was dead.

What the hell had happened here? Rivera swallowed uneasily, collected himself. There would be plenty of time to figure it out; what they had to do now, and do fast, was secure the area, deliver first aid, and evacuate the victims.

He raised his radio and gave the orders, and the SWAT team began moving down the main street in formation, at a trot. As they proceeded, the carnage became more evident. One of the SWAT team started praying under his breath over the frequency, until Rivera shut him up. He could hear other comments, whispered speculation, muttered maledictions. *What the hell?* he wondered. *Terrorists? Meth heads? Gang rampage?*

Rivera started to feel a little strange; the scene was utterly unreal. He could see from the hesitant, reluctant way his men were moving that, even if they'd never admit it, they were scared. This wasn't urban violence; this wasn't even war. It was something like...well, like a horror movie.

He tried to shake off his own feeling of dread and take firm charge of the situation. In as matter-of-fact a voice as he could muster, he rapped out orders, sending two-man teams left and right to secure the main street and side streets. The first body he came to was horribly mutilated, as if by a wild beast.

His radio began crackling with incoming reports. "Victim outside number eleven Main Street!" "Two victims in the Inn!" The calls were spotty at first, but people were soon talking over one another on the emergency frequency.

As if to push back against the chaos, Rivera watched his team carefully, making sure they were performing by the book: this was a big one, a very big one, and everything they did would be reviewed and re-reviewed. With relative efficiency, given the circumstances, his men established the perimeter, secured the area, and then called in the ambulances. No sirens. Within minutes, paramedics came in and rushed to the many victims, performing triage and, where necessary, first aid.

Not many, Rivera noticed, needed first aid.

Then it came time to clear the houses. There were about twenty of them on the main street. Three had their doors broken in, and in those houses they found more bodies. Even one or two pets had been killed.

In the rest, they found the living: whole families cowering in basements, or hiding in the attic or in various closets, so terrified they could hardly move or speak. And when they did, they spoke of glimpsing a creature: a demon with a tail and a dog's face. His men duly took down the information, shaking their heads with disbelief. In the storm, the darkness, and the power outage, no one seemed to have gotten a good look at it—at least, no one who survived.

In the thick of battles in Iraq, Rivera had experienced a kind of chaotic, collective terror, in which events were so fast-moving and scrambled that afterward nobody could say what had really happened. That seemed to be the case here. The survivors had nothing to say that was reliable or credible, even though their recollections were remarkably consistent on certain points. If only he could find someone who had gotten a good, long look at the killer...

As if on cue, Rivera heard a shout. Lurching from behind a house staggered the figure of a man, not exactly drunk, but not exactly sober, either: wild-eyed, shouting and waving. He spied Rivera and came rushing over, arms outspread, and before Rivera could react the figure had enveloped him in a panicked hug, like a drowning man clasping his rescuer. "Thank God, thank God!" he screamed. "It's the end times. The demons have been unleashed from hell!" Despite all that Rivera could do, the man knocked him down in his desperation.

Two members of his team came to Rivera's assistance and helped wrest the man off him, pinning him to the ground. He continued to thrash and shout.

Rivera rose, then bent over him, trying to speak in a calming voice. "What is your name?"

This was answered with a fresh gust of shouting. "What does it matter?" The man cried inconsolably. "The world is ending; nobody will have a name now!"

Rivera leaned closer and steadied the man's face with his hand. "I'm here to help you. My name's Lieutenant Rivera. *What is your name?*"

The man began to emerge from his mindless panic. He stared at Rivera, eyes bugging, sweat streaming down his face.

"It's not the end of the world," Rivera went on calmly. "I want you to listen. Are you hearing me? Nod if you understand."

The man stared and finally nodded.

"Your name, please?"

A croak. "Boyle."

"Mr. Boyle, *are you hurt?*"

The man shook his head.

"What did you see?"

He began to tremble. "Too much."

"Tell me."

"A...demon."

Rivera swallowed. "Could you please describe the attacker?"

"It...*he*...came down the street... He was running... And making a sound. He kept saying the same thing over and over again..."

"What was he saying?"

"Something like *son, son*... He was horrible, gigantic, seven feet tall. He had a dog's snout. Rotten teeth. Naked. Horrible yellow skin. And he stank. He stank like shit."

"Naked? In this weather?"

"Yes. And...he had a tail."

"A *tail*?" This was disappointing; the man was going to be about as useful as the others.

"A horrible tail, not like a real tail, it was dragging around behind him like a snake. And he had hands, giant hands that ripped people apart like they were nothing more than..." He was overtaken by a violent fit of trembling. "Oh, God... *Oh, God!*"

Rivera shook his head and rose. "Get this man into an ambulance. He's not sane."

52

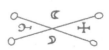

Gavin's gun went flying as the creature seized his wrist; he drew Gavin toward him with a growl, twisting the wrist hard as he did so. There was a faint crackle of tendons. Gavin grimaced in pain but did not scream; he stared, as if in shock.

Constance remained frozen. *So this*, she thought with a strange detachment, *is Morax—the demon.* And yet it was human, or mostly so. A tall man with a dreadfully deformed face: a prognathic snout, with projecting teeth that pushed out from behind rubbery lips, and a sloped forehead with a massive sagittal crest that rose up like a bony Mohawk across his knobby skull. His skin was sallow and streaked with filth, his yellow skin puckered with pustules, scabs, and a thousand tiny scars; his eyes were a dark orangey brown; his body was ropy; he was bald and naked; and his stink filled the perfumed confines of the altar room. But the tail—the tail—was what most arrested her attention. It wasn't a typical animal tail, but rather a long rope of pink flesh that was utterly limp, its club-like end bristling with wiry hairs. The tail had no life; it dragged behind him like a flaccid, paralyzed limb.

The man gripped Gavin's wrist with a hand as massive as a bear paw, with spade-like fingers terminating in brown nails. He stared at Gavin, his pupils contracted with hate. The two seemed momentarily frozen in a grotesque tableau.

And then the creature made a sound, an angry hissing sound, which broke the spell.

Gavin, wincing, spoke with remarkable presence of mind. "It's all right, Morax. Everything's going to be fine. You're home now. Let go of me, please."

Morax repeated the guttural hiss. It sounded like *shunnng*, or *sohnn*, but Constance couldn't catch it.

"You're hurting me," said Gavin. "Please let go."

In response, Morax gave Gavin's wrist another savage twist. There was a sharp cracking sound. The sergeant gasped, but—much to Constance's surprise—kept his composure.

Even if she had not heard Gavin's story, it would have been obvious that these two had a long and troubled history—a history, it seemed, that was about to reach its end, one way or another.

The two were so focused on each other that Constance realized she had an opportunity to escape—if she moved carefully. The way by which she had first entered the chamber, however, was blocked by the two antagonists. She would have to escape deeper into the tunnels.

She took a step back, and then another, careful to keep her eye on the confrontation.

"Morax," Gavin said, "I'm now the leader of the coven, which means that we're partners, in a way. It was wrong, what's been done to you over the years, and—"

With a sudden roar, the creature yanked Gavin's hand and wrenched it off as he might a turkey drumstick. Blood spurted from the ragged wrist. With a cry Gavin staggered back, frantically trying to stop the bleeding, now wide-eyed with terror. The demon roared again.

Constance walked calmly and slowly along the rear wall of the room. The two were so fixated on their struggle that they had forgotten about her completely. Whatever was going to happen to Gavin, it wasn't good, and she did not particularly wish to see it. The creature was as swollen as a toad with incandescent hatred.

"Please," Gavin said, his voice breaking. "We respect you, you're very important to us... I'm so, so sorry about what happened. It'll all be different now, with me in control." He held out his good hand in a gesture of supplication.

Morax, enraged by this speech, roared incoherently and seized the other wrist, twisting it hard; this time Gavin broke down, issuing a shrill scream and sinking to his knees; and that was the last Constance saw of him as she slipped around the corner into the darkness of the central corridor and the deeper tunnels beyond.

53

Pendergast paused at the lip of a low sand dune and gazed down into the ruins of Oldham, which lay in a scrubby hollow scattered with deformed pine trees. The storm was abating, with the rain having temporarily ceased and the wind dying. But the sea continued to pound the shingle beach with ferocity. A full moon appeared fitfully, casting a feeble gloom through the ruins, the walls half buried, the scattered cellar holes, the bits of crockery and sea glass gleaming dully in the wet sand.

The creature's tracks had been almost obliterated, but there were still indentations in the sand and shingle that Pendergast was able to follow—some of which were the creature's, along with smaller ones that he felt certain belonged to Constance.

From the position of the cellar holes, Pendergast was able to determine where the main street had once passed through town. At the far end he saw a broken brick wall on a larger foundation of granite blocks: undoubtedly the ruins of Oldham's church. He walked to the edge of the church's cellar hole, a deep basement area faced with cleaved blocks, scattered with loose bricks, wood planks, trash, and—at the rear—a rotten canvas sailcloth.

He climbed down into the ruined cellar and shone his light around, quickly focusing his attention on an uncovered iron plate at one end, near the sailcloth. Going over to it, he knelt and examined the hinges. A close examination revealed it had been used—and often. He lifted it carefully, making no noise, and shone his penlight in. A narrow stone staircase led down to a damp tunnel, which in turn snaked off into darkness.

Hooding his light, he slipped inside, easing the plate shut behind him. Switching off the light, he crouched on the stairs, listening intently; the sounds of the surf were now muffled, but no noise appeared to issue from underground: only the rising stench of death and decay, overlaid with a faint scent of burning wax.

He drew his Les Baer and listened once again. Still nothing.

Switching the penlight back on, he examined the stairs and saw clear signs of recent passage, including sand, moisture from the storm, and a partial—but clear—bare print. Once again, he felt a deep disturbance at this; it was an incontrovertible sign of how he had overlooked crucial evidence. But even as he sorted through that evidence in his mind, he could not arrive at an explanation for the sudden appearance of a monstrous, barefoot mass murderer in Exmouth, or why it had chosen this moment to unleash its ferocity on the town.

Deep anxiety for Constance's safety warred with caution inside him as he descended the stairs and crept forward, moving cat-like along the tunnel. Scratchings, both ancient and fresh—pictographs, demonic figures, symbols, odd Latin phrases—all mingled together on the walls.

And then he heard it: an animalistic murmur, a sibilant, quasi-human utterance. He froze, listening. The sound was distorted by the web of tunnels. Now came a voice, pleading and indistinct, again too unclear to make out the words or even the sex of the speaker.

A beast-like roar echoed through the tunnels. Another roar came rolling down, and then in response, a reasonable-sounding voice, pleading, first quietly and then louder and louder, ending at last in a high-pitched, horribly distorted scream.

Pendergast broke into a run; the tunnel divided and he took the right fork, heading in the direction the sound seemed to have issued from. But there was another fork in the tunnel, which he again took, only to be halted by a cul-de-sac. He turned and retraced his steps even as a second hideous scream reverberated; it was a male voice, he could tell that now, but its terror was so profound that its owner could never have been recognized.

But where was Constance?

Turning down yet another passageway, his flashlight beam reflected off what appeared to be a pool of blood; he raised the light to reveal two corpses, lying on their backs, limbs splayed, eyes wide open. He recognized them both as inhabitants of Exmouth: one was the fisherman who had given Constance a ride to the police station, the other he had seen one evening at the bar at the Inn. Both had been torn apart in the most horrifying and brutal way imaginable. Bloody bare footprints led away from the mess. Pendergast examined the scene with his flashlight. It told a horrifying story indeed.

And then, as if to underscore the horror, the fresh sounds of torture and pain came rolling down the tunnels.

Constance Greene felt her way along the slick walls of the tunnel with both hands. She had left behind what dim light there was, and she was now cloaked in a profound darkness. Her hands were still cuffed, and her stiletto was tucked once again into a pocket of her dress. The sounds of extreme agony and torture continued to echo through the tunnels. Constance had seen and heard many unpleasant things in her lifetime, but few if any were as sickening as what was clearly transpiring behind her.

The sounds were now dying out, as Gavin evidently sank into death. She turned her attention back to the problem at hand—escaping from this hellhole and the insane creature that tenanted it. She hoped—although common sense told her it was unlikely—there might be a second exit at the far end of the tunnels. If not, then perhaps there might be a place in which she could hide and wait for an opportunity to slip out.

As she moved deeper into the underground complex, the stench lessened somewhat, replaced with earthy smells of fungus, mold, and damp. The problem was that she had become disoriented in the darkness of this new set of tunnels, and was unsure how to return the way she had come. But the darkness did not frighten her—she was used to it and, in some ways, even found it a comfort—and she felt confident in her ability to merge with the dark, become one with the walls. In time, the disorientation would also turn to familiarity...if she were allowed that time.

And now, with one final chuckle of anguish from behind her, silence descended. The demon was finished with Gavin, and he was gone.

54

He held up his hands. They were red and wet. He licked them. They tasted like the bars of his cage. He looked down. The head of the Bad One lay upside down, tongue dangling, eyes open.

He smelled the air, and there were strange smells. The girl had run away.

He took his big toe and poked the head in the eye. He was looking at something far away. Very far away.

Where was the girl?

He sniffed the air. He wanted her out. This was his home. This was his territory. Not hers. He had gotten rid of the hated faces. They would come no more. This place was his now.

He walked past the altar and pinched out the light. Now it was dark. Darkness was his friend. It made others stupid and afraid.

The girl was going into the Dead Ends.

His chains were gone. The strange one had suddenly appeared, warning him of the Killing Men who were coming for him, and then broken his lock. He was free now. He could go anywhere—even to the Above Place. But he *had been to the Above Place...and it was not as they had promised. They had lied. What he had dreamed about all his life was a lie. Like everything else they said. The sun, they had called it. All the pain they caused him, the Blooding Knife and the rest, they said would be made up for when, one day, they would take him to the Sun, the warm fire in the sky. Darkness gone, light everywhere.*

Thinking of this, thinking of the pain, thinking of the lies, thinking of the cold blackness he had found in the Above Place, just like here, the rage came back. Stronger than ever.

He went toward the Dead Ends. After the woman.

55

∞

From the time of her childhood, Constance had been no stranger to the dark. Despite the disorientation, she moved with a sense of purpose.

The walls were damp and dripping. Sometimes her fingers encountered spiders or millipedes that scrambled off in a panic when she brushed past them. She could hear rats, too, rustling softly, squeaking and skittering out of her way. The air smelled increasingly of fungus, slime, and rot. There was no movement of air, less and less oxygen. Clearly, there was no outlet in this direction.

Feeling along the wall, she came to a corner. She paused, listening. The only sound she could hear was the low rumble of surf, the vibration moving through the ground itself, and the faint drip-drip of water. All was quiet.

She slipped around the corner, her feet finding purchase on the damp floor, her hands tracing the wall. She brushed past an insect—a centipede—and it fell down her sleeve, wriggling frantically against her skin, and she paused to gently shake it out. She once again considered trying to find a place to hide, but rejected that as a strategy of last resort;

the demon Morax certainly knew these tunnels better than she. With only a stiletto, and her hands shackled, she had no hope of killing him. After what he'd done to Gavin—what she had seen, and what she had heard—she knew she could expect the same from the creature.

There was no escape in this direction. She would have to get past Morax and get out the way she had come in.

A. X. L. Pendergast turned away from the two eviscerated bodies. He backtracked and ran down a side tunnel in the direction the screams had come from, even as they now died away with an ominous rapidity. But almost immediately he came to another division in the tunnel; he paused to listen intently, but in the fresh silence was no longer able to determine from which direction the screams had come.

The extent of the tunnels surprised him. They appeared to have been constructed over a long period of time, perhaps even centuries—clearly, the style of their building changed from one section to another, indicating the work of many years. They had a similar feeling to the catacombs that he had once explored in Rome: a secret place of worship. But there was more to these tunnels, as the bizarre symbols on the walls, the smell of occupation, and other stenches far worse, would attest.

Examining the ground, he took the left-hand branch, as that seemed to his eye the more traveled. It, too, branched several times, but he continued to stay on the more beaten path. After a few minutes, the tunnel turned a corner and he found himself staring at prison bars blocking the way ahead. Set into the bars was a metal door that yawned open. The smell emanating from the cul-de-sac beyond was so foul that it suggested long occupation with an utter lack of either hygiene or toilet facilities.

He flashed his light into the rude cell and saw it ran about a hundred feet back, ending in a wall, with a sleeping area of filthy straw, an overflowing hole for necessities, and a broken table. A steel collar, studded with sharp points, was fastened to a leash of metal links. It was hanging on one of the bare stone walls. Kneeling, he observed the traces of the occupant in the damp, sandy floor—a welter of human bare feet, matching the prints he had been tracking from Exmouth. This was where the killer had been locked up—for a very long time.

He straightened and, shining his penlight, glanced at the padlock that once held the door, now lying open on the ground. What had initially been a cursory inspection suddenly became riveted attention. He picked up the lock and gave it a minute inspection, at one point removing his portable loupe and examining the mechanism. It was an almost new Abloy shrouded steel padlock with a top-loading cylinder, invulnerable to bumping. A most serious lock indeed, and one that would have challenged even Pendergast himself. Yet he could see that it had been interfered with in a subtle, clever, and devious way, so as to make it appear locked when it wasn't.

Something about the particular method of interference seemed chillingly familiar.

After completing his inspection, he stepped inside the prison and walked to the far end of the cul-de-sac, stepping over filth, old chicken carcasses, pieces of rotting hide, and broken marrow bones. Greasy cockroaches scurried away from the beam of his light. Against the far wall, manacles, cuffs, and chains lay sprawled on the ground, open. These also were advanced, high-tech devices, of recent manufacture. Each manacle and cuff had its own small lock; Pendergast once again examined each lock in turn, his pale features becoming like marble.

The jailers had gone to great care and expense to keep the prisoner absolutely secure. But on their last approach to this jail, they would not have known the locks on the cuffs and manacles had been tampered with—that the creature would be able to free itself and attack them.

No doubt those jailers were the two bodies he had come across in an earlier passage.

As he examined the final lock, his normally steady hand began to tremble, and he dropped the chain. His knees gave way and he sank to the ground in disbelief.

A sound reached his ears. After a long moment, he shook off his paralysis and rose to his feet. Constance was still somewhere in this complex of tunnels—and now, it seemed she was in far greater danger than he had realized.

Forcing his mind back to the issue at hand, he leapt up and raced through the dank corridors, again following the main path, heedless now of the noise that he made. After several twists and turns he arrived at a wide passage leading to a large, ponderously decorated, pentagonal room, lit by candles and dominated by an altar. He stopped, peering around with his silvery eyes. A ropy tangle of flesh and bone lay on the altar. It was so distorted it took Pendergast a moment to realize the tangle had once been human. A muscle was still twitching: a neurological artifact. The man was very recently dead. But where was the killer who had just completed this work of death and dismemberment?

He spun around, Les Baer in hand, flicking his light into the darker alcoves as he moved across the altar room; but even before his light had reached the final alcove, the figure he had earlier seen assault Mourdock—naked, bestial, yellow—exploded out of a dark corner. Pendergast swung the handgun around and squeezed off a round, but the figure did a curious, cringing flip that avoided the shot while at the same time striking a blow at Pendergast with one foot, smashing the weapon out of his hand. Pendergast half turned to absorb the blow and dealt the man-creature a sharp punch to the midriff as he rotated past, tail lashing him across the face. Pendergast rolled, braced, then crouched, pulling a modified Fairbairn-Sykes fighting knife with a short fixed blade from its strap on one calf, but the creature took advantage of the movement to come back at him low, then leap at him with a growl. They fell to the ground, the creature on top of him; Pendergast tried to stick him with the knife but the brute seized the blade in a massive hand and tried to wrest it from his hand, gripping the steel, blood running freely. Forced to drop the flashlight, struggling to keep his attention on the fight at hand while holding his new, fresh concern at bay, Pendergast tried to work the blade through the clutching fingers. The flashlight rolled against the wall, still casting a feeble light. As they struggled over the knife, the stinking demon opened his muzzle and, with broken black teeth, seized the corner of Pendergast's ear and bit through it with a crunch of cartilage. The action momentarily relieved Pendergast of the pinning weight of the beast, and he kneed him in the chest with a sound of cracking ribs; with a roar the demon tore the knife out of Pendergast's hands, severing several of his own fingers in doing so, then lowered his head and attempted to ram Pendergast up against the wall. But Pendergast slipped sideways, more nimble than any bullfighter, and the demon rammed himself against the stone

56

It was textbook. As Rivera gazed out on the scene, it appeared just as in all the disaster and terrorist drills they had done dozens of times back in Lawrence and Boston. The entire town was essentially being treated as a crime scene, with MRAPs securing all points of ingress and egress, the medics clustered around the motionless bodies, the ambulances quietly coming and going, the SWAT team members engaged in patrol, questioning the unhurt victims, and surveillance in place on the chance the killer returned. It was the very picture of purposeful activity. An increasingly restive crowd of reporters and vans were being held back at the Metacomet Bridge, and they would have to be appeased soon or they would really go nuts. The airspace had been temporarily restricted over the town, but television choppers hovered over the marshes and circled about just outside the restricted zone, ready to rush in as soon as they were cleared.

The additional men, the strangely comforting routine, had helped take some of the edge off Rivera's undercurrent of tension—not to say anxiety—over just how strange this situation was. Despite everything, they were no closer to understanding what had actually happened, identifying the killer, or understanding his motive. If any of the witnesses were to be believed, it was a monstrous, humanoid creature, naked, filthy, with a snout and tail, that moved as fast as a wolf and dismembered its victims with massive, tearing hands.

Right.

Except that they had found countless size 16 footprints—bare—throughout the town, inside the homes that had been invaded, many printed in blood. One killer. Not a crazy mob, not a riot, not a rampaging gang of terrorists. Just one killer seemed to have done all this. As for witness descriptions of that killer, Rivera chalked a fair amount of that up to hysteria and terror. But not all of it. Some crazy, large, and undoubtedly costumed killer had rampaged through town. But who he was, why he had done it, where he had come from, and where he had gone were mysteries yet to be solved.

One killer. Rivera's nerves spiked again.

There had been a crucial development: one bright-eyed officer had noted a security camera in front of a clothing store that the killer must have passed several times. The camera was recording 24/7, and it was low-light capable. Best of all, it switched to battery backup during a power failure. Rivera's team had broken into the store and collected the digital footage, and they were now processing it at the mobile command center. The footage was overly dark due to the lack of ambient light, but it was currently being enhanced, and it was supposed to be ready...he checked his watch...now.

Until he could see that footage, Rivera simply refused to speculate on how a single individual, barefoot no less, could have perpetrated all this death and destruction. This was something completely outside his experience, and he needed to reserve judgment...at least until he had seen that footage with his own eyes.

He raised his radio. "Gil?"

"Yes, sir?"

"Is that footage ready?"

"Um, well, sort of, but I gotta tell you—"

"Don't tell me anything. I want to see it fresh, without any preconceptions."

"Right, sir."

Gil didn't sound his usual cocky self. Rivera hung up the radio and walked toward the command center: a mobile container set atop a tractor-trailer rig. He mounted the steps and entered to find things strangely silent. It didn't take ESP to sense that the level of tension in the room was through the roof.

"What do you have?" he asked.

A number of edgy glances were exchanged. Gil, the video operator, nodded toward a screen. "This is the feed from the store camera. It was dark, but all the digital information was there, waiting to come out. It covers the area in front of the store, the sidewalk and part of the street. It caught the, the perp both coming and going down the street. Time stamp's in the lower-right corner. The first segment starts at 21:23, and the next at 22:04."

"Let's see the first segment."

A hesitation. "Okay."

Rivera folded his arms and watched the monitor. At first there was nothing to see, just a fish-eye view of the empty sidewalk, the edge of the storefront, and the street. The town was in blackout and there were no streetlights, but the camera had recorded a grainy, reddish image that was surprisingly clear. Suddenly, there was a movement and a figure strode across the monitor. It took less than a second—but that was enough.

"What the *fuck*?" Rivera said.

Silence.

"It's a guy in a mask and suit," Rivera said.

No one responded until Gil, in a weak voice, said, "I'll go through it frame by frame."

Rivera stared as the feed was rerun and replayed, this time at one frame per second. The perp—if it could be called that—came into view again, walking in a fast shamble down the sidewalk toward town.

"Freeze it!" Rivera barked.

Gil froze the image.

"I don't believe this. Go one frame back."

The operator complied.

"I don't fucking believe it. Can you magnify that face?"

The face was magnified.

Rivera squinted, looking close. "That's no mask."

"No," Gil said.

No one else spoke.

Rivera licked dry lips. "Continue."

He watched the frame-by-frame in deepening shock and disbelief. It was pretty much as the witnesses had said—a deformed monster with a tail. No, he said to himself, *not* a monster: this was a human being, a freakishly deformed man. The view was from diagonally and above, which accentuated the doglike, bucktoothed snout. But instead of a dog's nose it had a human nose, squashed like a prizefighter's. The man's face was splattered with blood and gore, slowly being washed away by the rain. Its expression positively glowed with hatred, the eyes like slits, the mouth open, showing a swollen pink tongue from which hung a rope of drool. It strode along with a sense of purpose that chilled Rivera to the bone simply because it was so intentional. There was no insanity here, nothing random: this was a brute with a plan. And there they were—those gigantic, splayed bare feet with the three-inch toenails, the tracks of which they'd found everywhere.

Gil cleared his throat. "I'll advance it to the next segment, with him coming back after the massacre—"

Rivera straightened up. "I don't need to see any more. I want dogs. Tracking dogs. The son of a bitch went into the salt marshes and we're going after him."

"Lieutenant?"

He turned in time to see a striking, dark-skinned individual—who'd been in a far corner, giving a statement to one of Rivera's men—step forward.

"Who are you?" Rivera asked.

"Paul Silas. Live out past Dill Town. I couldn't help overhear what you just said. If you're going into the marshlands, you better have someone who knows his way around or you aren't ever gonna come out."

Rivera looked at the man. He had an air of quiet competence about him. "You telling me you know these marshes?"

"A bit. Nobody knows it all."

"You see that thing on the screen?"

"I did."

"And you still want to help us?"

Silas cast an eye out the command center, over the darkness of town, then turned back to Rivera. "I surely do."

57

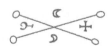

In the perfect dark, Constance listened to the sounds of the struggle. As intently as she listened, she couldn't determine who the demon was fighting, only that it must be someone tenacious and powerful. But as the clash of battle progressed, as the demon roared in what sounded like increasing triumph, she sensed the monster's foe was losing—and when the sounds died away and silence returned, it was only the demon's loud snuffling she heard. The other one was evidently dead, which did not surprise her.

Constance reviewed her situation. She had spent many of her younger years in a dark basement not unlike this one, and had once possessed an exquisite sense of hearing and smell, as well as keen night vision. She knew how to move in total silence. Those senses, dulled more than she'd expected by normal living, quickened somewhat in the dark and looming danger of the tunnels. She could not see—there was no light at all—but she could hear.

The creature was snuffling again, loudly, like a dog with its nose in the air, trying to catch a scent—her scent. But the air was dead, with no movement at all; that was to her advantage.

With extreme care she moved away from the sound, one hand sliding lightly along the wall as she went, feet probing gently ahead so as to make no noise. The wall of the tunnel made a turn, and another turn, and yet another; soon she came to a dead end and had to retrace her steps. At another point, she came to a heap of old bones that quietly crumbled under her touch while she worked her way past them.

She sensed she had entered an underground maze of crisscrossing tunnels, alcoves, and culs-de-sac. Again, the air was completely dead, the atmosphere one of staleness and desuetude. There was a lot of old refuse on the ground, and the walls were crawling with centipedes, spiders, and pill bugs. It seemed these were long-abandoned tunnels that, perhaps, the creature might be less familiar with. What she needed to do was maneuver past it, somehow, and then get out—with all possible speed.

As she listened, she heard more snuffling and labored breathing, and it occurred to her that the demon might be injured. She felt increasingly certain that it was looking for her.

She began moving again, not knowing where she was going, her aim now merely to keep away from the creature. But even as she moved, the sounds ceased. She continued down one long tunnel segment, then froze: she could hear him moving, breathing hard, ahead of her and headed in her direction. Pressing herself against the wall, she waited, holding her breath. The sounds came closer, along with a grotesque and now-familiar stench that seemed to envelop her...a shuffling of feet on the sandy floor...and then he had passed by, following the path of an intersecting tunnel.

She exhaled. The demon didn't seem to have as keen a sense of smell as she had feared. Or had it deliberately passed her by? Either way, this was her chance. If she moved in the

58

Rivera stood near Chief Mourdock's squad car, watching the handler work the dogs. The man had arrived in record time, accompanied by two powerful redbone coonhounds, which, he claimed, were especially suited for work in swamps and water. Rivera sure hoped so; even from here, he could see that the tide was coming in fast.

The enigmatic Paul Silas stood off to one side, tall and silent. Rivera wondered if he'd made the right choice in accepting his help. True, the man did have a faint air of the military about him. And as he looked out again over the dark salt marshes—thrashing in the wind, tatters of mist whisked along in the dying storm—he realized he had no desire to venture into that hell without guidance.

As he'd waited for the dog handler, he'd worked out the basic sequence. The killer, after first wreaking havoc in the town, had gone on to kill Chief Mourdock here on Dune Road, and then disappeared southward. With much loud baying the dogs had picked up the trail from the squad car and were even now beginning to follow it into the marsh.

Silas began following the dogs and Rivera hurried to catch

up to him, Rivera with a flashlight, Silas with a headlamp. They were preceded by five heavily armed members of the SWAT team and an officer carrying a powerful beacon that shot a brilliant beam of light a hundred yards ahead.

The dog handler was a big man with a red beard, wearing a Red Sox cap and bundled in a slicker. His name was Mike Kenney and he seemed to know what he was doing. The dogs, too, looked like they meant business. Kenney had them both on long leashes and was firmly in control. The dogs were following the trail without hesitation, charging ahead confidently and pulling Kenney along.

Rivera continued following the SWAT team, Silas at his side. He had a waterproof GPS that promised to show them exactly where they were.

"Any idea where he's headed?" Rivera asked Silas.

"He seems to be making a beeline across the marshes. Which would bring him out on Crow Island."

"And what's out there?"

"Nothing but scrub pines, sand dunes, some ruins, and a beach. Most of the island's a wildlife refuge."

"So what's ahead I ought to know about?" He was staring at his GPS, but he couldn't seem to translate the neat green-and-yellow map to the howling wilderness they were in. Kenney and the dogs had disappeared into a sea of salt grass, followed by the SWAT team, and he could hear the dogs baying up ahead. As they proceeded, the baying of the dogs seemed to ratchet up a notch.

"Well," said Silas, "if he keeps up this line, he's heading for the Stackyard Channel."

"Which is?"

"That's the main tidal channel of the marsh. The tide runs through there pretty hard. We're at three-quarter incoming tide, which is when the current peaks. It'll be running five, six knots."

"Can we wade it?"

Silas gave a snort. "At this tide you can't even swim it."

"So he'll be stopped? Turned aside?"

"If the killer came through an hour or two ago, say, the tide would've been a lot lower. So he maybe swam it. We'll need a boat."

Rivera cursed himself for not thinking of this before. He unhooked his radio and called the command center.

"Barber, I want you to get the two Zodiacs into the water, ASAP. Send them into the Stackyard Channel. You'll find it on the survey map."

He described what he wanted and, using his GPS, emailed waypoints to the command center showing exactly where they would need the boats. At least the team had brought a trailer with the two Zodiacs. They could be put in at the town landing in a matter of minutes, and—with their powerful engines and the tide in their favor—Rivera figured it would take less than ten minutes for them to reach the rendezvous point.

"Channel's up ahead," said Silas.

A moment later, Rivera and his men emerged onto the channel bank. He looked ahead across fifty feet of powerful, black, swift-moving current, its surface swirling with nasty eddies and upwellings. The wind howled across the water, lashing the cattails and bringing with it a gust of stinging rain. The beacon light pierced the gloom and illuminated the far embankment, where he could make out tracks in the mud.

"Looks like he swam," said Silas.

"It's going to be a bitch landing a boat along this embankment."

Silas nodded.

"You got any idea why he's heading out here? Seems he knows where he's going."

Silas shook his head.

Rivera gestured at the channel. "Any more like this?"

"Just a lot more marsh grass and a couple mudflats before you reach the scrub."

Kenney was struggling with the dogs now, trying to pull them back from the edge. The dogs sounded almost insane with frustration at not being allowed to leap into the water. Kenney, who until now had been speaking to them in a low calm voice, was starting to lose his cool.

Rivera went over. "We have two boats coming. Zodiacs."

"I hope to hell they get here soon," the handler replied. "I've never seen the dogs so excited."

More full-throated baying came from the dogs, who were pulling hard on the leashes. Kenney spoke to them sharply. The tide bore along, deep and powerful, between the banks; woe to any dog or man who was caught in it.

Rivera's radio crackled. "About half a mile from your waypoint," said the dispatcher. Rivera looked upstream and after a moment was able to glimpse, through the rain, a white light, flanked by green and red.

"Kenney," he said, "you and the dogs get in the first boat. We'll take the other."

"Right."

"Be careful. This is going to be a little hairy."

The lead Zodiac came into the beam of the beacon, the pilot bringing the boat past their position and then pushing the tiller to the right, turning the boat upcurrent and coming into the embankment at a slower pace, the engine raised slightly and churning the water.

"Dogs first!" Rivera shouted.

The boat moved parallel to shore, slipping closer. The dogs, still frenziedly pulling at their leashes, did not look like they knew what to do. Kenney reined the leashes in tight and ordered: "Jump in! Jump in!" For a moment, it looked like both animals were going to leap over the rubber gunnels at the same time, but then—at the last instant—one pulled back. With a shout, Kenney and the dog were thrown into the boiling water.

"Life ring!" Rivera cried. "Throw him the life ring!" By the harsh light of the beacon, Rivera could see Kenney's pale face sweeping along with the current. Not far away, the coonhound was paddling furiously and aimlessly, eyes bulging, screeching in terror, paws thumping the water. The dog, dragging its leash, was being spun around in a powerful eddy, its dangling tongue whipsawing, while Kenney tried to swim toward it. The dog's screech turned into a hideous gargle as the Zodiac pilot gunned the engine and headed toward Kenney, the other dog still in the boat, barking frantically and looking as if it would jump out at any moment. In seconds the Zodiac had closed in on Kenney and the life ring was tossed; Kenney seized it and was pulled close, then bodily hauled over the gunnel by the pilot and mate together.

"Get the dog!" he screamed.

The pilot swung the boat around, aiming for the churning, eddying white water. But even before they reached it the dog went under; the last thing Rivera saw were floppy ears and a lolling tongue, glistening in the beacon's brilliance; then, finally, two rotating paws that were quickly sucked beneath the gray, roiling surface.

Kenney let out a wail of despair and had to be restrained from jumping into the water after it; the boat circled and circled, but the dog did not reappear.

Rivera got on the radio. "Bring them to the other side," he told the pilot. "We've got to keep going, even with the one dog."

"Yes, sir."

"Bring the second boat in."

The second Zodiac, which had been too far away to assist, came in now and turned upcurrent, easing into shore. The men jumped in, Rivera last, and they set out across the channel. A moment later they buried their nose in the mud of the far embankment, next to the first Zodiac, and in another moment were back on land.

"My dog!" Kenney was screaming. "We've got to go back out and look for my dog!"

Rivera grabbed him by the arm and shook him. "Your dog's gone. We've got a job to do."

The man, his cap dripping wet, his clothes sodden, stared back at him uncomprehendingly. No way was he in any shape to continue. Rivera turned to one of the men. "Okay, take Mr. Kenney back to the command center. We're keeping the dog."

"No, no!" Kenney protested. "Only I handle the dogs!"

"Take Kenney back!" Rivera seized the leash. "Let's go."

They set off through the salt grass, Rivera leaving Kenney behind, protesting loudly. Silas, swift and silent, continued at his side. The remaining dog had picked up the trail again and was surging forward with a fresh frenzy of baying, his powerful stride practically eating up the ground as they moved along.

"Looks like he's definitely headed for the southern end of Crow Island," Silas said.

"Yeah, but what the hell is out there for him?" asked Rivera.

"Well, if we keep to this bearing, we'll end up in the ruins of Oldham."

"Oldham?"

"An ancient fishing village that washed away in a hurricane back in the '30s. Nothing there now but cellar holes and..."

"And what?"

Silas gave a snort of derision. "That depends on whether or not you believe the legends."

59

C onstance struggled only momentarily, as she felt a warm breath in her ear and the whispered word: "Aloysius."

She relaxed and he released her.

"We must get out," he whispered into her ear. "We're no match for the killer on his own ground."

"I quite agree," she said, feeling awkward despite the intense danger of the situation. "However, I'm lost."

"As am I, unfortunately."

This struck Constance as surprising. "You're lost?"

"I was...distracted. Do you know where the killer is?"

"He went past a few moments ago. Perhaps I can hear him. One moment." She fell silent. At the very edge of audibility she could hear the faint sounds of the creature, breathing hard and moving about. He was most certainly wounded. The sounds moved back and forth as the thing searched for them. "Do you hear that?" she asked.

"I'm afraid not. Your ears are keener than mine."

More silence as she listened. The sounds were distorted by the tunnels, and eventually they faded away. She waited, but they did not reappear.

"He seems to have moved away from us."

"As I feared."

She didn't ask what he feared; it was exactly the kind of question he would refuse to answer. He finally spoke, his voice remaining a whisper in her ear. "You have more experience in dark tunnels than I. Do you have any ideas on a way out?"

From this, Constance understood that, due to her many years of wandering the subterranean tunnels and basements of 891 Riverside Drive, the burden of escape was on her shoulders. "One, perhaps. Have you heard of John Pledge of Exeter, England?"

"No. Make the lesson short."

"Pledge was a hedge-maze enthusiast. He devised a way for anyone to get out of the hardest kind of disjoint maze. One starts in an arbitrary direction, keeping a hand on the right wall, and counting the turns. After four turns, if all are right angles, the hand is removed from the wall and one continues in the original direction until another wall—"

Constance felt Pendergast place his finger to her lips. "Just give me your hand and lead the way."

She gave him her hand and he murmured in surprise. "Your hands are shackled."

"Yes. And yours are wet. Is that blood?"

"It's nothing. Hold up your hands, please."

She felt him work on the cuffs. One dropped off, and then the other.

"Are you hurt?" she asked.

"I repeat: *it's nothing*." He spoke sharply. "Do not mention it again."

After a moment, he spoke once more. "Forgive my sharp tone. Constance…you were right and I was wrong. Things were happening here in Exmouth on two levels—one on a far deeper level of evil than the other. It's nothing I've come across in the serial-killer cases I have worked. I simply did not see it."

"Never mind," she replied, the feeling of awkwardness returning.

He hesitated, as if about to say something more, but instead simply indicated that she should lead the way.

She started down the passageway, feeling along the wall with one hand, holding Pendergast's hand with the other, and probing ahead with her feet. The tunnels were silent; the sounds of the demon had disappeared. She continued to follow the Pledge system, counting the turns, the task made much easier by the fact that almost all the corners were right angles.

Pendergast halted. "The air is fresher here," he said. "Less foul."

"So I noticed."

"Listen again, if you please," he whispered.

She listened, straining to hear any sound beyond the muffled vibration of surf and the dripping of water. "Nothing."

"I feared as much. I'm sure of it now: he's lying in wait. The logical place would be at the entrance to these tunnels. So here's what's going to happen: I will go first. He will attack. When he does, I will divert him while you run past and out. I will mount a rearguard action."

"You know quite well I won't leave you."

"If you don't, we'll both perish. Please do as I tell you."

"I have my knife."

"Give it to me."

She fumbled it out of the folds of her dress and handed it to him.

"I want your promise: you will run past and keep running."

"Very well," she lied.

Then, as she was about to lead onward, he hesitated again.

"What is it?" she asked.

"This is a damned awkward time to tell you this, but it must be said."

She felt her heart accelerate.

"You must be prepared for a confrontation, Constance."

"I'm ready."

There was a brief pause. "No. Not *this* confrontation. Another."

"I don't understand."

"If something should happen to me...assume nothing."

"What do you mean?"

Pendergast paused in the darkness. "Someone's been here. Someone I fear that I—that *we*—know only too well."

In the dark, Constance felt herself turn cold. "Who?" But from his voice she already had an idea who he meant. The cold abruptly became incendiary.

"I found the creature's shackles and the lock to his prison door had been tampered with. Most cleverly. Why? There's a perverse logic at work here...and I'm all too certain I know what that logic is."

"Does this have to do with the figure in the dunes?"

Pendergast shook away the question. "Yes, but there's no time to explain. Please listen. I have complete trust in Proctor. If something should happen to me, put yourself in his hands. He'll be to you all that I am now, your guardian and protector. And I repeat: no matter what happens, no matter how things seem, *assume nothing.*"

"But, Aloysius—" she began, but fell silent when she felt his finger on her lips.

Pendergast then pressed her hand, directing her to continue down the tunnel.

60

They continued their circuitous route, turn after turn after turn. It wasn't long until Constance noticed the air was cooler and appeared to have some movement: they must be very close to the entrance now. While fresher, it still had a foul reek to it—the same foul reek that came from the beast.

Pendergast, she realized, must have come to the same conclusion, because he stopped and—using touch alone—directed her to take a position behind him.

Moving slower, in absolute silence, they proceeded. They were now in a long, straight tunnel that, she assumed, led to the outside world. After a minute, she gestured for Pendergast to stop once again so that she could listen.

She could hear labored breathing. The beast was evidently trying to control it, but he couldn't quite stop the sound of wheezing. He was just ahead. She indicated his presence to Pendergast with a faint touch of hand pressure. Pressure back told her Pendergast had also heard it.

He released her hand and, tracing letters on her palm, spelled out with painstaking slowness:

ON THREE I RUSH
YOU FOLLOW
I ENGAGE
KEEP RUNNING

She squeezed her understanding. He held her hand, tapped out 1, 2, and 3—and then in a flash he seemed to disappear, as silent and quick as a bat in a cave. She followed at a run, blind, hands stretched out in front of her.

A sudden roar split the air right directly before her, followed by the sound of a knife ripping through flesh—a butcher-shop sound—and then the thud and crash of a desperate struggle. She ran past and was about to stop when she heard Pendergast shout: "Keep going, I'm right behind you!"

They sprinted on in the darkness, still blind, while, a moment later, Constance heard the creature renew its pursuit with high-pitched screams. It sounded as if Pendergast had dealt it a savage blow, but it was clearly far from being down.

And then Constance saw a glow of light ahead, and the stone stairs materialized. She stopped and turned to see Pendergast running toward her.

"Keep going!" he cried again, leaping past her, racing up the steps, and ramming open the iron trapdoor with one shoulder. He pivoted and pulled her up and out, slammed the iron door closed, and then hauled her out of the cellar hole and into the ruins of Oldham. As they ran toward the beach, Constance heard the demon burst through the iron door with an unholy screech.

They had just passed the dunes and reached the level beach when the demon caught up; Pendergast turned to face him with the knife, warning Constance to keep going. But instead she stopped and turned to see Pendergast and the demon come together with a violent clash, locking in a fearful embrace: Pendergast with the knife raised, Morax—missing two fingers now—struggling to disarm him, the whole ghastly scene illuminated in the predawn light of morning. The storm had abated but the surf remained violent; great rollers leapt up with blowing spume, then crashed down and swept their way up the beach. The air was full of atomized seawater.

She stared, unable for the moment to react. She saw with horror that Pendergast had been badly hurt. His shirtfront was torn, and one side of his face was cut and bleeding. The demon twisted and turned, the two struggling for dominance; but the huge demon prevailed and finally tore the stiletto away from Pendergast, throwing it into the sea. He swung at Pendergast with a great ropy arm; Pendergast dodged the blow but, clearly weakened by his injuries, was thrown off balance. The demon raked him cruelly with a massive hand, tearing through his clothing and reducing it to bloody tatters.

Pendergast retreated and the two parried and thrust, the fight driving both of them into the swash zone. Pendergast backed into the water, almost as a deliberate strategy, seeking some kind of advantage. But the strategy failed; with a mighty blow, Morax knocked Pendergast down into the surging water. As he struggled to regain his feet, the demon reared above him and raised a massive hand, preparing to deal the deathblow.

Constance lost her mind. In silent fury, she raced down the wet sand into the swash and sprang onto the demon's back, grabbing his skull with her fingers and sinking her teeth into his neck. The foul, rubbery taste of flesh filled her mouth. The creature, surprised by the ferocity of her attack, let out a scream and, swinging away from Pendergast, spun around and around, scrabbling at her, ripping at her clothes, trying to free himself. But she hung on tenaciously to his craggy brow; with a twist of her head she ripped the hunk of flesh free and spat it out, then bit down again, trying to reach the carotid artery. The demon, roaring with pain, staggered into the surf zone. A green roller reared up, then fell upon them; in a moment they were both engulfed in fierce, icy water. The shock of the water loosened her grip and tore her free from the demon. Unable to swim, she thrashed frantically in the boiling surf until she felt sand sucking under her feet and realized she was being carried onto the beach by the dying wave. She gripped the sand in the backrush, struggling to prevent herself from being dragged back into the maelstrom. Just as she felt the sand slide out from under her, strong arms gripped her and pulled her to her feet—and there was Pendergast, staring at her, a look of horror on his face. It took her a moment to understand why: in her terror, she had not realized she was still gripping a second gobbet of flesh between her teeth.

Meanwhile, Morax was struggling up from the surf, coming at them, face distorted in pain and fury. Pendergast rushed to put himself between Constance and the demon and, once again, the two came together with a bone-cracking thud. With a huge effort, Pendergast drove the demon back into the breaking surf, and in an instant both were engulfed in a gigantic, breaking wave.

The boiling white water swept Constance off her feet; she clawed at the sand to keep from being sucked back in the undertow, and this time managed to hold herself in place as the wave receded. Temporarily freed from the backwash, she crawled up the beach in the lull between waves and managed to get past the surf zone.

The sun was just breaking over a blood horizon, throwing pallid light onto her face. She blinked her eyes groggily. All she could see were great crimson rollers coming in, one after the other, crashing and thundering up the beach, then withdrawing again with a vast, dreary roar. And there, standing in the surf, was the demon. He had abruptly ceased all struggle and was staring into the rising sun in wonder, a twisted smile appearing on his face, arm outstretched as if to touch it, finger pointing, the swirling water around his legs reddening with arterial blood.

Where was Pendergast?

Where was Pendergast?

Constance rose, screaming: "Aloysius! Aloysius!"

She strained to look into the blinding orange surface of the sea—and then she saw him, his pale face rising and falling just beyond the break zone. His arms were barely moving.

"Aloysius!"

She took a few tentative steps into the water. He was struggling desperately to swim, but he was obviously weakened, gravely wounded, and the currents were now carrying him rapidly away from shore.

"Aloysius!"

Somewhere, vaguely, she heard the baying of a dog.

Morax collapsed into the bloody surf.

She stumbled down into the onrushing water, wading toward the struggling Pendergast despite her inability to swim, the torn, heavy dress impeding her progress.

"Stop her!" a voice cried from behind.

Suddenly there were people on both sides. One burly man seized her around the shoulders; another around the waist. She tried to twist away, but they hauled her out of the surf.

"Let me go!" she cried.

A male voice spoke out: "There's nothing you can do."

She fought like a banshee, screaming and twisting. "Can't you see him? He's too weak to swim!"

"We see him. We're calling a rescue boat."

She struggled afresh, but there were too many of them. "He's drowning! For the love of God, save him!"

"No one can go into that surf!" said the same male voice.

"Cowards!"

She tried to rush back into the water herself, but more men appeared and, despite her wild struggles, they managed to drag her out of the breaking surf and onto the dunes. Four more men in military fatigues appeared. Together, the group managed to hold her fast as she thrashed, spat, and kicked.

"I'll kill you! Let me go!"

"Jesus, what a tomcat! I can't believe it's taking half a dozen of us just to hold her down—!"

"We don't have time for this. Get the medical kit."

They wrestled her to the sand. She found herself pinned, face downward, cuffed and restrained, felt the sting of a cold needle on the back of her thigh...and then everything became far away and strange.

Epilogue

November

Quietly, Proctor eased open the double doors of the library to allow Mrs. Trask to pass through with a silver tray laden with a tea service.

The room was dim, lit only by the fire that guttered low in the hearth. Before it, in a wing chair, Proctor could see a motionless figure, indistinct in the faint light. Mrs. Trask walked over to the figure, placed the tray on a side table beside the chair.

"I thought you might like a cup of tea, Miss Greene," she said solicitously.

"No thank you, Mrs. Trask," came Constance's low voice.

"It's your favorite. Jasmine, first grade. I also brought you some madeleines. I baked them just this afternoon—I know how fond you are of them."

"I'm not particularly hungry," she answered. "Thank you for your trouble."

"Well, I'll just leave them here in case you change your mind." Mrs. Trask smiled maternally, turned, and headed for the library exit. By the time she reached Proctor, the smile had faded and the look on her face had grown worried once again.

"I'll only be gone a few days," she said to him in a low tone. "My sister should be home from the hospital by next weekend. Are you sure you'll be all right?"

Proctor nodded, then watched her bustle her way back toward the kitchen before returning his gaze to the figure in the wing chair.

It had been over two weeks since Constance had come back to the mansion at 891 Riverside Drive. She had returned, grim and silent, without Agent Pendergast, and with no explanation of what had happened. It had taken Proctor time, patience, and effort to coax the story out of her. Even now, the story made little sense and he was unsure what really happened. What he did know, however, was that the vast house, lacking Pendergast's presence, had changed—changed utterly. And so, too, had Constance.

When she'd first returned from Exmouth, Constance had locked herself in her room for days, taking meals only with the greatest reluctance. When she at last emerged, she seemed a different person: gaunt, spectral. Proctor had always known her to be coolheaded, reserved, and self-possessed. But in the days that followed, she was by turns listless and then suddenly full of restless, aimless energy, pacing about the halls and corridors as if looking for something. She abandoned all interest in the pastimes that had once so possessed her: researching the Pendergast family ancestry, antiquarian studies, reading, playing the harpsichord. After a few anxious visits from Lieutenant D'Agosta, Captain Laura Hayward, and Margo Green, she had refused to see anyone. She had also appeared to be—Proctor could think of no better way to put it—on her guard. The only times she showed a spark of her old self was on the rare occasions when the phone rang, or when Proctor brought the mail back from the post office box. Always, always, he knew, she was hoping for word from Pendergast. But there had been none.

Proctor had taken it upon himself to gather all the information he could about his employer's disappearance. The search for his body had lasted five days. Since the missing person was a federal agent, exceptional effort had been expended. Coast Guard cutters had searched the waters off Exmouth; local officers and National Guardsmen had combed the coastline from the New Hampshire border down to Cape Ann, looking for any sign of Pendergast—even so much as a shred of clothing. Divers had carefully examined rocks where the currents might have hung up a body, and the seafloor was scrutinized with sonar. But there had been nothing. The case remained officially open but, finally, became inactive. While the findings were inconclusive, the unspoken conclusion was that Pendergast—gravely wounded in his fight with the creature, struggling against a vicious tidal current, weakened by the continual battering of the waves, and subjected to the fifty-degree water—had been swept out to sea and drowned.

Now, quietly, Proctor approached and took a seat beside Constance. She glanced up at him briefly as he sat down, giving him the faintest smile. Then her gaze returned to the fire. The flickering light cast dark shadows over her violet eyes and her dark bobbed hair.

Since her return, Proctor had taken it upon himself to look after her, knowing that this was what his employer would have wanted. Her troubled state roused unexpected protective feelings within him—ironic, because under normal circumstances Constance was the last person to seek protection from another. And yet, without saying it, Constance seemed glad of his attentions.

He decided, once again, to try to draw her out of herself; to help free her, at least temporarily, from the cycle of guilt and loss that he sensed must be going through her mind.

"Constance?" he said gently.

"Yes?" she asked, eyes still on the fire.

"I wonder if you wouldn't mind telling me the last part of the story. I know you've said it before, but I still don't quite understand what happened—what really happened—in the struggle with that...creature called Morax—just who he was and how he was able to...to overcome Mr. Pendergast."

For a long time, she remained quiet. At last, she stirred and—still looking at the fire—began to speak. "I explained to you about the genetic abnormality, a vestigial tail, that caused Morax to look as he did; about how the Exmouth witches, in essence, enhanced the abnormality over the generations through breeding, as someone might a strain of dog. The witches were obsessed with his similarity to the images of Morax in old grimoires and demonic catalogs. The breeding line were treated as sub-humans, kept locked up in filthy conditions, used—I should say abused—for satanic rituals. That is why, once Morax got free, the main victims of his homicidal attention were members of the coven. The odd few were innocent bystanders, people who got in his way."

"But..." Proctor sought the right words. "How could this freak get the better of Mr. Pendergast?"

She glanced over the tea service for a moment before returning her gaze to the fire. "He didn't get the better of Aloysius. The creature perished."

"But Mr. Pendergast—"

"—is *not* dead." She finished his sentence sharply—but

for the first time, he heard an uncertain tone in her voice. Also, the guardedness she had exhibited since her return, Proctor noticed, had at last faded.

Proctor took a long breath. Once again, he tried to divert her thoughts. "But how did the brute manage to kill so many?"

"The treatment he endured turned him into a sociopathic beast. Only one thing kept him under control—beyond chains and whips, of course. And that was the promise they had apparently made to him, again and again, that one day they would take him above ground to see the sun, to bask in its warmth and light. He seems to have become obsessed with it. When he escaped the maze of subterranean tunnels—only to find a dark night with no moon—he thought he had been duped. And his anger burst all bounds." She paused. "He did get his wish, though...just before he died."

"Lot of good it did him."

Then she straightened in her chair. "Proctor, speaking of the subterranean...I've decided to go below."

The abrupt announcement took him aback. "You mean—down there, where you lived before?"

She said nothing.

"Why?"

"To...teach myself to accept the inevitable."

"Why can't you do that here, with us? You can't go down there again."

She turned and stared at him with such intensity that he was taken aback. He realized that it was hopeless to change her mind. At least this implied she was finally accepting that Pendergast was gone—that was progress, of sorts. Perhaps.

Now she rose from her chair. "I'll write a note for Mrs. Trask, instructing what clothes and necessities to leave inside the service elevator. I'll take one hot meal a day, at noontime. Left in a covered dish in the elevator."

Proctor rose as well. He took hold of her arm. "Constance, you must listen to me—"

She glanced down at his hand, and then up into his face with a look that prompted him to release his grasp immediately.

"Thank you, Proctor, for respecting my wishes."

Rising up on her toes, she surprised him again by lightly kissing his cheek. Then she turned, and—moving almost like a sleepwalker—headed to the far end of the library, where the service elevator was hidden behind a false bookcase. She swung open the case, slipped inside the waiting elevator, closed it behind her—and was gone.

Proctor stared at the spot for a long moment. This was crazy. He shook his head and turned away. Once again, the absence of Pendergast was like a shadow cast over the mansion—and over him. He felt a sense of failure with her. He needed time to be alone and think this through. He walked out of the library, took a turn down the hall, opened a door that led into a carpeted hallway, and mounted a crooked staircase leading to the old servants' quarters. Gaining the third-floor landing, he walked down another corridor until he reached the door to his small apartment of rooms. He opened it, stepped inside, closed it behind him.

He should have protested her plan more forcefully. With Pendergast gone, he was responsible for her. But he knew that nothing he said would have made any difference. Long ago he learned that, while he could handle almost anyone, he was hopeless against her. He also had other family business to worry about: most pressing was what to tell Tristram, Pendergast's son, who was away at school in Switzerland

and who knew nothing yet of his father's disappearance. He simply had to hope that, in time, Constance would face the reality and accept it—and rejoin the living...

A gloved hand whipped around from behind, seizing him around his rib cage and tightening with immense force.

Taken by surprise, Proctor nevertheless reacted instinctually with a sharp downward movement, attempting to throw the intruder off guard; but the man anticipated the reaction and thwarted it. Instantly, Proctor felt the sting of a needle jabbed deep into his neck. He froze.

"Movement is inadvisable," came a strange, silky voice that Proctor, with profound shock, recognized.

He did not move. It stunned him that a man—any man—had gotten the drop on him. How was it possible? He had been preoccupied, inattentive. He would never forgive himself for this. Especially because *this* man, he knew, was Pendergast's greatest enemy; returned, it seemed, from the dead.

"You're far better versed than I in the arts of physical combat," continued the smooth voice. "So I've taken the liberty of evening the odds. What you're feeling in your neck at the moment is a needle. I have not yet depressed the plunger. The syringe contains a dose of sodium pentothal—a very large dose. I will ask you once, and once only: signal your acquiescence by relaxing your body. How you react now will determine whether you receive a dose that is merely anesthetizing... or lethal."

Proctor considered his options. He let his body go limp.

"Excellent," said the voice. "The name is Proctor, I seem to recall?"

Proctor remained silent. There would be an opportunity to reverse the situation; there was always an opportunity. He only had to think.

"I've been observing the family manor for some time now. The man of the house is away—permanently, it would seem. It's as depressing as a tomb. You might as well all be wearing crepe."

Proctor's mind raced through various scenarios. He must pick one and execute it. He needed time, just a little time, a few seconds at most...

"Not in the mood for a chat? Just as well. I have a great many things to do, and so I bid you: *Good night.*"

As he felt the plunger slide home, Proctor realized his time was up—and that, to his vast surprise, he had failed.